Grantville Gazette VII

ERIC FLINT'S BESTSELLING
RING OF FIRE SERIES

1632 by Eric Flint
1633 by Eric Flint and David Weber
1634: The Baltic War by Eric Flint and David Weber
1634: The Galileo Affair by Eric Flint and Andrew Dennis
1634: The Bavarian Crisis by Eric Flint and Virginia DeMarce
1634: The Ram Rebellion by Eric Flint and Virginia DeMarce et al
1635: The Cannon Law by Eric Flint and Andrew Dennis
1635: The Dreeson Incident by Eric Flint and Virginia DeMarce
1635: The Eastern Front by Eric Flint
1635: The Papal Stakes by Eric Flint and Charles E. Gannon
1636: The Saxon Uprising by Eric Flint
1636: The Kremlin Games by Eric Flint and Gorg Huff & Paula Goodlett
1636: The Devil's Opera by Eric Flint and David Carrico
1636: Commander Cantrell in the West Indies by Eric Flint and Charles E. Gannon
1636: The Viennese Waltz by Eric Flint, Gorg Huff & Paula Goodlett
1636: The Cardinal Virtues by Eric Flint and Walter Hunt

Grantville Gazette I–V, ed. Eric Flint
Grantville Gazette VI–VII, ed. Eric Flint & Paula Goodlett
Ring of Fire I–III, ed. Eric Flint

1635: The Tangled Web by Virginia DeMarce
1636: Seas of Fortune by Iver P. Cooper

Time Spike by Eric Flint and Marilyn Kosmatka

Grantville Gazette VII

Created by ERIC FLINT

Edited by Eric Flint & Paula Goodlett

GRANTVILLE GAZETTE VII

This is a work of fiction. All the characters and events portrayed in this book are fictional, and any resemblance to real people or incidents is purely coincidental.

A Baen Books Original

Baen Publishing Enterprises
P.O. Box 1403
Riverdale, NY 10471
www.baen.com

ISBN: 978-1-4767-8029-0

Cover art by Tom Kidd

First printing, April 2015

Distributed by Simon & Schuster
1230 Avenue of the Americas
New York, NY 10020

Library of Congress Cataloging-in-Publication Data

Grantville Gazette VII / edited by Eric Flint and Paula Goodlett.
pages cm. — (The ring of fire ; 7)
Summary: "A cosmic accident sets the modern West Virginia town of Grantville down in war torn 17th century Europe. It will take all the gumption of the resourceful, freedom loving uptimers to find a way to flourish. Here are stories that fill in the pieces of the Ring of Fire political, social and cultural puzzle as supporting characters we meet in the novels get their own lives, loves and life changing stories"— Provided by publisher.
ISBN 978-1-4767-8029-0 (hardback)
1. Fantasy fiction, American. 2. Seventeenth century—Fiction. 3. Time travel—Fiction. 4. Alternative histories (Fiction), American. 5. Science fiction, American. I. Flint, Eric. II. Goodlett, Paula.
PS648.F3G757 2015
813'.54—dc23

2015002216

10 9 8 7 6 5 4 3 2 1

Pages by Joy Freeman (www.pagesbyjoy.com)
Printed in the United States of America

To the memory of Karen Bergstralh,

who is sorely missed.

Contents

Preface

Eric Flint

This is the seventh anthology of stories from the electronic magazine *The Grantville Gazette* that Baen Books has published. The first four were direct, one-to-one reissues of the first four volumes of the magazine. Thereafter, given the pace at which stories were being published in the magazine, we shifted to a "best of" format. *Grantville Gazette V* contained stories selected from issues 5–10 and *Grantville Gazette VI* contained stories selected from issues 11–19. This volume contains stories selected from issues 20–30.

If you're spotting a pattern here—the spread of issues selected from keeps getting bigger, from six to nine to eleven—you're right. The pace of the magazine has kept outrunning the anthologies. As of the publication date of the book in your hand, the electronic magazine just came out with its 59th issue.

This is the sort of problem created by success, which is a much nicer problem to be faced with than those produced by failure. But it's still a problem. We'll probably have to keep expanding the spread of issues we choose from in succeeding collections of stories from the *Gazette*. In the meantime, though, we have taken some steps to alleviate the backlog in other areas.

Last year, we launched a new publishing house, Ring of Fire Press. The "we" referred to consists of the many people who have participated in creating the 1632 series, either as authors or editors or technical advisers or—usually—a combination of all three. This series long ago became a collective enterprise in which I function as much as the literary analog to the conductor of an orchestra as I do as an author.

Ring of Fire Press works closely with Baen Books. Our arrangement is that Baen gets first choice of whatever they might want to publish for the first time—that would be all novels and many anthologies—or reissue from the electronic magazine. (That would be all the *Grantville Gazette* anthologies.) What's left is then selected from by Ring of Fire Press for publication as an e-book with, for those who prefer a paper edition, a print-on-demand option as well.

This material consists of two items. First, serialized stories that are simply too long to be included in an anthology published by Baen Books. Most of them are reissues of stories that were first published in the magazine, but some of them have been significantly rewritten. We are also now moving toward publishing some original stories as well. The material we publish includes collections of fact articles. Initially, with the first four *Grantville Gazette* anthologies published by Baen, we included fact articles along with fiction. But once we moved to a "best of" format beginning with *Grantville Gazette V*, space considerations required us to limit the collection to fiction only.

As of the publication of this volume, these are the titles available from Ring of Fire Press:

Kim Mackey, *Essen Steel*
Herbert Sakalaucks, *The Danish Scheme* (which includes a short story by Eric Flint, "Brave New World")
Douglas W. Jones, *Joseph Hanauer*
Kevin H. and Karen C. Evans, *No Ship for Tranquebar*
Wood Hughes, *Turn Your Radio On*
Various authors, *Medicine and Disease after the Ring of Fire*

You can buy the titles from Baen Books' Webscriptions in any format you choose, including Kindle and EPUB (which is the format used by Nook, Apple and Kobo). They are also available from Amazon or Barnes & Noble online. My preference, for whatever it's worth, is for people to buy through Baen Webscriptions. Leaving aside my longstanding, friendly and mutually beneficial relationship with Baen Books, its Webscriptions service charges us a considerably smaller distributor's fee than anyone else does.

And . . . I think that's it. I believe in keeping prefaces short anyway. I hope you enjoy these stories.

—Eric Flint, October, 2014

An Aukward Situation

Eric Flint

"Freddy's been murdered, Ludwig, and the police refuse to do anything about it!"

The countess of Schwarzburg-Rudolstadt flung herself into an armchair and glared at her husband, as if he were somehow responsible for the nefarious crime and the subsequent refusal of Magdeburg's police force to do their sworn and bounden duty. Luckily, given the force of her arrival in the piece of furniture in question, it was one of the new stuffed armchairs based on up-timer design. A traditional seventeenth-century "armchair"—even ones owned by royalty—were made of wood and had nothing more in the way of cushions than quilted padding on the seats.

"It was horrible!" Emelie continued. "He was strung up by the neck—left to hang from a post! And then the murderer disemboweled him!"

She shuddered. "I hate to think how poor Freddy must have suffered."

Count Ludwig Guenther of Schwarzburg-Rudolstadt studied his young wife for a moment. The count was well known for his prudence and good judgment. Now in his mid-fifties, Ludwig Guenther was more than three decades older than his spouse. All things considered, they got along quite well and there was a great deal of affection in their marriage. Still, there were moments when the emotional distance between a woman of twenty-one and a man of fifty-five was considerable.

This, he judged, was one of those moments. Caution was called for.

"That sounds dreadful indeed," he allowed. "Disemboweled, you say—in addition to being hanged? What reasons are the police giving for their refusal to investigate?"

"They say he's just a bird! It's ridiculous!"

The count took a moment to examine the situation from an unexpected direction. *Re-orient himself*, as an up-timer might put it.

"Ah . . ." In his mind, he ran through the names Emelie had given him of her charges. "Would you be referring to Kleine Friedrich? The—ah—junior of the three grand auks at the aviary?"

"They're great auks," Emelie said. "And yes. He's the one who was so horribly murdered. The poor creature—and he was so *young*."

She crossed her arms, shivering a little. That was not due to cold. It was a warm summer day. "I feel terrible about it, Ludwig. Freddy was so friendly—not at all like his parents. He was one of my favorites."

The feeling in the count's belly was now a sinking one. More like plunging, really.

"Yes, that's dreadful."

"Well, do something!"

"For Pete's sake!" exclaimed Gotthilf Hoch. The police sergeant threw up his hands. "It's just a bird!"

"Who is 'Pete'?" asked Simon Bayer.

Sitting at the basin Gotthilf had designed and made for her to use when she did kitchen work, Ursula Metzgerin broke off from plucking the chicken. "It's just an expression Gotthilf got from his partner Byron Chieske. Up-timers use it to avoid blasphemy."

Simon frowned. Like most youngsters—smart ones, at least—he had a tendency to ponder issues more thoroughly than they usually needed. "I didn't think up-timers worried about blasphemy at all. I've heard even their parsons take the name of the Lord in vain."

Gotthilf throttled his exasperation, lest he vent it on Simon. For that matter, he didn't want to vent it on Ursula either. The relationship among the three of them was somewhat fragile. He and Ursula were betrothed and it was agreed by all that as soon as they married they would adopt Simon. The orphan had been taken in by Ursula's brother Hans before he died.

But, for the moment, they did not have the long-established and well-buttressed family situation that allowed a paterfamilias to occasionally vent his spleen without causing undue alarm or producing badly hurt feelings.

"The up-timers have a history too, Simon," he said in a calm tone of voice. "In the world they came from—not even so long ago, by their reckoning—blasphemy was just as disapproved of as it is among us. So they developed—invented—words and phrases to circumvent the problem. They call them 'euphemisms.'"

"Yu-fa-misims." Simon rolled the word around on his tongue. "Yufe-am-issims."

Most of the difficulty he had with the pronunciation was caused by the fact that the word was English, not Amideutsch—and of Greek origin, to boot. Within a few years, of course, it would be absorbed into the new dialect of German emerging within the USE and would come trippingly off the tongue of lads his age. Those with some education, at any rate.

"Euphemisms," Gotthilf repeated.

Inspiration came to him, then. "Such as the euphemism"—he pointed at Ursula, now back to her work with the chicken—"of saying that Ursula is 'dressing' the chicken and 'preparing' it for our supper. When what she has actually done and will be doing is wringing the poor bird's neck, tearing out all its feathers, disemboweling the wretched creature and breaking many of its joints. That is to say, more-or-less exactly what was done to the bird in the zoo's aviary."

Here, a look of great and histrionic surprise came to his face. "Yet, imagine! No one proposes that the police investigate the horrid crime perpetrated on this chicken!"

Ursula smiled, but didn't look up from her plucking. "It's not the same, Gotthilf, and you know it. For one thing"—she held up the chicken by its neck—"*this* does not belong to an endangered species."

"Neither did the great auk in the aviary," said Gotthilf crossly. "I talked to one of the men from the expedition that brought the birds to the zoo. He told me the Faroe Islands are swarming with the things. They don't go extinct for another two or three centuries."

He threw up his hands again. "Up-timers! Sometimes I think they are downright mad! Here they are, in Magdeburg—a city whose population was butchered not five years ago—and they fret over the fate of some ugly birds!"

Too late, he spotted the pinched expression on Ursula's face.

She and her brother Hans had been part of the city's population during the siege. They'd managed to escape the slaughter committed by Tilly's troops, but in the process of doing so Ursula had suffered the injury that had left her partly-crippled to this day.

"That's one way of looking at it," she said, a bit tight-lipped. "But there's another way to look at it also, Gotthilf." She broke off from her work for a moment and lifted her head. "A folk that worries over the fate of birds is perhaps less likely to slaughter people too, wouldn't you think?"

Gotthilf made a face. "They're no saints," he protested. "I've learned a lot of their history from Byron. In the world they came from, they committed worse slaughters that we ever have."

"Than we ever have *yet,*" Simon qualified. His expression was now very solemn. "We're the same people that they are, just separated a bit by time. I know some of that up-time history myself. Pastor Gruber told me that the worst slaughter ever done was done right here in the Germanies. He said we Germans killed—would kill, however you say it right—millions of Jews. I didn't even know there that many Jews in the whole world."

"This conversation has become morbid," complained Gotthilf. "How did we get from one dead bird to millions of dead Jews?"

"There *is* a connection," insisted Ursula. She'd finished plucking the chicken and moved the basin aside. Cleverly, Gotthilf had designed it with wheels so she could continue to work without having to get her cane. She now reached for the cutting board that he'd also designed and made so it could be wheeled to and from her chair. He'd even built in a case to hold her cutting knives.

Ursula was quite in love with the man. But he could be obtuse, sometimes.

"And the connection is..."

"It's not that a crime was committed," she said. "Crimes happen. It's that nothing was done about it. Not at the time, anyway. *That's* the connection."

"I agree with her," Simon said stoutly. "You *should* do something about it, Gotthilf. That's what policemen are for."

Gotthilf looked at the chicken that Ursula was now spreading across the cutting board. In preparation for being disemboweled, mutilated...

He wondered what a great auk would taste like. In his exasperation, he was tempted to find out. The dead bird—*excuse me, the murdered avian*—was still in the police station, in a box filled with ice. Captain Reilly had wanted to just throw the thing out, of course, being a sensible man even if he was an up-timer. But there'd been enough of an outcry from the public—more precisely, that small but well-off and well-connected portion of the public that had financed the aviary to begin with—that the captain had decided to keep the carcass on ice for a while. Not because he expected he'd do anything about it, but simply so he could claim he might.

Fortunately, Ursula was an even-tempered woman. After drawing out a knife from the case, she turned her head and gave her betrothed a smile. It was a sweet smile, in a slightly sarcastic sort of way. "Since the horror of the deed itself doesn't move you, Gotthilf, you might want to consider the matter from a practical standpoint."

"Meaning what?"

"Meaning that you're always complaining that the police department doesn't have enough money in the budget to afford a full-time medical examiner. Which you need in order to be able to promptly investigate and solve crimes—murders, especially—for which there are no witnesses and no evidence beyond the remains of the victims themselves."

She went back to her work of "dressing" a chicken.

Gotthilf stared at her. His mouth was perhaps a bit ajar.

"You'll get flies in there," Simon warned.

"My dear, I'd like to introduce Sergeant Gotthilf Hoch, from the Magdeburg *Polizei*." Count Ludwig Guenther gestured toward the short, stocky man who'd come into the salon behind him.

Countess Emelie placed a slip of paper in the book she was reading and set the book on the side table next to her chair.

"Please have a seat, Sergeant." She nodded toward a chair across a low table from her. The piece of furniture was what up-timers persisted in calling a *coffee table*—rather to Emelie's annoyance because she detested the beverage. If she wanted to savor acidity and bitterness, she could invite any one of several relatives and acquaintances over for a chat.

After the policeman took his seat, the countess cocked her head sideways a bit. "Aren't you the one betrothed to the boxer's sister? The one with the orphan. I'm sorry, I don't recall their names."

"Ursula Metzgerin. Yes. I am. The boy's name is Simon Bayer."

There seemed to be an air of approval in Emelie's tone of voice, Ludwig-Guenther was relieved to note. The count had been afraid that his wife would prove hostile. At the moment, policemen generally ranked in her pantheon of virtue and rectitude somewhere on the same level as swindlers and considerably below fishwives.

"I heard the story from Lady Simpson." She bestowed a smile on the sergeant. "She quite approves of you, it seems."

"I'm pleased to hear that. Especially since it bears on the reason for my visit."

He cleared his throat. "You are of course aware of the unfortunate events at the gala opening of the new zoo. The, ah . . ."

"Murder," Emelie provided. Her smile was now a bit strained.

"Well . . ." Hoch seemed to come to a decision and squared his shoulders. "No, Your Ladyship," he said firmly. "The killing of the great auk known as Freddy does not constitute 'murder' under the laws of the USE. Or the laws of any other nation that I know of."

The countess's brow was lowering. Stoutly, the sergeant pressed on. "Nonetheless, it *was* a crime and it should be solved and the culprit or culprits brought to justice."

The brow paused in its fearsome lowering. "I distinctly recall your Captain Reilly telling me that there is no law against killing an animal in the USE."

"Well, no, there isn't. But there *are* laws—quite a few of them; some with severe penalties—governing the destruction of property. If you will detach yourself from your . . . ah . . ."

"'Personal and emotional involvement' is perhaps the phrase you are looking for," the countess supplied. Her tone of voice seemed considerably older than her actual years of life. And the brow was starting to come down again.

Slowly, though. Count Ludwig Guenther still had hopes this might turn out well.

"Ah, yes," said the sergeant. "Look at it for a moment from the standpoint of a magistrate. The death of a bird, in itself, is nothing to the law. But the death of a bird which cost a great deal of money to acquire for the zoo's aviary and whose loss will undoubtedly cause further pecuniary losses from lowered paid attendance at the aviary . . . Well. That's a different matter altogether. If there's one thing a German magistrate understands perfectly well, it's the loss of money."

The countess's brow began to rise and she leaned back in her chair, her expression now becoming pensive. "I . . . see. But then—why have you policemen been unwilling to investigate? Surely you don't refuse to do anything about burglary or swindling?"

"No, we don't. But this case, well, to be honest it caught us off-balance. Crimes against property don't normally take the form of—of—"

"A poor harmless innocent bird being foully done to death in a cruel and vicious manner."

"Ah. Yes. Usually it takes the form of thieving or perhaps arson."

The sergeant raised his hand. "But there's more to it, Your Ladyship. The other—and much bigger—problem is that we simply lack the resources we need to properly investigate the crime."

Down came the brow. But slowly, slowly.

"How so? You investigate other crimes against property. You just said so yourself."

"Yes, Your Ladyship. But with most crimes against property the motive is either greed or, in the case of vandalism, animosity against the owner. Usually it's greed, at least in part. So we investigate by following the money. Who gains from the criminal act? More often than not—far more often than not—that question will lead you directly to the culprit."

Hoch shrugged. "It's not much different with acts of vandalism. People don't usually destroy or deface someone else's property unless they are gripped by strong anger, hatred, jealousy or resentment. Such powerful emotions usually leave plenty of traces. Footprints of sentiment, you might call them."

He spread his hands. "Perhaps now you can see the problem we policemen face. No one seems to gain anything from the death of the bird Freddy. And while I suppose it could be an act of vandalism, who hates or resents the new zoo that much? No one that I can think of."

The count decided he could risk a small intervention. "Me, neither. You, Emelie? Perhaps an enemy of Lady Simpson's?"

He was pleased to see that the frown had completely left his wife's face. Her expression was now simply one of puzzlement.

"No . . . no." She smiled faintly. "Mind you, the dame of Magdeburg has plenty of enemies. You can start with the not-so-small horde of Freifrauen and Eminent Lutheran Ladies who resent Mary's informal title of 'Lady Simpson.'" She chuckled. "There being no such rank in the German nobility—but it doesn't matter, because she gets more respect than most margravines do."

She paused for a moment, thinking. "But . . . You have to understand the nature of the enmity and the sort of weapons and tactics it elicits. We enter a realm full of backbiting, gossip, calumny—oh, there's enough malice there to float a barge—but I can't imagine any of them slaughtering a *bird*. And for what? Yes, Mary was one of the chief fundraisers for the zoo, but it's not as if the aviary is especially associated with her. If it's associated with any prominent person in the capital, it'd be associated with *me*, since I volunteer to work there. But . . . but . . ."

Ludwig Guenther felt quite safe making another intervention. "How many bitter enemies could you have possibly made at your age? I won't even mention your cordial disposition."

His wife gave him a quick smile. But her attention was instantly back on the sergeant.

"No," she said, shaking her head. "I really can't see Freddy's murder"—here she made a quick exasperated gesture—"or call it whatever you will, being an act of vandalism. But then . . ."

Hoch nodded. "You see our problem. There were no witnesses. There seems to be no motive. That means the only avenue we could follow would be a careful examination of the physical evidence. First and foremost, the carcass of the bird itself."

"Yes. That makes sense. So why haven't you done so?"

Count Ludwig Guenther thought Hoch's ensuing sigh was overly theatrical. But, all in all, he was quite pleased with the sergeant's performance.

"Because, Your Ladyship, the Magdeburg police force does not have a medical examiner on our staff. True, the city has a coroner's office, but they are understaffed and we can only get their help on a few cases. We have asked for a medical examiner several times, but"—here he displayed an impressive frown of his own—"in their wisdom the city's authorities have refused to provide funds for the post in our budget."

But the frown that came now to the countess's brow was a wonder! Truly splendid.

"Why ever not?"

"Because—insofar as we humble policemen can follow their exalted logic—it seems they don't believe having a medical examiner will be of much assistance to the task of apprehending criminals and miscreants. One of the authorities involved went so far as to call it a frivolous request."

Emelie came to her feet. Very energetically. "We'll show them!" Just as vigorously, she rang the little bell on the side table. When the servant came into the room a few moments later, the countess said: "Never mind, Dorothea. I was going to have you send a message to Lady Simpson but I've decided just to walk over myself. It's not that far and it's a pleasant day."

She was already heading for the entrance to their town house. "Comc with me, Sergeant Hoch."

The maid barely managed to get ahead of her and open the door. As he followed Emelie, Hoch gave the count a thankful look.

Ludwig Guenther nodded solemnly in response. This was going quite well. So far, anyway.

After the countess of Schwarzburg-Rudolstadt finished her tale of woe and wonder at the folly of officialdom, Mary Simpson nodded.

"I'm glad you brought this matter to me, Emelie. I think we can use it to solve two problems at the same time. The despicable act against poor Freddy and the recalcitrance of modern—I use the term very, very loosely—society when it comes to gender affairs."

She looked up at Sergeant Hoch, who had remained standing while the countess explained the situation. Mrs. Simpson's brow carried a rather formidable frown of its own.

"I trust the police department does not share in the sexism of so many members of what is laughingly called 'proper society.'"

Hoch kept his face impassive while he tried to decipher the meaning of the term "sexism." The word was English, not Amideutsch. But, by now, as was true of any speaker of Amideutsch, Gotthilf had gained considerable fluency in his understanding of the complex permutations of English.

So, within seconds, the meaning of the term seemed clear enough. Misogyny—what Germans would call *Frauenhass* or *Weiberhass*—elevated to a philosophical plane. So to speak.

But he didn't see how the term applied in this context. Clearly, though, prudence was called for here. Not to mention adroitness.

"Ah . . ." Without thinking in time to stop himself, he scratched his head.

Mrs. Simpson snorted. "Baffled much? I swear, there are times I *really* miss my own century."

She sat up straighter in her chair, as if delivering a lecture. "What I am referring to, Sergeant, is that I have a protégée—a splendid young woman from Halle by the name of Ilse Vogler—who recently completed her medical education at the University of Jena. Against considerable resistance and animosity on the part of some members of the faculty, I might add. Now she's trying to find a job where she can use her newly-acquired skills. And—my, what a surprise!—she is encountering even more resistance and antagonism than she did at the university."

Things were becoming clearer. Gotthilf felt a hollow sensation in his belly. He did not like the direction this seemed—

"You understand where I'm going with this, I'm sure," said Mrs. Simpson. "I think it would be splendid if the police of our nation's capital and premier city were to make a woman its medical examiner. An example to encourage the others, as a French general might say."

The reference to French generals was meaningless to Gotthilf, but the rest was as clear as day.

"Ah . . ."

"If it's the budget problem you're concerned with . . ." Mrs. Simpson made a dismissive gesture. "You needn't concern yourself with that. Within a day—well, better give me two—I can have enough funds to provide Ilse with a year's salary. I am by no means the only prominent woman in this town who is displeased with the treatment Fräulein Vogler has received."

"What a superb idea!" the countess of Schwarzburg-Rudolstadt exclaimed. "We could call it the Freddy Fund."

Simpson nodded, but her gaze was still on Gotthilf. "Surely you don't object, Sergeant Hoch? I assure you, Ilse got excellent marks at the university."

There was nothing for it but to acquiesce. At least Captain Reilly and Byron Chieske probably wouldn't make a fuss. Unless . . .

Gotthilf kept his expression bland and unreadable. Unless the two American police officers decided Mrs. Simpson's proposal was an instance of that dreaded syndrome they called *political correctness*. A term whose heretofore murky meaning was becoming clearer to Gotthilf.

But all he said was: "By all means, let's see what she can do."

☆ ☆ ☆

Ilse Vogler proved to be quite a formidable young woman. Thin to the point of being gaunt; intense; inquisitive blue eyes peering from behind thick glasses at everything that drew her interest.

It didn't take her more than a few hours to solve the crime, after she began her examination of Freddy's carcass. Generically, at any rate. The police would still have to place a specific name on the villain, but the nature of the crime—its motive; its aim; all of it—was now quite clear.

Less than an hour examining the bird. Half an hour or so traveling from the police station to the zoo. A little over an hour examining the scene of the crime in the aviary.

"The bird's neck was broken further down than the ligature mark would indicate. See?" She pointed to details of the vertebra exposed by her scalpel. They meant nothing to Gotthilf.

"Ah . . ."

"Isn't it obvious? *First*, the bird's neck was broken. *Then*, the cord was tied around its neck and it was suspended where it was found."

"You're saying the bird was hung to disguise the real cause of its murd—ah, killing?"

"Precisely. Now take a look at this." Vogler held up the bird's feet. Looking closely—which he now realized he'd never done when the bird's carcass was first brought to the attention of the police—he could see stains on the great auk's talons and the webbing between them.

"Is that . . . ?"

"Yes, of course it's blood. We will test it to be sure, but I think it's obvious it must be human blood. No other birds were found injured—I asked already—and no other animals are allowed into the aviary. Then there's this. Follow me."

She moved over to a bench against one of the walls of the aviary. It was a nicely carved and decorated sitting bench, not a work surface. Gotthilf presumed it had been placed there to provide the patrons of the aviary with a place to sit and admire its feathered inhabitants.

"Look at this," she said, pointing to more dark stains on the surface and legs of the bench. "Here also." Now she indicated stains on the stone floor.

Her thin face was tight with aggravation. "The idiot cleaning staff obviously tried to remove the stains—you have to put a stop to that in the future, Sergeant Hoch! a crime scene must be inviolate until my examination is done—but blood is not so easy to remove."

She straightened up. "As you can now see, everything is clear. The bird was not the *victim* of a murder, except incidentally. No, it was the murder *weapon*. Well . . . assault weapon, rather. I don't think homicide was intended."

Gotthilf was still trying to catch up with her. "In other words, you're saying . . ."

"Oh, pfah! It's obvious. Emelie—the countess—told us the young bird Freddy was of a friendly disposition, didn't she? Always approaching people without fear or hesitation. So."

She looked around the aviary. "Picture someone sitting here on the bench. The opening gala is well underway and refreshments have been served in the zoo's central . . . whatever they call that thing. Square, plaza, whatever. Almost everyone has gathered there to eat and drink."

Abruptly, she held up a cautionary finger. "But not all! Two people—perhaps there were more, but I see no evidence of it—have remained here in the aviary. They are quarreling over something. One of them becomes enraged. Sadly for Freddy, the incautious bird has waddled over. The enraged party seizes Freddy by the neck and uses the bird to bludgeon the object of its fury."

She paused, her face growing momentarily pensive. "The great auk—he wasn't quite full-grown—weighed a little under four kilos."

Kilos was another term creeping into Amideutsch. Gotthilf translated the amount into familiar German weights. About as heavy as a grown cat.

"Easy to pick up, but not heavy enough to cause serious harm," he said.

Vogler shrugged. "Not unless it was as hard as a hammer. But, no, you're right. The bird's claws obviously inflicted some wounds, but they would have been superficial. There's not enough blood spilled here to have been life-threatening—*but!*"

Again, the abrupt cautionary finger came up. "There's still quite a bit more blood here than you'd expect—*except* from head wounds."

It was all finally coming into focus for Gotthilf. He was now getting excited, in his own phlegmatic way. "Yes. Yes. The sort of weapon a furious person might use to *punish* someone, or express great anger. But they didn't intend to commit murder. Well, except on the bird, and that's not legally murder. Then..."

He looked over to the post where the bird had been strung up by the neck and disemboweled. The aviary's cleaning staff had removed the entrails and scoured away what they could, but there were still bloodstains evident in the vicinity.

Not spread far, though. The blood had pooled below the carcass rather than being splattered all about.

"The rest of the bird's wounds came after it died," he said.

"We call it 'posthumous.' Yes." For the first time since they'd met, Vogler gave him an approving look.

Gotthilf looked back at the bench. "So, after the enraged party beats the other with the bird—killing Freddy in the process—the two of them conspire to disguise what really happened as a bizarre act of purposeless mayhem."

"Exactly."

The sergeant was now on familiar ground. "This was a domestic quarrel," he said confidently.

Vogler nodded. "Yes, that's what I think too. And with head wounds like that, he or she must have sought medical treatment afterward. They would have claimed it was an accident of some sort. You'll have to interview the city's doctors."

"Won't need to." Gotthilf used his thumb to indicate the passageway that connected the aviary to the rest of the zoo. "That's the only way out. Someone in the central—they call it the 'gallery,' I think—where the refreshments were being served must have noticed them leaving. One of them would have some sort of bandage on their face. I'll find out who it was soon enough."

He looked back at the new medical examiner. "Welcome to the Magdeburg police."

It was the first time he'd seen Vogler smile. Her lips were so thin the smile reminded him of a snake examining a nearby rat.

Which was all to the good, so far as Sergeant Gotthilf Hoch was concerned. Magdeburg was full of rats, a goodly number of them two-legged.

When his investigation was over, Gotthilf decided it would be wise to give Mary Simpson a full (though private and informal) report.

When he was finished, she gave him a shrewd look. "I notice that you avoided any names."

"It was part of the settlement that we would keep the matter from public display, Mrs. Simpson."

His own smile probably had a serpentine flavor to it. "Though I admit it pleased me—Captain Reilly and Lieutenant Chieske also—that one of the perpetrators was the same official fellow who pronounced our request that a medical examiner be provided for in our budget to be 'frivolous.'"

With her resources, if she chose to do so, Simpson could find out who that was. But, technically, Gotthilf had maintained the discretion agreed to in the final settlement.

Simpson leaned back in her chair, sipped from her cup of coffee, and shook her head. "A crime of passion, then. A wife infuriated by her husband's infidelity."

"Um. I wouldn't call it a crime of 'passion,' exactly. Countess von Mans—ah, the lady in question—seems to have been infuriated over the large sums of money her husband was showering on his mistress rather than—ah—"

Simpson smiled. "Yes. Quite, as an old English friend of mine would have said. There are still ways I haven't fully acculturated myself to the seventeenth century."

She set down the cup. "I take it you're pleased with Ilse Vogler."

"Oh, yes. Byron is starting to positively dote on her. That was part of the settlement we made with the count and—the persons involved. We agreed to keep the matter private, since the person physically injured chose not to file charges and the institution which suffered a monetary loss from the bird's death agreed to a settlement out of court. The aviary gets an annual stipend for the next twelve years and"—he couldn't help but grin—"the police department gets a medical examiner's salary paid for out of a special fund contributed by an anonymous donor. It's a bit irregular but quite legal."

Simpson chuckled. "I'm pretty sure I know who this unnamed count and countess were. Detestable people. And if I'm right, the countess must have protested loudly and bitterly before she finally succumbed to the inevitable."

"Oh, yes. She issued what you might call a great auk."

The Pitch

Domenic and DJ diCiacca

Today the road was perfect, dry enough for wagon wheels but not yet dusty. Ian, who had sold a few of the up-time plows that were in the fields, was delighted. He had a new product in the wagon that he said was a surefire-couldn't-miss item, and he and Bert were going to revolutionize a different part of society, a part as yet untouched by the ongoing industrial and agricultural revolution. This far out in the country, a lot had not yet changed.

They checked off the inventory, made sure the two goats were firmly hitched to the back of the wagon, and slapped the mule into motion. Ian called "Up, Napoleon!" and laughed. Bert had no idea what it meant. Ian had picked up all kinds of up-timer phrases and ideas. But the mule's name was Oliver.

Three days later they were still on the road. They had yet to make a sale. Oh, they'd had fair luck with other, smaller farm implements, and farm bulletins and pamphlets and plans. Dream Farms Holding Company lampwork glass beads were doing especially well. But they had sold no washing machine kits, which was the larger part of their inventory.

Ian was entirely upbeat. "Nothing to worry about. It takes time to develop a good pitch. A peddler hears 'no' a lot more often than he hears 'yes.' Once we sell the first one and word gets around, they'll fly off the back of the wagon. So relax, enjoy the ride, and enjoy the day. Life is short. Get happy. Everything is going fine." Ian was talking just to hear himself talk. Maybe he needed the pep talk as much as Bert did. Ian talked a lot, when he was inclined.

A smartass remark at the wrong time to the wrong people had cost Bert his tongue, years ago. While he could still make most sounds, he rarely said anything. He said even less now. He was grumpy. His butt hurt from sitting on the hard bench of the wagon, his feet hurt from walking, and his head hurt from the frustration of watching Ian make his pitch. In Bert's humble opinion, nothing was more tightly fisted, closed minded, mulishly stubborn, or suspiciously grim than the people in the little towns and hamlets like the ones they kept passing through.

Ian was the salesman, or peddler, or drummer, or bullshitter, whatever anyone wanted to call it. He seemed to like everybody he met. That was fine.

Bert was security. He was the muscle. This meant Bert did all the work while Ian talked. Ian talked, and Bert fed the goats. Ian talked, and Bert unloaded things from the wagon. He put the demonstration model together, if they got that far, and he went for water, and did every other damn thing, like unhitching the mule and setting camp or handing Ian the right display model or illustration, or mug of beer. All the while, Ian talked. And it didn't do a damn bit of good, as far as Bert could see.

Ian thought otherwise. He talked about weather, and war, and seed crops and hay, and tough times past and good times to come, and the hopes and fears of the average Joe. He avoided talk of the court, and politics, and religion, which of itself was a wonder, but probably a necessary one. He softened the waters for future sales of scissor cutters and hay rakes and hand tools and farm gadgets of all kinds, and he planted seeds of his own in fertile ground when he got the chance. But somehow or other, whenever he broached the subject of the washing machine he got stonewalled. Froze out. Stopped cold.

"We've got a laundry." Some communities had a communal laundry.

"My wife washes my clothes. She does just fine." Never tell a man to go ask his wife. About anything.

"We have a river right over there. What do we need that gadget for?"

"We just don't need it."

"It costs too much."

"Are you saying my clothes are dirty? You sayin' I stink?"

One time they had back-pedaled right out of town. Mostly they were treated fairly, and they were listened to, and they were given a polite "no." Even when they were enthusiastically received and did well with the other products, they received a firm no when they got to the washing machine. Mostly Ian talked to the men, while the women looked out of doorways and held the children back. Bert, of course, stayed silent.

Sometimes Bert juggled, and often in the evening he and Ian played penny whistles, and drank beer at the local pub, and made a few more sales—and probably a lot more future sales, according to Ian. But they sold no washing machines. Twice they were allowed to set up and demonstrate, and women watched and men stood about with sarcastic expressions, and children teased the goats and had to be scolded by apologetic parents, but after all the fuss and bother and activity, nothing happened. Ian was untroubled by this. His plan was to travel out for two weeks, planting seeds, and then turn around and retrace their steps, reaping harvest.

Bert had his own opinion about the plan. But over the next week, they worked up an act, and Bert began to enjoy himself, and they were more and more allowed to set up the demonstration model.

They would pull the mule to a stop in the middle of some dozen or two buildings, sometimes haphazardly placed, sometimes organized into a tidy square or main street, and Ian would introduce himself and comment about the weather and pass on whatever news they had picked up in the last little hamlet. Bert would look about for the nearest mud puddle and promptly trip over his own feet and fall into it. Or he would drop something heavy on his toe when he was unloading the wagon, and pinch his fingers while setting up the demonstration model. Once a goat nipped his ass, and they worked it into the act. Ian talked, and Bert did shtick, and he always did his best to make it look unintentional. He pantomimed with increasing skill, and he exaggerated his muteness, and when people laughed it made him unreasonably happy. Ian seemed satisfied, too. They enjoyed themselves, they made a profit, and they moved on, but they sold no washing machines.

They passed through the last little hamlet on their itinerary one lazy spring afternoon and a few hours later settled into a campsite where they would remain for three days. They fished, they sparred, they honed their fighting skills, they practiced with their penny whistles, they slept and they talked. Well, Ian talked. They tethered the critters on good pasture, they rubbed the mule down and checked his hooves and legs, they patched and greased tack and harness and wagon wheels, and they generally passed the time. Then they did a fresh inventory, hitched up the mule, tied the goats to the wagon, and started back. They passed through the same little hamlet without stopping, and without comment or incident.

Late that afternoon they reached the next, and they were spotted long before they reached the first building. They drove into the middle of town and found the road blocked by two men; men they had drunk beer with and shared news and gossip with, men who had been friendly when they parted. Now these same men stood with arms folded and dark scowls on their faces, blocking the wagon. When Ian pulled Oliver to a halt, other men emerged from various buildings to close off retreat. More joined the ones in front. Grim-faced women stepped out from doorways, or looked out of windows, determined and resolute, hands on hips or holding heavy ladles. One woman had a beauty of a shiner around one eye. She had a definite attitude and a heavy iron fire poker in her fist. She glared not at Ian and Bert, but at one of the men, most likely her husband. One of the angriest looking men had a dark bruise along one cheek.

Ian tied off the reins and sat up straighter, wearing his poker face. Bert, if he'd had a tongue, would have bitten it. It took every effort and a really hard self-inflicted pinch on his ear to keep from grinning. Grinning, he was sure, could be bad. They were on the verge of a riot.

Ian, his eyes flat and his face blank, leaned slightly toward Bert and spoke out of the side of his mouth. "Looks like we're about to make a sale."

And Bert figured it was true, and he pinched his ear again and bravely kept even a hint of a smile from his face. Later, perhaps, it would make a great story. But not now. When a dozen or so angry men surround you, it's best not to laugh just because they're not wearing trousers. And it was clear as sunshine that none of these men were going to be wearing trousers again until those very trousers had been washed in a reasonably priced, assemble-it-yourself, newfangled, goat-powered washing machine.

Venus and Mercury

Kirt Lee

Madame's earthly affairs had long been largely in order, but this latest bout, lasting weeks, came at a bad time. Events in England had erupted. Her incapacity had tragic consequence for Thomas' dear nephew, Adam, whom she loved as dearly as if he had been her own. She was now recovered sufficiently enough to give him her full attention. Given her condition—not to mention his—she dared no further delay. Perhaps the matter could yet be repaired.

The sweet child now stood at the door. "Come closer, dear Adam, so Madame can see you." Adam did so. "But the years pass so quickly. You are no longer a boy. Such happy years they were."

"Madame fares better?" English accent, with just a touch of Parisian.

"For today, child. But Madame forgets her manners. There is wine. Will you pour for us both?"

"Of course."

"And if you would also, to mine please add a measure of the medicine that you will find in the drawer to the left."

Adam opened the drawer and examined the medicine closely, tasting a bit. It was mercuric, and of high quality, the medicine of a syphilitic. Beside it, a spoon. "One of this measure, Madame?"

"Yes, thank you." She watched him stir the medicine into her wine.

"Madame finds the medicine more agreeable with wine?"

"I am French, child. If I wished to take hemlock, I would mix it with wine."

As he started to put the medicine back, she added, "Do take as much as you like for yourself, child. I'm sure you are at tight ends lately."

He paused. "Madame?"

"Wicked tongues delighted in bringing Madame this news."

Adam knew word would get around soon enough. Still, he had hoped it would not happen quite so quickly. He would have spared his late uncle's paramour this news. He gave her the cup, and sat without speaking.

"Tell Madame how this occurred."

"Does it matter now?"

"Speak."

"Madame knows of events in London?"

"On most days, Madame is uncertain of events in her own chambers."

"Charles Stuart ran amok, tossing accusations of treason with abandon. Father is dead, his estate confiscated. When the news got about, I was courted. I needed friends, so I consented. When a chancre appeared, I knew what it was." Adam had seen enough syphilis chancres. He had come to Paris to study medicine. "My 'friend' accused me of infecting him. It was quite a scene. He told the faculty at University, and they expelled me." His tone was a bit flat.

"You were had, child. The wicked man who sent word of your infection to Madame was one who sought revenge. He wishes to see that I suffer in my last days, but dared not attack one whose cousin is so close to *Le Cardinal*. Thus, he struck at you, while grief and need left you vulnerable. It would have been easy enough to find a desperate young man in need of medicine, willing to do such work. It was simple cruelty, well aimed."

"Name him. I will kill him." Adam's tone was still flat.

"You will not." As usual, Madame seemed quite certain of herself.

Adam stared sullenly.

"Obey me child. I have other purposes for you."

"Can I kill him and still fulfill these purposes?"

"He is Madame's privilege. Assassination has never been my way, but I have no time for more gracious means. He would soon have you killed, of course, since he will assume I have told you how you came by the syphilis. He will fear you will seek revenge. He will expect you. This is a matter for professionals, not revenge."

"Your privilege, Madame," Adam conceded.

Madame now studied him in a way he would have found ominous when younger, but now found pleasing. Whatever she planned for him, he would find it worthy.

"In the other drawer, you will find papers, some bound. Look first at the bound set."

Adam retrieved them. Next to them was another bottle of medicine, a year's supply at least, perhaps two, and a bag clearly filled with coin. He opened the bound volume.

"Sonnets: Bacon. Marlowe. de Vere. Others."

"Just so. You know them?"

"I do. The usual parlor amusements for those with the right training."

"And the rest?" Madame asked.

"More sonnets. Correspondence regarding business. I see little in them, Madame. More parlor amusements?"

"Another method is also present. Examine the last two pages."

He did. "An interesting variation . . . clever . . . it would be more compact. Certainly more laborious, but one could conceal more with it."

"Just so. Memorize the method, child, then toss those parts in the fire."

Adam needed but a moment; then the papers burned.

Madame continued. "It was a method Bacon shared with few. It will unlock all but the first three sonnets in that binding. Use the better known method for those, though you'll find little of interest in them. As you say, they are mere parlor amusements. I'm uncertain how many know the more difficult method. Some, I'm sure, but I would not know who. I am the last of my own acquaintance who I am certain can read those."

"And what will I find in those, Madame?"

"Scandal."

"Scandal?"

"Scandal, and more, some of which will still be fresh fifty years from now. Some date as far back as the reign of Elizabeth and concern Raleigh, Walsingham and others. Madame has added some work of more recent vintage, detailing some events in France. All the sonnets contain something in the simpler method. Most conceal something in the more difficult method. This is a lesson that will serve you well in life, child. Always keep some lesser coin where a thief can find it, but not too easily. Keep the better coin better hidden."

"True wisdom, Madame. And you wish me to . . . ?"

"To keep them safe. They are historical documents. One day, scholars will drool over them, smearing the ink. Madame would not have them lost, or the method forgotten. Who could I trust other than my dear late Thomas' nephew? Will you undertake this, and see that they are not misused?"

"I would be honored. But I must remind Madame, I share her malady."

"You must pass them down, as they were passed to me, as I pass them to you. Add to them if you wish."

"I would be honored, but . . . yes, I will undertake it."

"Good. Now examine the other papers."

He did, and as he did, grew perplexed. "Travel papers. Who is John Smith?"

"You are. Madame has done many favors over the years, and knows where many bodies are buried, if you take my meaning."

The old bird looked quite predatory. He wondered how many stories he would find in her papers. Too few, he was sure. Bacon's methods were flexible, but not thrifty. "Why would Madame wish me to go to Basel?"

"Read on, child."

"This man in Basel is to provide bank drafts and papers for me to travel to Grantville." He paused. "You mean for me to go to Grantville?"

"They have begun a medical school you know."

"Yes, it was all the talk among faculty and students."

"And why would I wish you to travel to Grantville, Adam?"

"To study medicine?" Light dawned. "Oh. Chloramphenicol."

"Unobtainable elsewhere. It is said to cure syphilis, not merely alleviate it. A student might have better access."

Adam considered. It was true. And he had no other prospects.

"The money is yours, whatever you choose. I have no heirs of my own. Take it, before the lawyers get it."

"I will do as you say. And I will see if I can find enough of this chloramphenicol for two."

"I may be no longer in need of it by then. In truth, it has become a rare day when I am so lucid. My concern now is for you, and for those papers. Take care of yourself, and them, and Madame will be well rewarded."

"Yes, Madame."

"Good. It is best you start soon. Tonight. Do not return to your rooms. Take up the coin and the medicine, then one last thing, before you go. Take down the sword above from the wall, please."

He did, looking closely. "It was Uncle's. He wore it on special occasions."

"It is a near match to the dirk your uncle gave you when you were twelve. The dirk was made for you. The sword is older."

"Uncle left it with you, Madame?"

"Yes. It was my father's. I gave it to Thomas. I wish you to have it now."

Adam bowed.

"We take care of our own, child. Never forget this. It is possible that you will find a new circle of friends in this Grantville. I cannot imagine a town of that importance without such prospects. Choose carefully. You now carry a great historical treasure, so give some thought to the future, and be watchful for opportunities."

"Yes, Madame."

"Go with God, Adam. Your uncle loved you, and so do I."

Madame received a kiss on the cheek, and the lad was gone.

A servant entered shortly after.

"Adam's visit was noticed, Andre?"

"By no one now living, Madame," Andre answered.

"Very good, Andre. Please gather up half of mother's silver from the basement. Take it to the Savoyard. Tell him the rest is his if the brings me the head of the Burgundian Stork before morning. Be certain he understands: Madame will only give the rest if she can see the head, and know its face. He must not mutilate the face."

"Yes, Madame. The Savoyard will be pleased." Andre looked pleased also. But then, he had always been fond of Adam.

For the first time in her long life, Madame would now be a killer. She rested more easily now, satisfied.

Adam left the house, looked at the sky, then started walking. With each step, he retreated deeper into himself.

A robot named Adam walked to Basel. Inside, a young man named Adam noted every house, every window, every cobblestone. He expected never to see them again.

☆ ☆ ☆

The robot named Adam had walked into Grantville. Inside, the young man named Adam resented every intrusion from the world outside.

He had read the words hidden in the archive of Madame, finding Bacon, Walsingham, Raleigh, Elizabeth, the Stuarts, the Valois, the Bourbon. It was beyond price. He wondered if it might be the only such archive outside the hands of monarchs.

Likely it was not, but being its custodian kept Adam alive. In that, as in all her efforts, Madame knew her business. He could not bear to think of such papers being lost or abused.

The robot now sat in a small examination room in Leahy Hospital awaiting a doctor. Safely inside, the young man watched with curiosity. How would the examination differ from those he knew? Would he be cured? Would he be tossed out? Fascinating questions.

The door opened and a man came in.

The man stared at Adam's sword hanging by the door, then at Adam. He looked at Adam's paperwork, and smiled oddly.

"Good morning, Adam Tyrrell. I am Dr. Balthazar Abrabanel." Mildly cheerful, English accent. There could only be one doctor by that name, with that accent. "I don't believe we've met, but would you be Thomas Tyrell's nephew?" Abrabanel pointed to Uncle Thomas' sword.

The robot was gone. The young man remained, naked. Abrabanel had served the court in England. He may have done intelligence work. Which factions, which sides had he been on over the years? What was he doing here? The voices of his elders flashed advice though his imagination.

From Father: Kick him in the stomach and run, boy!

From Uncle Thomas: Trip him up. Find the medicine. Then run.

From Madame: Offer him wine. Converse.

Then Adam got advice from himself: Father never would have known this man, so try Uncle's advice first. Then Madame's. Hold Father's in reserve.

"Madame Rossignol sent me," Adam said.

The smile left the doctor's face. Nothing took its place. "Beg pardon?"

"Madame Rossignol."

"I don't understand."

"You knew *her*." It wasn't a question, and Adam emphasized the pronoun.

"I knew Henri Rossignol well enough, but long ago. *He* was close to your uncle. Why would *Henri* send you?" The doctor emphasized the pronoun and the name.

"Chloramphenicol."

"I'd heard he had syphilis. He was the last of that circle, since your uncle died."

"Not quite the last."

Abrabanel digested that, then passed over it. "I understand your uncle fell at Breitenfeld?"

"Yes. He preferred an honorable end to a demented one."

Abrabanel digested that, too. "More syphilis?"

Adam nodded.

"What can you tell me of Henri's condition?"

Adam rendered a description that would have gotten a fair mark from a professor.

"Have you been studying medicine?" Abrabanel asked.

"Two years in Paris."

"You know the prognosis?"

"She may already be dead."

"Perhaps. We might get the medicine to him while he still lives, but you must understand... At best, it would only stop the disease from causing further harm. The injuries already done would remain. From your description, he would not live much longer in any event."

"I suspected as much, sir."

"But you had to try anyway. I understand. In your place, I would do the same."

"There's more, Doctor."

"Yes?"

"I have it, too."

"Syphilis? What symptoms have you had?"

While the doctor examined Adam, Adam examined the doctor's instruments. They were marvelous up-time devices. He was intrigued to find he understood most of them. He made a mental note to try to learn more about their construction.

When it was done, Abrabanel said, "No signs of it just now, but the university doctors are good. You can put your clothes back on." There was still no expression on his face.

"You can cure this?"

The doctor nodded.

"I have coin. A legacy from Madame."

The doctor ignored that. "You've been taking mercury?"

"Yes."

"Stop. It's nearly as bad as the malady. Give it to me. We'll use chloramphenicol, but it's short just now. Sieges breed epidemics, so we sent much to Amsterdam. Emergencies only at the moment. In three weeks, perhaps four, we'll have more."

Adam deflated. He would live.

Uncle had walked into a block of pikes, and died. Adam had walked into Grantville, and would live. He considered that a moment, and decided it might be good to live. It would make it easier to preserve Madame's papers.

"Thank you. Should I apply to medical school elsewhere if I mean to continue my education?" Adam surprised himself. He hadn't known he would say that.

"We can speak of that later."

"I'll be grateful if you can just rid me of the syphilis." Yes, It felt good to live.

"Chloram will fix that, well enough. Do we need to discuss anything else at the moment?"

"No."

The doctor took a piece of paper and wrote. "Very well. This is my prescription until then. Where are you staying?"

"I'm at the Y."

"Your uncle was a very talented man, Adam Tyrrell. Henri more so. I will send word to you at the Y when we have the drug." As he left, the doctor looked at Adam's sword hanging by the wall. "Do keep it sheathed, lad."

Perhaps he meant the sword. Perhaps. There was no trace of humor in his voice.

Adam looked at the prescription. The top was typeset:

"From the desk of Balthazar Abrabanel, MD. Prescription:"

Below, handwritten:

"Essay a composition on the book *And the Band Played On*, by Randy Shilts, to be found in the Medical Reading Room, third floor, Leahy."

Curious title. Likely a morality lesson.

Adam returned to the front desk and asked where he might find the reading room.

☆ ☆ ☆

Adam had an early lunch in the Leahy cafeteria before going to the reading room. where he presented his "prescription." The librarian seemed to find nothing odd about it. He received the book, and settled in a comfortable chair by a window. A laudably quiet up-time clock behind the librarian's desk showed the time just before noon.

He made many trips to the dictionary chained to the desk.

Much later, he stopped and closed his eyes. It was dark outside. He had not finished the book, and did not care to continue just now. He could see that this project was big. Four weeks might do. Maybe.

Early the next morning, he stopped at the stationer across from the downtown library. He bought a folder, filled it with paper and chose a partly used up-time pencil. He did not care to mix bottles of ink with priceless books.

He noted that the up-time lady ahead of him had brought in a handful of well used pencils with no erasers. She left with two fresh pencils with erasers, muttering angrily. He filed this away in his growing collection of anecdotes.

At Leahy, Adam started the book fresh, this time using the dictionary more carefully. He learned new words, and new uses for old words. He wrote down references to other publications. He marveled at the index in the back. He seldom spoke to anyone. Others politely left him to his work.

Inside the book's cover were notations and a pocket indicating that it had once been in the collection of the high school. Adam checked with the librarian, and learned that yes, that meant it had been freely available to any adolescent in town. The book did not look well used. He added this to his list of curiosities.

Had the University of Paris possessed this book, it would have been heavily restricted, solely for professional use. The entire faculty would have had apoplexy over the author's presentation of sodomites, but on no account would it have been discarded.

It was not a medical book, but a popular account of the AIDS epidemic, written by a journalist.

What was Abrabanel's purpose in assigning it to Adam? Surely the man knew what was in it. The parallels to syphilis were glaringly obvious. He wanted Adam to learn a practical lesson, to go with moral teachings. But the rest?

Whatever moral or professional lessons Abrabanel was offering, another thing was clear enough: the doctor needed help with this, whether he knew it or not. As a gay syphilitic, Adam had a certain perspective on this topic.

He learned that up-time attitudes toward sodomites had been evolving, amid great social contention. There was a Sodomite movement! Sodomites had attacked police outside an American tavern, and boasted of it!

Madame would never have approved. Uncle Thomas? A more interesting question, but he was no longer around to ask.

Adam added a problem to his notes: how to discreetly research sexual topics.

He preferred handling leeches to that book.

Adam left a note for the doctor: How many cases were there in Grantville?

The answer: One known, now deceased. More were very unlikely. The note offered no further comment.

Adam did more reading at Leahy when he finished the Shilts book, then shifted to the other libraries. The Leahy reading room had been decorous. The SoTF State Library, though, was a mob scene. The wait for the encyclopedias, in particular, was lengthy.

Periodicals were easier to browse at leisure, and the collection included more than two decades of *Time* magazine. Adam's notes from Shilts included some references from that publication.

Time was eclectic. Politics. War. Entertainment. Science. Medicine. Business. People. Even the very price on the cover suggested new lines of up-time research, as it increased over time. Amazingly, it was vastly cheaper if home delivered. Down-time, these magazines were treasure beyond even that carried by the Spanish Caribbean fleets. Up-time, they had been as disposable as an old man's apple core. He could write one hundred learned commentaries, and still only scratch the tip of this one collection of magazines.

Adam added to his growing list for future research. The Cold War. Republicans and Democrats. Punk rock. Disneyland. Oil sheiks. Gates, Wozniak and Jobs.

Most of the world, including Europe, seemed to have lost its aristocracy. The noble families were covered in the same pages as theater and music, rather than politics. It was a stunning world, but in the pages of the magazines, it seemed as ordinary as a woman beating a rug in Southwark.

His most shocking discovery? Grantville was a rural backwater. Certainly that was common knowledge, but after a few dozen issues of *Time* magazine, Adam knew it in his bones. He did not see it merely in terms of technology or history. He saw it in terms of culture and society. These vaunted up-timers would have been judged backward by the twentieth-century sophisticates of New York City or Paris.

He started going through the *Time* collection issue by issue, starting in 1980, just before the AIDS epidemic was discovered. He made a fast note of each title and topic as he went, regardless of relevance to this assignment, building his own index. He slowed only to read the articles relevant to the AIDS epidemic thoroughly and abstract them. Time enough for the rest later.

More paper. Another pencil. Always another puzzle on the next page.

Shilts had died in 1994. Some important material dated after his book had been published in 1988. Adam saw that the story could not be understood from the book alone. Had any down-timer done this additional research yet? The up-timers must already know the story, but AIDS, far more than syphilis, was a disease of pariahs. Would this blind them to its lessons?

The library never closed and was always crowded. Even in that busy place—no, especially there—people began to notice that Adam was on a quest. Finally another researcher approached him.

"You seem to find the magazine collection useful. Perhaps you are compiling an index. If so, I would find ways to be grateful if you would share it."

Adam made a noncommittal answer, but began to surface from the magazines and books more often to take notice of his surroundings. After a day of that, he stopped and just looked at where he'd been working.

Some patrons, especially up-timers, just seemed to be reading. Others, both up-timers and down-timers, read and wrote more furtively. This was made easier by the rows of carrels, almost booths, for the researchers, Without that added privacy, the situation would have been intolerable. Some cast challenging glances at any who looked too closely. Many, very many, shielded their materials from others. A few of the researchers had men with them, humorless men, who seemed to be there only to keep prying eyes at a distance. Other researchers acted like spies from a poorly written comedy.

These men were not hiding their work from the authorities so much as from each other.

Adam had never seen a library with a bouncer before. This library had more than one.

Adam speculated that the cloak check at the entrance collected blades for reasons beyond preventing patrons from using them on books. The stakes were high indeed. *Monarchs* paid some of these researchers, seeking to gain some advantage of history or technology over their rivals. The outcome of wars might be decided in these rooms.

He was sure it was the largest collection of learned spies ever assembled. Certainly it was the most industrious—and most ironic. What they were "spying out" was free for the taking!

What did this say about the authorities who permitted it? It couldn't be stupidity. It must be a statement of strength, or perhaps of arrogance. Or was there some deeper game here? Adam was accustomed to deeper games.

From the door, a woman's voice called out, "Roach coach!" The midnight meal wagon had arrived. People began drifting outside. Some left a friend behind to guard their work.

Uncle Thomas would have loved this, had he only lived to see it. Madame would have set up court in a corner, reading romances while directing her mignons in their research. Adam wished for their advice.

Yes. It felt good to be alive, and more so each day.

"Pizza. Italian food!" A young man, Tuscan by his accent, smiled at Adam. "An excellent choice." He sat next to Adam uninvited, but not entirely unwelcome. They ate outside the library in darkness broken by gas lights.

"I grew weary of sausage and sauerkraut." Adam's conversation skills felt rusty. For weeks, he had avoided conversation.

"My card." The young man handed it to Adam.

Stephano Vasari
Grantville Library Research
Specializing in History & Biography
Best Rates—Can you afford not to ask?

"I'm Adam. How's business, Stephano?" Adam was genuinely interested in the answer. If he were judged morally unfit for medical training, he would need other work.

"The usual for a freelance researcher with no great or wealthy patron. Castoff questions not wanted by researchers with better sponsors." Stephano assumed a bored voice: "How will my children fare? Should I invest in Virginia? Will the siege of Amsterdam destroy the tulip market, or create a shortage? Is there anything I should know about Lord Him or Lady Her that will help me gain favor? They seldom phrase that question so baldly, but it's clear what they want. All very predictable. I hope one or another of them will be so pleased with my answers as to refer me to a patron with real money and better questions. I'm seldom so lucky as to find an inquiry from someone who is in the encyclopedias. I seldom even bother to cover my work. I should have listened to my mother, finished my education, and become an attorney." Stephano rolled his eyes to indicate his opinion of that option.

"It all sounds terribly tedious."

Stephano shrugged. "It can be. The speculation is that you are compiling a magazine index. If you are generous with it, you might find many willing to share information or hire you in times of need, but be advised, few are willing to share patrons. Of course, you may already have one—not that I would pry."

"Actually, I'm at loose ends. I intend to petition to study medicine."

"You invest your idle days shrewdly, friend."

"So I'm learning."

Stephano finished his pizza. "And now, back to work. I have to find a way to tell an abbot in Campania that I can not find for him the current whereabouts of Prester John. I fear he will not pay well for that news, if he pays at all."

Adam decided he liked Stephano. Perhaps it was the charmingly downscale American Western garb. It might have been fun to prowl Southwark with him. He made a mental note to watch for *Time* magazine references to Prester John.

Adam remembered Stephano's remark about "Italian food," and made another note in his future research list, adding "Hamburgers," "French Toast" and "French Fries." Americans and their culture, even their food, were the proverbial child of a thousand fathers.

His research list was getting long. He was not sure of a market for it.

Adam had enough material for his commentary on AIDS. The epidemiology aspect was obvious, but he would write a much longer paper. He began writing it the next afternoon. It would have been a much shorter paper without the magazines.

Several days later, he dropped the essay off at Leahy for Dr. Abrabanel. He was told it would still be a few days before the doctor had his medicine, so he went back to the library. Stephano had recommended music by the Village People, so he signed up for a CD player.

The Village People lyrics were suggestive, and the costumes more so. Adjust for period and Adam could imagine those Village People fishing the piers of London—with their hooks baited for sailors. But Adam found he could "stop the music" and did. The librarian suggested Steeleye Span, which turned out to be more agreeable, and quite fascinating to an Englishman.

Adam had several references to the Village People in his magazine index. He gave the dates and page numbers to Stephano without comment. The Village People were gay icons.

Adam wondered when *gay* had replaced *sodomite* in his mind. Recently, to be sure. The change had not happened easily, but he now found that he occasionally felt "uppity."

Adam lay in his bunk, listening to a dozen neighbors breathe, snore, and turn. They didn't keep him awake. Something else nagged him.

The lady with the pencils.

Erasers. Ballpoint pens. Light bulbs. A child bawling over a deflated bicycle tire. Amid this, monarchs moved spies through the libraries like chess pieces.

He got up, dressed, and stepped out into the night. Clear sky. Gas lights.

Gas lights. Not electric.

He went to the library, and sat at a picnic table near his usual gas light. Within the building, Prometheus.

Instead, Stephano emerged. He must have been sitting near a window, watching. This pleased Adam.

"Pondering the night, Adam?" he asked.

"One should, from time to time. Will you walk with me, Stephano?"

They meandered quietly from one gas light to the next, never very close to the lights, never very far.

After a time, Adam spoke, "Grantville."

"Yes," Stephano replied. "Grantville."

"They are Prometheus, Stephano."

"Bringers of light. Yes."

"And you know what happened to Prometheus? Look in the library, Stephano, and see the vultures."

"Grantville isn't bound yet. They still stand defiant. But look again, Adam. When I see Grantville, I sometimes see the city of Rome. You know what they say of Rome these days?"

Adam shook his head.

"I would render it poetically: Where barbarians failed, Barbarini prevailed. Today's Romans use the monuments of the Caesars as quarries."

"I'm afraid I've never been to Rome, Stephano."

"I would love to show it to you some day, Adam. But here, have you seen the streetcars? The airplanes? The APCs? They had none of it when they arrived. All of it, quarried from whatever they found in their pockets. How long can they do this?"

"I've been so buried in my own affairs. I hadn't noticed. But yes, I see it now. And it's of a part with all the frantic work. Steel. Chemicals. Guns."

"Have you heard of their Granges, Adam? One of their major works is preserving their stock. They have refined seed and livestock breeds, but some of it hangs by a thread. There are not enough of the cattle, for instance, so they must breed carefully."

"The large horses, also?"

"Yes."

"The vision of Prometheus came to me earlier. But there was more to it, Stephano. Look closely at the vultures feeding on the liver of this town, and what do you see? Indigestion."

Stephano considered a moment. "Yes, it is true. It is such a delicious irony, such a magnificent jest. The Grantvillers could not be more clear than if they had hung a sign over the door. 'Heads I win. Tails you lose. Take what you like.' It must be galling."

"Look deeper still, Stephano. Have you studied the nations of their world? There's not an important monarchy remaining except maybe in Arab lands."

"True. Galling indeed."

"And how did that happen, Stephano?"

"That's the big question, my friend. You'll hear it discussed among researchers, if you sit at the right tables for lunch."

"It almost doesn't matter. Whatever did it, it's right there in that library, being copied and spread round the world by the very spies who seek to stop it. An information plague, like one of their computer viruses. That's why they keep the library open to all."

Stephano went dumb. Then it sank in. "My God! Can this be true?"

"I'm sure of it. I think I may even have some grip on the details."

"Adam, you're a very rich young man if you do."

"Rich? Did Cassandra prosper? Stephano, to understand what they do, it helps to study epidemics. Look closely and see this one spreading. The CoCs. The Granges. The Ram and the Ewe. Religious toleration. Women in pulpits. Jews in Prague taking up arms and tearing down ghetto walls. They're spreading a cultural contagion that touches anything, everything."

"And the library is the center of all this? I don't buy that, Adam."

"The people take part also, just by the way they speak and carry themselves, Stephano. The library is how they persuade the great and mighty to steal it!"

"You may be right, friend. It would explain much. But forgive me if I keep some skepticism."

"Not at all."

They walked more.

"Did you expect all this when you set out for Grantville?" Adam waved around.

"No. I met an up-timer in Rome named Harry Lefferts, who spoke of the medicines. I came for chloramphenicol and stayed for the library."

"I'm on the chloramphenicol waiting list. Soon, I hope."

They stopped and looked at one another, each waiting for the other to speak first.

After a very tense moment, Stephano suddenly grinned rakishly and sang. "YYYYY-EMMM-CEEE-AAAAAA."

A dam burst inside Adam. He fell to the ground convulsed in laughter.

Stephano stood looking down at him. "Damned gas lights," he said mournfully. He then winked brightly. "But as Grandmother always said, chloramphenicol first."

When Adam's laughter had run its course, Stephano helped him up. "Adam, when I went in for treatment, I got Dr. Nichols. He's not an easy man to fool." He paused a painful moment, then said, "So they know about me. Hang around me too much and... I suppose I should go now."

"Wait." Adam considered a moment. "Adam and Stephano. I like the sound of that. Do you?"

Stephano smiled. "I do. You make fine company, Adam."

That was what Adam had needed to hear. "I think we need to find a more profitable line of work."

"How?" Stephano asked. "As researchers?"

"In a manner of speaking. I need to know if you've been working for anyone, Stephano. Will anyone object if you strike out on your own?"

"There's nothing I can't clean up in a few days, then I'm free. I'm tired of living on the castoffs of others. And you?"

"The same, and worse. I've no family, no home. I will adopt this place as my home if I can."

"Agreed. I would not leave the libraries willingly. Have you found a patron, Adam?"

"No. We can do better than that, I think. I have enough money to get us started."

Stephano shrugged. "May I hope for intrigue, danger, excitement?"

"I mean to reach high, Stephano." Adam stared at him appraisingly.

"Adam, talk to Stephano."

"Wait till you see some of the things I've found in the library."

"Adam, should your Stephano be worried now?"

Adam was pleased to see that *his* Stephano looked worried, a bit, but very interested as well.

"I've been working on some essays I'd like you to read, Stephano. Perhaps they'll attract the desired attention."

They were still plotting when the sun rose.

Days later, Adam and Stephano stepped out of the library.

"I'm tired of the roach coach," Stephano complained. "I hear they have excellent lunchtime entertainment at Cora's lately: improvisational comedy from a female impersonator who calls herself Veda Mae Culpa. Shall we research it?" Veda Mae Haggerty, Grantville's loudest gossip, had become a running joke with Stephano.

"That sounds fine, but she's a lady, not an impersonator."

"I mean to check her for an Adam's apple. Either way, she's no lady."

"She's had no apples from me," Adam said virtuously. "I need to stop by the Y on the way."

At the Y, Adam found a message waiting for him. "It would seem I'm going to Leahy this afternoon. They have the curenstoff."

"We'll eat first. Trust me, it will be good for your nerves. Then we'll go to Leahy."

"We?"

"We."

Adam didn't argue. He'd be glad of the company.

The Veda Mae Show helped his nerves. Stephano's rather loud donkey impressions helped more, since Veda Mae seemed oblivious of their intent. In the end, they agreed that it would require a medical examination to pass judgment on whether that was an Adam's apple on her throat.

The walk to Leahy did not last long enough for Adam's taste.

The door to the examination room opened. Dr. Abrabanel entered.

"Good afternoon, Adam. I have your medicine." Abrabanel placed it on the table. "You swallow it. Again, you understand that there's a small risk? One person in several thousand dies of it. I have not yet seen this happen. I judge the risk favorable, compared to your illness, but the decision is yours."

Adam solemnly took the medicine.

"I'll want you to visit every third day for three weeks, to monitor your progress. Now, I'd like to discuss your commentary on Shilts."

"Certainly."

"Let's allow the hospital to have their examination room back. We'll speak in my office."

Adam's essay was in Abrabanel's office. The doctor took it up, and glanced at the first pages.

"I keep an easy schedule these days. Some teaching. Some patients. You're not the first I've assigned this book. I see that you've noted AIDS as an epidemiological example. From there, most students go on to write about the disease itself. You've included some of this. Like most others, you've compared AIDS to syphilis. You've also compared that epidemic to the epidemics of our own time. At this point, some students append sermons. You haven't. Instead, you continue to study the course of the epidemic well beyond the period covered by the book, almost until the Ring of Fire." The doctor looked up.

"The magazines ran out at that point, with no cure found."

"Just so. You've noted that it first came to light in a pariah population, and that distaste for homosexuals hampered early understanding and efforts. You note that homosexual distrust of authority was also a complication in controlling the disease, even when it was better understood. You recount the development of organizations to help those with the disease, and the rise of protest movements. I find it interesting that you invested several paragraphs on a description of the American tradition of nonviolent civil rights movements, and how the AIDS movements followed in that tradition." The doctor looked up again. The doctor pronounced *homosexual* like it was an unfamiliar diagnosis. At least he wasn't using *sodomite*.

"It's an integral part of the story, sir."

"Yes. I'd heard some of this from the up-time doctors and staff. If any students found that material, they didn't include it. Only you wrote of it as anything other than a sermon. You expressed no opinions."

"I found the subject awkward, sir."

"I can imagine. Would you care to express an opinion now, Adam?"

Adam had rehearsed several answers to that question, should it arise. But what came out was, "It made me angry, and frightened."

"A physician is required to control his emotions." Abrabanel gave Adam a professional look.

"Of course, Doctor. But have you seen a food riot?"

"Not up close."

"Nor I, up close. But I ask myself what happens in an epidemic when the chloramphenicol runs out."

"Then we will do what we can. I'll expect you back in three days, Adam."

Adam rose to leave, then hesitated at the door. "You gave me chloramphenicol."

"Yes." The doctor looked up at Adam.

"It's scarce. Someone else didn't get it. That person may die in my place."

"If there were more urgent need, I'd have waited to treat you."

"I'm no longer sure I wish to study medicine, doctor. Perhaps later, if they'll have a former syphilitic."

"There is no record of your infection. And as for the cost of the medicine, it would seem I lost some chloramphenicol in an accident. Clumsy of me. That was good research, lad. You earned it. Return in three days. And while you wait, consider your life, Adam Tyrrell. Do not travel the road of your uncle and Henri Rossignol."

"Yes. Chloramphenicol may not always be available."

"I mean . . . consider marriage." The doctor returned his attention to some papers on his desk.

Adam found Stephano in the cafeteria. As they walked, Adam spoke. "It would seem the doctor disapproves of sodomy."

"Does he know about you?" Stephano asked.

"He counseled me regarding marriage. It may merely have been his idea of fatherly advice, being as I've no family now."

"Kind of him," Stephano said.

"He offended me," Adam replied. Which felt odd, considering that the doctor was also saving his life.

When Adam returned for his first follow-up, he gave the doctor a short paper on the economic troubles of the United States in the last quarter of the twentieth century as reported in *Time* magazine. On his next visit, he gave the doctor a paper comparing the development of the microcomputer industry to various enterprises in Grantville, including the role of four up-time teenagers in the development of a sewing machine industry. Adam had been careful to emphasize the role and nature of geeks in both developments.

Adam repeated this brand-building process until his last follow-up visit. On that day, he first visited the library to verify that a certain science fiction book was still on the shelves and in the catalog. He then went to Leahy and gave the doctor his commentary on the book. Afterward, he returned immediately to the library, where he found the book gone, along with its catalog entries.

He collected Stephano from a carrel and took him outside.

"I've dangled the bait. He—or apparently they—took it," Adam reported.

"I watched a librarian remove the book. So, we wait?" Stephano asked.

"We wait."

"If it goes bad, do you think they will let us share a jail cell?"

"Let's not wait to find out. The doctor pronounced me cured. Take me home," Adam said, adamantly.

Stephano smiled. "At least that part of the waiting is over."

Later, in Stephano's rooms, Adam felt himself retreating back inside the robot again. This frightened him, but Stephano was patient. Flesh is stronger than armor.

The next morning, they went to the Y to collect Adam's belongings. He was moving in with Stephano. As they walked, Adam said, "It would seem that no ruffians broke down our door last night."

"I had thought they wouldn't. Door breaking doesn't seem common here," Stephano said. "But I'm never certain with these Americans. Just when I think I know them, I find they still surprise me."

"Political weather changes, even in their world. Consider their Ku Klux Klan, their McCarthy hearings, which they even called 'witch hunts,'" Adam said. "And let's not forget their military was still witch-hunting gays up until the Ring of Fire. The up-timers are under great stress here in Grantville. We need friends. Somewhere here, there are people of great subtlety. Finding and courting them may take some time, but I judge that the up-timers prefer spirit to servility. Let us start boldly, and see how it goes."

"It's worth a try," Stephano agreed.

At the Y, Adam found a message waiting for him, asking to him see Dr. Abrabanel at Leahy. Adam didn't have much to move, so they did that first. They both wanted that to be done, to be made official. Then they went to see Dr. Abrabanel. They entered the doctor's office together.

"Perhaps your friend could wait for you in the cafeteria," the doctor suggested pleasantly.

"If this is about my treatment, I'd prefer that Stephano stay. If it's about that last book report, I insist he stay."

Stephano closed the door from the inside, not making a move to leave.

"He's read the book?" the doctor asked.

"And my report," Adam answered. "I gather that the librarians don't take science fiction seriously. This was a large book. Huff-duff, and how to recognize a huff-duff antenna by its movements. Radio intercepts. Signal traffic analysis. Computer-assisted crypt-analysis, with some hints regarding early computer design. The Pearl Harbor intercepts. The Yamamoto killing. The battle of the Atlantic. Pseudo-random number generation for one time pads by way of Riemann-Zeta functions, with suggestions how they might be computed without electronic assistance. Hints about proper generation of random numbers and other cipher keys. Large number factoring. Allusions to game theory, information and coding theory. Operational security. Portable radios that can reach from Naples to London. Names of cryptographers, some real. You might wish to remove the Alan Turing biography. I found it fascinating, also. Mostly it was just hints, but there was enough detail for years of research."

"I liked the part about allowing a ship to be captured with its code books so they could replace some codes so that the Germans would not guess that the English had learned by cryptanalysis that the codes were compromised. With a little more work, the author might try writing a history of the de Medici," Stephano said wistfully, in his thickest Tuscan accent.

The doctor looked pinched, but said nothing.

Adam looked at Abrabanel. "Who is the last survivor of Madame Rossignol's circle?"

"How much did they teach you, Adam?"

"Enough. Lord Bacon himself was among my teachers. I remember him fondly. Would you believe it? I used to puddle in his lap when I was small. Are you qualified to test me?"

"That could be arranged," the doctor said, sitting back.

"Cipher cracking is a rare skill, Doctor," Adam pointed out.

"I know it," the doctor acknowledged.

"And you have much need of it here, given the activity in that library," Adam added. "You'd need the largest Black Chamber in Europe to handle that much suspicious mail."

"Understand this, Adam Tyrrell. They have a constitution here that guarantees against unreasonable search and seizure. Opening mail without a warrant is a serious crime. The up-timers won't want their fingerprints on that. It would be politically dangerous."

"So there are rules. It still needs..." Adam stopped. Fingerprints? That would be another up-time expression, and one with some real meaning. He made yet another mental note, then continued, "It still needs the largest Black Chamber in Europe just to handle the ones known to be working for hostile powers."

"You wish to offer your services?" Abrabanel asked.

"Will that buy us protection from official harassment?" Adam spread his hands in an inquiring gesture. "In Paris and London, I'm a known homosexual. That information could easily arrive here. My boyfriend . . ." Adam pointed a thumb over his shoulder. ". . . is known here, in Florence and perhaps Rome as well."

"Maybe Rome," Stephano shrugged. "Definitely here. Dr. Nichols is an insightful man."

"We need the usual assurances regarding official harassment and blackmail," Adam finished. "Delivered in person by someone of convincing rank."

This protection was Adam's true goal. It would make it possible to stay in Grantville, near the precious libraries. He and the doctor stared at each other for a moment, appraisingly.

"I will make inquiries," the doctor finally said.

"Are we done, Adam?" Stephano asked, adding, "I'm hungry."

"Yes, I think so. Doctor? The usual assurances, given in person by someone of very convincing rank?"

"I'll get back to you, Adam."

As they left, Adam said, "Speaking plainly feels good."

"Yes," Stephano agreed. "But let's not do it often, shall we?"

"It's hardly necessary. The idea of gay liberation is in the same libraries along with all the rest of the stuff they're spreading. They can't erase it any more than they can expunge references to Elvis Presley."

"Do you think they'll go for our ideas?"

"Whoever 'they' are, I think they'll at least test me. Truly, I'll be satisfied if they merely leave us alone. Now, I need to do some research. I think I've overlooked something."

Fingerprints.

Stephano hadn't been allowed in this room.

The man behind the desk had the look and manners of a clerk. The man behind the man behind the desk looked more like some nightmare from Scandinavian mythology. Adam resolved to make no sudden moves.

"You are Adam Tyrrell, of London, son of William Tyrrell of London, until recently medical student in Paris," the man read, droning. Definitely a clerk, and either a very good sport, or very dangerous. The clerk's Swedish accent and the troll behind him argued for the latter. "You claim past association with Francis Bacon, Henri Rossignol, and Thomas Tyrrell, all late of the Black Chamber of Francis Bacon during the reign of James Stuart, King of England and Scotland."

"And before that during the reign of Elizabeth. Does the gentleman there speak English?" Adam pointed to the . . . uh . . . man.

"I'm not certain he even speaks Swedish. Definitely not English. Ignore him. You claim to be a cryptanalyst, trained by the above named persons."

"That's correct."

"Describe those persons, Mr. Tyrrell." The clerk took up a quill, clearly not as bored as he pretended.

"In what manner? Their appearances?"

"In whatever manner you please, Mr. Tyrrell." No, he was not bored. He was displeased.

Adam described their appearances, also adding some description of their homes while the clerk made notes.

"Examine these papers, Mr. Tyrrell." He pushed them across the desk with a grim smile.

Adam took the papers. Most contained jumbled letters and numbers, apparent cipher texts. "May I ask who you are?" Adam asked.

"I am a clerk. Do what you can with those. Paper and ink there. I will return with lunch and to examine your progress." He might have offered a pencil, rather than ink. The clerk got up and walked to the door, then gestured to the troll.

"Come!" the clerk barked at the dangerous one.

Adam began to examine the papers more closely.

"Stand! Stay!" the clerk pointed the troll to a spot just outside the door before closing it. "Stay!"

Nice theater that. Adam resolved not to need a chamber pot until the clerk returned, then made a note to find his own troll someday, should he be lucky enough to live so long. He turned his attention back to the work, choosing the easiest looking ones.

The room had none of those wonderful up-time clocks. Some indefinable time later, the door opened and the clerk entered. "Your lunch. Show me your progress."

"Thank you." Adam took the food and pointed to his solutions so far, then decided this was a good time to ask after the pot. The troll accompanied him without obvious instruction, causing Adam to nearly dry up. When Adam returned, the clerk was glowering at his work. He left without comment. Adam went back to work.

It was late afternoon when the door opened again. An obviously higher ranking man led the clerk back in. The man sat behind the desk. The clerk stood to one side. The troll stayed outside. Adam pegged the new man as a Swedish officer.

This man, who had a badly crippled arm, looked Adam's work over. Then he looked at the clerk and said, "That will be all."

The man stiffly left, causing Adam to remember advertisements for something called Preparation H, the last of which was rumored to rival chloramphenicol in price. The clerk looked like he could use some.

The man with the crippled arm sat back and grew something that might pass for a smile. "I remember the statuette of Harmodius and Aristogeiton in Bacon's study. It was quite unique, an inspired piece, but also slightly embarrassing. They needn't have been portrayed quite so . . . affectionately. But I remember no black Japanese vase featuring women with umbrellas."

"The doomed but triumphant lovers. I loved that piece. You must have visited after May 1620, when I broke the vase," Adam relaxed into his chair a bit. "I'm not likely to forget that date. My father had the vase glued back together and placed in our parlor as a chastisement." Adam grimaced at the thought, then wondered if the man knew that Harmodius and Aristogeiton were tyrannicides. "I've never broken a bit of pottery since."

"A hard lesson. I visited in 1622, as I recall. I will also confess that I was at first quite fooled by 'Madame Rossignol.' I was trying to place 'her' in the Rossignol family tree and wondering if all their women had such large Adam's apples." The man indicated that item on his own throat.

"The up-time term is 'drag queen,' sir, and I've no idea where they got that term. More politely, they use 'transgendered.' Madame is a cousin of Antoine Rossignol, Cardinal Richelieu's cryptanalyst. Or perhaps was his cousin. She was dying when I last saw her. Please understand that Madame was not affiliated with any faction of King Louis' court. She was of the circle of Francis Bacon, as was her lover, my Uncle Thomas. They retired to Paris when

Bacon fell from favor, where they lived private lives, not caring to choose among the various factions."

"That matches my information. Can you recommend replacements for two of my codes?" The man waved a couple of Adam's solutions in the air.

"Certainly, sir."

"Good. Now, what am I to do with Adam Tyrrell?" He stared fixedly at Adam.

"I have some suggestions, sir, but... ah... I don't believe we've met."

"Colonel Erik Haakenson Hand, at your service."

"A colonel?"

"What, you expected maybe His Majesty's cousin?"

"Oh, not at all. I am seeking someone who can... ah..."

"Who can protect a sodomite from the law?" Now that definitely was a smile, twisted, but nonetheless a smile.

Sometimes speaking plainly was more frightening than fun, but Adam managed to keep an even disposition. "Yes, Colonel. I seek protection for myself and any associates."

"Well then, how about His Majesty's cousin?"

"Probably such a man would do, if he's not out of favor. But can you make such an introduction?"

"I just did." Yes, a very twisted smile. The colonel had a refined sense of humor.

"Oh." Adam realized he was in the Swedish Consulate, sitting across a desk from His Majesty's Royal Cousin. He mentally filed this under "Be Careful What You Ask For."

"So I ask again, what is His Majesty's Trusted Kinsman to do with Adam Tyrrell?" Hand was a man who could insert Capital Letters into his words, without raising his voice.

"I... uh... have a list of... suggestions right... uh..." Adam found it, "right here." He handed it to Hand. It was several pages. "Have you read my other essays, Colonel?"

"I have." Hand began reading, nodding, hmm-ing, then chuckling. Then...

"*Damn!*" He had reached the fourth page. "Fingerprints?"

"Fingerprints."

"And Black Chamber personnel may be leaving fingerprints on letters they read?"

"The books say they should. Fingerprint references are all

over the library: encyclopedias, dictionaries, novels . . . especially detective stories. I begin to believe that to remove all sensitive references of that sort, not just regarding fingerprints but huff-duff for example, would gut the library. If the fingerprinting idea isn't known widely yet, it is only a matter of time. Gloves will soon be standard in all Black Chambers. Notice also that the books say the prints may linger for years. So those who have kept their correspondence might dust their collections. In that paper, I describe how the fingerprinting of incoming correspondence might be used as a sort of device—like the up-time passive sonar—to probe the existence, sizes and interests of mail opening operations around Europe. It seems a simple enough process, but then, one might think the same of the airplanes. I hear that the airplanes are not as simple as the books make them sound."

"What is passive sonar?" Hand glanced through the pages, looking for it.

"It's not in that paper. It's a device for listening for submarines, which can give the direction of any noise heard. I have taken some notes on it if you wish to see them, Colonel."

"Yes, please. Who else have you discussed this with?" Hand asked.

"Only my friend. He helped do the research. The library is rather large."

"They think it is small, Adam." Hand resumed reading Adam's proposal. When he reached the end, he put the papers down, looked across the desk and said, "Adam Tyrrell, if I truly am the first you've spoken to regarding this material, you have earned some protection already."

"And my friend as well?"

"Yes. The Lefferto is to be part of this project?"

"He is, and we may need to hire others. They may or may not know that the work has intelligence value."

"And you mean this to be an independent espionage research and development firm, rather than a governmental Black Chamber?"

"Yes sir. I suspect the up-timers had such firms. I believe we can make it pay by publishing surplus library research in a magazine format, which will also serve as a legitimate business cover."

"So you need no money from me until you have results?" Hand raised an eyebrow.

"Probably no money, Colonel, but we will need legal protection.

Also, a computer, instruction in its use, access to any cryptography books that they may have taken off the shelves, and assistance learning the up-time math. If things progress well, we may need consultants in a variety of fields, such as radio or chemistry."

"I can't promise a computer, but could press for it. The books may not be difficult, at least for me. The math instruction is routine. And this magazine you propose to publish, it can also be used to disseminate propaganda?"

"Oh, yes, sir! That's part of the fun."

"This fingerprint game sounds intriguing, if it works. I see I have two choices, Adam Tyrrell. I can hire you to keep you from working for someone else, or I can lock you up to keep you from working for someone else."

Adam nodded—sagely, he hoped. "May I ask, Colonel, if anyone else had already reached that conclusion?"

"Dr. Abrabanel seemed to think you should be taken seriously, otherwise, no."

Adam felt mildly offended. Perhaps it showed.

"Understand this, Adam Tyrrell," Hand said in his best Stern Colonel voice. "His Majesty is a deeply Pious Man who will Not Approve of you and your friend. But His Majesty is also a Practical Man who understands that sometimes the Needs of the Realm have their own logic. Results Matter. You will not allow me to regret helping you. You and your friend or friends will Be Discreet. Practice discretion, and I may be willing to offer assistance if needed. You understand?"

"Don't Ask, Don't Tell, Colonel?"

"Let me be very, very clear. I do not ask. I insist. You Will Tell Me these things, so that any problems can be nipped in the bud. Do You Understand, Adam Tyrrell?"

"Of course, Colonel." Adam said, relieved to finally find someone who spoke his language.

"And since you must stay in Grantville to do this, we will have to bring the up-timers in on it. They control the computers in any event. Where I might settle for an oath, they may insist on more, perhaps citizenship. Also, they are very strict about mail privacy. Any mail you open will be your own, or given to you at my direction."

"Of course, Colonel."

"You will have a Swedish assistant."

"As you wish, Colonel." Adam imagined a troll.

"I hope you like blonds."

"Beg pardon, Colonel?" Adam shook his head to clear it.

"He's blond. Also, his loyalty is beyond question. He was to learn radio soon, so we'll just bring him here early. It will take a couple of weeks. He will find lodging in your quarters. Did I mention you are advertising for a lodger?" The colonel had a sweet smile when he wished. He was almost displaying it now.

"Our quarters are not large, Colonel." Adam hoped he didn't look as taken aback as he felt.

"Then perhaps you are also seeking larger quarters. But that would be none of my affair." Then the colonel sat up straight with a sudden inspiration. "On second thought, it is my affair. You will work where you live, and someone trustworthy will be there at all times. I will arrange rooms for you and the Lefferto—and for your new Swedish friend—in a very nice, modern building, with excellent plumbing. You and your friend will like it very much."

The colonel sat back with a look of pure pleasure. "It's about time someone lit a fire under some dithering asses in this town. Your project sounds like just the spark. After all, you managed to cut through the red tape this far."

"Uncle Thomas was better at it, Colonel. I wasn't sure I had succeeded at all." Adam was now wondering if he was pleased to have succeeded.

"You nearly didn't. May I ask why you bothered? With your Rossignol connection, you might have gotten a good offer in Paris."

"They didn't have chloramphenicol, and their library isn't as good." Adam paused for emphasis. "Besides, the factions there have a way of getting a bit rough, even inelegant. Here, I have some hope of staying aloof from any factional fighting, although Stephano and I were rather concerned about the up-timer tendency toward witch-hunting. Finding some patron of high rank seemed prudent."

"Witch-hunting? They're adamantly against the practice!"

"They no longer believe in witches, sir, so they substitute others. In the 1950s, it was Communists. Homosexuals are a traditional target for some, especially in their military. The victims even call it 'witch-hunting,' though there are no witches. The analogy is exact. I suppose the practice is common to all peoples. I've been working on a essay on the subject if you would like to read it."

"Yes, please."

"Have you heard the way they use the word 'faggot,' especially around the 250 Club?" Adam shrank a bit.

"Oh. Them." Hand sneered.

"We hear it elsewhere, as well, but it's more frightening from that lot," Adam grimaced.

"So you are scared of them."

"Sometimes, Colonel. But more often, I just feel sorry for them," Adam said.

"Sorry? Why?" The colonel looked closely at Adam.

"They've lost everything, sir. It's quite pathetic. The stress must be intolerable at times."

"Bear in mind that I can get you out of jail far more easily than I can get you out of a lynching. Bring your friend tomorrow morning," Hand said, waving dismissal.

"How did it go?" Stephano asked.

"It would appear we have caught a big one. A Swede, not an up-timer," Adam said dryly.

"How big?"

Silence.

"Adam, talk to Stephano..."

"He will find us larger quarters. We will live and work there, with a blond Swedish friend." Adam shifted on his feet nervously.

"Adam, you frighten Stephano..."

The Up-time Reader's Monthly

VOLUME 1, ISSUE 1

Editor-In-Chief: Huckleberry Finn
Chief Researcher: Tom Sawyer

An eclectic monthly compendium of snippets and observations gleaned from the up-time libraries of Grantville, Thuringia (formerly Grantville, West Virginia), with an emphasis on a larger understanding of the culture and times of the up-time world that was and will now never be, presented for the educated reader.

Limited copies of this, our debut edition, are distributed free at USE embassies and other select locations. To purchase extra copies and subscriptions see back cover.

Free referrals to reputable researchers and copyists on request, but the Editors cannot assume responsibility for private transactions.

IN THIS ISSUE:

The Stark Depiction Of War In Up-time Literature

Reviews of three famous up-time novels of war: *The Red Badge of Courage*, *All Quiet on the Western Front*, and *The Cruel Sea*, which depict the progressively greater horrors of up-time war through tales of the nineteenth-century American Civil War and the two World Wars of the twentieth century.

Fields Of Study

We begin our taxonomy of up-time academia with brief descriptions of the subjects of Physics, Chemistry, Biology and Economics. In future editions, these and others will be examined in closer detail, with discussion of sub-fields.

When You Come To A Fork In The Road . . .

In this first installment of our examination of colorful American expressions, we consider the wit and wisdom of up-time sportsman Yogi Berra.

The Reference Desk

Descriptions of the famous Grantville collection of Encyclopedias, with usage notes and sample passages. In future editions, we will present commentaries on other valuable reference books such as *Roget's Thesaurus* and *Robert's Rules of Order*.

Historical Notes

In this issue, we outline the unification of the Germanies during the nineteenth century. In the next issue, the Italian Unification.

Letters To The Editors

In future issues, we will print reader comments on our articles and essay answers to some of your research questions.

☆ ☆ ☆

Adam and Stephano each had a couple of magnifying lenses and wore silk gloves to avoid adding their own fingerprints to any that might be found on their mail. They added each letter to indices by date, name and subject. They debated while opening the letters. It was the old argument.

"All of the research in the first issue is yours, so I must be The Editor," Stephano insisted, while examining an envelope.

"Remember that I paid for this issue, so that means I'm The Editor. Besides you're doing more of the research now," Adam reasoned.

"Very well, I'm Tom Sawyer. And I'm starting a new column called *The Picket Fence*."

"You'll paint that column yourself. I've read that book," Adam said, peering through his strongest magnifier.

"We have a new order here," Stephano said, reading a letter he'd just extracted. "Fifteen additional copies of Issue 1 plus nine subscriptions, all from the same person. Someone named Reubens in Haarlem."

"Mail gets to Haarlem fine. Reubens works for the cardinal-infante. Put it in the boast stack. I mean to brag about it. And we'll definitely want to check that one for fingerprints."

Stephano opened the next one, and whistled. "One hundred first issues plus fifty subscriptions from Morris Roth in Prague."

"All for himself? He must be forwarding them somewhere. And we'll have to check that one thoroughly for fingerprints as well. Roth will want to know if anyone, like Wallenstein, is reading his mail." Adam examined another letter for signs that he was not the first to open it, then carefully opened it. "I have another research request for you in this letter, Stephano. Someone wants an explanation of baseball."

"Already written." Stephano waved dismissal. "We can put in The Editor's Reply in the next issue. I expected that one."

Adam held up the next letter. "And here, Stephano, I have another request for a copy of *The Cruel Sea*."

"Another anti-submarine warfare researcher." Stephano moaned. "They do take the long view. I'll send him a note saying that he can buy a printed copy next month. Better yet, we'll just put a notice in the next issue. Perhaps we could start a 'Recently Republished' column."

"We should demand kickbacks from the printers," Adam observed.

"It's called 'paid advertising.' And we should also charge them to review the books they are reprinting. Ah! I have a research request just for you, Adam!" Stephano looked cheerfully mischievous.

Adam looked across the table glumly. "Let's hear it."

"It would seem there's an abbot in Campania looking for Prester John."

"Him again? Perhaps we can refer that to someone. Do you suppose Veda Mae would be interested in moonlighting as a researcher?"

"Why not? She's the reason Prester John fled to Ethiopia in the first place." Stephano logged the letter and placed it in the finished stack, with an exaggerated gesture of finality.

Life for Adam was good again, but he did wish Madame and Uncle Thomas were around to share it. They would have so loved Stephano. Across the table, Stephano was frowning at the next letter.

Yes, it was very good to be alive.

In the back of his mind, Adam considered some nagging cipher problems from Colonel Hand's most recent bundle.

Yes, Dear

Terry Howard and James Copley

"Wives... more trouble than the Methodist church."
—The Devil, in *Damned Yankees.*

Lili Trainer entered the office and without a word to the receptionist, the clerk or Dwight Rogers' secretary, walked straight into the site manager's private office. When your husband is the manager's boss and your late father owned part of the company—which you expect to inherit when the estate gets through probate—you can get away with doing things like that.

"Dwight, I'm sick and tired of the mud and the dust, and tripping on the damned cobblestones. Do something about it." There was cobblestone on the old part of the street in a little village just outside of Celle where the oil company had leased land to build an office and some modern housing for senior staff. The new section of the street was just packed dirt. The duke owned the village and he hadn't done anything about extending the paving.

"I suppose we could put down oil on the roads for the dust."

"Now that would be a waste of oil." Lili made it sound like an accusation.

"Not really. Bunker fuel is too heavy for diesels. The steamboats out of the naval yard can burn it, what we don't burn to run the refinery. That still leaves the stuff that is too thick to be bunker fuel and too light to be tar."

Lili shook her head, "You'd end up with oil getting tracked

into the houses. Then when it rains it just makes the mud worse. You've got that asphalt stuff. Don't tell me it's not asphalt! I looked it up! It's that bitamen stuff they make asphalt with! Don't tell me that isn't what you've got in those big thatch-covered piles, at Weitze. Why can't you spread it over the roads?"

Dwight sighed. He had just had this same argument with the army liaison when he came to negotiate their fuel prices. "Lili, that's impossible right now." He began his well-rehearsed explanation. "It isn't that simple. What we need to do is mix the 'bitumen' with aggregate, to make bitmac. Even then you can't just spread it on the ground, and believe me it's not as simple as just pouring it like cement. You first have to have the proper road base, which means you need surveyors because once you put in a hard road it's kind of permanent. So after the road is staked, then it has to be graded and stabilized. Ideally that calls for stabilized gravel, over a bed of larger stone. Stabilized gravel means gravel with sand and the right clay in the right mix. Then you can put down the bitmac."

"So do it."

"Happy to. I don't like muddy streets either. Tell your husband to get me a steady supply of gravel in different grades, plenty of sand, and the right kind of clay." Dwight ticked off the items on his fingers.

"Along with an endless supply of gravel and sand, I'll need a roller, and scrapers. And we'll need culverts for the cross streets and some way to get an even layer of asphalt spread over large areas. An asphalt laying machine would be nice. Bradford Steam Works in Grantville can build one, but for now we don't have one. Nobody does.

"Get me my shopping list and I'll get started. Until then the bitumen is just going to sit there."

"Is that all, Dwight? I thought you said it was impossible."

"It isn't going to be easy or cheap, which is the same thing as impossible."

"No it isn't, Dwight. It's not anywhere near close to being the same thing. You and Jerry, two big-shot engineers! How many times have I heard you two say that the first step in solving a problem is stating it clearly? You might as well be talking about an alcoholics' anonymous twelve-step program. The first step is admitting that you have a problem. Well, at least you've admitted it. But from your *shopping list* I don't see why it's a problem at all."

"Lili, we'll have to reinvent some of the equipment, 'cause Grantville sure isn't going to give up any of its up-time equipment just so we can have a smooth ride. Besides, the county's hot asphalt machine wasn't inside the ring, so they don't have one to loan us anyway."

"I still don't see why we can't do it. We've got the asphalt. We know how to do it. Grantville has paved roads. Why can't we?" Lili walked out into the heat of an August summer.

Dwight rolled his eyes skyward.

The sunshine announced it was Sunday morning, a lazy time to lay about and take it easy. The Baptists in the area decided one Sunday service was enough and that an afternoon service was more amenable. They had to gather from Wietze to Celle and beyond. Since the sermons were kept short and the Baptists were willing to share the pulpit, the English speakers came together every Sunday. It wasn't just the Church of Christ and the Methodists who turned up. Some Lutherans and Catholics, and some un-churched showed up too. Worshipping in German or Latin, on top of living in German and polyglot jargon, just wasn't the same as back up-time. Besides, the ladies arranged for an old-fashioned West Virginia dinner to be served up after the service. People had been known to socialize until they had to leave to be home by dark.

Perhaps the oddest thing about it was the number of down-time English speakers who showed up. As long as they stuck to English they were welcome. The old deacon, Doty Maze, had held a German-language Baptist worship service for his growing class of converts on Sunday morning until he got shot and killed. Then a down-timer took over as pastor. Without the old deacon to link them together they were two different congregations now.

Helga, the Trainer family's maid, knew that on Sunday mornings breakfast didn't happen on a schedule, but hot biscuits were not required. A short order menu was fine. Often a pastry bought on Saturday from the bakery in Celle was all she needed. She knew Mr. Trainer would still wake up at five o'clock. He would hit the bathroom, brush his teeth and go back to bed and back to sleep. Around seven Mrs. Trainer would wake her husband up. Helga would become aware of them whenever they came down for breakfast.

On the last Sunday morning in August 1636, Helga did not have to wait for them to come downstairs. The whole house, from basement to attic, was very aware of Mr. and Mrs. Trainer—starting at twelve minutes after seven.

Helga heard it all. At a volume that would not stop rising until it was rattling the shingles, Lili started with: "Jerry Trainer, you ungrateful, selfish pig! I've given you the best years of my life! I even got a job to pay the bills so you could get your masters degree! I'm not asking for all that much, just a decent, civilized place to live with a few basic amenities! It's not surprising you like the mud; you're a pig. A selfish, self-centered, arrogant pig! Don't tell me it can't be done. Dwight says he can do it!"

"I didn't say it can't be done. I said it can't be done right now!"

"Dwight says it can!"

"Well, he doesn't have to pay for it!"

"Neither do you! It's company money we're talking about here. My money! Not yours!"

"It isn't your money until the probate is settled. It can't be settled until the court rules on the claim your dad was co-mingling public and private funds. Then there's the charges of profiteering, and conflict of interest! That will take a while. The probate is a mess."

"So what?" Lili crossed her arms as she looked away. "That just means it'll take longer for me to pay it back to the company."

That didn't make any sense at all to Jerry. Did she think she could spend some portion of the company's money as she wished and in advance? Clearly the facts were whatever she wanted them to be and when she looked away like that he knew there was absolutely no way of getting her to see reason.

"Even if your mother does go ahead and sign her interests over to you like she says she's going to, if and when she actually gets any, you still won't own anywhere near a majority."

His arms waved wildly as he emphasized his point. "Even if you did, you couldn't do whatever you want! It's a publicly traded company! I know your dad acted like he owned it all. That's what all the fuss is about. At the time nobody cared as long as he got the oil flowing. Now, it's the money flow they're interested in. I can't run the company that way. I've got to look out for everybody's interests, what is best for the bottom line. Paving the street in front of the office and our homes is out of the question!"

"Dwight says it isn't. Dwight says all he needs is gravel!"

"Well, if that's what Dwight said, then Dwight is an even bigger idiot than you are or he's lying through his teeth just to get your goat!"

Oops. It really wasn't wise to make a remark like that. Jerry knew that as well as he knew his name.

"I'm an idiot? I'm an idiot?" Her volume climbed with every repetition.

"Lili, look. We'll be putting down gravel this spring. Okay?"

"Why stop there when we've got all of that stuff on hand that can be asphalt as soon as you add gravel?"

"Time, trained people, and equipment that we don't have and can't get!"

"Dwight says we can get it."

"Laura Lee Trainer!" His voice was straining with exasperation. "Just who is going to pay for it? I can't justify spending company money on it!"

"But, Dwight said..."

"I don't care what Dwight said!" Jerry replied, barely restraining himself. "It isn't going to happen! It costs too much!"

"Jerry, that's your answer to everything! I'm damned lucky you wanted flush plumbing and hot running water or that would have cost too much, too!" Lili's voice was practically a howling growl. "It's your answer to everything. If you don't want it, then it costs too much. But you can always seem to find a way to do it if it is something you want. That golf course you laid out between the oil wells was the dumbest thing I ever heard of! But I guess it didn't *cost too much*!" The last part was a rising shriek.

"All right! Listen, we've got gravel coming. I've got to pay the crews to put it down anyway. I tell you what, Miss Smarty Pants. If you think it is just that simple, you figure a way to pay for the asphalt machine and I'll find a way to cover the other costs! Okay?"

"And you think I can't, don't you? You just make sure you keep your end of the deal!"

"Yes, dear!" Jerry snarled.

Helga watched Jerry grab his golf clubs and stomp out of the house. He didn't come home for lunch and he didn't show up at church that night either. When he did come home he slept on the couch.

☆ ☆ ☆

"Dwight? Why in hell did you tell my wife you could pave the streets if I wasn't being a stubborn, pigheaded idiot about getting you the gravel you needed?"

"I never said that."

"Yeah, well what did you say?"

"I said I'd need aggregate, scrapers, rollers, a paving machine, surveyors, a trained labor force and lots of time."

"Do you have any idea what that is going to cost? Shoot, just getting the equipment made up is going to cost a fortune."

"Sure, I know that. That's why we haven't done it already. I told your wife as much."

"Well, she didn't hear that part of it. All she seems to have heard is that you can do it if I get you the gravel."

"Sorry, Jerry."

"Shoot, Dwight, I know it's not your fault. The woman has selective hearing. I know; I've lived with her for years. But since her father died and she knows she's going to own a big chunk of the company she acts like she owns the world."

"Ha!" Dwight snorted. "Can you imagine what she'd do if she did? We'd be out of a job in a hurry!"

"Nah!" Jerry got a shit-eatin' grin on his face and dropped into a hillbilly cant, which he only did when he was wantin' ta be nasty and ridicule someone, "She'd miss us. Come a light bulb needin' changed, we'd be back on suffer'ce. Just you watch..."

After a quiet breakfast in the solar, Georg, Duke of Kalenberg sat reading dispatches from the engineers at Wietz, while his wife, Anna Eleanor, busily applied embroidery to one of her daughter's new dresses.

"Georg, I was talking to Mrs. Trainer. Wouldn't it be nice to have an asphalt road, like they have in Grantville, from the docks to the manor? I wonder what it would be like to have roads that didn't wash away or turn to mud," she said as she glanced his way. "Darling, you said so yourself when we were in Grantville that the roads there were superb. And I, for one, think it would be a fine investment, what with all the new trade going on down by the river.

"What a market district we could have. And surely it would draw some of that Grantville business you've been harping about."

"Yes, dear," Georg replied, without really listening to what his wife was saying.

"I can't imagine it would be too expensive to get it done. A good portion of the things we need are right here."

"Hmm..."

"Then I can go ahead and order it done?"

Georg mumbled something indecipherable. It might have been, "Yes, dear."

"Also, Mrs. Trainer was telling me that they will need a machine or two that they don't have but could get made in Grantville, and some rock and such from the quarry.

"Oh, and this should make even a pfennig-pincher like you happy; Lili said if we paid for the machines then the oil company would undertake the cost of scouting out and training the crews and working out the... 'bugs' is what she said. I think she may mean the new machines might have problems and they would have to work them out."

Grumble... Mumble...

"Thank you, darling, you're such a dear. It's so nice to talk to you in the mornings." She gathered up her sewing and left the room.

"Huh? What was that, love?" Georg looked up. Anna Eleanor wasn't in the room.

On April first, a servant hurried into the telegraph office just outside of Celle in Oil Town. "I need to send a telegram," he said. "Then I will wait for a reply."

Somewhere near Grantville a telephone rang, "Good afternoon, Bradford Steam Works. How may I help you?"

"That you, Anna?"

"What's up, Maria?"

"Got a telegram for you. You want it over the phone? Or you can pay to have it hand-delivered, or you can send someone to pick it up."

"Give it to me over the phone. And hold the hard copy. Someone will pick it up maybe tomorrow."

"Doesn't sound like a happy customer. It says: 'To: Bradford Steam Works, New Street, Schwarza. From: Georg, Duke of Kalenberg, Celle. One April 1637. You want how much? Stop. For what? Stop. End.'"

"Anna, let me call you back after I check this out."

☆ ☆ ☆

— A T & L TELEGRAPH —

TO: GEORG, DUKE OF KALENBERG, CELLE

FROM: BRADFORD STEAM WORKS, NEW STREET, SCHWARZA

DATE: 1 APRIL 1637

MESSAGE:

WE'RE READY TO DELIVER THE ASPHALT PAVING EQUIPMENT YOU ORDERED —STOP—

THE BALANCE IS DUE AND PAYABLE UPON DELIVERY —STOP—

END

— A T & L TELEGRAPH —

TO: BRADFORD STEAM WORKS, NEW STREET, SCHWARZA

FROM: GEORG, DUKE OF KALENBURG, CELLE

DATE: 2 APRIL 1637

MESSAGE:

I NEVER ORDERED ANY ASPHALT PAVING EQUIPMENT —STOP—

WHAT IS ASPHALT PAVING EQUIPMENT —STOP—

I DON'T EVEN KNOW WHAT ASPHALT IS —STOP—

END

— A T & L TELEGRAPH —

TO: GEORG, DUKE OF KALENBURG, CELLE

FROM: BRADFORD STEAM WORKS, NEW STREET, SCHWARZA

DATE: 2 APRIL 1637

MESSAGE:

WE ARE IN RECEIPT OF AN ORDER SIGNED BY DUCHESS ANNA ELEANOR ALONG WITH A DRAFT ON AN ACCOUNT WITH OPM FOR MATERIALS COST —STOP—

AS VERIFIED PREVIOUSLY, DUCHESS ANNA ELEANOR IS AUTHORIZED TO DRAW UPON SAID ACCOUNT —STOP—

OPM REQUIRES THAT FINAL PAYMENT BE MADE BY YOU DIRECTLY OR ADDITIONAL APPROVAL DOCUMENTS MUST BE PROVIDED TO THEM, DUE TO OPM'S WITHDRAWAL RESTRICTIONS —STOP—

END

Georg scrubbed his face hard after placing the telegraph form back onto the table. The servant who delivered it, anxiety showing on his face, slowly started to slide away along the wall as he attempted to avoid his lord's wrath.

With a deep sigh, the duke placed his hands flat on the table, and raised his head, piercing the servant with his gaze.

"Would you kindly request that the Duchess Anna attend me here at once." It was a capital O Order, not a request.

Hearing more than a little steel in the voice, the servant scampered off, relieved the lord's wrath would strike elsewhere.

"Anna, what has possessed you? Because of your order, our investment account at OPM has reduced by *half!*" Georg ground his teeth as his wife calmly entered the study and gracefully ignored his outburst of anger. She looked over the papers sitting on his desk, noting the telegrams from Grantville.

"Anna! You simply cannot do something like that without my permission."

"Don't you remember? I asked you about this, over breakfast, months ago, back in September! You didn't object then, and besides, it's a wonderful investment. Imagine the prestige of being the only city outside of Grantville with asphalt roads."

"We can't just build roads wherever we want! Agreements must be negotiated, documents drawn up, approved and signed. I have no right to—"

"And who tells the duke what to do in his own duchy? Are you a duke or a mouse? If you want to build a road, you simply buy the rights to build a road. Simple, no?"

"Simple? Yes, if want to start a revolt. But that is beside the point. Are you trying to bankrupt me? Why should we spend money on asphalt? We have plenty of roads, and the streets by the docks are just that, by the docks! Who cares if they're muddy? You don't have to walk in them!"

Anna's eyes grew flinty. "Bankrupt you? Whose dowry money do you think is in that account in the first place? An account, dear husband, you refused to even think of putting any of *your* money into. You called it 'that up-time foolery,' as I recall!"

Georg screwed his eyes shut for a moment, realizing he might have gone a bit far. "But, Anna, dearest, *I* am the person who is responsible for your fortune, and I *have* to take better care of your money than of my own. It really would be irresponsible of me to let you risk more than just a very little of it on untried, harebrained schemes. We had this discussion when you insisted on investing some of your money in that crazy, up-time foolery. I only very reluctantly acquiesced with your wishes. It seems I may have been wrong, at least so far, anyway. You've been getting a very good return. At least up to now. *But then you go and spend half of it without even asking me.* It's not like the law allows you to make this sort of transactions without my consent—*except, it seems*—in Grantville. This paving machine you ordered is ridiculous. I didn't realize you would be able to access that account like this without my consent."

The storm clouds over Anna's head darkened even further. Georg could feel the growing threat to his domestic tranquility like cold juices running up his spine to shoot icy fingers into his brain that hurt like daggers. He recalled how Anna had threatened to seek financial "emancipation" when she insisted on making the investment in OPM. If she did, especially now that the first investment worked out so well, he would be a laughingstock.

"Don't 'but, Anna' me, Georg! You let me have joint access to that account because, and I quote, 'You might as well control it, there won't be anything left in six months anyway!' Well, you were wrong about that, and you are wrong about this, too. That paving machine is going to be the second best thing that ever happened to you. The only thing better was the day my father—who must have been dead drunk at the time—agreed to let you marry me.

"Just because a bit of your family's lands has suddenly become supremely useful, does not suddenly make you the smartest man of means in Kalenberg. If my family had not assisted you in the initial finance of the oil fields, you too would be simply looking in from the outside! Ownership or not!"

Georg felt an urgent desire to flee back to his troops in Gustav's service where all he had to worry about was getting shot to death. *There at least I know what I am doing, charge when you can win and retreat when you can't. But modern finances are a bottomless quagmire. Life had been so much simpler in those days. Lord in Heaven, give me a nice, simple, peaceful war.*

Anna never even slowed down.

"I talked about things with Mrs. Trainer and some other ladies from Grantville, back when you were being stubborn about investing in OPM, Georg. They told me, if I go to Magdeburg or Thuringia-Franconia, I can have a divorce just by asking for one. I wouldn't even have to prove you were spending all of my money on, as Lili put it, fast horses and wild women.

"Then I could establish my own power over all my property! My family already has an estate in Franconia, so I don't even need to establish residency. I am already arguably a native of that state.

"It's only these benighted places like Duchies of Luneburg and Brunswick where a woman is always under some man's guardianship. Well, my high and mighty lord and master, as duke of Luneburg and Brunswick you can legislate that old-fashioned stupidity away. And I fully intend to see that you do. And you will. Because if you don't, well, I *will* go to my home in Franconia. Do you really want me to divorce you? I can and you know it!"

Georg's mind went back, yet again, for a time beyond counting: to the day when he and his brothers drew lots twenty years earlier to decide which one of them would marry so the family's wealth would be preserved in one line instead of being subdivided into ever smaller separate bits and pieces. *Why did I have to lose by winning? I'd be free to have mistresses and no commitments. I could hunt and travel and enjoy life. I'd have a free rein with the stuff of wine cellars.* His thoughts took a turn back to reality. *Yes and I'd have gout in my feet like August, which is not so good after all. The winning lot could have fallen to Fritz. He would have done well with it. But, then I wouldn't have my delightful children. I'd be just an uncle. I'd miss having kids.*

A man needs to have harmony at home, how else am I going to preserve our dynasty's power, to serve the emperor and the true faith, and to ensure a good future to my sons? "Anna, quit being silly. There is no need for talk about a divorce. I only want the best for you and our children."

The duchess, somewhat mollified, admitted, "So do I. I don't really want a divorce. Even after comparing notes with the ladies from Grantville, I still know very well that I've invested the best years of my life in you. And I've finally gotten you relatively well trained, as much as any man can be. But you *will* see to it that the law is changed."

Georg decided to keep his mouth shut. But he couldn't help but wonder. *Trained? Like a hunting dog? Like a horse? Is it that how she sees me? Is that really how women see their husbands?*

Anna continued, "Most of my fortune is safely in real estate anyway. Real estate always survives. Cash money can be invested in riskier ventures; the higher the risks, the higher the return. I can afford to lose it. None of it is borrowed; none of the properties are at risk. It might take two or three good crop years but I can replace what I lose, if I do indeed lose anything. Which I won't! Georg, this paving machine is going to be a gold mine!

"Besides, even if I don't make any money back, I will still get a good paved road from here to the river. That is something I am more than willing to pay for."

"But, the costs..."

"Oh, bother the costs. We would finally be able to ride from the valley to the river without once getting out while the carriage was pulled out of the mud, or having our teeth rattled out of our heads." Anna rose and began to stride out of the room... "That by itself will be a wonder."

Jerry Trainer came home for a quiet, relaxing lunch and walked into a beehive of activity. Lili was supervising half a dozen women busily scrubbing the house down, top to bottom.

"I thought you decided, last year, to leave the spring cleaning until after the streets dried up," Jerry said as he pecked his wife on the cheek.

"Oh, that? Well the mud won't be a problem this year and we have an important guest coming so I want the house to shine."

Jerry heard two alarms in his head and decided to check out the safer one first. "Who's coming?"

"Anna Eleanor, the wife of Duke Georg. You've met her before."

"The duchess? Why is she coming? Her husband isn't, is he?" Jerry felt the cold chill of uncertainty running down his back. They were leasing the mineral rights to the oilfields from the duke at a flat percentage of gross sales. He had been very helpful in getting access rights to the drilling sites, which was separate and different from the mineral rights, along with the lease on the land the refinery was on down by the river. There for a while it really had looked as though they would never get a lease for enough land to build the complex everyone was calling Oil Town. Then the duke intervened. But even when he was being supremely helpful, no one likes a surprise visit from the landlord.

"No, dear, her husband isn't coming. Anna Eleanor wants to be here when her asphalt paving machine arrives. That should be next Tuesday or Wednesday. So I want the house looking its best."

Jerry's face became very calm, which it often did just before he blew up. In an unnaturally steady voice, Jerry asked, "Why is the duchess having a paving machine delivered here?"

"So we can use it while hiring and training a crew. Don't you remember? You said if I got the paving machine you would take care of everything else."

Lili looked at the expression on her husband's face. "Jerry? You aren't thinking of welshing on our deal are you? You can't, Jerry. I took you at your word. I promised Anna Eleanor that if she bought the machine we would train the crew for her for free. Of course while we're training them, we can get the streets paved, right?" Lili smiled. "You promised, Jerry. A deal is a deal."

Jerry clamped his jaw closed tight, did an about face, and marched out of the house without another word.

When he walked through the front door of the office, the receptionist took one look and ducked back to her typewriter, pounding away furiously. Her father had had a look much like that just before he took his belt off to teach someone a lesson.

With the inner office door closed, Jerry sat down and let out a long breath. "Dwight, we have a big problem!"

Dwight sat behind his desk, working a pencil back and forth between his hands, and waited without saying anything.

"Remember when Lili wanted the streets paved? I told her we couldn't afford it and we had a big fight. Well, to get her off of my back I said if she could come up with a paving machine I could take care of the rest.

"Dwight, there was no way in the world she was going to raise the money to have a paving machine built. Right?" Jerry waited for Dwight to nod.

"Well, she couldn't, and she didn't, but she got the wife of Duke Georg to do it for her. It's going to arrive next week and Lili promised the duchess we would hire and train the crew for her.

"It's not in the budget. What in the world am I going to do? I could tell Lili I was wrong..." Jerry plopped down in a chair in front of Dwight's desk. "She'd make me miserable, but I could do it. I could string her out and take forever with one delay after another and just put up with the constant nagging. But I can't do that with the duke's wife.

"Dwight, please, gim'me a miracle." Jerry's language was slipping. "It's not like you ain't done it before." Dwight was one of the few up-timers with hands-on oil experience. On several occasions when the theory didn't seem to be working he had looked the situation over, made one or two small changes and everything else fell into place.

Dwight carefully placed his pencil down on the desk. "Jerry, calm down. It might not be as bad as you think. Look, we've got a hot lay asphalt paving machine that we didn't know we had. Seems to me, we can manage to pave some of the street here in Oil Town."

Jerry shook his head glumly, "I don't see how."

"What Lili was really complaining about was that the mud was getting tracked into the buildings. Right?"

"Well, that and the dust."

Dwight waved a hand in dismissal. "It's the mud that's the problem. Look, the old street is already cobblestone, and most of the new buildings have boardwalk fronts instead of sidewalks. But people pick up mud on their shoes when they cross the streets. Let's take what we've got and pave the intersections so people can cross the street and only have to deal with the mud that falls off of the wheels."

"Even that is going to cost more than we've budgeted," Jerry objected.

"If this works, once we get things rolling, I betcha the only limit will be how fast we can produce the bitmac. Yeah, we've got a stockpile, but if we pave the street here...once word gets out, I bet that new machine will be so busy with orders we'll run out before the end of the season. If that's the case we'll have enough of a windfall that we can buy enough gravel to do like we planned on with this round and gravel the road down to the refinery by fall. Be nice to have it paved too.

"Look, Jerry," Dwight continued, "the duchess has a paving machine and she is going to be buying bitumen. We can tap the research and development budget for some of the shortfall. Heck, if we work it right, we might even squeeze out enough to pave all of the street in front of the new buildings!"

Reaching into a desk drawer, Dwight brought out his old solar-powered calculator. He'd found it in the back of a junk drawer at home. He could have sold it for hundreds, if not thousands of dollars. Instead he kept it. He was good at math, but he hated it.

"One sec, Jerry, while I do some numbers..." Grabbing the budget spreadsheet, he began punching numbers into the calculator. "Okay... There's that... And... per crew..."

Jerry began to fidget, picking up an old ceramic coffee mug on the desk that Dwight used as a pen holder. He noticed a few ballpoint pens that still worked and one of the new and expensive fountain pens.

"And... *done!*" Dwight did a double-take at his calculator as he wrote the final figures onto his notepad. "Well I'll be damned... not bad. In fact it's downright affordable."

Jerry looked at the figure. "That's still too high, Dwight. I can't justify that big of an unbudgeted expenditure. I guess I'm gonna have to go talk to Lili..."

"Hold on, Jerry. You didn't let me finish. That price is if we were purchasing the materials. We already have most of the gravel on hand, and sand is, pardon the pun, dirt cheap.

"We're getting about five percent of bitumen per barrel of crude and we aren't selling very much of it. We haven't had much luck making inroads on the existing pitch markets. They're just a little afraid to try something new and we're a long way from any large users, so the transportation cost would eat us alive. I figure we can up the price when we sell it to the duchess, hey, one job and we'll be making money! There's your budget adjustment.... Just call it development costs!"

Jerry's eyes had gotten brighter and brighter as the information worked its way through his mind. He was not a greedy type, but if this got him out from between the rock that was his wife and the hard place that was the company's shareholders, he was all for it.

Jerry jumped out of the chair, his mind racing. Visions of road crews in orange vests and projections of the next quarterly report flipped back and forth through his mind.

"Of course!" He walked to the large slate mounted on the wall, looking at manning requirements that had been chalked onto the makeshift planning calendar.

"Hot damn, Dwight! I think we gots ourselves a business here! We might want to buy our own paving machine!"

"Wait a minute, Jerry. Remember, it's only cheap for us until we run out of gravel, plus we'd have to commit a lot of money if we buy a paver. Let's just let the duchess do her thing, and we'll make money selling her the asphalt."

"Yeah, you're probably right..."

"So, what ya' gonna tell Lili?"

Jerry chuckled, and an evil grin grew on his face. He turned to Dwight.

"Ain't gonna tell 'er nuttin'," Jerry said in a redneck leer. "You don't think I'm going to encourage her to say, 'I told you so,' do you?"

"You mean just like you never told her we really didn't actually have to have a hot-paving machine? Yeah, we need one, to get the best results, but we could have made do."

"Shhhh!" Jerry said. "Things are bad enough as it is."

Lili stood on a boardwalk facing the first paved section of Oil Town's street and watched the workmen putting blacktop on the second section while another crew packed the gravel on the third so it would be ready for asphalt; a fourth section was being dug down with horse-drawn scrapers.

Lili smiled. "See, dear," she said, squeezing her husband's hand, "Dwight was right. We *can* do it."

Jerry wasn't paying attention to his wife. His thoughts and eyes were on Anna Eleanor and the guests she had invited to watch the process after there was a finished section for them to see. Jerry was listening carefully to overhear the conversation the duchess was having with the duke.

"Georg, quit worrying. I already have three contracts lined up for the new company."

"But the air force is considering the possibility of requisitioning the use of the paving machine and they're insisting they have a priority claim on the stockpiled bitumen."

This didn't bother the duchess in the least. She was more than ready to rent the machine and its crew to the air force at crew cost. "Good. When we get it back, the demand, and the price, and the *profit* will all be just that much higher. It will be the final proof that there was no finer road surface in the world. If that happens, you can think of a score of people who will absolutely have to have it right now. As for the bitumen, well, I had someone look it up for me in the library in Grantville. There were other sources for asphalt if it ever comes down to that and Mrs. Trainer says she will get me the right of first refusal on sales here. It is really just tar after all. And the up-timers aren't the only source of tar, now are they? I've already put in an order for two more machines."

"You what?" Georg's startled voice caused heads to turn.

"Yes, dear. It is obvious this one is going to pay for itself in short order. Unless I want someone else having them made up," Anna Eleanor said, "I need to keep the machine builder busy. I want a solid lock on the business before I have to deal with competition. So I ordered one for next year and another for the year after."

Georg put a hand to his forehead and dragged it down to his face.

"You'll see. It will work out."

Jerry could see Georg taking note of how many people were looking at them. It was clear he wanted to have a fight with his wife, but not in public. What could a man say at a time like that . . . ?

Jerry chuckled. The additional costs to pave and upgrade Main Street of Oil Town were fully justifiable as a promotional expense. They could quit trying to market it as a pitch substitute, because it looked like the duchess was ready to buy all they could refine. He could foresee the day when there would be a waiting list.

Lili heard him chuckle and asked, "What? Jerry? Are you listening to me? Jerry?" There was a tug on his hand. "Earth to Jerry, come in?"

"Hum?" He quit counting the un-hatched chickens in his mind and turned to his wife. "What, dear?"

"I said," Lili's voice was a touch stern, after all, no one likes being ignored, "Dwight was right. We *can* do it."

Jerry smiled and took a lesson from Duke Georg of Kalenberg, a grandfather of the George kings of England in a history which now would never be. At a time like this there really was only one thing a man could safely say to a question like that from his wife.

"Yes, dear."

High Road to Venice

Gorg Huff and Paula Goodlett

Merton Smith rolled his wheel chair over to the phone and called up the weather service. "Hi, Dan. How's it look for a flight to Venice?"

"Not horrible. The reports from the weather stations are mostly in. There is a warm front that was moving in from the west but it seems to have stalled. We don't know why, but we suspect that something is going on in the east. I wish we still had the stations in Saxony and Brandenburg."

"Politics." Merton snorted. "They screw up everything. So what do you figure is out east that Saxony and Brandenburg aren't reporting?"

"It's a cold front, Merton. We just don't know how big it is."

"Okay. How's it look on the south side of the Alps?"

"That's the good news. Clear and sunny all the way to Rome. Bolzano is reporting light winds through the pass and wants to know when you guys are coming."

"Looks like today's a go," Merton told him.

Johan Schroeder did the walkaround. He was the pilot, Merton the co. Besides, Merton couldn't walk, at least not all that well. Merton had gotten new fiberglass prosthetics but wasn't all that used to them yet. Honestly, Johan wasn't all that comfortable with Merton. A man who was missing both legs to above the knee shouldn't be piloting an airplane even if he was an up-timer and familiar with the engines. Johan checked the bag for leaks. It was double thick canvas with tar between the layers and oiled leather at the bottom where it contacted the ground, where the greatest wear would occur. He wiggled the flaps and the rudders. Checked for dings in the wings, body, and tail. Checked the bag fan, then climbed the step ladder and went aboard the plane where Merton was already in the right seat. By tradition, the left seat in a fixed wing was the pilot's seat. Johan headed back and checked the cargo. "So what do we have?"

Merton turned in his seat and read off the passenger list. "Eight passengers plus the cargo has us traveling a bit heavy, Captain. We have two Venetian bigwigs that were in Grantville for shopping and business. Lucco Ricci and Alberto DeLuca. DeLuca is the redhead. There's a little boy that was sent here for surgery on a deviated septum. His dad is some sort of muckety-muck or something in France, so they sent him to Grantville by way of Venice. He's five, and I've been calling him Frankie. His nanny, Mademoiselle Babin, isn't crazy about that, lemme tell you."

Johan caught sight of a really differently dressed stranger. "Who's the guy in the robes?"

"Magdalena said he's a sultan or something from Algiers, or North Africa anyway, who wanted a look at the library in Grantville. Can't pronounce it right. Hafsid Bey Sidi Uthman, that's it. Peter back there is a certified electrician the sultan hired to wire his palace. The blond guy is Matthew Howard, English kid on his grand tour."

"I heard about him," Johan said. "He cut quite a swath through the young women in Grantville. Good thing he didn't stay more than a month."

"Yeah, he's headed to Rome, he said. And the last is David Bartley, who's going to Venice for a week on some business."

"About standard," Johan said. "Half a million in cargo and five million in ransoms." Then he waved to Magdalena that they were ready and the passengers started to board.

"Welcome aboard, sir, ma'am." Johan got the passengers settled in then headed up front for the usual speech. "Folks, we're not having box lunches this trip. Nürnberg is only eighty-five miles away and we have to stop to refuel, since the trip is about four hundred miles. TransEuropean Airlines will have a catered lunch waiting for us when we get there. There will be snacks and drinks for the long leg of the trip, which is the one to Bolzano, where we refuel again. Then it's just a hop, skip and jump to Venice. We should be there before sundown."

Sidi Uthman asked, "This lunch? I did explain my dietary requirements..."

"I'm sure our office sent word ahead, sir." Johan made his way back up front, resenting a bit that it was him acting as greeter. He wished again that they could afford the weight of a stewardess. But these weren't up-time passenger planes. They were more like an air-going stagecoach in the amount they could carry. They were roomier per pound or passenger they could carry than an up-time aircraft would be, which made them pretty luxurious stagecoaches. But that was because they had less lift for their size.

About a quarter hour later, they were in the air and headed south.

"Stop that squirming, Francois!" Mme. Badin snapped. "Can't you just look out the window?"

Francois tried but he really had to go. He'd been too excited to visit the restroom before they took off. Then Mr. David Bartley leaned over the seat in front of him and said, "I need to go use the facilities. I'll take him, if you like."

Mme. Badin gave Mr. Bartley a measuring look. Francois knew that she was uncomfortable with airplanes, and the idea of getting up and walking around in them made her even more nervous. He squirmed some more. "I really need to go."

"Very well. But be careful."

The young Englishman stood up and headed to the can, just beating Mr. Bartley and Francois. "*Don't* push the red button!" Mr. Bartley said and Francois looked up in time to see that Mr. Bartley was grinning.

"No fear," Matthew said. "I've been told all about the red button."

Francois looked up at the two men. He hadn't been told about the red button. He wondered what it did. He knew enough to know that red buttons did bad things.

"Just not till we get out of range of Grantville," Mr. Bartley explained. "You don't want your poop landing on the head of someone who'll complain to the mayor, do you?"

Francois felt his eyes get even wider. Then Matthew came out and agreed. "Yes. The red button opens a hole in the bottom of the plane. Then poof! Everything that's, ah, collected during a flight will fall down out of the sky. Best to do that over a forest or something, so you don't drop it on someone's head."

Francois went in and spent some time looking for the red button but didn't find it. He became convinced that Mr. Bartley and the Englishman were playing with him. Then he spent some time giggling about how it would work. He was still giggling when he got back to his seat. His nanny, after he told her the story, turned around and gave Matthew and David a very stern look. They glanced at each other, trying to hold back the laughs. It wasn't true, of course. The toilet in the Monster was emptied on the ground by much more conventional means. But it made a fun story for Francois.

Shortly after that Francois got to visit the cockpit where they steered the plane. It was big, almost as big as the cabin. There were cabinets and things where they stored stuff for the plane. There were two chairs. At first Francois thought they weren't locked to the floor like the seats in the cabin were. But they showed him the little rails that let the seats be moved, then be locked down again. So that the copilot could be navigating when he wasn't copiloting and the pilot could handle the radio and stuff. But the chairs were still attached to the floor.

It was while Francois was down on the floor looking at the rails that he saw the copilot's feet. Now Francois was greatly impressed with the medical know-how of the doctors in Grantville. They had fixed his deviated septum. The idea that they could make legs that were real legs seemed to him quite likely. Besides, these didn't look at all like the peg legs he had seen. They had feet. It also seemed quite a neat thing to have. "Did the doctors fix your legs like they fixed my seppum? Did they hurt after they sewed them on?"

"No, I'm afraid not. The guy who designed the Monster had more to do with my legs than the doctors did. They aren't sewn on; I take them off at night like shoes," the copilot explained. "They are made of a composite, the same as the airplane."

"Why not just use wood?"

"Wood is heavy and artificial legs don't have muscles in them. Well, these have springs in them which help, but they aren't really the same as muscles. So Georg used composites to keep the weight down. I'm still getting used to them but they are better than sitting in a chair all the time." They didn't explain to him that Merton the copilot had been in an accident at a machine shop a couple of years ago and had lost both legs above the knee. The loss of his legs had been especially hard on Merton, and the Ring of Fire had made it harder still, because it had turned back the clock in the field of prosthetics. It had never occurred to Merton before the accident that the switch from "disabled" to "physically-challenged" had been anything but political correctness. The difference between a peg leg and an up-time prosthetic limb was the difference between a disability and a challenge. At least in Merton's case. It was, for all practical purposes, impossible to walk on a couple of peg legs that started above the knee. That was not true with up-time prosthetics.

The composite legs that Georg had made for Merton at Farrell's request fell somewhere in between an up-time prosthetic and a peg leg but rather closer to the up-time product. They allowed Merton to walk with the aid of something to hold on to. He'd been told that once he got a bit more used to them he might even be able to get by with a couple of canes instead of a walker.

Francois spent the rest of the hour and a half flight to Nürnberg looking out the window, mostly at clouds. When that got old he looked at the passengers. Francois was a child of nobility. But for most of his life he had been a hidden-away child. Not that his parents didn't love him. They did. Still, he had been sick most of his life, so he hadn't been able to play much. He had met more people in the hospital than in France. All he really knew of France was Mama, Papa and Mme. Badin . . . well, and a few doctors that Papa had had look at him. Not being sick was quite a novelty in itself. So was being able to breathe through his nose. During his recovery from the surgery he had gone from shy to curious, perhaps even overly curious.

"Ah." Sidi Uthman pushed his chair back and burped delicately. "Most interesting, indeed."

The meal had been leg of lamb with mint jelly, not something Merton much cared for at the best of times. But, he figured, whatever it took to make a passenger happy. Gods knew, they paid enough for this treatment. For him there was a large pot of coffee, which he appreciated.

"More please," Frankie said. David Bartley poured himself and the kid another cup of cocoa, while his nanny enjoyed a glass of wine with the Italian merchants. Peter Hartz stuck to beer.

"Merton," Johan called, "time to preflight."

Back in the air, Johan pointed the nose a bit west of south. "That cold front must be weaker than they predicted," he said. "We came in a bit farther east than I thought we would."

"What is taking you to Venice, Herr Bartley?" Alberto DeLuca asked. He was a portly man in his late thirties or early forties.

David looked at him then smiled. "Ships. OPM has been asked to invest in a shipping concern, so I'll be looking at ships. And talking to people about what it should cost to refit them with some up-time devices that should allow smaller crews."

"What sort of devices?" asked Lucco Ricci.

"Electric winches, batteries and a drag generator."

"What is a drag generator?"

"It's what Brent Partow calls a small generator that you drag behind a sailing ship. It uses the motion of the ship through the water to charge the batteries. The idea is that a ship rigged with the system would be able to use the wind indirectly to raise the sails and a few other things, decreasing the crew size from a third to half. We're not entirely sure it will work or how big the units would be. I'll also be pricing glass and silks."

The conversation went from there. With David talking about silk and glass while DeLuca and Ricci tried in vain to move the discussion back to the availability of the shipboard power system. Every once in a while David would let slip some tidbit about how the initial investment would be significant but the savings in crew cost would probably pay for it in the course of a single journey, then go back to talking about the price of silk. All in all David thought it was going very well.

About an hour and a half later, Merton started getting worried. "Shouldn't we have seen Munich by now, Johan?"

"It's the damned clouds," Johan muttered. "Can't see properly half the time."

"Point it a bit farther east," Merton said. "It can't be that far."

☆ ☆ ☆

"Still no Munich," Johan whispered.

"Maybe we better land and ask?" Merton suggested.

"Not in Bavaria." Johan shuddered. "You *don't* want to set down in Bavaria. Not ever."

"We can't be that far off course," Merton said.

"Far enough that we don't know exactly where we are," Johan said. "Keep looking."

Merton suppressed the urge to stick his tongue out at Johan, and kept looking. They were passing over the foothills of the Italian Alps. That was clear enough, but where? "Turn right and follow the valley?" Johan had made this trip a lot more often than Merton had.

"Might as well. I don't have a clue where we are, but I wonder where it leads."

"Bolzano, I hope. But at the very least, I hope it's within Duchess Claudia's lands. We should be safe as long as we land in the Tyrol somewhere."

"There's an outpost," Johan said, pointing to a building below. "Might be a customs station."

"And you'd better turn north and follow that pass," Merton grunted. "I'm really not liking this at all. Much more of this and we'll have to land, no matter where we are."

"Well, do we take the chance?" Johan's voice was worried.

"It's a lake. We know we can land there," Merton pointed out. "All we have to do is find out where we are, then we can plot a course to Bolzano. We're not hurting for fuel yet, but if we keep flying around like this we will be."

There wasn't much help for it. They had to know where they were. As it was, the passengers were getting restless, probably catching their own tension.

"Going down," Johan said. The clouds were low and spotty over the lakes, more mist than anything else, but they could see enough of the lakes to be sure of their outline and one thing about water landings, the water was flat. "Give me twenty percent flaps. I want time to look around a bit as we come down. We'll turn at the end of the lake and come back for landing."

Merton set the flaps and the Monster slowed.

☆ ☆ ☆

"Folks, make sure your seat belts are fastened," Merton announced. "We're going to land for a bit. Just as soon as we clear up the problem we're having, we'll be on our way again."

"What's the problem?" Matthew said.

"Probably something electrical." Peter grinned. "Luckily, I can help with that."

"Are we lost?" Frankie's face was aflame with curiosity. "Are we stopping to ask directions?"

David Bartley and Sidi Uthman shared a look. "Certainly not."

Nanny snorted. "Men never ask for directions. They'd rather ride—or fly—around in circles all day." Then, as the implications of what she had said occurred to her the joke seemed to lose its humor. If they weren't stopping to ask for directions, what was wrong?

Matthew looked over at their only female companion, who'd gone white around the lips. "It'll be fine, Miss. The engines are running steady. It's probably just a an odd reading on an indicator or something." He started trying to distract her with stories while the rest of the passengers looked out the windows.

Hearing the conversation through the open cockpit door, Johan said, "Time to 'fess up. Hold her steady for a minute." Then he got up and went back to face the music. "Ladies and gentlemen, I'm afraid Frankie is right. We've missed a couple of our check points, probably because of the spotty visibility we've had today. So we're going to land at a small village on the edge of the lake and ask for directions. It should be no more than a chance to stretch your legs for a few minutes. Then we'll be on our way."

Frankie crowed. "I was right!" And started giggling.

"Amazing!" Nanny laughed.

"Captain!" Mr. Bartley protested. "You're letting down all mankind," though to Frankie he didn't really sound displeased.

Slightly red-faced because it was always embarrassing to admit they were lost, Johan said, "Our director, Magdalena Van de Passe, made stopping to ask directions airline policy."

"Ah, that explains it," Alberto DeLuca proclaimed jovially. "Our pilot and copilot are true men, self-sufficient in all ways, but like all gentlemen they must yield to the quirks of the ladies." He gave a florid bow to Nanny.

Blushing harder, Johan retreated to the cockpit and went back to the controls. By now they had flown over the village and he turned around to take up their landing approach. By they time they had finished the turn they were five hundred feet above the ground and losing about fifty feet a minute.

"Forty percent flaps," Johan told Merton and he throttled back the engines. The Monster slowed as they came back into the mist over the water. It was the wrong order. A mistake no bush pilot would make, nor any pilot with experience landing pontoon planes, but neither Johan or Merton had that sort of experience. Compared to just about any up-time multiengine pilot they were rank amateurs. What they had seen was the air cushion landing gear go over bumps and ditches on land and logs floating in water without missing a beat. They had over flown the lake just like they were supposed to and it looked clear. With the patchy mist, shadows from the mountains, and the altitude of their flyover, it wasn't what a bush pilot would consider a proper examination. In fact, for half the flyover Johan had been calming the passengers rather than looking out the windows for debris or boats on the lake.

"Inflate the bag," Johan said and Merton started the motor that would fill the ACLG.

A few seconds later Merton reported, "Bag deployed." They were now a hovercraft—or would be in a few seconds. They were almost half a mile from land, down to ten or so feet over the water and sinking slowly on flare effect. "Jesus! Pull up. Pull up! There's a boat!"

Johan jerked the stick back.

The last thing Thoman Klein expected was for a monster of any sort to drop on his head. Much less a monster that made those hideous growling noises.

It was the noise that drew his attention. Normally Lake Heiterwanger, especially this far from shore, was dead quiet. All the better for "not really fishing" as far as Thoman was concerned. He just had to get away from his wife, his mother and their constant chatter now and then.

When he turned to see what was making the noise, all the blood drained from the upper part of his body. A massive, rawhide-colored . . . thing was coming right at him. And above the thing, which looked like a lobed bag of some sort, was a bright blue . . . other thing. With wings. Four wings.

Thoman grabbed his oars, but it was too late. He jumped.

☆ ☆ ☆

The Monster did miss Thoman, but just barely. The landing gear, made only of leather and canvas, caught the bow of his boat. The plane was traveling at over thirty miles per hour; the leather balloon—or at least a portion of it—wrapped around the bow of the skiff and flipped it neat as you please, lifting the starboard side up into the undercarriage of the plane. There was a loud bump followed by shouts from the passengers but the air cushion had cushioned the blow. Not without damage. A rip over ten feet long was torn in the bottom of the bag. Then they were down, trailing strips of leather and a shattered skiff. Now the water itself made up the bottom of the bag, plugging the major leak and leaving only the minor ones. The largest of which was a tear about a foot wide in the rear wall of the bag. They weren't going to sink. Heck, they wouldn't sink even if the bag were removed entirely. They would become, in essence, a flat-bottomed boat. With most of the bag still in place and the bag motor running they were still a hovercraft, just not a very efficient one. The skirt on a hovercraft is supposed to leak; that's what makes it slip over the surface with very little drag. It just wasn't supposed to leak quite as much as it was at the moment.

Johan made a wide circle on the water and headed back to look for survivors. He saw a head bobbing in the water. "Take the stick, Merton, and get us up beside that guy. I'll go out and throw him a rope."

"I have the stick."

Johan got up, opened the emergency locker and grabbed a rope, then went through the opened door into the passenger compartment. "Keep your seats, folks. We had a problem on landing." The door to the cockpit was generally left open in flight. It was there primarily as an extra security measure when the plane was on the ground, making it a bit harder for someone to steal it by climbing aboard and flying off. "Folks, we hit a boat. Apparently someone was doing a bit of fishing. We're going back now to pick up the survivor." Then he opened the door and stepped out onto the bottom wing.

He watched as the plane approached the man in the water. Who was swimming like hell in the other direction. "Hold up there. I'll throw you a rope," Johan shouted over the noise of the engines.

Thoman looked over his shoulder to see the thing approaching him and a man standing on it with a rope in his hand. In the blink of an eye he went from being more scared than he had ever been in his life to more angry. They had almost killed him. Thoman didn't have the words for what these up-timers were and he could cuss for half an hour without repeating himself. He was so mad he almost didn't grab the rope that was thrown to him. The man on the machine pulled him toward it and he almost let go. The water around it bubbled and foamed like a witches' brew. But he was a quarter mile out from shore and the water was cold. He wasn't at all sure he could make it back to shore. The man who pulled him up was well-dressed, if in a strange style.

Damned up-timers and their flying machines. "You wrecked my boat," he yelled as soon as he was out of the water. "You lost me my trolling rig and my lunch. You soaked my clothes and almost killed me. I want restitution." There were faces in the doorway by now, watching the show. Then one of them spoke.

"Clearly he doesn't know his place," the man in the funny hat said. "You ought to throw him back in and be done with it."

The man who had pulled Thoman out of the water gave the fellow in the funny hat a look, then said, "Was there anyone else on the boat?"

Thoman shook his head.

"We can talk about restitution once we get you back to shore. Meanwhile, step inside where it's warm."

It actually was warm inside the thing. And the seat the man showed him to was comfortable, although he didn't much like the seat belt. And he wasn't too impressed with the giggling little boy who kept peering at him from between the seats in front of him. And sticking out his tongue.

Plus, there were too many languages being spoken—particularly by the man in the funny hat. Who kept looking at Thoman and sneering.

Not to mention, he was still angry about the boat. These people were going to pay for that boat. Or else.

In a day of strange happenings, probably the strangest was after they'd gotten this monster machine to shore and unloaded. A man came struggling out of the front of the machine, using a very odd contraption that he called a walker. A man with, of all things, fake feet. Thoman had seen a peg leg before. But never fake feet.

"My name is Merton Smith. What is the lake called?" the man with fake legs asked.

"Heiterwanger See," Thoman told him.

"Where's the nearest large town?"

"Why do you want to know?"

Merton Smith gave Thoman an apologetic look. "We got off course. We were landing here to ask for directions. It's happened before and usually it's no problem, but the mist hid your skiff."

"Well, you'll get nothing more out of me or the rest of the village, either. Not until you've paid for my boat and for nearly killing me."

"How much?" Lucco Ricci, one of the businessmen from Venice, squeaked. "For *that*?" *That* was what was left of Maximilian I's rustic cabin. Located outside the village of Heiterwang; it was not in good repair.

"This is a small village, milord. There is no inn. And Her Grace's letter of transit doesn't give you the right to just take what you want. You could, if you like, sleep in that contraption you arrived in." It was said with all the proper deference but it translated to: Take it or leave it.

The very scruffy—and quite sharp—headman of the village gave Ricci a look. One that David could understand. It was a small village and you could tell it didn't have an easy time of things in general. Plus, here in the late spring, there wasn't a lot of surplus food to be found in most places. Still, David thought the villagers were making a mistake. He looked around. While not the best time of year, this was a beautiful place. The fact that Maximilian I had liked it for trout fishing suggested that with a little work it would make quite a nice resort, with fishing in summer and skiing in winter. Which would be a really nice source of additional income for the village. Lucco Ricci looked over to Johan.

"They have canvas and leather that we can buy. We can fix the bag with that and the patch kit and a bit of help sewing from the villagers," Johan said. "It'll take some time, though, so you may as well take their offer. We won't be able to leave until tomorrow. If then."

Lucco Ricci nodded and gave over the coins. The village had insisted on silver, not trusting USE dollars. Luckily Lucco had been in Grantville doing a bit of arbitrage. He had brought a couple of hundred thousand USE dollars to Grantville and used them to buy silver, which he was taking back to Venice. Most in slugs of ninety-nine percent pure silver electrically separated from copper, but some in silver coins of various denominations and from various mints. It was all destined to make Venetian coins.

Merton and Johan had gone through their books and charts and found what they thought was the right lake. There were two of them connected by a narrow waterway, the Plansee and the Heiterwanger See. "See" apparently designated a mountain lake. The village that the Monster was sitting near was called Heiterwang, which fit. If that was where they were, they were over forty miles west of where they were supposed to be.

"Can I help?" David asked.

"Yeah," Merton said. "You can help me get back to the plane. I'll be spending the night guarding the cargo. These are Claudia de Medici's lands, but considering the attitude of these people, better safe than sorry."

With a lot of help from the villagers—some of who seemed to really be enjoying the novelty—they'd managed to get the plane up on jacks. Johan and some of the local men who sewed sails were working on repairing the bag.

It was a long, cold night.

No one but Signore DeLuca had very much in the way of coins. And while they grumbled, the right of transit document that Claudia de Medici had given them did stop the villagers from trying to impound the plane and hold them all prisoner. Still, Johan had to sign a promissory note with Signore DeLuca for funds to pay for the damned boat and their lodgings and food. Probably it wouldn't be a problem, since they truly didn't have much choice. Magdalena would understand that they had to do what they had to do.

Sultan or vizier or whatever-he-was Sidi Uthman was very unhappy with the provisions they found. He was happy to make that displeasure known, too, and kept threatening to sue.

Johan could hardly wait to get out of Heiterwang.

"Magdalena! *Magdalena!* Venice wants to know if the plane took off on time."

"Certainly it did." Magdalena van de Passe looked up from the invoices and other assorted paperwork on her desk. "It arrived in Nürnberg on time, too, and departed nearly on time. Why?" Magdalena didn't panic. It was quite common for their flights to be off-schedule. It had happened before, and was very likely to happen again. Almost anything could cause a delay, from sudden storms to adverse winds.

"Because it hasn't arrived in Bolzano yet. And Duchess Claudia was expected at a dinner in Venice tomorrow night. She was planning to take the Monster from Bolzano." Which Magdalena knew was a hundred miles even as the Monster flew. There was no way Duchess Claudia would make her dinner party if the plane was delayed too long. And that could well have political consequences.

Magdalena looked at the clock, then did some calculations. Really, the Monster should certainly have been in Bolzano by now. "If it hasn't arrived in another two hours, then I'll worry," she thought.

Actually, she worried every time the plane took off. It was the only plane TransEuropean Airlines owned. Markgraf Smith Aviation nearly had a two-engine model, the Neptune, ready for test flights, but it would be at least a month before that plane was ready.

Magdalena didn't get back to the paperwork. The first call came from Delia Higgins, wondering if she'd heard that the plane had arrived in Venice. She was worried about her grandson, David Bartley.

The next call was from Farrell Smith, worried about Merton.

The calls kept coming for the rest of the afternoon, then stopped as all the people concerned drifted over to the airline's offices, waiting for news.

Magdalena and her secretary stayed busy serving refreshments and trying to reassure everyone that things were all right.

"Perhaps they had to set down at one of the customs stations. We have an agreement with Duchess Claudia, but the radios don't always work well in the mountains."

"Oh, I'm sure everything is fine. It's probably interference from the storm."

By the time darkness fell and there hadn't been any news, Magdalena was finding it very hard to reassure anyone. Including herself.

"Is there any word?"

Farrell Smith looked like he hadn't slept a wink. Magdalena figured he probably hadn't. Neither had she. "Not yet, Farrell."

"There's so much that can go wrong . . ."

"Merton and Johan are experienced, Farrell. As experienced as any of us. You know that."

"Yes. But..."

"All we can do is wait, Farrell. Someone will be at the radio twenty-four hours a day until we hear."

Not much got done at Markgraf Smith Aviation that day. Farrell Smith was too worried to leave the radio shack and go work on building another airplane. Delia Higgins joined him, along with Johan's wife and a number of others.

It didn't help matters that the press had gotten hold of the story, either. Nosy reporters were constantly asking family members how they felt, which at one point almost caused Farrell Smith to bloody a nose. *The Street*'s headline read DAVID BARTLEY MISSING and the *National Inquisitor* asked WHAT'S REALLY IN THAT SKY? Both headlines were in 32 point type and hard to miss.

By the beginning of the third day, none of the crew or passengers could wait to get out of Heiterwang.

"Let's just get in the damn thing and go," Merton said. "I'm getting tired of being looked at like I'm a freak, for one thing. For another, I'm sick of dried fish and peas. Rain or no rain, cold or no cold, let's get out of here before we have to pay three times the going rate for something else."

"Amen," Matthew said. "I'm deadly tired of this backwater."

Johan checked the bag one more time. It was holding air. Sort of. Just at the moment, it was still leaking in some places it wasn't supposed to—but they still had a bag. Then he looked up at the sky. The weather was a concern, but he had flown in rain before. Just not very often. Still... He signaled Merton cut the air cushion fan, then he and the passengers climbed aboard.

"Fasten your seat belts folks." Johan smiled. "We are *so* out of here."

Merton had already restarted the fan when Johan took his seat. "Give the bag a bit more power, Merton."

It was choppy almost from the moment they left the ground. Turbulence was coming off the back slope of the mountains. Johan tried to climb above it and ran into a monstrous head wind. The valley had clearly been protecting them from the worst of the storm. The Monster clawed its way east for about twenty minutes, then sleet started falling. The icy rain from the north that had been blocked by the ridge on their left was blocked no more. They started looking for a place to land. But it was hard to see with the icy rain. They kept flying with their wings getting heavier from the ice every minute. Wing icing was a danger to aircraft and passengers because it added weight and disrupted air flow over the wings. It could also literally freeze the control surfaces in one position. The Monster didn't have deicing systems. They had to land soon or they would crash.

"Grantville Base, Grantville Base. Jupiter One, Jupiter One." Merton tried to radio, but he was needed to help control the plane. They had no way of knowing if any of their message got through.

It was several minutes later when they found a flattish piece of ground. The landing wasn't a problem. And there were a couple buildings off in the distance. They used the bag to get close. No one was out in this whether and the wind hid the sound of the engines.

Once they got close to the houses, they cut power to the bag and settled. Then Johan went out and tied the plane down.

It wasn't a village; it was a high pasture with some woodcutters in residence. The sheep would be coming up in a few weeks. Perhaps because they hadn't landed on anyone's head, the people seemed much more friendly. The villagers were willing enough to take USE dollars, but only at a lousy rate of exchange. The crew and passengers spent a fairly comfortable night and the next day, waiting for the storm to pass. Johan stayed on board the plane that first night and Merton the second.

"The storm is getting worse, according to Bolzano."

Delia Higgins' face went even paler, but Magdalena kept on. "Bolzano also says that they got what they think is a message from them. But there's a lot of interference from that storm. We just don't know yet."

The newspaper headlines that day were even worse. And they had reporters hanging around looking for comments.

Siegfried looked at the plane. "I'm not sure about this, Karl." He had had a tour that afternoon. It was impressive. What they called the cockpit was more of a cabin. The whole plane was roomy. "It's one thing to pick up a bit of the readies knocking off the occasional stranger on the Brenner Pass. But these are important people."

"Important people bring big ransoms. Now shut up and help me up onto the wing." Siegfried made a cup of his hands and Karl climbed up. The plane wobbled a bit, not much.

Merton wouldn't have noticed the plane wobble if he had been asleep but the cold weather was making his stumps ache. He looked out the window thinking the wind might be picking up again. But it was still as death. Then the plane shook again. Someone was on the wing. A little nervous, but mostly embarrassed, Merton closed the cockpit door and started putting his legs on. He started to call a greeting but checked himself. What would anyone be doing out at the plane at this time of night? He checked the clock. It was three in the morning. Well, three fifteen.

"I don't see the cripple they left guarding the plane, Karl."

"Will you shut up," hissed another voice. "We want him alive. He's an up-timer and they're all rich, so he will be worth a good ransom."

Merton forgot about his right artificial leg and opened the gun case just as quietly as he could. The gun case had four Suhl revolvers and a 30.06 for just this sort of situation. He managed to get the case opened while Karl and whoever it was continued to argue about whether this was a good idea and whether they should take the risk of trying to take him alive or just cut his throat. He gathered that there had been an ongoing debate about whether to rob them since they had arrived. Their planned morning departure had brought things to a head.

Merton was sitting in the copilot's seat by then, with it turned to face the cockpit door, a blanket on his lap and a six-shooter under the blanket. He'd been as quiet as he could. The plane itself, to prevent engine noise from bothering the passengers and because it was a natural function of the way the body of the plane was made, was pretty close to soundproof. But the partition between the cabin and the cockpit was about as soundproof as a Japanese paper wall.

Merton was sitting in the cockpit wondering what he could do. When the cockpit door was pulled open, he saw the long knife silhouetted by a lamp, and reacted. The barrel of the forty caliber six-shot revolver came up two inches. He squeezed the trigger and the hammer fell. From four feet away the bullet hit the center of the sternum and didn't even slow much. Instead, both bullet and sternum disintegrated into an expanding shock wave that went a long way toward destroying both lungs and the heart of the knife-carrying bandit.

As the first bandit fell out of his sight picture, Merton fired again. It wasn't until later that he realized that the second bandit was not advancing, but stood still in shock, perhaps beginning to bring his weapon up or perhaps just raising his hands to surrender. Merton would never be sure which and the question would haunt his dreams.

But that would come later. For right now Merton needed to find out what was going on. He finished putting on his legs, cursing the darkness but afraid to turn on a light. The lamp had gone out when the second fellow dropped it. He stuck another couple of pistols in his coat pockets and grabbed the 30.06. Then he checked the windows. The sleet had given over to rain that afternoon and by now the ground was muddy, not icy. It was black as a pit. He couldn't see a damned thing. Stepping over the bodies of Karl and his whiny friend was a chore in itself with his walker and his fiberglass legs.

The Monster had two doors, the passenger hatch and an emergency exit/cargo hatch on the other side in the back. The passenger hatch let the passengers step out onto the wing on the right side of the plane, the cargo hatch was behind the wings which meant its bottom was about five feet off the ground. As might be expected, Merton much preferred the passenger hatch. But the passenger hatch was the one that the bandits had entered and, more importantly, it was visible from the buildings.

Merton went to the cargo door in the back. He opened it and hung on and lowered himself to the ground. As he was trying to manhandle his walker out of the cargo hatch he slipped on the wet ground and landed on his ass.

"What's taking so long?" Herman asked, more to himself than anyone else. This wasn't their usual mode of operation. Herman had figured that the plane was the greatest danger, or at least the most unknown. Who knew what it could do with a pilot on board?

The plan was to have Siegfried and Karl secure the plane, then Siegfried would report back and the rest of them would take the passengers. But they had been gone . . . it seemed like an hour, but honestly was probably closer to half of that. Still, they should have been back by now. And there were the sounds muffled by the rain but they might have been gun shots. And Herman had told Karl and Siegfried to be quiet about it. Could the pilot have gotten the drop on them? No, he couldn't have. He was a cripple and even if he had gotten a shot off, the other one would have gotten him. But it was taking too long. "Albrecht. Go check on those idiots. Find out what's taking so long. If they're going through the goods without the rest of us, they'll regret it."

Albrecht grunted and nodded. Then stomped out into the dark.

Francois had to pee. He was a big boy now so he got up without waking Nanny Badin. They were all sleeping in the one big room but there was a nice fireplace. What Francois was a little nervous about was going out to the outhouse on his own. He wished there was a chamber pot or that he knew where it was. After due consideration he went looking. In the process he inadvertently stepped on Sidi Uthman, then tripped and fell on David Bartley. Who jerked up in surprise, which woke Lucco Ricci.

The noise woke Nanny Badin, who directed Francois to the chamber pot. By then everyone was awake.

Merton froze when he saw the light. The Monster was positioned for takeoff first thing in the morning, which meant it was facing down a slight grade and facing mostly away from the woodcutters' cabin. To make it a short walk for the passengers, it was placed close to the cabin. The lamp and the man carrying it came into sight heading for the passenger door of the plane. Merton was standing in the open with his walker between the tail of the plane and back corner of the cabin. Which fortunately meant that the man with the lamp was facing away from him.

About the time Francois was doing his business, Albrecht was discovering a much worse mess on the floor of the passenger section of the plane. The door to the cockpit was closed and from the position of the bodies the last mistake Karl and Siegfried had ever made was to open it. It wasn't a mistake that Albrecht was anxious to repeat. He rushed back to report to Herman that everything wasn't going exactly according to plan.

Merton moved as fast as his walker would take him as soon as the man with the lamp reached the door of the plane. But Merton couldn't move fast. He had barely rounded the corner of the cabin…

☆ ☆ ☆

Master Uthman, a Bey of Tunisia and member of the Hafsid family, didn't fly well and was not nearly as comfortable among heathens as he had expected to be when he volunteered to undertake this journey for his family. It wasn't that he was treated badly. In fact, he had been treated extremely well . . . but flying terrified him. He wasn't used to feeling helpless and at the mercy of others. So he had lashed out, which he sort of regretted. Sort of. The notion that he terrified a little boy didn't appeal to him. Made it hard for him to sleep. Not that he could apologize. A person in his position didn't do that. But he found that he wasn't sleepy after the little boy woke him. Rather than lie there, he got up and found a seat in a corner to think.

He had just sat down when the woodcutters came though the door armed with pistols and knives. Which, as it turned out, was a very good thing. He wasn't where they were expecting him to be and he was armed. Unlike an airplane bumping around over hills and dales in the sky that couldn't be seen, this was a danger that Uthman could deal with. It was almost with a sense of joy that he reached into his robe and pulled out his brand new Suhl revolver. The bandits were looking at the passengers sleeping on the floor of the large room. And Uthman didn't hesitate or ask them to put down their weapons. He started shooting.

Blam. Aim. *Blam*. Aim.

Now the bandits were reacting, turning in his direction. That's when Bartley opened up, followed a second later by Peter. Lucco Ricci and Alberto DeLuca had their guns out, but by then there was nothing left to shoot at. Matthew Howard had put himself between Miss Badin and the bandits, the last few of whom had turned tail and run.

The room was full of gunpowder smoke. Uthman was shocked at the amount of firepower a few people with revolvers had compared to single shot weapons. Four men lay dead . . . more than dead. Ground up for sausage. Then he heard more shots from outside.

Merton had almost reached the back door when he heard the shooting and turned in time to see the bad guys making a quick exit. They were running away from the cabin and didn't seem to want to get close to the Monster either. He pulled a pistol from his coat pocket and fired off a few rounds. He doubted if he hit anything. They kept running anyway. "Hello in the house!"

"That you, Merton?" Johan's voice.

"Yeah. Everybody all right in there?"

"It appears to be. Come ahead."

Merton made his way into the building to a scene of carnage. And a room full of armed people. "Where did all the guns come from?"

"Who would go all the way to Grantville and fail to buy a repeating pistol?" Sidi Uthman said.

David Bartley snorted. "He's right. I'd be surprised if Frankie doesn't have one."

"It's in his luggage. For when he's older," Miss Badin acknowledged, still holding the small lady's gun that she had failed to bring into action. All the guns were on the small side, suitable for hiding in a large pocket or a shoulder holster. Concealed weapons. Holdout guns.

"Turns out me and Frankie were the only ones in the room that weren't packing," Johan said. "And it's the last time I'm not going to be packing for some time to come."

David looked at Merton. "Johan Kipper got mine for me years ago. He's told me more times than I can count that I have to be ready to be my own last line of defense. It was probably true up-time too, but having money makes you a target. I suspect that most of your passengers have been armed, just not in a hurry to advertise how."

Johan and Peter removed the bodies from the Monster, while Uthman, David Bartley and Merton kept watch.

"You did well, Mr. Bartley," Uthman said.

"If money makes you a target it can also provide you with excellent training." David smiled. "Johan Kipper insisted that I take advantage of that training. He provided most of it. I'll probably hear I-told-you-so for the next year, about his not being along. I assured him that flying was perfectly safe."

Uthman snorted, amused at the notion that anything in life was safe. He also realized that the safest he had been in the last few days was while he was in the air. It wasn't going up into the air that should frighten him, it was coming back down to the ground.

They took off with the sunrise, not seeing any sign of the bandits. The weather was clear and cold with only high clouds so they climbed looking for landmarks and found what they figured had to be Innsbruck. So they turned south along the Isarco River valley. When they saw the Torre delle Dodici and Reifenstein Castle they knew they were back on course.

Merton checked the fuel gauges "From what I can tell getting lost didn't cost us much fuel. Mostly landing and taking off."

"Bolzano Base, Bolzano Base. This is Jupiter One. We're about fifteen minutes out," Johan radioed.

"Grantville will be glad to hear that, Jupiter One," a voice reported. "You've had half the world in a fizz. What the hell happened to you?"

Johan glanced back toward the passenger compartment. Mr. Howard and Miss Badin were sitting next each other, which amused little Frankie no end.

"It's a long story," Johan replied. "Mostly weather."

"Man, I need a shave," David said, rubbing his chin. "And a shower. A hot shower. Real soon."

Uthman laughed. "If you'd only grow a proper beard, Herr David, you'd only need the shower."

David glanced around at the passengers who were debarking. "None of us look any too pure, I guess. But we did get here."

"Well, not quite yet. We still have to fly from Bolzano to Venice. Still, Her Grace keeps a house especially for air travelers. Electricity, hot and cold running water and quite a nice restaurant."

"We got word from Bolzano. They're down and safe. Everybody is fine. No details yet."

Oh, thank God, Magdalena thought as she fought to keep from bursting into tears. That wouldn't do at all. She had to go to the waiting room and reassure the people who'd been waiting for nearly five days. She also had an airline to run, so while she had the radio on the line, and before the morning window closed she said, "Find out what the delay was if you would and how soon they can be back here. This has thrown our schedule all to hell. Oh, and if you could, see who is going to sue us over the delay." Magdalena didn't realize that she came off as awfully hardnosed about it all. And in truth she didn't, not more than the radio operator thought she should. She came across as what she had become. The Boss.

☆ ☆ ☆

"So, you had interesting times, I hear." Duchess Claudia took a sip from her wine glass. "But all is well that ends well."

"I'm glad your agent was able to reimburse Don DeLuca," Johan said. "There are a number of things I'm going to recommend to Fräulein van de Passe when we get back. We've become too accustomed to dealing in USE dollars and forgot that not everyone is willing to deal in them."

"The villagers in Heiterwang are going to soon receive a . . . ah . . . visitation." The duchess sniffed. "All of my people should know by now that I believe in business. Running off business on their part does nothing to improve the duchy. Should you ever happen to land there again, I can assure you of a better reception."

"I wouldn't be too harsh on them, Your Grace," David Bartley said. "All in all their attitude was understandable, if not the wisest in the long term. They overcharged but didn't threaten, at least not after they saw your letter of transit. And overcharging travelers in distress is a tradition of long standing . . . plus it's one that continued into the twentieth century." He snorted. "Even Herr Klein's attitude was understandable, given the circumstances. What I'm worried about is the 'woodcutters' at the second landing. We shouldn't have run into bandits in a random landing. It's not just finding a needle in a hay stack. It's sitting in a hay stack and finding the needle the hard way. Which suggests that they might actually have been woodcutters and if your woodcutters are moonlighting as bandits, you have a real problem."

She paused a moment. "As for the woodcutters, I appreciate your actions. And I'll be sending people to investigate that, as well."

"I won't say we got them all," Merton said. "But we got a lot of them. We'll write it up in detail while we're in Venice, but, we've got to get going." He held up the radio telegram. "We're behind schedule, you know."

Duchess Claudia nodded. "Please do get us a report, as soon as you have the chance. Meanwhile I need a ride to Venice. I will have to apologize for missing the dinner last week."

"Well, I'd better get out to the plane." Merton got to his feet and grabbed his walker. Then he headed to the refueled plane and got back aboard ahead of the passengers.

Johan was checking the plane out as thoroughly as he could here. Due to all the bouncing around, both in the air and in the water—not to mention on the ground—he was concerned about cracks in the body. He was particularly careful around the fuel tanks, since they'd found out the hard way that the fuel could essentially melt their composite. The last leg to Venice had been blissfully uneventful. Still, Johan wanted to know what he was working with as much as possible before they took off for the return trip. Safety protocols from the up-timers were making their way into the down-timer consciousness. "Looks okay." Merton said after looking over the lists.

"Yes it does." Johan agreed. "I'm a bit surprised."

"Wood and glue are easier to maintain, Uncle Hal says. But they also take more maintenance too. What surprises me is how little flack we've gotten from the passengers. Granted, everyone was getting along all right by the end of the trip but I would have expected some heat after we got where it was safe."

Johan looked up from his examination in confusion. "Why?"

"Why?" Merton's confusion was clear on his face. "We crashed! Then we landed in a nest of bandits!"

"Yes. So? No one died in the crash. No one was even that shaken up thanks to the seat belts. Wagon wheels come off all the time; horses go lame or step in a hole and throw their rider to the ground; people sometimes die and are always thrown around. And most people think themselves lucky if they make a four hundred mile trip without running into bandits."

What was confusing Johan and, for that matter, Merton was a difference in world view. One that had been shrinking since the Ring of Fire but was still there. Call it a difference in "comfort level with risk." Not that West Virginia miners were a particularly risk-averse group by up-time standards. By the standards of people who had grown up in war torn seventeenth-century Germany, the up-time attitude toward risk versus reward—even among West Virginia coal miners—was a bit on the squeamish side. Of course, an average up-timer would see the large majority of down-timers as shell-shocked adrenaline junkies with no regard for safety or even sanity.

Still, people adapt. Johan was still willing to take what an up-timer might consider insane risks if there was a profit to be made in the doing—but at least now he studied the risks so he knew what they were. And Merton was willing to get back in the

Monster and fly back to Grantville; he was just surprised that the passengers were not screaming bloody murder.

About then a woman showed up. Nose in the air. "Signore Lucco Ricci informs me that if one is to travel to Grantville, this device is the best means."

The woman so obviously felt superior that Johan took a step he knew was going to get him a dirty look from Merton. He cast a quick glance at Merton, then spoke quickly—before Merton could stick his foot in his mouth. "I'm glad Lucco enjoyed the trip. I'm Captain Johan Schroeder. This is my copilot Merton Smith von Up-time."

Sure enough, Merton started to open his mouth and blow the whole gig, but Johan gave him his best glare and he settled back down. Johan knew that Merton figured the whole "von Up-time" thing was silly, but he also knew that most people considered matters of rank vitally important. Johan's rank as captain gave him a degree of social position, but not as much as the von Up-time gave Merton. It was another area where up-time and down-time attitudes were at odds.

Johan smiled his own superior smile. "We do have a couple of seats available for the next flight to Grantville. We leave on Tuesday, but you'll want to buy your tickets now."

The Royal and Ancient Game

Mark H. Huston

St. Andrews, Scotland, Winter 1634

James O'Fehl, the butler of Ramsay Manor, wearily tugged open the heavy wooden door to Andrew's bedchamber. He could see faint streaks of morning light through gaps in the drawn draperies. Andrew was sleeping soundly in the center of his large bed. James shuffled across the room, and briefly paused to steel himself against what he knew must be done. He took a deep breath, shook Andrew's shoulder, and quietly announced, "The package ha' arrived, milord."

Andrew, the son of Lord Ramsay, sat upright, instantly awake "Here? In the castle?"

"Aye, milord."

Andrew tossed back the covers, peeled his nightshirt off in one swift motion and began to pull on his clothing. The January air chilled the bed chamber, and he shivered with cold. *Or maybe excitement*, James thought dryly.

"Just in time for today! Perfect, James! Have you told my father?"

James lit more candles in the room. "No, milord. You wanted me to wake you first, if they arrived tonight. The messenger brought them out in darkness, sir. It was quite expensive to have them delivered at this hour. They got to the village last night, I'm told."

"Does anyone in the village know of this?" Andrew hopped

on one foot as he pulled on a stocking, finally steadying himself on the bedpost.

"No, sir. Other than it was a very special package, and had to be delivered to you as soon as possible." James picked up a doublet, and held it so Andrew could put his arms into it. "That has happened before, with other packets and letters for your father. While this is somewhat larger, we aroused no undue suspicion."

Andrew ignored the doublet, threw a splash of water on his face, and turned to James. "Did anyone know they were from Germany, specifically Grantville?"

"The writing on the package was somewhat strange, but it is unlikely anyone noticed, or could deduce the contents."

Andrew smiled and clapped James on the back. "This is going to be one of the best days of my life. I cannot wait to see the look on Foreman's face. He's Spottiswoode's man, you know. Nobody has beaten him in a year and a half. But today. Hah! Today will be different. We must wake my father."

Laird Ramsay dashed down the stairs and joined his son and James in the main hall. Laird Ramsay hadn't bothered to dress; he was still in his nightclothes. The crate was half opened by the time he arrived. It was not yet fully light, and flickering candles in the great hall created twisted and dancing shadows as the men worked. Laird Ramsay dashed to the fireplace, snatched the massive family claymore from over the mantle, and used it to hack away some of the last bindings.

At last. They had them. From Grantville, the future. They lay exposed, in their bag.

Laird Ramsay handed the heavy sword to his son, and knelt in front of the open crate. He carefully lifted out a long bag. It rattled mysteriously. Father and son looked at each other with a mix of anticipation, joy and disbelief. Andrew was clenching the massive claymore in both hands, breathless with anticipation. The two men grinned at each other, a wide silly grin.

Laird Ramsay reached inside the bag and grasped a shiny metal shaft. He pulled it out of the bag, and looked at it in wonder. "Look how long this is!" He held it up to a candle, and looked at it closely. There were cushioned grips! At the opposite end, where the gleaming metal shaft blossomed out to a bulbous shape, were the deeply embossed words *Titanium* and *Wilson Pro Golf*. It was a three wood. Made of metal. The rarest metal in the world. "They mus' be strong, named afta' the Titans," he muttered

Andrew nodded, and then hastily looked at the other clubs in the bag: the massive driver, the irons, and the curious short and flat-faced putter, all purpose-built for the greatest game in the universe.

"This," said Laird Ramsay, his voice quavering with excitement, "this is what we will use to finally defeat that dammed Spottiswoode." He looked as his son a little guiltily. "S'pose I shouldn't call him dammed. He is the archbishop of St. Andrews *and* Lord Chancellor, after all. But his men Forman and Hannay have beaten us for the last time."

This was a rivalry that went far, wide and deep. The noblemen had their pride. The men of the kirk had the same. Both groups struggled against the sin, and in most other areas of their lives all were successful at being good, modest, and solid Christians.

However . . .

This was golf, and their struggles against the sin of pride were less successful here.

The kirk/noble game had been going on every Monday morning, weather and course allowing, for the last three years. It had been two years since Lord Ramsay had carried the day. Two years of itchy, scratchy, rubbed-raw-with-dirty-burlap humility. It was time. Past time. A man can only take so much humility.

Andrew was still clutching a putter. "We should challenge them to a wager. Something significant, something the preacher and his kirk golfers will have to live down. Something embarrassing." He handed the putter to James and turned to his father conspiratorially. "What should it be, Father?"

Laird Ramsay held up his hand and got far off look in his eyes. "I have just the thing. Something no bishop's man should ever do. Aye." He nodded his head slowly. "Aye, 'tis perfect."

"I've seen that smile on your face before, Father. Whatever it is, you are scheming. That much I know for sure."

"Aye, lad. And we must make the wager before they see the clubs, or hear of their existence. It must be today." He held the club in his grip, wiggling it. "See how it flexes, boy, so much more than the old ash? We will be able to hit the ball so much farther. We will have one shot for two of theirs. 'Twill be a slaughter, it will."

Andrew had been digging in the crate and the golf bag, going through the zippered pockets. "Look, Father. Balls! They sent us up-time balls, too. These will work better than the feather stuffed balls we use."

The father lifted his son's face to his, each man holding a club, and solemnly said, "Lad. We both know it takes balls to play this game of golf."

James O'Fehl almost stifled his laugh, but wasn't quite successful. The laird and his son glared at him.

Later, the sun was shining brightly for a Monday morning in January. Cold but unusually clear. Brisk. Perfect weather for golf. Just a touch of wind from the sea.

Spottiswoode and his men Foreman and Hannay were already waiting on the first tee at St. Andrews. At sixty-eight years of age, Spottiswoode had withdrawn from active competition in the last year, although he still played occasionally. He nearly always came out to walk a few holes, and offer encouragement to his two associates.

Laird Ramsay and his son strode confidently to the tee, carrying their same old clubs. They bowed slightly to Spottiswoode. "Good morning, Archbishop and Lord Chancellor. It is a pleasure to see you in fine form this morning." Laird Ramsay turned to Foreman and Hannay, and nodded to them. "Gentlemen, you too are looking fine this morning. Beautiful day, no?" The nobleman smiled beatifically.

Hannay looked suspiciously at Laird Ramsay. "You are in quite a mood today, milord. 'Tis been a while since I have seen you this chipper for our weekly match." He turned to his partner Foreman. "What d'ye think?"

Foreman smiled. "I think it will be different at the end of the day, after we finish, and he pays us the wagers he has lost. Like every other day."

Hannay piped up. "'Tis for a good cause tho, lads. Ye be supporting the kirk." The two churchmen laughed. Spottiswoode frowned slightly at his subordinates. They were rubbing it in too hard.

The silly smile did not leave Laird Ramsay's face. "I feel lucky today, lads. Very lucky. So does Andrew, don't ye, Son?"

"Aye, Father."

Laird Ramsay continued, "So lucky I want to raise the wager, gentlemen. Today, we have decided to go 'all or nothing' as it were."

Archbishop Spottiswoode wondered what they were up to. He raised both hands in front of him, as if to give a blessing. "Gentlemen, I must maintain my—let us call it *distance*. I am, after all, the king's hands, eyes and ears for Scotland, and the head of her church. It might appear unseemly of me if I should be partaking, or supporting the partaking, of wagering on the golf course." He looked at the carriages a few yards away, and pointed. "I am going to walk over there, so I do not witness these untoward actions between my senior churchmen and members of a noble family. It might be too much for me to bear. Let me know when it is time to return, I will be waiting." As he walked away, he turned and looked over his shoulder with a twinkle in his eye.

He waited a few minutes more than he thought he might. There was some discussion of the wager between the men, and Laird Ramsay looked to be raising the stakes even more, sweetening the deal. Finally an agreement was reached, and all shook hands. Spottiswoode then returned to the four men, while the caddy for the Ramsays trotted off. "Are you finished with your discussions of the game, gentlemen? It does grow late, and I want to walk all twenty-two holes today."

Foreman leaned toward him and said, "These two are up to something today, Your Grace. I don't know what, but there is some sort of nonsense. The wager they made is—"

"Tut-tut, Foreman. I will hear nothing of any wagers."

"But—"

"Nothing, Foreman."

"Yes, Your Grace."

Spottiswoode squinted off in the distance. "What is it your caddy is carrying there, Ramsay? What a large bag!"

Ramsay smiled his silly smile again. "Oh, nothing. Just some new clubs and balls we are trying out today."

Foreman snorted a laugh. "Hah. If this is anything like the time you soaked your golf balls in fish oil to get additional yardage off of the tee, you *are* going to owe us, Ramsay." He turned to Hannay. "That only caused the ball to explode after he hit it the third time. Quite a mess with feathers and stink all over."

Laird Ramsay continued to smile. "Say what you will, Foreman. Take a look at what we have obtained." The caddy stood the golf bag up in front of Laird Ramsay. "Up-time golf clubs. And balls. Regulation equipment, from the future." Laird Ramsay got just a touch of gloating in his voice. "I don't think you lads are going to stand a chance against us today. Not a chance." Laird Ramsay then took out the driver and danced around a little bit, humming a tune, and occasionally stopping to take a joyous practice swing.

Andrew looked a little sheepish, and just shrugged at the churchmen. "We got them last night, we did."

While his opponents stood shocked and looking worried, Andrew explained to Spottiswoode how he had acquired the club set. An old lady had bought them, right after the Ring of Fire as an investment, and kept them unused in her home until they were discovered by a Scotsman, who told his captain, who immediately wrote to Ramsay. The amount of money exchanged was—well, Laird Ramsay could afford it.

Spottiswoode and his two men admired the clubs, oohed and ahhed at the balls, and flexed the shafts. They tried a couple of swings. They looked even more worried.

"You say you got these last night?" Spottiswoode asked as he carefully examined the balls and the curious titanium driver.

"Aye, that's true," replied Andrew.

"This says it is made of metal named after the Titans."

Andrew nodded his head. "Very strong, ye know, the Titans."

Spottiswoode felt a bit happier. "Aye, lad. Very strong. Primitive. Clumsy, some would say." He turned to his two assistants, who were looking on with elevated concern. "I don't think you have much to worry about today, lads."

The two churchmen looked at their leader with surprise, their expressions clearly indicating that the good archbishop had lost his ability to observe and reason. Foreman swallowed and bravely went first. "Begging Your Grace's pardon, but I think we are going to be spanked by this new kit."

"Spanked good," added Hannay.

"Patience, my sons, patience. Play your own game; let them play their own game." Spottiswoode smiled broadly at his two charges.

Hannay and Foreman teed off first. The first hole was a short one, a little over one hundred yards. Both hit good shots, and then waited for the Ramsays.

Spottiswoode got the feeling that Laird Ramsay was not about to let this opportunity get away. Ramsay used one of the new balls, one of the golf tees that were sent to be used in place of the small piles of sand usually pulled from the hole, but most interestingly, he grabbed the largest club in the bag to hit his first shot. Spottiswoode smiled as Andrew, seeing the club, tried to stop his father. Andrew must have read these clubs could hit a ball well over three hundred yards, and the first hole was only a little over one hundred, and the second was only another hundred yards beyond the first. But Spottiswoode had seen this look in Lord Ramsay's eyes before. The look of certainty bordering on rapture. A glorious certainty, wrapped in layers of three years of chaffing rough burlap. The protest died on Andrew's lips. The boy must know that it was hopeless.

Laird Ramsay took a couple of practice swings, stepped up to the ball after glancing over his shoulder at his opponents, and swung at it with all of his might.

The laird was a fine athlete, powerful, and had a good swing. When he connected, the club hitting the ball made a fascinating metallic and musical *ping*, and it took off like some sort of holiday firework, rocketing down the fairway. It passed over the hole where it had been aimed, and continued to rise. But then it did a most curious thing.

The ball turned right. Toward the sea. One moment it was climbing, well on its way to—well, the *third* hole and then, slowly at first, it turned off target. The farther right it turned, the faster it seemed to go. The five men watched it rocket at what was now a ninety degree angle to the original path. They watched in amazement as the ball finally lost momentum, dropped down near the shore, disappeared for a heartbeat, and then bounced high into the air with a solid thwack as it rebounded off of a rock, and finally finished with a quiet *plop*, a good twenty yards into the sea.

They could all see the concentric rings radiating outward from where the little white ball disappeared beneath the sea. It was a few moments before anyone spoke.

Finally, Spottiswoode broke the reverie. "That is the singularly most impressive out of bounds shot I have ever seen."

Laird Ramsay looked at the golf club in his hands as if it were some bewitched stick. He then looked at the archbishop. Then to his son. "Wa' hae I done, lad?"

"Wee bit too much club, Da."

The rest of the round wasn't much better, and the laird and his son were soundly defeated. They couldn't adjust to the new technology and sliced and hooked and overshot their way to the worst defeat ever. It was not pretty.

They were honorable men, the Ramsays. They paid their debt the next week. Half of the village turned out to watch the match. Bravely, father and son doffed their clothing and began to play in the nude. Since it was so very cold that day, Spottiswoode took pity on them, and only made them play the first two holes in the buff. They refused his suggestion, and played an additional hole to prove their resolve.

From the day of the fateful match forward, when the Ramsays played their three holes in the buff, the putter, which is the shortest club in a set, was henceforth known as the "Naked Ramsay."

A Bell for St. Vasili's

Keith Robertsson

November 1633

"*Ux Te!*" Kseniya hadn't at all expected what she was seeing.

When Princess Natalia Petrovna hired Father Gavril to come to Grantville and set up a church for the people who were coming to study, she'd mentioned that her brother Vladimir had bought a home. She'd even put Kseniya "on salary" as the housekeeper, since Kseniya would of course come to Grantville with her husband.

But, a home *wasn't* supposed to be the size of the Kremlin.

March 1634, The Rezidentz's Kitchen Office

Kseniya slammed the pen on the desk. "*Durag nummers.*"

Though Kseniya was a merchant's daughter and had been raised to expect a certain level of comfort and the responsibility that went with it, she was never expected to manage what amounted to a small business on her own. Hadn't her father married her off to a priest with the prospects of good parishes? The Grantville *rezidentz* was big, as big as one of these up-timer hotels. Impossible for one woman to handle, simply impossible.

Prince Vladimir had gone all out. The house—if house was the proper term at all—covered what she'd learned to call a "block." It was built to take advantage of natural light, two rooms and a hall wide, and two stories high, on each wing. The four wings made a large square, with a private garden in the center. A large private garden. Some of it was given over to decorative gardens, some was kitchen garden, and they had some chickens for eggs. The back wing was the stables and residential area for some of the servants, the east wing was offices, the west, rooms for guests. The south wing was formal reception rooms, more offices and the private quarters for the prince. And his soon-to-be bride, Brandy Bates.

As she was ruminating, a knock came on the door to her cubbyhole office.

"Hi, Mrs. Kotova," said the young lady at the door. "Do you have a moment? I need to borrow some of your brains."

"Good afternoon, *Gospazha* Brandy," Kseniya said. "My time is your time. But are you sure you need to speak to me?" In the months that Kseniya had been in residence, she'd grown close to Brandy and liked the young woman quite a bit.

"Well, Mrs. K, if there's another female Russian in this house who's older than me, tell me who she is," Brandy said.

"*Nu*, if you make those qualifications, I'm the only one in the *rezidentz* or Grantville who fits them," Kseniya said. "Tell me why do you need to 'borrow' some of my brains? I didn't know I had any to spare."

"It goes back to something I heard years ago. If you don't have a lot of brain power but are a good judge of character, you can always borrow or hire the brains. It's a matter of being able to trust your sources."

"Thank you, *moiya gospazha*, for your confidence in me," Kseniya said. "From the sound of it, I think we need a pot of tea. Pardon me for a moment."

When Kseniya returned to her seat, Brandy took a deep breath and plunged into her not-so carefully planned presentation.

"Mrs. K., I feel like a stranger in a strange land. I love Vladimir to pieces and I can't think of life without him. But sometimes, I think I'm about to go nuts here. I don't know enough Russian, for one thing. Then there's running this house. It's not a house. It's enormous. I'm a reference librarian, not Martha Stewart. I don't know how to manage a household the size of Kudzu Werke. Like Charlie Brown used to say, '*Arrgh*.'"

Somewhere, in her venting, Brandy started to cry. Not much, just a few sniffles and enough moisture to cause a need of a handkerchief.

Maria, the maid, arrived then with their refreshments. While Brandy snuffled, Kseniya got up and took the tray, motioning for Maria to leave quickly. She was relieved that she wasn't the only person who was having problems with this situation.

"*Oy*, you do have some problems, don't you? But we're in the same boat, I'm afraid. I wasn't trained for this, either. Your first problem is easy to solve. I can help you with your Russian; you can help me with my English and German."

"Okay," Brandy said. She stopped sniffling and picked up a cup of the tea Kseniya poured. "That will help a lot."

"I agree with you about your other problems. You'll be the *gospazha* of the household. As that, you have a staff working for you. Right now, Gregorii is your major domo. He's reporting directly to the prince. While my husband is your chaplain, I am the head of the kitchen and female staff. But, like you, I am in over my head," Kseniya said.

"We'll just have to figure something out. Do you have any ideas?"

"I'm not really trained to run a kitchen of this size. It's not just the cooking . . . that I can do. It's also the buying from the different sellers. And I'm not used to all these modern conveniences. I grew up cooking on an open hearth and in a *pech*, a big stove . . . not like the cook stove we have here."

"We need help. Let's think about it and do some investigating. Right now, though, I have to go see Vlad. He got another batch of letters from home. And from the czar. And the bureaus. And, and, and!" Brandy threw her hands in the air. "It never stops."

"In that case, you must be on your way. *S' Bogom* . . . go with God."

"*S' Bogom*, Kseniya," Brandy said. "Oh, yeah . . . could you please send Maria to the office with something to eat in about a half hour?"

"Of course, Branya." Kseniya was still surprised by the offhanded politeness of the up-timers she'd met.

"Come on in, Brandy," Vladimir called.

The couple embraced and exchanged a kiss or two.

Brandy whispered, "*Ya lublu tebya*."

"Your pronunciation is getting better. Who's been teaching my girl Russian?"

Brandy said, "Mrs. Kotova and Vladimir Troshin."

"I thought I knew all of the Russians in Grantville. Most of them live in this building. *Who* is this Troshin?" Vladimir asked, putting on his Rezident's hat.

"A singer on a record I borrowed from Ms. Mailey's collection," Brandy said. "While she's in England, Dr. Nichols is house-sitting for her. He lent it to me."

"You learned Russian from a singer?"

"At least the pronunciation," Brandy said. "The record is all Russian big band music."

"We'll have to listen to it when I go into Grantville Saturday. I want to hear your other Vladimir," Vladimir said.

"Sure thing. I think you'll like it. 'Sides, it's danceable. But enough about music. What came in today's mail?"

"Mostly the usual contradictory stuff, one office not telling the other what I sent them, so the other writes asking for information I sent months ago. Here's a stack of inquiries. I've made marginal translations for you."

Taking their seats on either side of a partners desk, the pair set to work. A soft knock came at the study door. Maria had arrived with the tea tray.

"*Mein Herr und Fräulein*, where do you want the tray?" said Maria.

"Here, please, Maria," Brandy said.

Maria placed the tray on the indicated empty spot on the desk.

"Thank you," Brandy said. "Dear, do you want honey on your biscuit?"

"*Da*," Vladimir said, deep in a piece of what was probably arrant nonsense that needed a diplomatic answer.

Brandy gave the stack of correspondence a glare, then repressed a sigh. *Might as well get it done.*

"Vlad, it's getting on to six o'clock. I need to get back into town."

"Do you really need to go?" asked Vladimir.

Laughing at Vlad's oft repeated query, Brandy said, "I told you I won't have breakfast in this house until after the wedding. Cora would be sure to spread the news all over Grantville. Besides, I'm meeting the girls at Tyler's tonight. Dinner and a brain picking session."

"What do you mean 'brain picking' session?"

"I talked to Mrs. Kotova this afternoon. I found out I need to get my ducks in a row if I am going to be the *gospazha* here," Brandy said. "The girls know folks I don't. And I know folks they don't."

"If you must, you must," Vlad said. "But I'll be glad when the day comes that you don't." He wiggled his eyebrows in a suggestive manner.

Brandy laughed again. "Just hold your horses, fella. It'll happen soon enough. *S' Bogom*, honey."

The next Monday afternoon

"Miss Garrett, this lady is Mrs. Kseniya Kotova. Mrs. Kotova, this is Tate Garrett," Brandy said.

As Brandy closed the door, Kseniya gave Tate a once over. She was short for an up-timer, maybe five and four of their feet and inches, solidly built, not too skinny and not too fat, with short, muddy-colored blond hair. And a look of leadership in her eyes.

"Pleased to meet you, Mrs. Kotova," said Tate.

"As am I," Kseniya said, a bit flustered. The girl was much younger than she'd expected.

"Tate, we've got a problem. And I think you're the solution to it," Brandy said. "I asked some people I know and your name came up as some one with the needed skills and experience."

Tate looked startled. "Skills and experience? Brandy . . . Miss Bates, I'm the junior assistant manager at the Willard Hotel. What do I know that you can use?"

"We know that. How big do you think Grantville is?" Brandy grinned.

Brandy wasn't being nearly as formal as Kseniya thought she should be with a possible future employee. Up-timers were very odd that way. "Miss Garrett, we know where you presently work. *Gospazha* Brandy knows of your education and where you planned on going to school after graduation. Someplace called Johnson and Wales . . . and something called hospitality arts?"

"Boy, you ladies really do know about me. Are you sure there's no KGB agents stationed here?"

Brandy laughed. "Who needs the KGB when you've got the Barbie Consortium? We need someone to help Mrs. Kotova. And me, for that matter. You'll be *chef de cuisine* and other duties as assigned. This place is like a hotel, only with both permanent residents and transient guests. Not to mention, you'll have a wedding to cater in the not-too-distant future. We are also taking you on because you know the food suppliers in West Virginia County. What do you think? Want a job?"

"Good night, Brandy! Most chefs have to spend years to get the position you're offering. You're darn right I want it," Tate said.

"Good to have you with us." Brandy grinned and extended her hand.

"*Da*," Kseniya said. "I'm happy to have the help."

Three weeks later

To the casual observer, the kitchen looked the same as it did a month ago. However, Kseniya saw minor yet practical changes. Over in at the baker's station, Maria was weighing out the ingredients for the afternoon's baking. The prince liked warm fresh baked goods on his supper table. He'd even fallen in love with American-style fruit pies for his dessert. So, he was happy. Everyone else was eating better and she was staying inside her kitchen budget. For that, Kseniya decided to stop by the makeshift chapel and light three candles before the icon of Saint Vasili. Her thinking was interrupted by a shout.

"Good afternoon, Mrs. K. How you doin'?" Tate asked.

"Fine, Chef, *slava bogu* . . . errm, praise God. And you? The kitchen looks a bit more polished," Kseniya said.

"Ahh, it wasn't any thing a bit of elbow grease and some chlorine bleach solution couldn't cure. The scullery crew needed a bit of encouragement to clean the corners," said Tate. "Are we still having tea with Colonel Makoveev?"

"Yes. He may be a *streletz*, but I don't think he is a colonel. Maybe a captain or a colonel's nephew," Kseniya said.

"What's a *streletz*, Mrs. K?"

"The *streletzi* are the czar's musketeers. The *streletzi* regiments form the czar's guard regiments and the garrisons of the larger cities in Russia," replied Kseniya.

"So, what makes you think he is a fake?" said Tate.

"There are only so many *streletzi* colonels. They are all old, fat and in Russia. This Colonel Timofei Makoveev is too thin and too young to be a colonel and he's here."

Tate laughed. "Let's go in to the office; the mice have ears," she said. Then she waved at Maria. "Maria, have the usual setup brought to the office."

"Yes, Chef."

"Agreed. After you, Chef," Kseniya said.

The ladies entered the kitchen office and fell to examining the accounts ledger. Kseniya was pleasantly surprised to see the neatness and completeness of the book. She was very pleasantly surprised to see the reduction in costs. One of the scullery crew brought the tea into the office and they came up for air and poured their cups of tea.

"What is keeping Makoveev? I'm on my second cup," Kseniya said. "You'd think his mother taught him better than to let a lady wait."

"I don't know." Tate shrugged. "Do you want me to send out a search party?"

Just then came two raps on the office door.

"Mrs. Kotova, Chef Garrett, I apologize for being late. I was out at the range with the Junior ROTC." Colonel Timofei Makoveev had a pleasant baritone. He also held a full cup of tea, procured from the kitchen's common tea pot, in his hand.

"Good afternoon, Colonel," Kseniya said. "Tell us, please, what in the world were you doing with a bunch of teenagers?"

"Some one talked Prince Vladimir into volunteering me as a range safety officer. I guess with a red coat and yellow boots, the instructors think I didn't look like a target. Now, how can I help you ladies?"

Tate said, "First, Colonel, in this office, unless one of our subordinates is present, we're on an informal basis. Here, I'm Tate, this is Mrs. K, and you're Tim . . . or Colonel Tim if you insist."

The soldier thought for a moment and said, "So, this is something like the Officers' Mess they talk about down at the American Legion Hall."

"*Da*, you're correct, Tima," Kseniya said. "We're here to support the prince and *Gospazha* Brandy. I am happy to see you are familiar with the American Legion."

"As the representative of the *Streletzi* Bureau, I need to make contacts with the various military related organizations in Grantville."

"Tim, I need a date to tomorrow's Legion pastrami roll lunch. I'm not a vet. The vets I know are all too old. If they're young and still free, I've turned them down in high school," Tate said.

Timofei looked the woman sitting behind the desk in her

double-breasted chef's jacket. She was young, easy on the eyes but not drop dead beautiful, and wore a uniform with Prince Vladimir's crest embroidered on it. All things considered, a worthy lunch companion. And there was just something about a girl in uniform . . . "I'll be happy to be your escort for lunch, Tate. Due to the ways armies are organized these days, the Legion allows men from friendly services to buy affiliated memberships. I get to eat and drink there but not vote."

"Tima, I saw that look in your eye. Don't get any ideas about Tate. If she tells me you got out of line, *ya Mama*. I'm mother around here," Kseniya said in full mother-bear mode. "Do you understand me?"

"*Da*, Mama Kotova. I hear and will obey," said Timofei. He looked like a mischievous boy who'd been caught with his hand in the cookie jar.

"Good, I'll watch over the kitchen for lunch," Kseniya said. "Tima, tell Old Sasha to have the carriage ready to take you to the Legion Hall at, say, about eleven o'clock tomorrow morning."

"Yes, Mrs. Kotova," Tim and Tate chorused.

"Colonel, let's get out of here so Chef Garrett can get supper ready."

10:30 AM, Saturday

Colonel Makoveev said, "Sasha, I won't need a driver today. Just hitch up the buggy."

"Vanya, you heard the colonel. Get the buggy ready," Sasha ordered.

Old Sasha watched Makoveev as the buggy was readied and saw the look of a man on a trail.

"Sasha, what do you think of these Grantville horses?"

"Colonel, I never thought I'd be working with so many head of quality horse flesh. These Morgan crosses are beautiful," Sasha said.

"I need a saddle horse for my own use. Keep your eyes out for me," Tim instructed.

"Do you want a fighter or a rider, sir?"

"A rider," Timofei said. "I leave the fighting to the Scots and Finns. Also, find me a decent saddle. After four hundred years, you'd think there'd be some improvements."

As the two dove deep into a discussion of horses and tack,

Tate walked into the stable yard ready for her trip into town. She expected to ride in the two-horse carriage. Instead she saw the two-seat buggy all hitched up and ready to go.

"Okay, Colonel Timofei Ivanovich Makoveev, what's with the seduction rig?" Tate said.

"Good morning, Chef Garrett," Timofei replied. "I thought we'd leave the larger rig for the prince's use. The post was built for cars, not carriages."

"I guess the good thing about driving a horse is you need both hands. The boys I knew couldn't keep both hands on the steering wheel," Tate said.

Timofei said, "Don't worry on that account. I remember Mama Kotova and I want to live."

Sasha helped Tate up into the buggy, while Timofei climbed into the driver's position.

"Thank you, Sasha, for your help," Tate said.

Sasha gave the couple a polite bow as they drove off into Grantville.

11:20 AM, Saturday

The carriage drew up before the whitewashed building. Timofei handed the reins to the hostler and helped Tate down. A sign beside the front door read: "Pastrami Roll Lunch 1100–1300 hours: $4.00 members and guests, $6.00 Unescorted Visitors, Benefits Grantville JROTC Scholarship Program."

"That looks like a good price, Timofei," said Tate.

"It is. The price includes cole slaw, potato chips and the first beer," said Tim. "Let's go in. I'm hungry."

The pair went through the door. They checked their overcoats and hats with the cloakroom girl.

"'Morning, Colonel McCoy," said a voice to their right.

"Good Morning, Mr. Kindred, and it's Makoveev," said Timofei.

"Sorry, I never could wrap my tongue around those Russki names. Who's this young lady? I've always seen you on your own," Kindred said.

"This is Tate Garrett. She's the new chef for Prince Vladimir. Chef Garrett, this is J.P. Kindred."

"Tate Nadine, isn't it?" J. P asked. "It's good to see you again. You've sure grown up since I saw you last."

"Hi, Mr. Kindred. You're right; it's been a long time."

"I figure you're old enough to buy me a beer back in West Virginia. So, you can call me 'JP.' The same goes for you, son," said J.P. "Please join me. I'd like to eat my lunch without an old codger who wants to re-fight Omaha Beach with the ketchup and mustard."

"We'd be happy to join you, J.P.," said Tate.

Tate, Tim and J.P. found an empty corner table. With a courtly gesture, J.P. seated Tate in the metal folding chair. Their orders were taken by the waitress and they settled into conversation.

Tate looked around the room. "J.P. this place hasn't changed all that much. But, what's with the Imperial Legion posters?"

"It's like this. The boys decided they could either die as American Legion Post 238 or we could live on as Imperial Legion Post 2. We'd have been number one, but Jackson and his gang formed their post up in Magdeburg before we got our act together."

"J.P., you know pretty much all the legionnaires and what they might have in their attics don't you?" Tate asked.

"Well, I know the members. But I don't know all that much about their attics," said J.P.

"Like Colonel Tim said, that Russian prince over in Castle Hills has hired me to run his kitchen. I need to get the place up to speed. Not to mention, the kitchen will be catering Brandy Bates' wedding..."

"Yeah, I heard about that. How can the Legion help you?"

"A few years back, I read in one of those food industry trade magazines about the Armed Forces Recipe Cards," Tate said. "The article said there are over a thousand cards and that they cover every course from soup to nuts. I figure I could use a set, even if it's just for daily meals. Of course, for the fancy stuff, they probably won't be much help. But we're cooking for a hundred or so for every meal up there."

J.P. said, "I know a couple of guys who retired out as cooks. Maybe one of them has a set in the attic. Can you give me a day or two to ask around?"

"Sure, J.P.," said Tate. "A day or two won't hurt. But, I'd like to know one way or another if a set came through."

"Since I can charge this to the *Streletzi* Bureau, how about another beer?" said Timofei.

Three Days Later, Kseniya's New Office

Kseniya reached for the teapot. "Another cup of tea, Mr. Kindred, Father Gavril? We'd like to thank very much for the help you and the Legion have given us."

"It wasn't all that much, Mrs. Kotova," said J.P. "In fact, it turned out easier than I thought. Back in the '80s, a legionnaire was a cook in the Army National Guard. He donated a set to the post that the Army had declared obsolete and replaced."

"Do you need the set back soon?" inquired Kseniya. "If the post can wait, we would like to copy them so it we can have a complete set."

"Not a problem," J.P. said. "Just give them back when you're done."

Since her husband wasn't talking much, Kseniya tried to bring him into the conversation. "Father, they tell Chef Garrett she'll need twenty-four pounds of ground meat to make enough *golubtsi* for a hundred."

J.P. said, "What are those? I never saw them on a dining hall menu."

"Sorry," Kseniya said, "that's stuffed cabbage rolls."

"And one of my favorites," Father Gavril said. He finally started talking more. Really, he was going to have to get comfortable with up-timers.

"I'm a bookish sort. If God had allowed it, I'd be in a monastery surrounded by books," Father Gavril said. "However, God in His providence brought Kseniya into my life. I also have a talent for languages. I have the best of all worlds, Kseniya, my two sons and the libraries of Grantville."

J.P. followed up by asking, "I thought married Orthodox priests were parish priests. Does your research interfere with your parish responsibilities?"

"No, not really. I only have twenty or so parishioners at the moment. Most are Russians, but there are a few from the various Orthodox churches who came back in the Ring of Fire. Grantville is much quieter and cleaner than the parishes I would have served in Mother Russia."

"Father, where do you hold services? I don't see any onion domes around here," said J.P.

Gavril smiled. "Prince Vladimir has made room for me in the

ballroom. It's not the best but it will do for the moment. We, easterners, stand during services, so there is no need for space-eating pews."

"Do you plan on building a church and have you decided on a name for it?" asked J.P.

"Oh, yes. It will be dedicated to Saint Vasili the Fool for Christ. The patriarch decreed if the name was good enough for a cathedral in Moscow, it would be good enough for a parish in Grantville," Father Gavril said. "We pray it will be completed in time for the prince's wedding in June."

"Is that a likely date?" asked J.P.

"It is a wishful date. We have few funds from Moscow, my parishioners are few, and time is short," Father Gavril said.

J.P. looked at the clock on the wall. He saw he needed to leave if he wanted to get his story in by the deadline for the late edition. He hadn't bothered to mention that he was an old newspaperman. And, now and then, he still did a human interest story. The first Orthodox church in Grantville certainly sounded interesting to him.

"Father, Mrs. Kotova, I'm happy the post could help you." J.P. stood up. "I need to be getting back into town, so, I better say good-bye now."

"May God bless you for your service to Him," Father Gavril said as he made the sign of the Cross.

Kseniya reached one of the pull ropes hanging on the wall. Three sharp tugs sounded a bell in the kitchen. One of the duty footmen soon appeared in her doorway.

"Mr. Kindred, Vanya will show you the way to the door," Kseniya said. "The *rezidentz* can be confusing to visitors."

J.P. followed Vanya to the front entrance. He went down to the corner and caught a streetcar back into town. During the ride, he mentally wrote the story. Soon, he was at the keyboard of his loyal Royal typewriter pounding out it out.

That night in the Kotovs' bedroom

Kseniya looked over at her husband. He was still awake after what she knew to be a long day of work. "Gavra, what's the matter? Your tossing and turning is keeping me awake."

"Dearest, after Mr. Kindred left, I realized we have a problem.

When will she be baptized? And what name should we use? Brandy is not an acceptable name. You know the rules."

"I think, Gavra, we need to light candles to Our Lady and Saint Vasili asking God for wisdom. And I need to borrow some brains," Kseniya said. "Now, we need some sleep to face tomorrow. Good night, husband."

"Good night, my dear."

The next morning

"Gregorii, go find Father Gavril, tell him his presence is requested and required in my office," Vladimir said. "Also find out if *Gospazha* Brandy is here and relay the same message to her. If she is not, let me know."

"I hear and obey," Vladimir's major domo said.

Soon a knock came at the open office door.

"You sent for me, sir?" Father Gavril said.

"Come here; look at these newspapers," Vladimir ordered.

Gavril read the first paper in the stack and his face took on a serious set. "I can see why you are concerned."

"Those are only the morning German papers," Vladimir said. "I sent for Brandy to help interpret the English paper where this story first appeared."

The office door slammed open. A "serious as a heart attack" Brandy Bates stormed in. "Vladimir Yaroslav, this house had better be under attack by the Tartars," she said. "Who do you think you are? My commanding officer?"

Oops. Vlad had forgotten that Brandy could get a bit testy when he "went all over princey," as she called it. "The *rezidentz* is not under physical attack. However, it has made the newspapers without my knowledge."

"I'll grant that those can be as dangerous as the Tartars," Brandy said. "But Greg told me my 'presence was requested and required.' I think you've been reading too many Hornblower books, buddy boy." She picked up yesterday's evening edition of the *Grantville Times*.

"Father Gavril made the papers," she said. "Not you. And what's the problem, anyway?"

"My wife invited Mr. Kindred over yesterday to thank him for the help he gave Chef Garrett," Father Gavril said. "Something about recipe cards, I gathered. Anyway he started asking questions about the chapel. Kseniya and I didn't think what we said would appear in the papers."

"Still," Vladimir said. "We made the papers without my knowledge. That is a problem."

"Honey, there is no such thing as bad publicity as long as they spell your name right," Brandy said. "The *Times* printed it as a human interest story. J.P. must have liked our kitchen's biscuits, 'cause, he wrote a really positive article."

"We will see how this all develops. Father, no more newspaper interviews without my knowledge and permission," Vladimir said.

"I hear and obey, sir," said Gavril.

"Brandy, I understand you have scheduled us to visit the KudzuWerke showroom," Vladimir said. "If so, we better get going."

Brandy came up to Vladimir and hugged him. She said, "Yes, I did. But ease up on the princey stuff, dude. You're creeping me out." Brandy then gave Vladimir a good kiss on the lips which he enthusiastically returned.

Father Gavril studied the Robin of the CoC cartoon strip in the *Daily News* during the exchange.

The afternoon of the following day

Father Gavril and Kseniya entered the prince's office. Kseniya knew something was up from the way the tradesmen treated her. However, her German and English weren't up to catching their shades of meaning. The pair saw Brandy sitting with her chair to one side of the desk. Her presence would temper the prince's actions.

"There have been developments from that story," Vladimir said. "Look at this stack of mail."

"Now, Vladimir, be nice," Brandy said. "Good afternoon, Father Gavril, Mrs. K. Yes, there have been developments. Positive developments."

"You're right, my dear. Positive, indeed," Vladimir said. "Take a look at these letters."

Gavril and Kseniya sorted through the partially opened mail. The letters were addressed to St. Vasili Orthodox Church, The Fool for Christ Church, Father Kotov, Father Gavril, Father G, The Russian Church, or some other variation. All conveyed the best wishes and prayers of the sender. Some contained donations large and small. Father Gavril was surprised by the number of checks drawn on the Grantville banks. Others had pledges of material support.

"*Gospazha* Brandy, what is this backhoe service?" Gavril asked.

"Here is someone offering a load of bricks," Kseniya said.

"I think we need to get this mess organized," Brandy said.

Vladimir agreed. "Make it so."

"Gag a maggot, Vlad. First, you're Hornblower, now Picard," Brandy said. "I need to keep a closer watch on your reading and TV." She wagged a finger at him. "If you start introducing your gun as 'Clyde,' I'm calling off the wedding."

Kseniya's Office

"Tate, you can't believe the offers we've received to help build my husband's chapel," Kseniya said.

"Yeah," Brandy said. "It's turned into a community project. Not only did folks send in money, but Father Gavril got pledges of material, building equipment and labor."

"Sadly, the only item not pledged is a bell. And we don't have the money to buy one already cast or the time to wait for one before the chapel's dedication," Kseniya said.

"Brandy, have you thought about having a fundraiser for the bell?" said Tate. "Other churches have them all the time. We should be able to put one on here; the place is plenty big enough. We could do a Russian feast; maybe even get some of the food donated. That will help with the profit margin. I know the local fish mongers throw away the roe. We can get the makings for some nice caviar for free."

"You're right, Tate," Brandy said. "Vlad could buy a bell, though..."

"For a cause like this," Tate pointed out, "well, it's a community thing. If we let people help, we make more friends, let people get used to our ways. We can make it a 'Night in Moscow.' We'll have Russian food and music."

"This sounds like nothing we did in the old country," Kseniya said. "There we could count on the czar or somebody important to give a new church its bell."

Tate grinned. "There's an old saying. The czar is very far away. Besides, Brandy, you and Vlad need to entertain. He's basically the Russian ambassador here, you know."

"Jeez, Tate," Brandy said. "Vlad's almost as bad about publicity as, as . . . well, whatever. St. Vasili is going to get some more. Even if Vlad hates to read about the *rezidentz* in the papers without knowing about it first."

Tate winked at her.

Brandy's sitting room

"Brandy, a problem with your baptism has come up," Kseniya said.

"What's the problem, Kseniya? This will be the first time I've been baptized in any church. Vlad and I settled this long ago," Brandy said.

"It's not the rite itself. The problem is your baptismal name," Kseniya said. "According to the rules, you need a qualified name. That's 'qualified according to church law.' My husband says 'Brandy' is unacceptable."

"Now, that's a problem we never thought of," Brandy said.

"It's also a matter of you're starting, spiritually that is, a new life," Kseniya said.

"You're right. Something other than 'Brandy' would show the change. Now what can we come up with that will qualify?"

"Branya," said a now relaxed Kseniya, "your people usually have two given names, right?"

"Sure a first and middle name," Brandy said. "I hate mine; it sounds so old fashioned."

"Well, what is it?" asked Kseniya.

"Margaret. Momma said I got it in honor of Margaret Truman," Brandy said. "I think it smells like mothballs."

"Branya, the name may smell like mothballs to you," Kseniya said. "To me it sounds like a solution to the problem."

"How can the name of a dead president's daughter be a solution?"

"Margaret is the name of a saint, Saint Margaret the Virgin of Antioch. It will work perfectly. Even better, you were planning on a June wedding. We both know St. Vasili's won't be ready for a wedding by then."

"Yeah, that is a bummer," Brandy said. "I guess we'll have to have it in the garden."

"Can you survive a seventeen-day delay? Saint Margaret's feast day is July seventeenth. That will give Gavra two more weeks to get the chapel ready."

Prince Vladimir's office

St. Vasili's building committee was in session. Not that it was a large committee. In fact, it consisted of Brandy, Vladimir, the Kotovs and Pete Enriques.

"Father Gavril, Prince Vladimir, ladies," Pete said. "I've taken a look at the materials given or pledged for this project. It looks like you have enough to build a basic structure."

"How big a building?" asked Vladimir.

"I'd say about twenty by thirty feet. Call it five hundred square feet. It will be cozy but not too small," Pete said.

"I don't know about square feet," said Gavril. "Please tell me how many people will be able to get inside."

"Remember, Pete, Russians stand for their services. So you don't need to figure in room for pews or chairs," Brandy said.

Pete thought for a moment and scribbled some numbers down. "How, does eighty comfortably or a hundred smooshed in sound to you? That's with leaving space for the altar and other pieces of furniture."

"That sounds like it will be more than sufficient for our needs," Vladimir said.

"What about a bell?" Pete asked. "Nothing in the budget for one of those, yet."

"We plan on having a fundraising dinner. We hope we can get the money from that," Kseniya said.

"By the first part of July? I checked around; the foundries won't be able to deliver in that time frame, they said."

"Then we need a miracle. Let's pray for the Holy Mother's and Saint Vasili's intervention," Father Gavril said.

"Amen, Father," chorused Kseniya, Vladimir and Brandy. Pete kept his mouth shut. As a Grantviller, he wanted to help his neighbors. As a Pentecostal, he wasn't going to amen prayers to the virgin and a saint.

The Day Before a Night in Old Moscow

Timofei walked up to the kitchen's outside table. He knew Tate usually sat out here for her noon meal. The girl was getting to be a nuisance. Why he was trailing after her he didn't know. However, Timofei knew Tate was not only easy on the eyes but easy to talk to. That she was more than just competent at her job was another plus in her favor.

Tate was eating a meat pie when she heard Tim's military tread on the gravel. The man was getting to be annoying. Sure, he was a colonel, though Mrs. K. had her doubts as to his exact rank. But, he was cute in a Slavic kind of way.

"Tate, may I join you?" Timofei asked.

"Sure, Tim," Tate said. "Take a load off."

"It's a pity we're both going to be on duty tomorrow night," Tim said. "Otherwise, I'd ask if you would do me the honor of being my escort to the dinner."

Tate said, "Yes, it's a pity. Because I'd say yes. I hear the Old Folks Band is playing. Maybe we can steal a dance."

"It will have to be a slow one. I have two left feet," Timofei said.

A Night in Old Moscow

The interior courtyard was ablaze with torches and electric lights. Tables were set up in a horseshoe. The stage and food tables took up the fourth side.

Prince Vladimir climbed onto the stage and said, "Ladies and gentlemen, I want to thank you for coming out tonight for a time in Old Moscow. This occasion could not have come about without the efforts and hard work of many people.

"In particular, we owe our thanks to Chef Tate Garrett and the kitchen staff for the food, to Mrs. Kseniya Kotova and the decorating committee for all of the finery you see displayed, and, last but not least, to *Gospazha* Brandy for keeping this whole enterprise together. Now, I'll ask Father Gavril to ask God's blessing on tonight."

Gavril came to the front of the stage. In Russian, English and German, he gave thanks to God for the food, the hands that prepared it, and for the money brought in by the tickets.

Timofei surveyed the security detail. His men and women were without work tonight. He could begin to like these Grantville parties. Nobody was using the festivities as a reason to be drunk and obnoxious. Even Tate was pleased with the food service. She relaxed, standing over to the side. *I think I can dance to this music.* Timofei sent up a fast prayer of thanksgiving. The dance music was up-time ballroom and Brandy had insisted on dance lessons for the senior staff.

Timofei bowed. "Chef Garrett, would you do me the honor of this dance?"

Tate, in her best Scarlett O'Hara manner, curtsied and replied, "Why, Colonel, it would be my pleasure."

Timofei and Tate foxtrotted onto the dance floor to "Moscow Nights."

Tate whispered, "Honey, you don't have two left feet. You're not in Federico's class, true. But not everyone is the second coming of Fred Astaire."

"I guess my other left foot stayed in Moscow," Timofei murmured back. "I do have a question. If you promise not to get offended . . ."

"Tim, you'd have to work hard at offending me," Tate said.

"Good. Since you call me 'honey,' may I call you Tatia?"

"Of course. Turn about is fair play."

Kseniya walked through the tables, greeting the guests while she kept an eye on the men and women on serving duty.

Good. All of the tables have full beer pitchers. She moved towards the buffet tables. The scouts from Troop 9 busied themselves toting the heavier trays from the outdoor grills and the kitchen. The girl scouts from Troop 29 smiled as they dished out the food to the donors.

"Good evening, Mr. Bolender, Mrs. Walker," Kseniya said. "I want to thank you. Your scouts are a great help. Prince Vladimir is very impressed."

"You're welcome, Mrs. Kotova," said the Troop 29 scoutmaster. "A couple of our scouts are using this as their community service projects. If we had known about it earlier, one of the scouts would have used it for his Eagle Scout project."

"Likewise," said the Girl Scout Leader. "Though I think you need to thank Ulrich. He's the one keeping things moving. He's over there by the fire extinguishers."

"Thank you, Herr Schwarz," Kseniya called over.

Not leaving his post, Ulrich called back, "You're welcome."

"Please excuse me, I need to visit with the others," Kseniya said.

"We understand, Mrs. Kotova," said Evangeline. "Our troops also appreciate Prince Vladimir's donation."

"You're welcome. Though, the idea of donating in return for your help was J.P. Kindred's idea. You need to thank him," Kseniya said.

At that moment, Kseniya spotted J.P. He was sitting with a group of his fellow veterans and their wives.

Walking over to the group, Kseniya saw a small wooden crate on the ground beside the table. It looked rather heavy.

I wonder how these grandpas got that in here. Does the colonel know it's here? Kseniya wondered.

"Hey there, Mrs. K." said J.P. "This is a great fundraiser. Who'd of thought Russians were into barbecue."

"J.P., this isn't barbecue. It's meat on a stick," said one of J.P.'s tablemates.

"Welcome to the *rezidentz*," Kseniya said. "In Russian, this meat on a stick is called 'shaslik.'"

"What ever you call it. It's good chow," said the unknown tablemate.

"Mrs. K, let me introduce Chief Warrant Officer Louis Tillman," said Kindred. "Boats, this is Mrs. Kseniya Kotova. She's sort of the first lieutenant around this place."

"Pleased to make your acquaintance, ma'am," said Louis. "We have something that will interest your husband."

"You do?"

"Yes, ma'am. It's sitting in this crate," said Louis. "If Colonel Makoveev will lend me couple of strong backs, we can get it out where every one can see it."

Kseniya looked around for the *streletz*. He was standing so close that she knew he was in on this deal.

The colonel called out in his best parade ground voice, "Bondarev, Antonov, come here. Ivanov, bring a crowbar."

Two Russians, with help from the older scouts, easily moved the wooden crate in front of the stage.

Kseniya joined her husband, the prince and Brandy beside the crate.

Boats Tillman bellowed out, "Ladies and gentlemen, your attention please." With fewer decibels, he said, "Men, loosen up the nails in the crate."

Tillman continued, "The Legion would like to present a memorial gift to the Chapel of St. Vasili. All we ask is there be a plaque located nearby to identify the gift as being given in memory of those who gave their all for their country. Father Gavril, please open the crate."

Gavril took the crowbar from Antonov and started ripping off the boards. The scouts helped him by lifting off the top and removing the sides as the last nails were pulled out.

When the work party moved away, there stood a ship's bell.

"Folks, for years my wife and I went around to different antique shows and flea markets. And you know how I am about naval memorabilia."

The Grantvillers in the crowd laughed. They certainly did, since most of them had been treated to Louis' stories whether they wanted to be or not.

He gave them a grin. "We were in Pennsylvania when I spotted this bell. It comes from a decommissioned Coast Guard cutter, the *Tupelo*."

Father Gavril fell on the old salt's shoulders, babbling, "It's a miracle! Praise God, a bell for Saint Vasili."

Kseniya looked over at Brandy and Vlad. They were both beaming. And over in the corner, Colonel Tim and Tate were having an intense conversation. She smiled. There might be yet another wedding here at the *rezidentz*.

By Hook or by Crook

Victoria L'Ecuyer

Hamburg, January 1633

Someone grabbed Annabet Nutsch and covered her eyes. "Guess who!"

Annabet stiffened. She recognized the voice and jabbed her elbow into her brother's ribs. "Grow up, Johann." She wrestled free and shook her finger at the tall, gangly young man with light brown shaggy hair. "You should be in Jena doing your journeyman's work." She tucked her blond hair back under the cap he'd knocked askew.

"And you should be a housewife with a child on leading strings." He grinned at her, green eyes filled with mischief. "Look at this and tell me what you think."

Annabet shoved her baby brother out of the way. "I'm working."

"Just take a look!"

Annabet snorted. "Fine. A quick look, then you have to leave. My mistress is not an understanding woman." She dumped an armload of clothes in a wash tub and shoved them in the soapy water. "Rinse the linens, Wilhelmina, while I deal with my brother," she told the young maid who was helping her. Annabet took Johann's arm and towed him to a corner where they could talk unheard. "What is it?"

"American lace." Johann grinned.

Annabet looked at the long, narrow band of lace. It was made of very fine yarn that was twisted and tangled in a regular fashion.

It should have looked ugly, but it didn't. "This is nothing I have seen before." She stretched it flat to better see the stitches.

"It's from the future. I learned how to make this from an American woman in Grantville," Johann said. "She had this lace everywhere! It was on her tables and chairs and on the bottom of her curtains." He reached in and pulled out a ball of string and a fist full of hooks. They were all a different size and none bigger than a thin tree branch. "I whittled these for you. They are called *crochet hooks*." He reached into his bag again and pulled out a handful of papers with sketches and strange lettering. "Here are instructions. I cannot read the English, but I can tell what each step means. The lady I bought these from could barely speak German, let alone write it. I will need your help translating this."

"Johann, you know I don't read English!"

"But you do know what women call things." Johann grinned. "The lady taught me how to *crochet*. If I do what each picture shows, you can tell me how to write instructions." He sent her a pleading look when she remained silent. He rifled through his sketches and found one with a simple lace edging on the collar. "Look. She said you can make a collar like this in three days. Lace edging for sleeves would take maybe a day. Two, if you're slow. A collar as wide as your hand is long would take a week. Three at the very most. I can engrave the pictures easily. Now that I have a press, I can set the instructions and print the patterns myself."

Annabet scowled. She had heard her father carrying on about her brother's new press and his Committee and their dreams for revolution. She agreed with her father's skepticism. It sounded too good to be true. But this . . . She took the paper with the design. Johann was a good artist and his sketch was clear. The collar was simple, almost plain, but it was still lace. Annabet was torn. The American lace sounded like a get rich quick scheme, but this was lace. The wealthy matron who employed her as a maid of all work only had it on her very best clothes. "I will look at this. Tonight." Annabet stuffed the paper and all the rest back in his bag. "Don't assume I will fall in with your plans. Now go before Frau Koch sees you."

Johann hesitated, possibly to argue and wheedle her into loafing, but Annabet knew she was pushing her good luck by letting him stay as long as she had. She shoved him out the door.

☆ ☆ ☆

Annabet met her brother when he came home from the tavern that afternoon. She watched in satisfaction as their mother grabbed his ear and twisted it.

"Ow!" He fell to his knees when the pressure increased. "I'm sorry. Whatever it was I did, I'm sorry!"

"Not as sorry as you will be when Papa gets home," Annabet told him. "Frau Koch isn't going to renew my contract when it expires. And it expires real soon! She said it was because I had suspicious young men visiting me. When I told her you were my brother she didn't care. I shouldn't have been wasting my time and her money talking to you." Her fists curled. She wanted to twist his ear, too. And pinch and slap and kick and pummel him black and blue. She took a deep breath instead.

She needed the coin. She had spent all of her money on supplies to make things for her dower chest. As long as it was taking Gottfried to save up his mercenary's pay, she was certain that it would be her money that would allow them to get married. When he managed to return. His occasional notes with vague promises had stopped coming. She was worried he was spending all he had earned. "I keep hearing how your Committee of Correspondence encourages women to be as free as men. Not that I believed it.

"Unfortunately for me, it looks like I will be finding out sooner instead of later. I am your first committee member here in Hamburg whether I like it or not. You will print lace patterns before you print anything else. I will sell them for you and you will pay me the same as you would any other shop help."

That night, Annabet frowned as she watched her brother crochet. He was clumsy and slow. She doubted his claim of a lace collar in three days. Annabet turned to the pictures that gave instruction and scowled at them.

Sighing at herself as much as at him, she began to follow the pictures in the instructions, squinting, muttering to herself as she went. Johann offered advice and additional coaching, hindering as much as helping. After some time, a few shushings, and a kick to Johann's shin, Annabet mastered the basic stitches. Before too much longer, she was making a row of loops and picots on top of a simple filet crochet band that looked like a long, thin ladder.

"Hmphf." She finished her lace cuff and put it next to the hem of her sleeve. "It's like knitting, but not." Annabet started a second cuff. Now that she knew what she was doing, it went much faster. She could do a collar in three days, even if her brother couldn't. "Johann, you may not be an idiot after all."

He grinned. "Then you can help me write the instructions for the patterns? And make lots of lace to display?"

"Yes." She scowled. "But if my eyes cross because of it, I will beat you. You may be bigger, but I'm still older."

Johann laughed. "By the time I finish setting up my printing press, I will have two things to print! A broadsheet for the Committees and a lace pattern for women." He rolled up his project and went to his sister. "I'll be rich!"

Annabet frowned. "If you don't get a broken head first. Those who are in charge will *not* like this. The people who owe favors to them will like it even less. You know that the city leaders aren't at all sure about those crazy Americans. Plus, you've never run a printing press before!"

He waved her concerns aside and got paper from his pack. "Describe the first picture. How many chain stitches did it take to go around your arm?"

A week later, Annabet walked into her brother's shop on the outskirts of Hamburg. The bell over the door, missing its clapper, *tonked* when the door hit it. Johann yelped, brandishing a tool. She frowned at him before she set her basket down and straightened her lace collar. She removed her shawl, now trimmed with lace, and tucked it into the basket. "Why are you so jumpy? Who has been here?"

"Annabet. What are you doing here?"

She noticed his evasion, but let it slide in favor or more important things. "You need to have your landlord fix the bell and that broken window. This shop may be cheap because it's on the edge of town, but that's no reason for it to be shabby and in bad repair." Annabet looked around, spotted what she was looking for and crossed to the shelves. "I'm getting more patterns. All the women I know want one of each, even though they complain mightily about how hard it is to read them. I ran out." She reached in her pocket and pulled out a small purse. "Here's the money left over after I ordered more hooks. The patterns sell better if I have them.

"And do something about the printing. The ink is too blotchy;

the lines are too close together." She squinted at the example in her hand. "Make the spaces between the words wider, too." She went back to the stacks of paper.

A bit desperate, Johann took the money and her elbow. "I'll bring some home tonight." He started to drag her to the door.

Annabet shook him off. "What did you do? These pages are all tumbled." She pulled more off the shelf. "These are crumpled." She slapped his hand when he grabbed her. "Johann, what happened? Who's been here?"

"Nothing." Johann couldn't meet her eyes. "It was an accident," he lied.

She put her fists on her hips and glared at him. "What kind of accident?"

"I stumbled and hit the shelf. It fell." He met her eyes, finally. "Go home, Annabet. I'll bring the patterns tonight."

She recognized that look. "You are lying." Annabet narrowed her eyes. "Did someone from the city council come here?"

Johann grabbed sheaves of patterns and put them in her basket. "If you want the patterns now, you'll have to sort them yourself." He shoved a second stack in her basket then grabbed her arm in a fierce grip and dragged her to the door. "Go. Home. Annabet."

The next morning, Annabet answered the door to her parents' house and found her best friend, Bertha, hand in hand with Karl, Bertha's fiancé. "You're back! This is wonderful! Where's Gottfried? You went to war together. Did you get separated?" She went to hug him, then stopped. His face was solemn and Bertha was teary-eyed. "What's wrong?"

"May we come in?" Karl asked.

Annabet lost her smile. She stepped back and held the door open.

She showed them to chairs. Karl dragged his hat off his head, crumpling it in his big fists. He looked at Bertha in desperation, but she was crying.

Annabet hid her fists in the folds of her skirt and took a deep breath. "Gottfried's dead." She said it for him.

Karl nodded. Bertha dried her face and got up to put her arms around Annabet.

Annabet just stood there staring through the wall. "I had hoped he was whoring and too embarrassed to tell me he'd spent all his pay." She heard Karl clear his throat and focused on him.

"Gottfried was killed at . . ." He stopped when Annabet shook her head.

"It doesn't matter," she said. "He's dead. What good is he to me now?" Annabet was aware of Bertha and Karl communicating with grimaces and head jerks, but ignored them.

Karl eventually left. Bertha stayed long enough for Annabet's mother to return from the market. After a whispered conversation, Bertha left as well. Annabet let her mother guide her to a chair, but ignored her fussing in favor of staring out the window.

Annabet shrugged off her mother's urging to lie down. She did move, though, to a corner, where she stared at a half-finished cuff made of lace shells instead. It hurt to see what she couldn't have.

Johann clattered in that evening and crouched at her feet. He frowned at her expression. "Why the face? I brought you more patterns. One of them is new."

She started keening.

"Annabet?"

She curled into a ball. "Go away."

He swore. "Why are you crying? Did someone hurt you?" When she didn't answer, he shook her. "Who?"

"Gottfried." She blew her nose.

"Gottfried Groenenbach?"

Annabet stared at him, confused. "No, not the mayor's enforcer." She scrubbed her face. "My betrothed, Gottfried Mueller. He's dead. Now I'll never get married!"

"Dead? How?"

Annabet twisted her handkerchief. "How do soldiers usually die? In a battle. Somewhere." She ignored the tears rolling down her face. "Almost six months gone."

"Why so long to get the news?"

"Gottfried could barely read and didn't see the point in writing. He only did it because I made him." Annabet started sobbing again. "Karl didn't know how to put the news in a letter to Bertha, so he waited until he came back."

Johann put his arms around Annabet. He rested his forehead on her hair. "Is Bertha the one who used to pinch my cheeks?"

Annabet nodded and bawled. "She said she wanted a child just like you. I don't know why."

After a while, she pulled back and wiped her face with the

sodden cloth. Johan dug out his handkerchief, and the light fell across his face.

Annabet grabbed his chin. “Why do you have a black eye?”

“I ran into someone,” he said. “It doesn’t matter. What did Mama and Papa say about the news?”

A few days later, the door to Johann’s shop was locked.

“Are you certain he’s here?” Bertha asked. She kept one eye on the half-shuttered windows in the nearby shops, and wrinkled her nose at a pile of garbage scenting the air with more than a hint of rot.

“Yes,” Annabet replied. “He spends all of his time here or at the tavern talking about the Committees of Correspondence.” She pounded on the door. “Johann! Open up!”

“I don’t think he’s here,” Bertha said. “I don’t think we should be here, either. This isn’t a very good part of town.”

Annabet huffed and knocked on the door again. “Johann!”

The door jerked open and stopped partway. Johann blocked the opening. “What?”

Annabet pushed on the door. “What were you doing?”

Johann pushed back. “Working,” he said. “Go away.”

Annabet pushed harder. “Open the door.”

Johann glared. “No.”

Her eyes narrowed. When Johann didn’t back down, Annabet demanded, “What is wrong with you?”

“Nothing.” He shoved his jaw out in the stubborn expression that Annabet recognized all too well.

“We’ll see about that.” Annabet threw her weight on the door. “Bertha, don’t just stand there! Help me.”

Bertha added her weight. Johann held them off for a moment but ended up slipping back a step or two.

Johann gave up. “Stop.”

Annabet squinted with suspicion, but stopped. Johann shoved something aside and opened the door.

Annabet stepped over the threshold, then stopped. Bertha followed, trying to peer around her. The shop was covered with spilled ink and scattered papers.

Annabet picked up a ruined pattern. “What happened?”

Johann kicked at a pile of ink-splattered paper. “A group of men from the city council.” He shrugged and surveyed his shop. “They ruined all my paper and spilled the ink, then left me with a warning.”

"Be glad they didn't do more," Bertha said. "They normally break heads."

Annabet paused her prodding of the nearest mess and looked up at him. "What kind of warning?"

"Get out of the Committee or suffer the consequences."

Annabet snorted and started to pick up papers. "What did you expect?"

"Not this. I expected other journeymen and apprentices to join me." He sighed. "I hoped they would help me spread democracy."

Annabet clucked. "Always the dreamer."

Johann kept silent and continued cleaning. The women followed suit, at least until it came time to mop up the ink.

"Do you have enough money to buy more supplies?" Annabet asked.

His gaze slid away then he forced it back. "No," Johann said. "That is what part of the mess is from. I fought to save what I had."

Bertha sniffed. "He's ruined."

Annabet sent her an angry look. "That's very helpful of you." She considered the blotches on the floor. "Tomorrow. Tomorrow, I will think more clearly. Today, we will clean this up."

Johann crossed his arms, trying to look as forbidding as their father. "No. You will stay out of this!"

Annabet just looked at him. "You are not Papa to order me around. You are not my betrothed, either. You are just my baby brother, and you need help." A tear slid out of the corner of her eye. "I need something to work toward, something to hope for." She took a deep breath. "Please?"

Johann swore. "Fine." He uncrossed his arms and went back to work.

Bertha just patted him on the shoulder as she went to look for a mop. "You're a good boy. Stupid, but good."

Annabet met Johann when he came home the next night. He had no more bruises, but he did have a fresh scowl. He slammed the door behind him.

"What's wrong, now?" she asked.

He kicked a chair. "No one will give me paper or ink on credit. I have nothing to print on."

"You will." Annabet took the heavy purse she'd been carrying all day out of her apron pocket. "I want to go into business with you. I want to be a full partner and not just your clerk."

"What do you mean?"

"I sold all the linens from my dowry chest," she said. "One of the cooks where Bertha works is fumbled-fingered when it comes to fancy work. But she's thrifty and has plenty of coin instead. She's also in love, and her sweetheart just made master. He's ready to marry, and her dower chest was half empty. I emptied mine and filled hers for a good price. That, added to the money I earned working for Frau Koch . . ." She grinned while he gawped. "I will buy the paper and ink and give you half for your Committees of Correspondence. You will use the rest to print patterns for me."

Johann stared at her. "Why?"

Annabet's mouth pinched. "I grieve less for Gottfried than I do for the house we would have had and the children. All the men my age are either betrothed or married. I don't want to wait for a young one to earn enough to take a wife. That leaves widowers with children." She shrugged. "It's not my first choice, but I'm tired of being considered a child when I'm not.

"I will have a better chance of getting married quickly if I have money rather than goods." She held out her arms, fingering the hems of her sleeves. "With this American lace, I will look wealthy. By selling your patterns and making my own, I will be wealthy." She looked at her brother then picked up a pamphlet. "I read your *Rights of Man* and *Common Sense*. It's starting to make sense." She dared him with a glare of her own. "Will you deny me the same chances because I am a woman?"

Johann closed his mouth and swallowed. "No." He looked at her then began to grin. He grabbed her in a hug. "We will change Hamburg!"

Annabet snorted. "We'll try."

"Annabet, where are we going?" Bertha asked the next evening.

"To check on Johann's shop while he is traveling." Annabet met a drunkard's leer with a glower. "He managed to buy supplies, despite the council's orders that the paper and ink sellers were not to do business with him."

"That's to be expected." Bertha watched the street while Annabet wrestled with the key. "They like money, too. So why are you checking on his shop?"

"Johann is like a new mother with her first baby. He is afraid something will happen to his press while he is gone. He had to go to Grantville to buy more lace patterns." She shoved the door open. "He is hoping to bring back double what he did last time."

Once inside, Bertha looked around. "I expected more mess."

Annabet lifted the canvas sheet covering her brother's machine. "No one has broken the press. Yet."

"Give them time."

Annabet settled on a stool by the window and pulled out her latest crochet project.

"What are you doing?"

"You've seen me crochet."

Bertha tapped her toe. "Why are you doing it here?"

"I promised Johann I would watch his shop." She looked up and saw her friend's expression. "No, I am not getting softheaded. If the city council's thugs come with hammers and pry bars, I won't get in their way. I'll just offer to sell their wives and sweethearts my lace." She tipped her basket to show off the tidy bundles of crocheted edgings.

Bertha regarded Annabet for several minutes then dragged a bench into the light and pulled out her spinning. "I didn't know foolishness was contagious."

Three days later, Annabet looked up to see a very large man with a crowbar and ink-stained hands blocking the door. Two men with cudgels stood behind him.

"Is the printer here?"

Annabet realized that talking bravado was different from facing down thugs. She lowered her work to her lap wishing Bertha, anyone, was with her. "No."

The crowbar-wielding man looked at the sheet-covered press before examining her. "Where is he?"

"Halfway to Grantville."

"When is he coming back?"

"I don't know," Annabet said.

The city council's enforcers muttered back and forth between themselves, then left. The remaining man stepped in and closed the door. "When did he leave?"

Annabet looked him in the eye and lied. "Two weeks ago."

The man frowned at her. The door swung open and hit the stranger in the back. He spun to face his attacker.

"Annabet! Annabet, you must help me." Wilhelmina dodged around the man. "How do I fix this?" She thrust a knitted object at Annabet. "It's all matted." The maid that followed her looked frightened. She skittered her way past him.

Annabet glanced at the scarf. "You scrubbed it in hot water, didn't you?"

"My little sister smeared jam on the end. How else . . ." Wilhelmina broke off and bit her lip.

Annabet sighed. "Once wool is fullered into felt, you can't undo it. Scrub the whole thing until it's even. Then when it's—"

"Quiet," the man bellowed. "Is this a print shop or a sewing circle?"

"Neither. It's a crocheting circle," Annabet told him. "And a lace shop." She shook out her work before folding it and tucking it into her basket. "You may as well sit. I won't have time to speak with you until I help these girls with their problems." Ignoring him and his dumbfounded expression, she turned back to Wilhelmina. "Fuller the whole length. Dry it, then bring it back. Close your mouth, child. You look like a fish."

Wilhelmina, glancing from the man, who was still standing, to Annabet and back, did as she was told, then babbled and shoved her friend forward. Tongue-tied, the girl just thrust a wad of string at Annabet.

Annabet rolled her eyes. She untangled the project and found a misshapen lace collar. She smoothed it out on her lap, examining the design. "You are decreasing here and here." She pointed at the mistakes. "Do not do that. When you get to the end of each row, chain three, turn it around, then continue the pattern. You must always chain up to the next row." She handed it back. "Rip it out and start over." She scowled at the girl's moan. "Don't argue. You'll never get wed with that in your dower chest."

"But I followed the instructions!" The maid dug in her bag and pulled out a battered piece of paper. "Here."

Annabet read the paper and sighed. She pulled another one out of her basket and checked her notes. "You must have bought an early pattern. Johann fixed that mistake when he printed it the second time." Annabet exchanged the bad pattern for a good one, then shooed the girls off. She turned back to the stranger and made a point of straightening her elaborate lace cuffs and smoothing her apron, which was edged with wide bands of more lace.

"Is there something you want?"

"That printing press."

Annabet gave the man a second, closer look. He had ink-stained clothes and looked old enough to be a master. If so, he was one of the young ones.

"It belongs to my brother," Annabet said. "I'm not allowed to sell it."

"Are you allowed to talk about the Committees of Correspondence?"

Annabet considered the man a third time. From the age and amount of stains on his clothes, she thought he was married to a lazy wife—if he was married at all. She started toying with her crochet hook.

"Who is your master?"

"Herr Groenenbach."

"Friend to the mayor and uncle to Gottfried?"

The journeyman printer sneered, but nodded. "My name is Paul Klaussen. Herr Groenenbach is too lazy to want to train a new apprentice and too cheap to let me do it for him." His sneer turned into a snarl. "But he's more than willing to buy his friends on the council round after round of beer." He bit off the rest of what he was going to say.

Annabet stared at the crumpled, nearly illegible pattern in her basket while she twirled the hook in her fingers. Then she considered Klaussen one last time. She read his sullen expression easily. Her dead fiancé wore that same look often before he ran off to be a mercenary.

"My brother, Johann, left for Grantville four days ago. I don't know how long it will take him to walk there, buy patterns, and walk back. I don't even know that I trust the Americans when they say they want equality for all.

"I do know this. The Committee of Correspondence has given me work when no one else would."

"Then we will speak of work." He sat down next to her and shoved the pry bar under the bench. "Show me the pattern your brother messed up."

Five days later, Karl entered the shop. He trailed Bertha and carried a short bench over his shoulder with one hand and held a tall, narrow table with the other. Two youngish maids took them with a glad cry. The small cluster of women rearranged themselves and reapportioned the lamps, each one trying for the best light.

"Klaussen is not lying to you," Karl told Annabet. He took a seat close to Bertha and accepted a batch of narrow wooden rods from her. He began whittling them into hooks.

"So we have a printer who knows how to print." Annabet waited for the excited whispers to die down. "We still have to deal with the Groenenbachs and the city council. If they suspect anything, we will still lose the press."

Bertha, searching through her bag for her misplaced hook, said, "So hide it."

Two weeks later, the door to the shop slammed open again. Gottfried Groenenbach swaggered in backed by five bravos. "Where's the printer?"

Twelve women scrambled to keep their lights from being blown out by the wind gusting in. Annabet ordered him to shut the door. "Were you raised in a barn?"

She had the pleasure of seeing him gape at the freshly painted walls. Racks of spindles, knitting needles, crochet hooks and sewing scissors were on the wall opposite the door. There were bundles of prepared fiber waiting to be spun. Stiff paper bobbins that held various kinds of crocheted lace filled in any gaps. It was a craft woman's dream and a bully boy's ultimate confusion.

"Well, were you?" Annabet demanded.

"This is a print shop!"

The women tittered. The bravos shifted uneasily.

"Does this look like a print shop?" Annabet asked.

Gottfried looked around and tromped through the assembled maids.

The women drew their feet back and pulled their skirts out of his path, much like they would do for a filthy, snarling mongrel.

"You're up to something," he said.

"Yes," Annabet agreed. "I am up to teaching crochet. Would you like to learn? I charge by the hour."

Gottfried snarled at the sniggerer by the door. He gave the shop one last glare then stomped out.

Bertha, who sat by the window, watched the council's enforcers leave. "They're gone."

Paul opened the hidden door to the back room. "You were

right, Annabet. Fresh paint does cover up the smell of ink." He sat in the space cleared for him and continued to read aloud the latest news from the Committees of Correspondence.

Johann returned a week later. Tired and dirty, he looked from Bertha to Annabet with the biggest smile he could muster. "I have more patterns." He started to say more, but the door opened. Two girls walked in, followed moments later by two more. He looked around, confused at the changes. "Annabet, what's going on?"

The girls ignored him. They moved a bench into the light, then set out tapers in simple clay holders on one of a handful of tall stools. The women opened their work baskets and made themselves at home. One sent him a quick glance. The other frowned at a lacy circle.

"I'm giving crochet lessons. Not everyone can make sense of the instructions." Annabet shooed him off.

"In my shop!?" he asked in a near-bellow.

"Don't yell," Bertha said. "You weren't here. And it's her shop as much as yours now."

Annabet sighed. "It kept your precious printing press together. We hid it in the back. And watching for an attack is not that different from waiting for someone to return from war. Hand work makes the time pass." She turned to her students, then had to rap one of them on her head to get her attention back on the lesson. "A double crochet stitch there, not a treble, Wilhelmina."

Bertha made a rude sound. "Who is going to suspect a lace shop, Johann? We're just girls, after all. No Committee here." She put on a dumb look, then laughed at his expression. "Don't worry. Everyone here is a member of the Committee. Annabet makes Karl and Paul check to make sure no new members are spies for the city council."

"Who is Paul?" Johann asked.

"Paul Klaussen. Who happens to be a real printer," Annabet said. "He's as excitable about the Committees as you are."

Johann made a face at her, then went to check the printing press for damage. Not finding any, he collected his pack and crouched beside Annabet. "I found something else while I was gone."

She looked at him with suspicion. "What is it this time?"

He handed her a hank of fine wool thread. "A peddler was selling this. I thought you might like the color. It's a thank you gift for helping me. Not that I expected this much help."

Bertha leaned closer. "What an odd shade of pink."

Annabet squinted at the label wrapped around the yarn. "'Brillo's Best,'" she read aloud. "'Common Wool for the Common Man. Color: *Mauve*. Product of *Lothlorien* Farbenwerke.'" She fingered the wool. "What kind of name is '*Lothlorien*'?"

Bertha took it from her. "What kind word is *mauve*?" she grimaced. "Scratchy. I've seen better wool." She passed it on.

"But the color!" one girl cooed. "So pretty."

"How much will you pay me for it?" Annabet asked.

Johann squawked, outraged.

She glanced over at him. "I agree with Bertha. If I am going to work with wool, it has to be softer than that."

The girl named a price and dug for coins. Johann blinked and held his tongue when the other two young maids also offered to buy the yarn at the same price. By the time the women were ready to leave, he was left with an empty pack and a bemused expression.

As he and Annabet walked home, he finally spoke. "They paid more than I did."

"So when you go for more patterns, buy more Brillo's Best."

The next evening, Annabet watched Johann and Paul circle each other like strange dogs, ruffs raised and ready to snarl.

"This shop is not a bone," she said. "One of you can't print and the other can't draw. My lace patterns need both. So does the Committee."

When they didn't leave off the posturing she stepped between them and shoved Johann toward the door to the printing room. "Show Paul your letters from the Committee. Tell him about Grantville, too, while you're at it. I want you out of my hair until the women come. Three or four of them said they will be bringing their sweethearts."

They turned to her in unison. "How do you know?" Johann asked.

"Women talk in the market place as much as men gossip in the tavern." When they just stood there, she assigned sweeping and dusting.

Both men balked and headed for the press room. All three kept busy getting ready for that evening's Committee meeting. Sixteen women and girls, not counting Bertha, showed up. Half of them brought their sweethearts. Some brought hampers in addition to work bags. Others brought flasks and before long it was share and share alike.

People were reduced to sitting on the floor, and Karl eyed the walls and muttered about benches. Bertha told him to save his carpentry work for a shop in a better part of town.

Annabet stood by the door, brow wrinkled as she listened to Karl describe his experiences with the Americans to the newest Committee members. Crochet hooks flew while women grilled Johann about Grantville ladies. She glanced over when Paul joined her.

"Bertha is right. We should move the shop. We would get more business."

Annabet shook her head. "We don't have enough money saved to rent a better place. Plus, looking too prosperous will get us more attention from the city's councilmen than is safe right now. If Groenenbach comes by with his bully boys, we can say this is a gathering of friends and get away with it."

Paul thought about it then grunted an assent. He called the meeting to order.

A week and a half later, Paul hauled Johann into the family parlor and laid him on the floor in front of the hearth.

"Where did you find him?" Annabet asked. She reached for the medicines and cloths she had arranged and rearranged while she waited. Her mother came in and helped Annabet tend Johann, stitching him up where necessary.

"In an alley," Paul said. "On the way back from the shop. Groenenbach and his henchmen had just finished the beating and were getting ready to use knives. I bribed some drunks to go down the alley so Groenenbach wouldn't linger. Karl and your father went to the taverns Johann visits. I paid an urchin to find them with the news."

Annabet and her mother worked while Paul kept checking doors and windows.

"He can't stay here," Annabet said. "They'll kill him." She looked at Paul. "They'll kill you, too."

Paul crouched next to her. "So send him to Grantville for more lace patterns. He's a journeyman. Let him journey. I'll just pretend to court you."

Annabet glared at him.

"My master has no daughters and his wife is dead. His sons are apprenticed to other trades. I've been looking for my own wife. I don't see why it can't be you as well as another." He met her frown with a calm look. "It makes a good story and keeps you safe as well. Or do you think Gottfried Groenenbach won't beat women? Or worse."

"Listen to the man, Annabet," her mother said.

Two weeks later Karl and Bertha slipped into the shop. For once, Bertha carried everything, leaving Karl unhindered. He peered into the dark before closing the door. Annabet sent them a questioning look from across the crowded room.

"Gottfried Groenenbach has been asking questions about me and Paul," Karl said. "Someone saw Paul help Johann and reported it to the city council."

Paul swore. "Did they follow you?"

"I think so," Karl said.

"A strange man has been lurking in the neighborhood, too," Bertha added. "I thought I saw him on our way here."

Annabet grabbed spindles off the wall and bundles of unspun fibers from bins. She pulled the Committee of Correspondence's pamphlets from the hands of the women and filled them with supplies.

"Spin," she ordered. "Don't gape. Work."

Next, Annabet pointed at the new members and the males with nothing in their hands. "You, you and you, go to the press room. Karl, stay put. We know they saw you walk in. You will spend the evening telling war stories to Paul and the other men who are making something. We women will talk of spinning and lace."

Everyone stared at her. She grabbed the ear of a young apprentice and hauled him to his feet.

"Move!"

Everyone obeyed. The room rearranged and formed a scene like a cross between a family's gathering room and a well-lit tavern. The conversation was stilted. People kept looking at the windows. When the door didn't slam open right away, the Committee relaxed and conversation became more general. The apprentice cracked open the hidden door and begged a couple more lamps for the back room so they could read easier.

Paul grabbed Annabet as she paced among the benches and made her sit beside him. He shoved her work basket in her hands. Annabet muttered under her breath, but took out her latest project—a curtain, like the one her brother told her about.

The door slammed open. People jumped. Gottfried Groenenbach and his wrecking crew armed with cudgels swaggered in. Everyone drew back.

"Plotting revolution?" he asked.

Annabet held the lace panel up to the light to judge her progress. "Making frillies." She switched her gaze to the enforcer. "Gossiping. Female things."

"And you, Herr Klaussen?"

Paul met Groenenbach's look, then took a pull from his flask. "I am the only non-betrothed rooster in a room full of hens. Who needs revolution when there are women running loose?"

Groenenbach looked around again. "Why these women?"

Paul smiled and tugged on Annabet's lace-edged cap. "I like my pullets to have fine feathers." He grunted when Annabet's elbow connected with his ribs. "And be full of spice. I will be a master some day so I might as well start looking for a wife sooner rather than later."

Groenenbach sneered at that. He and his men tromped through the women, kicking over baskets and upending work bags, searching. They loomed over the men, Karl in particular.

Karl ignored them and kept sanding his latest crochet hook.

Not finding anything but patterns and simple tools, Groenenbach menaced the group for a bit then left.

Johann stepped inside the door of the Nutsch family parlor almost three weeks later. He growled and dropped his pack.

Annabet frowned at him. "What is wrong with you?"

Johann pointed at Paul. "What is he doing here?"

"Talking about the Committees of Correspondence."

Paul merely drank from his mug. "I'm also courting your sister."

Annabet swatted him. She had learned Paul liked to tease people. He especially liked to tease her. "He is keeping up the charade we agreed on."

"No one only visits their sweetheart at their shop," Paul added.

Johann just looked at him with suspicion.

Paul smiled. "How many patterns did you bring back? More

and more women want American lace. Annabet can't make her own patterns fast enough."

"Lots. The lady let me copy a whole book this time." Johann opened his pack and took a thick sheaf of paper out before tossing several rollags of mauve wool to Annabet.

"They had no spun wool," Johann told her. "I did manage to convince the owner of Lothlorien Faberwerks that all women know how to spin. All they wanted were the new colors." He pulled out more bundles of unspun wool. These were smaller and in a variety of vivid, nearly eye-searing colors Annabet had never seen before. "He got excited and talked into some device. Then he sold me all the samples my bag would hold and asked that I tell him what the women liked best." Next he pulled out more paper.

"Are those the patterns?" Paul asked.

Johann grinned. "Oh, no. We have much work to do. While I was in Grantville, there were many stories being told about Brillo the Ram." He nodded when Annabet raised her eyebrows in a question and pointed at the wool piled in her lap. "That Brillo, yes. If Brillo were a man and not a ram, he would be leading the Committees of Correspondence.

"I collected all the stories I could since I think they will be very popular here. I also started sketching illustrations for them. I think I could make them into books for children. Listen." He read *"Schade,* Brillo! *Schade!"* aloud to them. "It's never too early to start teaching people about freedom."

Annabet and Paul exchanged looks. Annabet blushed and fingered the wool in her lap. "The earlier the better," she said. She straightened her shoulders. "It is our duty to instruct children how to be good adults. If we should ever have them."

Paul smiled at her and raised his mug in a toast.

Annabet blushed and went back to her handwork.

Paul stopped teasing her, for the time being, and looked at Johann. "Show me your sketches, then read us the next story."

Water Conservation

Ray Christiansen

It might be said truthfully that in those days the young limbs of two branches of that great tree that is the House of Hapsburg were joyfully entwined.

—from *The Flowering of a New Kingdom: The early reign of Ferdinand and Marianne in the Netherlands* by Carolus van Loon, University of Antwerp Press, 1702

Queen Maria Anna strode quickly and triumphantly through the hallways in her home at Brussels. As they approached her suite in the royal apartments, she waved off her escorts, and bestowed a particularly warm smile on the young guardsman who opened the door to her suite for her.

When the door closed behind her, she spied a lone maid curtseying before her, and said, "Oh get up, Annette, and congratulate me. It was a fabulous victory! And in straight sets, too! You should have seen me fly across the court. I was magnificent today!" She carefully placed her tennis racket on the bench near the door and began dancing around the room.

Annette rose and replied, "Indeed, Your Majesty. That is marvelous, but I wondered why you were gone so long."

"Not so long as all that."

"But, you and His Majesty do have a state luncheon today with the burghers, guild masters, and university rectors. The cardinal and his sister will be there as well. I am sure you must remember."

Looking around, the young queen saw the formal court dress lying on the bed, and asked, "And Susanna is . . . ?"

"Waiting for your command. I am to fetch her and the others at your return."

"I don't suppose I have time for a bath before I need to dress?"

"I think not, Your Majesty."

"Oh well," she sighed, "before you go, please help me out of my tennis costume and into a robe. I am quite warm and need to cool off before I get into all that." She pointed toward the elaborate gown and its attendant layers of clothing.

"Yes, Your Majesty."

As Annette knelt to begin untying her tennis shoes, Maria Anna removed her hat and let her mind wander. She thought again about missing the bath she'd been hoping for.

When Fernando saw the way the improved sanitation edicts inspired by the up-timers had saved lives inside the city during the siege of Amsterdam, he had issued decrees governing cleanliness and sanitation throughout the whole of his new kingdom. He had also thought to lead by example, and brought a team of up-timers from Grantville to install a very modern bathing chamber in the royal apartments while improving the plumbing in the palace.

She remembered the seemingly endless weeks of workmen moving walls, laying in pipes and drains, the nuisance of finding new quarters for some of the servants as the boiler and cisterns were inserted into the attics, and the construction of the very clever pump house. There was, however, the rather peculiar suggestion of Herr Swiger's that their "Dutch mansion" would look "cute" with a windmill to run the pumps while they waited for the steam engine to be delivered and installed. Even *she* knew that a good team of oxen would be more dependable than the wind.

Her times relaxing in the very *regal* bathtub that had been installed had only been made more pleasurable by the gift of some scented "bubble bath" solution from one of the ladies in the Essen trade delegation some weeks back. Court gossips insisted that they "knew" she bathed for hours each day. In truth, she only indulged herself once or twice a week, if her schedule permitted, and she nearly felt like confessing to a sin, but she couldn't think of one that applied. Besides, she did get clean in body and relaxed in mind each time.

☆ ☆ ☆

As she mused on the wonders of the finished bathing chamber, another thought occurred. Of course, the showering cabinet that Fernando somehow preferred to the bathtub.

"Annette, I would have time to take a shower, wouldn't I?"

"I suspect so, Your Majesty, if you didn't take too long."

"Excellent! Fetch my showering cap and help me cover my hair."

Quickly opening a wardrobe, Annette returned with a rather large, plain bonnet whose only benefit to the wearer was the fact that it was waterproof. Working together, the two soon covered the queen's hair and tied the several tapes and ribbons to close the cap close to her head.

"This will be the perfect solution," the queen said, catching a glimpse of herself in the mirror.

Seeing her court dress reflected in the glass, she asked, "Was my nosegay delivered while I was out?"

Annette looked around quickly, and in a worried tone, replied, "No, my lady. I hadn't noticed that it was not here."

"Well, I must have flowers to carry that match the flowers on the banqueting tables."

"Yes, Your Majesty. Shall I send . . . ?"

"No, you must go yourself. Go to the chief steward and ask where my flowers have gone to, then go get them from, well, wherever they are, and bring them here as quick as you can."

Seeing her young maid's hesitation, the queen gave the girl her warmest smile and said in a low voice, "Please, Annette. I know that the steward can be a bit of a tyrant, but you are going at my command, and, besides, I trust you to find my flowers and make sure they are correct and arranged the way I like them. Now, do me this favor, and hurry, please, and bring them back for me."

"But Your Majesty, I need to help you get ready for your bath."

"No, I am quite able to finish undressing and putting on a robe by myself. Now go, fetch the flowers, please, and bring Susanna and the other maids and the ladies-in-waiting back with you."

"Yes, Your Majesty. Thank you, Your Majesty," the girl burbled as she tried to bow, open the door, and back out of the room, all at the same time.

As the door closed, the queen chuckled to herself and continued removing the last of her tennis garb, donned light slippers and a robe, and walked through the suite to the bathing chamber door.

☆ ☆ ☆

When she opened the door, she was surprised to hear both the sound of cascading water, and of a light baritone singing a rather improper song. Off-key. In Spanish!

Stepping in and closing the door, she drew herself up to her full height, cleared her throat, and in her best imperial tones declaimed, "Stop wasting all the hot water, you Spanish oaf!"

The sound of water (and singing) abruptly ceased, the shower cabinet door opened, and a rather handsome head topped by a showering cap not too unlike her own popped out, and its owner said, "Why, good morning, my dear. How was your tennis match?"

"Don't 'my dear' me," she replied with a stern look that was spoiled by a half-smile. Tapping her foot, she continued, "Time is short, and I simply must bathe before we greet our guests. Oh, and yes, I won."

"Congratulations, love. I, too, had a most successful morning."

"Nonsense. You were probably lounging about all morning."

"Not so. I spent the morning honing my martial skills at the Academy, and the masters praised my growing abilities and devotion to training."

"The only reason they asked you to join was so they could have a royal patron, and have someone to pay for the trophy swords and awards for the next tournament."

"That may be true in part, but I do need something to do on those mornings you go off to play tennis and I don't have pressing kingly duties to attend to. I do sometimes miss our morning walks and rides together. But more to the point, the Academy masters teach fencing in the Spanish style that I learned at my father's court, and I enjoy fencing with opponents who see me as a fellow student or as an apt pupil and not as a king or commander, just as some of your opponents and partners see you as an equally talented player and student of the game."

"Very well, I surrender. Your exercises are as important as mine, but please hurry, Ferdy, and do save me some of the hot water."

With a mischievous smile Fernando eyed his wife's robe-clad form, and suggested, "We could save some time *and* water if we showered together."

Taken aback, Maria Anna thought for an instant, and then with a dreamy smile looked over her shoulder to make sure she had closed the door. Before she could turn back completely, a rather imperious voice ordered with a chuckle, "Come, wench. Your king commands your presence within."

With a broad smile she quickly removed her slippers and robe, rushed into the shower cabinet, and shut the door. Shortly, the room was filled again with the sounds of cascading water, along with some giggles, a slap, and some other low, indistinguishable sounds.

Soon, her soft voice might be heard beneath the sound of the water, "You know, Ferdy, we will be terribly late," followed by the equally soft reply, "Yes, my love, but think of the water we'll be saving."

Later that evening in his own quarters, the chief steward of the palace reflected on a most satisfying day over an excellent glass of hock. The state luncheon was the highlight of course, but under his steady direction and keen eye for detail, all went off smoothly, despite a flurry of interruptions. The only flaw was the delay in starting, but the king and queen could, of course, be a bit late, and needed to offer *him* no explanation.

Affairs of state, he concluded, affairs of state.

An Electrifying Experience

Jack Carroll

Somewhere in the eastern Harz mountains, 1635

Something's burning! Stefan Leichtfuss stopped in his tracks to sniff, and began slowly scanning his eyes all around. *There!* A wisp of smoke was rising out of that new wooden cabinet mounted on the post! Before he could move, there was a loud humming, and then a rising screech from the machine on the floor. He was halfway across the mill before the two sacks he'd been carrying hit the floor and spilled. He paid no attention to that—in one fluid motion, he snatched up the grain shovel leaning against the wall and swung it at the leather belt. It popped clear of the pulley and hung down. He shouted out the door, "Herr Hartmann! Stop the wheel!"

The first thing Gerd Hartmann heard was a howl like an outraged cat. He was already moving when Stefan yelled. In three fast strides he reached the headrace gate, seized the lever in both hands, and slammed it shut. The flow over the spillway rose, while the wheel rumbled to a halt. As Gerd ran through the door, Stefan stuttered, "I-I'm sorry, Herr Hartmann, I know it's not my place to give orders."

"Never mind, I stopped it because I trust you. I would have anyway, I heard it too. Now... what happened?"

Stefan pointed to the box. "I saw smoke starting to come out of there, and then the belt started slipping on the pulley. I knew something was wrong."

"The generator pulley?"

"Yes."

Gerd unhooked the latches on the side of the cabinet and swung the front cover open. He didn't know what the insides were supposed to look like, but it surely wasn't this. The pivoted copper bars with the wooden handle were tarnished, almost black in places, and the metal was still hot—he could smell it. There was some kind of covering over some of the wires, looking frayed and charred. Something black had dripped down to the bottom of the case, and there were tiny flames dancing on the liquid pool, licking against the wood at the back.

"Quick! A bucket of water!" He pushed the cover shut to contain the flames.

The only bucket handy was full of freshly ground flour. Stefan dumped it back in the bin at the foot of the grindstones, and ran outside to the brook. He was back in seconds. Gerd opened the box again and started tossing the water in, a little at a time, until the black stuff hardened and the charred wood was damp.

When Theodor Dränitz heard the call from down the shaft to try it again, he'd gone outside the mine entrance, and waved to Hartmann down by the mill. Hartmann waved back and started the wheel.

Theodor went back in with his lantern and climbed down the upper shaft. He'd gone twenty feet along the tunnel, when there was a strange snapping and hissing sound, and an orange glow appeared between the boards of the wooden covering over the wires. Then he smelled smoke, and flame blossomed at one spot.

He took a short-handled pick and started to knock loose the burning board, before the fire could spread. Flaming fragments and splinters rained down on his left hand. He shook them off and kept swinging. Suddenly the dull orange glow from two of the newly exposed wires faded to black, and the noises stopped after a few seconds. He stamped out the burning wood, and looked to make sure no other pieces were on fire.

He went back up as fast as he could with his burned hand, and ran outside—Hartmann wasn't in sight. He hurried down the hillside to tell him not to start again, until they could figure out what had gone wrong.

All the way up at the house, Marta Seidelin heard the shouting. This scheme of Winkler's had her a little nervous to begin with. She rushed down to the mill to find her husband Gerd and his apprentice Stefan looking into a ruined-looking complicated thing on the post, along with Theodor Dränitz from the mine. There was a big puddle of water on the floor. Then she saw the condition of Dränitz's hand. There were raw, red patches, blisters forming, and dirt all over it.

"Theodor! That looks terrible! It must hurt!"

"Oh, it's not so bad."

"Well, it will be if it gets infected. The newspaper had an article about burns. Come up to the house with me and I'll take care of it."

Stepping back outside, she looked up to the house, and saw her daughter at the door. "Ilsabe! Ilsabe! Take two cups of boiling water from the pot and set them to cool!" Ilsabe waved and went inside.

Stefan was unlacing the belt when old Winkler arrived from down in the mine. "What's your apprentice doing over there, Hartmann?"

Can't even call Stefan by his name. Gerd snorted. "What does it look like, Horst? He's taking down the belt from that generator of yours."

"Hah? What about the test run? I'm certainly not going to pay you if you don't turn it."

"I'd like to get paid, all right, but I haven't the least desire to have my mill burned down. Take a look at this. Take a *good* look. This thing was on fire when we stopped it."

"The switchboard? On fire? What did you do?"

"We started the wheel when your foreman Theodor signaled. Then we stopped it when the pulley started screeching and this thing caught fire, and we put out the flames. Enough, Winkler! I'm through letting you and your men just try things in my mill with this new machinery when you obviously don't know what you're doing. Get somebody up here who understands this." His voice rose to a roar. "And by God, no more 'quick tests' without a proper belt release lever!"

The shouting match went on for ten minutes while Stefan finished taking down the belt and stowed it behind the generator.

"*Well?* What's wrong here?"

Winkler was standing with his arms folded and a scowl on his bewhiskered face.

Gerd silently fumed. This was just typical. *What a way to speak to a man who came all this way to help!*

The young Dutchman—he'd introduced himself as Jan Willem Bosboom, a "field engineer" from American Electric Works—straightened up from examining the insides of the switchboard. He just shook his head. "Quite a lot, Herr Winkler. Quite a lot. But *this*—" He pointed at a large porcelain block. "—is why the damage went so far. These load wires are supposed to be connected to the bottom end of the fuse holder. They're connected to the top instead."

"We tried that. Those little pewter ribbons on it are too weak. They kept melting."

"Well, I should *hope* so! That's what they're there for. They're supposed to disconnect the circuit when the load is too great, so that *this*—" Bosboom gestured openhanded toward the remains. "—doesn't happen. The instruction sheet explains all that. You did read it, didn't you?"

"No," Gerd said in a dangerous voice. "Herr Winkler has that. His men did everything, except for adding a pulley and belt to my main shaft."

"Oh? I see. Well, others are selling the services of their water wheels to generate a little electricity, and there's no reason you shouldn't do the same. But *this*... Well, I'll go over the owner's manuals later with both of you, but for now, let's finish the initial inspection before the day gets any further along. I'll get my hand lamp. We can follow the wiring down into the mine, and then we'll see what the pump looks like."

Gerd took a deep breath. "I think I'd better come along and see all of it for myself."

Winkler looked up sharply. "Eh? As you wish. Mind your head in the tunnels."

Bosboom reached down to his tool case and took out a small varnished wooden box. They started up the hillside to the mine entrance, Bosboom looking speculatively at the line of poles as they went.

Meanwhile he flipped out a crank on the side of his lamp, and with a *skkrrrk* spun it for a minute or so. Finally he flipped a little lever. A soft whirring noise started up inside, and a narrow beam of yellowish light sprang out through a window on the front. Gerd looked curiously at the thing. "Is that one of those marvelous portable lights I've been hearing about?"

"An up-time electric flashlight? Not quite. They can't duplicate those yet, but somebody found a good use for the half-million or so Christmas tree bulbs they have."

"Christmas tree bulbs? What are they?"

"Well, during the Christmas holidays, they decorate their houses by bringing in a small fir tree and stringing colored ornaments and tiny electric lights all over it. Supposedly it was originally a German custom, but they used little candles in the old days."

Winkler looked blank. "German? Not from around here. What a strange habit!"

"Oh, I agree," he laughed. "A street full of houses with Christmas trees in the windows is a sight to treasure forever, though."

The boss was coming up the hill. Gerd Hartmann was with him, looking like he was ready to spit thunderbolts. The stranger behind them must be the foreign expert to figure out what was wrong with this new pumping machinery... what was he supposed to be again? Some new kind of mine engineer? Theodor Dränitz picked up the lantern at his feet and lit a second one from it. He handed it to Herr Winkler as they reached the entrance, but it was Hartmann who performed the introductions.

Theodor led the way to the shaft head, and began descending the ladder. The miller followed him down, and then the visiting engineer. Finally the boss started down. The engineer was still ten feet up on the ladder when a sudden realization struck Theodor. "Herr Bosboom, wait!"

Crack! There was a clatter and a muffled exclamation. The beam from the odd-looking lamp swung around wildly.

"Hold on, I'm coming back up. Here, I'll guide your foot to a solid rung."

He braced himself between the ladder and the opposite side of the shaft, and lifted. The light steadied above him.

"Are you all right?"

"I think so," came out with a hiss. "It feels like I strained my left shoulder. I should have let the lamp fall and grabbed on with both hands."

"I'm sorry about this. I've been meaning to replace that weak rung. All this confusion . . . Can you make it down the rest of the way now?"

"Yes, but give me a moment."

Bosboom slowly descended the last few feet. Herr Winkler came down, and Theodor led the party off along the tunnel. By now the whirring from Bosboom's lamp was slowing down, and it was starting to get dim. Hartmann asked, "Herr Bosboom, would you like me to wind that for you?"

"Thank you, yes. I wish I had some ice for this shoulder."

Theodor replied, "The water in the flooded shaft is almost as cold as ice. I can dip a rag in it for you when we get there, if that will help."

"It's worth a try."

Bosboom stopped when he saw the charred fragments lying on the tunnel floor. "What happened here?"

Theodor said, "One of the cover boards caught fire when all this happened. I knocked it off so the flames wouldn't spread. That's when I got this burn."

Bosboom looked down at the bandage on Theodor's hand, then turned and raised his lamp. Herr Winkler didn't seem to notice when the engineer stiffened. Hartmann did. He asked, "What do you see there, Herr Bosboom?"

"These wires here look like iron. They should be copper. That's one major problem right there."

Herr Winkler snapped, "There's no copper wire made around here. We were told that iron could be used to carry electricity."

Bosboom looked over his shoulder at him. "That's a common mistake, unfortunately. Our instruction sheets warn against it. Besides all the other reasons not to use it, iron wires would have to be at least two and a half times this diameter to carry the current. That's why they got so hot and started a fire."

Winkler waved his hand at the wires. "The smith charged me enough for the iron wire. Copper would have been unbelievable. That would have to come all the way from Saalfeld!"

"Actually, no. We have plenty of it at the sales offices in Halle and Magdeburg, and there are others selling it too. That's not the worst problem I see here, either. Well, let's continue the inspection."

Theodor answered, "This way, then, Herr Bosboom," and stepped forward.

As the party moved through the tunnels, Bosboom kept looking around at the bends, the drain channels, and the wooden covering over the electrical wiring.

Finally they came to another shaft, filled with water almost to the top. Theodor reached down into the water with a rag, and handed it to the engineer. Bosboom clapped it to his shoulder, and began examining the equipment lying on the tunnel floor, moving his lamp around as he did.

There was a cast iron pump secured to a hoisting rig, connected to a long canvas hose stretched out along the tunnel, and a loose coil of electrical cable running down from the end of the wooden raceway. The engineer looked it all over. Then he knelt down and took a close look at the pump.

He sniffed at it. "What on earth? *Ohhhhh.*"

The boss snapped, "What now?"

"Just a moment, while I make certain." Bosboom took the rag off his shoulder and wiped the nameplate clean. He brought his lamp up close.

"Well. To start with, this isn't a mine pump. It's for a village water supply system, and it's only meant for clean water with no muck in it. If the length of that discharge hose is any indication, it can't possibly force water up from anything like the depth of this shaft, and I don't see the pressure relief valve it's supposed to have in case of a blocked outlet line. That's why it stalled out and overloaded the wiring. There's no fused disconnect switch on the wall here. Now that I think of it, I didn't see one at the mine entrance either. On top of everything else, you had the fuses at the generator bypassed. This motor smells like it's cooked."

Winkler looked wide-eyed at him. "*Cooked?* Why would anybody cook a motor?"

Bosboom's shoulders shook for a moment. He coughed, then got out, "Sorry. A figure of speech I heard at the factory. It means it was probably ruined by overheating."

"So what does this mean? How do I make this pump the water out of here so we can get down to the ore seam?"

"With *this* pump alone? You can't. It's impossible. The most it could do is push the water up the entrance shaft and out of the mine, if you didn't have a drain tunnel at this level."

"What? This is supposed to be a good pump. It cost enough!"

"It *is* a good pump, or it was. It's just not the right pump for this job. It's not even the right kind of pump. All right, I've seen what I need to. Let's climb back up and go over what has to be done. We'll start by going through the instruction sheets for the equipment in the mill, I think."

Theodor dipped the rag in the shaft again and handed it back to him. "I'll climb right below you, in case you need help on the ladder. I'm very sorry about the fall."

Winkler stalked off down the tunnel.

Ilsabe nestled the covered pot into the coals, and scooped more coals onto the lid. "That will do it for now, Mama."

"Good. Why don't you go tell Papa and Stefan when we'll be eating? Peter will be back by then, if I know your brother." She winked.

"All right, Mama."

She walked downhill to the mill and stepped inside. The stranger kneeling on the floor must be the expert Papa was expecting. He was doing something to that machine of Herr Winkler's that had caused so much trouble. There were tools and small parts lying around it.

Papa was saying, "Stefan, his shoulder is hurt. Go help him."

"Don't you want me to finish getting this load under cover before dark, Herr Hartmann?"

"Well . . ."

"Papa, I can help."

Papa looked over in surprise. "Oh, Ilsabe. I thought you were busy in the kitchen."

"No, most of that is done. Mama sent me to tell you that supper will be ready in about an hour. I can stay and help here if you need me."

"Well, yes, you came at a good time. Ilsabe, this is Herr Jan Willem Bosboom. He's here from the company that made all this electrical machinery. Herr Bosboom, this is my daughter Ilsabe."

The stranger looked up. "I'm pleased to meet you, Fräulein Hartmann."

"Pleased to meet you, Herr Bosboom. What would you like me to do?"

"I need you to pick up one end of this generator while I put a block of wood under it. Then the other end, and I'll prop that side up as well. After that you can take off these nuts and we'll pull it apart."

Papa picked up his grease pot again and went back to the mill machinery.

She knelt down and took a grip. It looked like a lot of iron, but... "Oh. This isn't as heavy as it looks. If you're quick with the sticks, I can pick it up all at once."

"All right." He put the blocks in place against the side. "Ready."

A second later it was propped up with its ends clear of the floor. He handed her a wrench and gestured with his hand. "You turn the nuts *this* way to take them off. I'll hold this down. Once that's done, you can slide off the end bells and we'll pull the rotor out."

She looked at the wrench in her hand. It shone like a mirror, and there wasn't a hammer mark on it anywhere—except... "Herr Bosboom, what's this here?"

"That? That's a kudzu leaf. It's the maker's hallmark."

"They must be great craftsmen. This is a beautiful piece of work."

He glanced up at her. "You appreciate fine tools?"

"Naturally. I grew up in this mill."

She turned to the generator, and set the wrench in place on the first nut. She gave it an experimental tug to get the feel, then braced her knee against the side and gave a solid pull. Two minutes later the insides were exposed to view, and she was lifting the pieces one at a time to a cloth spread out on a bench.

Ilsabe watched curiously while Herr Bosboom blew the dust away and started playing his lamp over the parts. She pointed to the wires wound around a stack of thin iron plates. "This looks very carefully made. What do all these pieces do?"

"Well..."

Winkler and Dränitz came back to the mill with a handful of thick pamphlets. Gerd came over to the bench to see, with Ilsabe beside him. Bosboom spread out the papers for the generator and the switchboard, and looked up in surprise. "Herr Winkler, these are in Italian! Do you read Italian? Do you, Herr Dränitz?"

"No, but there are plenty of pictures. We just went by those, and the tables."

"*Whooh*. So, you didn't get any of the cautions and the explanations. That explains a lot. The instruction sheets in German weren't packed with this equipment, obviously. I don't know how that happened, but I'll leave you my copies. But why didn't you just send for the right ones, before doing all this work?"

Winkler flung up his arms. "That would have taken a week or more for the post to go back and forth. I needed to get on with this, so my men could start mining."

"I see. Well, you would have saved a great deal of time, and a lot of money besides, if you'd sent for instruction sheets you and your men could read. Haste makes waste—it certainly has here. While you were gone, I inspected and tested the generator with Fräulein Hartmann's kind help." He nodded to her. "Except for that and a few bits and pieces, there isn't much here that can be saved."

"What! I wrote to the company to send somebody who could get this working, not to be told there is nothing to be done."

Bosboom straightened up and faced Winkler, his hand resting on the open leaflet. His voice went flat. "Herr Winkler, this trip up here is costing my company a day and a half of my time, and if you're being charged for it, I haven't heard about it. My job is to tell you the truth, not wave my hands in the air and magically turn it into something else. So I suggest you start taking detailed notes of this discussion, if you want to accomplish anything.

"Now, then. There's a great deal that can be done. In fact, this can be made to work. The basic idea is right, an electric pump is by far the most practical solution, with so little left of the old pumping machinery, especially everything there was above ground. But the system has to be engineered correctly. The pump company has people who can do that for you, and their consulting rates are reasonable.

"But the worst problem I see from the electrical side is that knob-and-tube wiring you have in the mine. That only belongs inside a dry building. It's dangerous anywhere in a damp tunnel, but you have it running right above open drain channels. Let a discharge line burst, and it's a death trap. Besides that, you have outdoor pole lines, and those don't look like they're up to standard either.

"There are just too many pitfalls here for inexperienced workmen. You need the services of a licensed electrician to direct the rebuilding, otherwise somebody's sure to be killed."

"An *electrician*? There isn't one within forty miles of here! It would take days to get one, and they charge a fortune! If you're such an expert—"

Bosboom clenched one hand on the edge of the bench.

"Herr Winkler. My employers make a point of maintaining a professional demeanor and sticking to technical matters when speaking with a customer."

"Well, of course!"

He looked unblinking at Winkler for a good two seconds, then growled, "I could make an exception in your case."

"*What?* What do you mean?"

"You asked for help. I've been patiently explaining what it will take to get the results you want, and make this pumping system safe for you and your men to be around. You stand here brushing aside what I'm telling you, as if a loud voice will change the facts to suit your convenience. *It won't.* We all had to begin from the beginning, but what seriously disturbs me is your unwillingness to learn when you have the chance. Do you expect to make this work without taking the trouble to get the right equipment and install it properly? For that matter, don't you care at all about the lives of your miners? Or your own life?"

"You expect me to throw money around like water? And take who-knows-how-long to do all this?"

"You don't like the cost of safe wiring? Would you rather pay to restore the old pumping system from before the war, with all the push rods and bell cranks? Would you like to pay to rebuild the dam so you could get power to drive it? No? I didn't think so. I can see the answer on your face."

Winkler was turning red. "Who are you, you young puppy, to talk to the head of an enterprise like this?"

Bosboom fixed Winkler with an icy glare and slammed his open hand down on the Italian installation manual. "Who am I, Herr Winkler? The examiners at Leiden consider me a civil engineer. Mr. Reardon is satisfied that I know enough about electricity to give sound advice to his customers. I'm the man who can tell you how to keep from walking into a worse disaster than the one you've already suffered. *The Lord protect your men!* What you have here would never have been built in any of the mines around Grantville. If the state inspectors didn't stop it, the UMWA would."

"Now what are you saying? Are you threatening me with the UMWA?"

"Oh, be serious! The UMWA isn't so foolish as to rely on companies or their representatives to tell them about dangerous mines. Now if you're through trying to bully us into rebuilding this whole thing without charging for it, you can start taking notes, and we'll discuss practical action to get your mine pumped out without killing anyone."

Winkler went growling and sputtering back to his office with his papers and notes.

Gerd watched the engineer for a minute as he started packing up his tools, still working one-handed. Finally he said, "Herr Bosboom, I don't think I've ever heard a speech like that one. Certainly not to old Winkler."

"I hope I did right. I hope I got through to him."

"What was it that made you so upset?"

"Herr Hartmann, I've seen the consequences of refusing to face facts." He shuddered.

"When I was nine years old, I wanted to see what my uncle Hannes did. One day he let me come with him to a job site, where he'd just been engaged as the supervising engineer. You can imagine what a treat that was for me. A canal lock was to be repaired and enlarged, so bigger barges could go through. When we arrived that morning, it had been all pumped out, and the masons were ready to go in and examine the wall.

"Uncle Hannes took a good look around, as he always does. Then he went over by the gate, and looked closer. You know how wood will start to take up a bend, when it's been under too much load for too long? Well, the top beam looked like that. He dug his knife into it, and it went in much too easily. The steward was there, representing the owners. Uncle Hannes stood up and shouted to him that the gate was rotten and not safe. He said it needed to be replaced before anybody could go into the lock with water on the other side of the gate. The simplest way would have been to block the canal with a temporary dam of rocks and dirt.

"But the steward wouldn't hear of it. He answered that the gate had held for forty years, and sent the men in.

"No more than two hours later, it broke open right in front of us. It all happened in a few seconds. Men ran for the walls and tried to ride the rush of water. All of us on the bank grabbed ropes, boards, whatever was within reach, and pulled men out, or just held them up until others could help. But there were two that nobody could find in time, with all the debris and muddy water in that lock.

"So, I broke a company rule just now. Deliberately. I couldn't just ignore a fatal accident waiting to happen, and not try my best to stop it. I wouldn't want that on my conscience. And nobody in the company wants a reputation for making things that kill people."

Gerd was silent again, thinking. He cupped his chin in his hand.

"Herr Bosboom, if I understand the lesson in all this, it's that I can't afford to allow this generator here unless I know enough about it to make it safe. I have to control what's in my mill."

Bosboom nodded his head. "That's a logical conclusion, for certain. I couldn't agree more."

"But you said other millers own these machines, and they're making money with them?"

"That's right, it's starting to happen. I think within a year there will be a sudden increase in that business. The problems of manufacturing light bulbs at prices people can afford are close to being solved."

"I see. That means we have some important decisions to make here. I'd appreciate a chance to ask you a good many more questions. Would you accept an offer of supper with my family and me, and a place to sleep tonight?"

"That's very kind. I wasn't really looking forward to going back down the road, with evening coming on. Maybe my shoulder will feel better after a night's rest, too. Can you accommodate the mule I rented to get up here?"

"Of course. Wagon drivers sometimes have to stay over."

"Thank you, then."

"Ilsabe, *liebchen*, go tell Mama we'll have a guest tonight."

With a thumping of boots Peter was back from his errand in the village. His eye fastened on the platter of fresh bread in the middle of the table, and Marta's eye fastened just as quickly on him. She reached across with the long wooden spoon in her hand, barring his way. "You'll sit and eat at the table with the rest of us, you wolf cub."

"Mama, I'm starved!"

"Oh, right, I can see your ribs. Papa and the men from the

mill will be here in no time. Then we'll all eat. And nobody will starve. Go wash up."

Then Stefan came in, and a minute later Gerd was there with their guest. He seemed a pleasant young man, with a ready smile and an air of intelligence. The cut of his clothes was something like the uniforms the army teamsters wore, but in different colors. His trousers were made of a heavy dark blue fabric with copper rivets at the pocket corners, and he wore a rugged-looking red and black checked shirt. He took off a broad-brimmed hat in a style she hadn't seen before. *Someone with tales from far away, perhaps?*

"... my wife Marta Seidelin, and our son Peter.

"Marta, a man of virtue stands before us."

She cocked her head, with an expectant half-smile.

"Old Winkler drove him to fury."

"Heh-heh-heh. I can't imagine how that could have happened. So then what?"

"Anyone else might have come out with a curse. Herr Bosboom here pronounced a blessing."

This time it was the guest who showed a half-smile—a puzzled one.

"You did! You prayed for the safety of the miners!"

Jan Willem's hand went over his mouth, and his eyes crinkled. "What? Oh. Yes, I suppose I did."

"And I assume you sincerely wished them well, when you called on the Lord to save them from Winkler's foolishness?"

"Well, of course. I wouldn't want anybody to be electrocuted."

"So, there you are. You pronounced a blessing."

"*Pffff!* A civil engineer is supposed to do a lot more than just pray."

Marta laughed as she ladled out the soup, and gestured for everyone to sit down. "Well, husband, what's the news?"

"Marta..." He sighed. "We have a problem. It will be weeks before Winkler will be in any position to make use of that generator of his, and even that might be too optimistic. Herr Bosboom says everything has to be rebuilt, and before that can even start, there are other experts Winkler needs to consult. So he won't be paying us to drive it, for as long as that takes."

"Oh, Gerd, we were counting on that money. What do we do now?"

"For now, let's enjoy the food in front of us and our company. We can talk later about how to finish paying the carpenters."

Bosboom asked, "The carpenters?"

"It's no secret. A storm last winter brought down a big tree, right on top of the mill. We were keeping ahead of expenses, until that happened. It's repaired now, and the mill is working again, but it cost a lot. The carpenters have been patient, but they naturally want their money."

"It sounds like a difficult situation. I'm sorry to hear it."

"Well, thank you. Gerd and I really hoped you'd be able to tell Winkler and his foreman what to do to get everything working."

"It's a little too complicated for that, Frau Seidelin," he said with a downcast look. "It involves a lot more than just telling them how to install the equipment my company supplied. That would be hard enough, with what they're trying to do. But there's all the pump and plumbing work to plan over from the beginning, and Herr Winkler seemed to think I could do a mine electrician's job too."

Gerd paused with his spoon in the air. "Mine electrician? There's a trade by that name?"

"Well, in a way. There are some special things to know about wiring in mines. One of Grantville's better-known citizens started out as a mine electrician. I haven't met her, though. She's been away on business since before I came to the company."

Clink! Ilsabe was sitting bolt-upright. The spoon had dropped from her hand. "Herr Bosboom! Did I hear you right? Did you just say that women work in this 'electrician' trade? This trade that Herr Winkler said draws such high wages?"

Marta understood in a flash. "Your dowry. You're thinking of how to earn your dowry."

"Yes, Mama! Instead of some dull job in service somewhere, struggling to save anything at all, maybe I could have a real trade? Herr Bosboom, is that what this means?"

"Well, if you decide that's what you want to do, I'd say it's a real possibility. You're quick enough with unfamiliar tools. If you can do as well with book learning, you could get accepted into an electrical apprenticeship program easily enough. The up-timers are absolutely desperate to train enough of them."

"And because of that, they accept girls?" Marta asked.

"That would be logical enough, but it's not the reason. They had an equal opportunity law before they were ever flung into our midst, and they declared it still in effect before the guilds knew what was going on. Anybody who can show a record book with the required experience can sit for the state examination for journeyman or master, and get the license. A licensed electrician can work anywhere in Thuringia and Franconia."

"But we're not in their state, up here."

"No, but let me tell you, a customer with any sense will ask to see a Thuringian license."

Marta looked at him pensively. "And it's a respectable trade? A better opportunity for our Ilsabe?"

"Oh, for certain. Hard work sometimes, but your daughter is a big, strong girl." He turned to Ilsabe. "Look, if you're at all serious about this, I'd be happy to write a letter of introduction for you."

"Oh, thank you!" Ilsabe's smile glowed. "I don't know what to say. Yes, I'd like very much to go see what this trade is really like."

"Yes, Herr Bosboom. I think we all would like to know that."

"Marta, that isn't all Herr Bosboom has to tell us. He said down at the mill that these generators are making money for other millers." Turning to their guest, he continued, "What's that all about? What makes this an attractive proposition?"

"Well. There's one simple fact about electricity. It's the cheapest and most convenient way to move a lot of mechanical power from where it is to where you want it. That pumping problem Winkler has is just one example. His little generator could equally well supply electric lights to a village of a dozen houses. And that's the smallest model our company makes. Seventeen of our big ones run all of Grantville."

"Electric lights in houses. Yes, I can see what that means, steady income all year round, doesn't it? But if we turned all the power of our wheel into electricity and sold it, there would be nothing left to run the mill."

"Actually, the usual kind of wheel captures less than half the power of the water running over it. And a lot more is lost in the runs along the brook from one mill wheel to the next. There's a fellow teaching water power the way they did it in their nineteenth century. I've attended some of his lectures. That brook out there could deliver at least ten times as much power as you're getting now, if you used all of their tricks."

☆ ☆ ☆

There was more. A great deal more. As much as Marta wanted to ask the foreign visitor about his family, his life, all the places he'd been, she put it aside. There was just too much that could be vital to her own family's future. She could see her husband too, struggling to make sense of all these new thoughts fighting for room in his head.

Finally Bosboom sat back and stretched. "Well, thank you very much for all your hospitality. I really should get some sleep now. I need to be on my way soon after sunrise."

Marta answered, "Oh, it was a pleasure. You've been generous to let us ask you so many questions. I'll have a bit of cheese and bread ready in the morning for you to take along. Stefan, show Herr Bosboom where he can sleep tonight."

Their footsteps faded out, up the stairs.

Marta stayed seated, staring across the room at the hearth, her chin cradled in her folded hands. "Gerd . . ."

"What is it?"

"He said we could sell enough power to light a village, and still have enough to run the mill."

"Well, yes . . ."

"Think what that means. Our water rights are enough to make electricity to sell, and still run a mill. That mill could be just as easily run *by electricity, somewhere else*."

"But, why . . ."

"Ours isn't the only wheel on this stream. Somebody else could put in a generator and sell enough electricity to run a mill, and send it down to the village and run a mill there. And then the farmers wouldn't have to cart their grain all the way up here."

Gerd froze. "Marta! If that happened, we'd be ruined!"

"*Unless* we did it first. Gerd, maybe this is only a fantasy. But if electricity means the mill could be away from the brook and put where the farmers are, then we must be the ones to do it."

"But, wait a minute. We have the only milling rights around here."

"You've been reading the newspapers as much as I have. As strong as the free trade factions have become in Parliament, how much can we really count on that, any more?"

Gerd began to pace. "If, if, if. So on one hand, if we do nothing, all these changes could wash over us and take away our business. But if we do all this and it doesn't work, we could spend a lot of money and get nothing back from it. And we're already short of money. I don't know what we're going to do about a coat for Peter, he's grown so much lately. What have these strange people done, Marta? Made us some bizarre kind of offer we can't refuse?"

"More like . . . given us an opportunity we'd be fools to ignore. But what we *must* do is find out the truth about all of this. The one thing we can't afford to do is guess."

Thump. Rustle.

"Urrr. Are you still tossing and turning?"

"I can't sleep, Marta. I don't know what's going to happen to us."

"Well, it isn't going to happen tomorrow, or probably even next year. Meanwhile, if it's slipped your fevered mind, there's the flour order for that mysterious army camp on the mountain. And they pay on time, if we ship on time. So the first thing to do is get your sleep."

"Yes, I know. But still . . ."

"Still. Yes." She chuckled softly. "Well, I know what will make you sleep." She snuggled closer. She laid her fingertips on his chest. She nibbled his ear. "Hmmm?"

"Mmm . . ."

Their guest came downstairs just as the family was settling down to breakfast. Marta picked up a package wrapped in newspaper and handed it to him. "This should help you keep body and soul together on the way back. How is your shoulder this morning?"

"Better, but I still feel it. I should be able to ride all right, though."

"I'm glad to hear it. Here, sit down." She busied herself setting another place next to Stefan. She looked across the table. Well, Gerd was looking a lot calmer this morning.

A few minutes passed in silence. Gerd looked up from his plate. "Herr Bosboom, we're going to look into all this. I think before we visit any of these places you told us about, we ought to read up as much as we can first, so we understand what we're seeing. You mentioned books. Which ones would you suggest I order?"

"Hmm. I think, to start with, I'd suggest *The Modern Millwright's Electrical Guide,* and *Installing Antique Wiring.* Maybe the *Thuringia Electrical Code.* They're all available in German."

"*Antique? What?* Are you saying the ancients did this kind of thing?"

"Hah, no." The engineer laughed. "The up-timer electrician who wrote it has a slightly twisted sense of humor. You see, they can't make the materials for the kind of wiring they're used to. Not yet, anyway. So they had to go back to the forgotten methods of their great-grandfathers, and there weren't any books around to describe them. Not in enough detail, anyway. They had to examine surviving examples in a few old barns, and figure out how it was done."

"They didn't pass their skills down? I never heard of such a trade."

"Oh, they did, they did, from one generation to the next one, and that's the funny thing. The materials and the methods changed fast. Very fast. That seems to happen, when the up-timer Americans are involved. After a hundred years, everything was completely different, and there was no use for the older ways.

"So now, they're trying to get back to where they were in just a few years. It's learn the trade, and then every time something new comes along, read another book or manual. I'll tell you, it never gets boring."

Gerd ruefully scratched his head. "No, I don't suppose it does. Things are changing all around us, since those people appeared."

"True. But, you know? We lived in changing times before any of this happened." He laughed. "They've certainly made it blindingly obvious, though."

Three months later

Marta was down at the mill keeping a close eye on things. The batch of coarse meal Stefan was grinding looked satisfactory enough. She glanced over at the new switchboard, with the metal case and the circuit breaker handle sticking out the front, that Gerd had insisted on after he got his hands on an electrical supply catalog. Winkler had squawked like a chicken over that one, but Gerd had roared like a bear. Well, he could look like a bear when he wanted to. The front panel had meters, too—she could see that the frequency was holding right on the mark. She returned her attention to the ledger in front of her.

Halfway down a column of figures, Marta glanced up with a momentary flicker of annoyance as Peter stuck his head out the door for what must be the tenth time that morning.

"Mama! They're coming!"

She put down the ledger and hurried outside, with Stefan right behind her. There Gerd and Ilsabe were, just coming into sight around the bend in the road. They waved, and walked a little faster. Half a minute later they were dropping their traveling bags at their feet, and Marta was seizing them both in a two-armed embrace.

"I've read all your letters over and over. Oh, Fräulein Apprentice Electrician, I'm so proud of you!"

"I'm not an apprentice yet, Mama. I still have to take the entrance examinations. The man at the power company said it will take a couple of months of study here at home, before I'll be ready for that."

"But the director of training was very complimentary, Marta. He said Ilsabe has the skill and the strength of character to take on the responsibilities of an electrician, and that's what they value most. He promised her a place as soon as she passes the tests."

"What an honor for you, Ilsabe!"

"And now . . ." He reached into his bag and pulled out a bank draft. "Look at this!"

She took it with an indrawn breath. "Oh, Gerd! This is most of what we owe. And now that Winkler is paying us, it won't take long to pay off the rest. You wrote about this, but just how did you manage to come home with more money than you started out with?"

"Luck was on our side, for once. You knew that Herr Bosboom advised us to go see the water works at the Braun and Scharff machine tool factory, so we could understand what water power can really do?"

She nodded.

"Well, it was the head millwright who showed us everything and explained how it all works. That was more of Herr Bosboom's doing. Their wheel is so small I could get my two arms around it, and it gives them hundreds of horsepower. Amazing! Anyway, it came out in conversation that he was short of temporary help to get a new part of the building running, and here we were with mill experience. So he hired the two of us for a month's work at good wages, helping his men hang line shafts and doing other mechanical work. We've missed you all terribly, but this was an opportunity we couldn't let slip away. Peter, I think you're taller."

Ilsabe broke in, "One of the men showed me how they put up electric lights, and I did a few myself."

"So she's done a little of the work with her own hands, and liked it. So, I consented to the apprenticeship."

Marta hugged them again. "I'm so glad you're home. You must both be ravenous after walking all the way from the train station. Stefan, you can stop the millstones now. We'll go eat, and then we'll talk."

"Oh, yes, Marta. There's so much to talk about."

Gerd eyed the pole and crossarm lying on the ground. Peter was taking a turn with the tools Theodor Dränitz had borrowed from the mine. He slammed the heavy bar into the bottom of the hole once more, and worked it around to loosen the dirt. *That boy is getting strong!* Stefan moved in with a post hole digger to lift out what Peter had loosened—a wonderful tool.

"That's deep enough, boys."

The four of them took their places around the pole and picked it up. Into the hole went the butt. Theodor, Gerd, and Stefan pushed up the top end as far as they could while Peter took up the slack in the tackle hitched part way up and belayed it. Then Gerd ran around and helped him haul the pole upright, while Theodor and Stefan steadied it from the side. Gerd walked around with a plumb line, making hand motions until the pole was vertical.

"Okay, Peter, it's straight. You can back fill it."

"It looks okay to me too, and I can tell where you've been lately!"

Gerd looked over his shoulder in surprise. It was Jan Willem Bosboom, riding up the road. Gerd's face lit up with a lopsided grin and a mischievous gleam in his eye. "Oh, yeah? I wasn't expecting to see you, though. What brings you up here?"

"I have a customer to visit nearby, and your mill isn't far out of the way. I thought I'd see how things are going." He dismounted and came over to shake hands.

"Things are going in directions I never imagined. Marta and I were only thinking of buying a generator of our own, you know, and selling what power we could spare from our own wheel."

Bosboom nodded.

"Did you know what all those people you arranged for us to see in Grantville have in mind?"

"Not exactly, but I thought they'd tell you what you wanted to know, so you could decide what to do."

"Hmmph. It seems they weren't interested in anything as modest as that. The government wants some little commercial power plants up here in the mountains, to help the mines get going again. Tiny by their standards, but a lot bigger than we could run with only our family water rights. There are investors ready to finance it, if we can show them a business plan that makes sense. So I asked them why they would think of coming to us to put something like that together, and do you know what they said?"

Bosboom shook his head.

"They said, 'There's nobody else to do it.' I think it must be their favorite saying down there."

"Now that you mention it, you're right. That's just about what they said to me when I was hired."

"So Marta and I have been asking around to get an idea who might buy electricity if we go ahead with all this, and we've been talking to our neighbors up and down this brook to see what kind of deal we might be able to make to combine some water rights. You know that phrase 'sweet-talking' some of the up-timers use? She has a talent for it. And meanwhile, we're learning all we can about running a power plant, while it's still mostly on Winkler's pfennig."

Bosboom threw his head back and laughed. A second later everybody else was laughing too. He waved his hand toward the pole. "So what's this for?"

"We're putting up a power line to the house. We only need two poles and a small transformer. We'll have one light in the kitchen and one over the dining table. After all, who would take us seriously if we couldn't show electricity working in our own home?"

"Who, indeed?"

"So, will you stay for dinner?"

"I'm sorry, they're expecting me up ahead. I'll just pay my respects to Frau Seidelin, and then I have to be on my way."

"No more Herr Hartmann and Frau Seidelin from you, with all you've done for us! It's Gerd and Marta from now on."

"Well, then, call me Jan Willem." He put out his hand to shake again.

Theodor said, "Herr Bosboom, I'm glad you came by. There's something I'd like to ask you about."

"Yes, what is it?"

"Well, Herr Winkler has been talking about another mining improvement he's heard of, that he thinks will help us dig the ore out much faster." He paused. "Do you know anything about something called nitroglycerin?"

The Pessimist's Daughter

Mark Huston

May 1635, Grantville, High Street Mansion, SoTF Government Building

"Hello, Ursula." The up-time woman smiled from her office, as she had done for nearly every afternoon for the last two years.

Ursula Volz lowered her plain eyes, nodded her head imperceptibly, and mumbled a quiet, "Good afternoon, Mrs. Carstairs," as she came into the back hall.

Ursula rapidly stepped by the lady in her office, past a large kitchen, and then threaded her way through a narrow hallway, arriving at the front foyer of the old mansion.

There was a guard station in what used to be the front hall. The regular night guard, Marcus Sauber, was sitting in a chair behind the desk. He was positioned facing the front of the building, where the public would normally enter. Ursula had entered by the employee and service entrance, at the back of the house.

The guard turned in his chair. "Hello, Ursula."

"Good evening, Herr Sauber."

"Right on time as always. Here is the note from the office manager; she tells me someone spilled coffee in the second floor hallway and it needs to be cleaned up tonight." He handed her a note. "It's always something, isn't it? Spills or messes to be cleaned up. Night janitor is never a fun job, right, Ursula?"

"I don't mind it, Herr Sauber." She paused at the desk and signed in on the log book that Marcus Sauber kept.

"Good afternoon, Herr Sauber." Keeping her eyes turned to the floor, she turned to the staircase to the left of the desk and headed toward the back stairs leading to the basement, taking a candle from the side table and lighting it as she went. There were no offices in the basement, because there were almost no windows. She went down the gloomy and musty stairs, and looked around. Something about being in a cellar always bothered her. The only things down here were storage for files and the cleaning supply closet, which was near the stairs.

Ursula gathered up her things from the supply closet and trudged up the stairs. She usually started on the first floor, in the public spaces, and then moved to the offices in the later afternoon and evening. She began her work in the lobby, by the guard station. It had rained during the day, and people had tracked mud into the hallway. With a mop and bucket, she started to scrub.

It was a good job, and Ursula liked it. It was quiet, especially later in the evening when everyone went home. It was interesting working at the High Street Mansion. It was built back when Grantville was a "boom town," owned by a man and his family who made toilets. When Ursula had seen it for the first time, she could not believe it was only for one man and his family. It took her almost a week to learn all the rooms. It was broken up into even smaller areas for more offices and rooms. The home was mostly empty when it came through the Ring of Fire, no one living there, and most of the contents had been auctioned off. Since it was big, and had plenty of light and windows, it was appropriated by the government as offices. Nobody bothered her much at this job, and she liked that too. The only thing a little bit irritating was—

"Ursula! Oh, I'm so sorry I'm late. Sorry, sorry, sorry. I got delayed at dinner with . . . umm . . . my mother. *Aaand* . . . she wanted to talk . . . about her new boyfriend."

Margit. Her co-worker. She finally arrived. About a half hour late, as usual. Ursula sighed. Margit always had excuses, and some of them were very entertaining. But tonight, Ursula was not in the mood. "I will finish this; you can start on the back hallway."

"Don't you want to hear about my mother's new boyfriend?"

"Not especially, Margit. And you used that excuse last month."

"Oh."

"Back hallway, Margit?"

"Okay. Let me get my stuff from downstairs. Back in a minute." She turned and half-skipped down the hall, humming a little tune. Ursula smiled just a little as she watched her disappear around the corner.

After finishing the public spaces and the offices on the first floor, they started up the stairs to the second, where more offices and desks were packed into rooms. Margit leaned over to Ursula. "Are you going out after work tonight, Ursula? You never go, and we have so much fun." Margit turned and bounced mischievously in her stride.

Ursula looked at her and shook her head. "I need to be home and to sleep so I can help my mother with the sewing as soon as it gets light."

Margit frowned. "Ursula, when are you going to have some fun in your life? How do you expect to meet anyone if all you do is work here in the afternoon, go home and sleep, then sew with your mother from first light until you come to work again? You are what? Twenty-one? Twenty-two?"

"I'm very plain, Margit. Who would ever want me? My father is a casket maker. He has no social rank."

Margit stopped on the stairs and blocked Ursula's path. "How many times have I told you it doesn't matter here? It must be a thousand times by now." She changed the tone of her voice, deepening it with authority. "Ursula, it doesn't matter here." She changed back to her impish grin. "There. One thousand and one."

Ursula paused. "Twenty-five. Almost twenty-six."

"What?"

"I will be twenty-six in two months."

Margit's hand went to her mouth. "I'm so sorry, Ursula. I had no idea you were ahhh—were that—ummm..." Margit stuttered some more, and after a pause she half-heartedly added, "You look remarkably young for your age..." Margit turned red behind her grimace.

Ursula looked at her with a frown. Margit was almost a full head shorter than she, and here on the stairs they were eye to eye. Margit always had several boyfriends, she was always talking about them. Ursula sighed.

"There was a boy in Magdeburg, before the war. But my father said he was not worthy. Since then there has been no real time or stability—we moved so many times to stay ahead of the wars."

"Wait just a second, Ursula. You've been here for two years. And you've been working this awful schedule that prevents you from meeting anyone. You've had plenty of time to meet someone." She turned coyly. "Or even several some ones." She finished with a girlish giggle.

Ursula had little patience with girlish giggles. "Life is what it is, and life is what it shall be. And that's all there is to it. No more. No less. That's all life is." She shrugged and began to climb the stairs.

Margit trotted past Ursula and once again blocked her path. "That's your father talking. The famous Eeyore Volz. The man with the darkest disposition in town."

"He's a very practical man, Margit. He's provided for us even in the worst of times, since before Magdeburg. You know he got my mother and me out of the city before the siege. He sold everything, cancelled his lease, and moved away. He had the foresight to act before..."

Margit grew quiet. "I had a cousin and an uncle there."

"My father is very smart, Margit. We were in three different cities and towns before we moved to Magdeburg. In each one of them, we moved out before something terrible happened. Papa was able to figure it out, before it happened. We think he is very smart, and that has kept us alive and together as a family."

"But he never smiles. I have never once seen him smile. People stay away from him."

"People don't talk to Papa very often. Mr. Blackwell, who owns the funeral home where Papa works, said most people won't talk to you much when they find out what you do. I'm sure that's why. And we never really had many friends, no matter where we lived. Papa said that suits him just fine, too."

Margit put her hands on her hips and looked Ursula in the eyes. Her short red hair and freckles made her look far younger than she really was. "What am I going to do with you, Ursula Volz?"

"There is nothing you need to do. Things are just fine the way they are."

Margit turned and began bouncing up the stairs. "Maybe. Maybe not." She turned and looked back at Ursula. "But I am not going to let you be an old maid without getting you to have some fun." She skipped off around the corner.

Ursula stood on the stairs for a moment before heading up after Margit. Together they found the spill in the hallway, and then, as usual, Ursula continued to the third floor of the mansion, where they told her the "ballroom" used to be.

Rolf Burger, the night guard, was at his post. He had a tiny desk and chair with a logbook where people signed in and out. His post at the top of the stairs put him between a heavy door and the hallway. Ursula was never really sure why they had the extra guard up here. The Department of Economic Affairs had something to do with money, she supposed from the name. Although she never saw any money there. As he saw her coming around the corner, he was already taking the keys off of his belt.

"So how is my fine, beautiful Ursula Volz this evening?" Rolf Burger was pushing sixty-five; he had no teeth, and a twinkle in his eye. A mixer. That's what Ursula's mother had said when she described him. A mixer. Mostly harmless.

"I am fine, Herr Burger."

"What's a beautiful girl like you doing in a place like this?"

"Working at her job, Herr Burger." She signed in on his log book. As he let her in, purposely he brushed against her as he backed the door open. He grinned a toothless smile at her as she stepped back. She cast her eyes at the floor and went into the hallway. There was a long hall with a half-dozen doors on both sides. She sat about her tasks as quickly and efficiently as possible, methodically working through one office at a time. Trash, feather dust, sweep, repeat. She settled into a calm rhythm, so when she opened one of the doors to what she thought was an empty office, she was startled to see a huskily built man hunched in front of one of the computers. The screen cast the only light in the office.

"Oh. Excuse me. I didn't know you were here. I can come back later—"

"No. That's quite all right. I don't think we've met before. What's your name?" He stood.

Ursula was still surprised by the up-timer forwardness. The man was very friendly; all up-timers seemed to be. At least the ones she had met. She quickly looked at his hand to see if he had one of the up-time marriage bands. She was relieved when she saw he did. When her eyes went back to his face, they were observing her carefully. She immediately felt the blush, and looked at the floor. "Ursula Volz, sir."

"My name is Grady. Dennis Grady. Nice to meet you, Ursula. I'm sorry I startled you. I was just finishing up some work. You can just skip my office for tonight."

She had heard of him. His wife Maureen was the head of what was called the Department of Social Services. Grady himself was rumored to have been a policeman before he came to their Department of Economic Affairs.

"Yes, sir." She backed out of the room and closed the door. In a few more minutes she had completed the floor, and she headed for the guard station. She opened the door to find Rolf sipping a hot beverage, with an up-time device steaming in the background. "Cup of coffee?"

Ursula's eyebrows raised. "Where in the world did you get that thing?"

"One of the ladies in the kitchen gave it to me. She said it was broken, so I took it to the tinker. You know we have one here now? He fixed it. The original glass is broken, so I use this ceramic mug. It only makes two cups at a time. This is the first night I have brought it to work."

"That's nice, Rolf. It smells good, too."

From behind her a masculine voice spoke up. "It sure does, Rolf. Smells darn good." Dennis Grady inhaled through his nose, enjoying the aroma.

"Hi, Mr. Grady. Do you want some too?"

Grady looked at the mug wishfully. "Going to have to take a pass. I need that stuff in the morning, not last thing at night before I go to bed. Sure smells good though."

Rolf's rubbery face lit up, and he turned to Ursula. "I have made this for my Ursula tonight, too. She knows I am in love with her, but she will never acknowledge it."

Ursula blushed and looked at the floor, as the old mercenary soldier flirted shamelessly. "Herr Burger, you are full of—poop, as the Americans say." She looked up at him and smiled, like she usually did. "How is your wife at home? I hear she was feeling ill last week? And your grandchildren, how are they?" She quickly glanced over to Herr Grady, and he smiled at her. She blushed again.

Rolf put his hand to his heart and looked crushed. "Oh, Ursula, what am I to do? You are about the only person who comes up here to see me at night. You never ask about how poor old Rolf is doing, you ask about my wife, my grandchildren, but not poor old Rolf. What am I to do?" His rubbery face was pouting and grinning all at the same time.

"Herr Burger. I ask about your wife and grandchildren to remind you it is not polite to flirt with younger women, especially single younger women. One of these days I will tell your wife how you are a shameless flirt with me."

The active rubbery grin left Rolf's face, and left only a pout with twinkling eyes remaining. "She already knows I'm an old goat, my dear." He laughed. "Just don't tell Eeyore, he might look at me and after a while I would jump off the ring wall cliff, I would be so depressed." He continued to grin.

Rolf seldom mentioned her father. Her mild irritation with the old guard was usually playful, but tonight, between him and Margit, Grady, and the spill, she'd had about enough. "My father is a good man who provides an important service to the town. He is not this 'Eeyore'; he is wise. And you should remember that, Herr Burger."

He looked hurt, his pout disappeared, and his eyes softened. "I meant no offense; it's just he is always so pessimistic. So sad. And it rubs off on you too, my dear; you are too young for that. Live a little, have some fun. Soon you will be old like me, and your life will be gone." He brightened and sat with mock suggestiveness on his stool. "However, I am not dead yet, my dear. Come and sit on my lap and—"

She turned on her heel and stormed down the stairs, leaving the two men. She was headed for the basement where she could cool off and put her equipment away. She knew she shouldn't let Rolf get to her that way, especially in front of an important up-timer. When she came down the first floor steps, she saw Margit sitting casually on the guard's desk, swinging her feet. She stopped at the bottom of the stairs and looked at Margit. Happy, carefree Margit.

And she was old stick-in-the-mud Ursula.

Ursula thought.

She made a decision.

Quickly, before Ursula could change her mind, she stalked over to where Margit was sitting, still swinging her legs like a ten-year-old. "Tonight," she whispered darkly to Margit, "we go out after work."

As Ursula walked away from Margit and Marcus, she turned and looked back. Both looked stunned.

☆ ☆ ☆

"Hey, everyone. I want you to meet my friend Ursula. Everyone, say hi to Ursula!" The little Sycamore Street Pub erupted in smiles and "Hello, Fräulein Ursula" from everyone who was there. Margit pushed Ursula from behind, and she stumbled into the room. She hadn't been in a place like this since she had been asked to fetch her father from a pub when she was a girl. She couldn't have been more than six or seven. She remembered the smell of the stale beer spilled on the coarse wood floor, the almost choking cloud of tobacco smoke, and the close feeling of the air inside. She hesitated again, and began to turn toward the door. Margit grabbed her and spun her back around.

"No, you don't, girl. You said you were coming in here with me, and I am making you keep your word."

"I have kept my word. I have come in. Now I want to leave."

"Not until you have one drink, and meet my new boyfriend. I know he has friends here tonight. He is *sooooo* cute. He's French, you know. I think he's a spy." Margit giggled at Ursula. "C'mon, just one drink."

"Why would you go out with him if you thought he was a spy?"

"Don't be silly. Almost everyone in here is a spy. For one side or the other, sometimes three or four sides at once. Good Lord, Ursula, if they threw all of the spies out of Grantville, there wouldn't be enough men to go around."

"But, spies, Margit? It doesn't seem right to fraternize with the spies."

"Follow me." Margit took her in tow, and dragged her toward a table in the back of the dimly lit bar. "I want you to meet someone."

"But, but—"

Margit dragged her to a table with three men sitting around it. One was older, maybe in his mid-thirties, tall and with a handsome face. At least the amount of face she could see in the dim lighting of the lamps. The other two were younger, in their early- or mid-twenties. They were dressed in plain clothing. Not something a laborer would wear, but more like traveling clothes. Practical, and not fancy. They all knew Margit. One of the younger men stood as Margit approached.

"Here you are, my dear Margit. Who's your most charming friend? Is this the beautiful Ursula we have been hearing about?" Ursula was glad it was dark, as she could feel her face glowing with embarrassment.

"Francois, this is why I love you. You are the consummate male."

"Is it my French accent, or my other . . . 'special powers of love' . . . that make you love me so?"

Margit drew herself up to her full five feet, and presented the Frenchman with a visage as haughty as a diminutive German farm girl could possibly make, and said. "If you think you are ever getting into my knickers without a betrothal, Francois, then you have not been paying attention these last two months." The other two at the table laughed out loud, and Francois looked hurt.

"I only have eyes for you, Margit."

"Nice try, Francois. The answer is still no."

The other men within earshot laughed as loud as the two who were at the table. Margit grabbed a chair from nearby, shoved it up to the table between the older man and Francois, and pushed Ursula unceremoniously onto the seat. "Sit here, girl. You have met Francois, across from you is Pitor, and next to you is Ian." Ursula recovered enough to respond with a bit of dignity. "Herr Ian. Herr Pitor, how very nice to meet you both." She turned to Margit. "Can we go now?"

Margit plopped herself down on Francois' lap and put her arms around his neck. "Not yet. You promised to have a drink first. Who's buying it?" She looked at Ian and nodded. "I think its Ian's turn at the bar."

Ian nodded in her direction, and replied with a subtle hint of sarcasm. "Of course, Margit, anything for you." He turned to Ursula. He seemed a little more reserved than the other two, and he had a distinguished-sounding English accent, very different from the up-timers. "Ursula, what can I get for you?"

His gaze was gentle but penetrating. His voice had a lyrical quality that surprised her. Masculine and wise. Not wise like her father, but wise is a different way. Worldly, strong. She caught herself blushing, and instantly felt like a duck out of water, awkward and stumbling around on webbed feet. She desperately tried to think of what she should order. She felt rising panic. Then he spoke again.

"Tell you what. I'll get you what I think you might like. I'll order for you. Will that be all right?"

She was certain her blush would be illuminating the room, and everyone at the table could hear her heart thumping loudly in her chest. Then she thought of Rolf, the guard at the mansion. Ursula was determined not to be an old maid, not if she could help it. She took a breath, found the will, and looked up at Ian. "Th-thank you. That would be very nice."

"No, I don't think so Ian," interrupted Margit. She turned to Ursula. "The last time he ordered for me, he came back with a tankard of some homegrown redeye made by the Haygood clan. Almost knocked me off of my chair with the first drink."

Ian looked rather betrayed at the accusation. "That was a drink for you, Margit. This lady is obviously very different, and respectable. I was going to get her one of the house pilsner, like the Yanks drink." He stood and turned to go to the bar, subtly winking at Ursula as he rose from his seat.

Margit shifted in Francois' lap. "Did he just say I'm not respectable?"

"I'm sure not," replied Francois with a grin. "However, you may remember the Haygood Redeye was meant to be sipped. As I recall, my love, you took a prodigious swig the first time he gave it to you." He turned to the others at the table. "It wasn't pretty."

Everyone laughed, including Ursula, who gasped when she realized she was having fun! Her! Ursula Volz, the one who never had any fun. The daughter of Eeyore Volz. She was still frightened, shy, even overwhelmed . . . but. She was having fun. A gleeful and satisfied smile was creeping onto her face when she turned and looked at Ian, returning to the table with their drinks. Her heart started thumping again, quite on its own accord.

June 1635, Grantville

Karol Volz was not feeling like a happy man. That, by itself, was perfectly normal. Karol Volz was never happy. But today, very early in the dark of the morning, he was more unhappy than usual, to the point of upset. Over the past two months, his daughter Ursula had been coming home from work later than was normal. It started out just once in a while at first, then it became more and more frequent. Now, for the first time, she had stayed out for five nights in a row. She always helped her mother with the sewing, just as she should, without fail. She always made it home, but she smelled of pipe smoke and beer. Karol knew she was meeting friends after work, at a small pub called the Sycamore Street Pub, which as one could tell from the clever name, was located on Sycamore Street. Karol harrumphed. This wasn't the sort of thing a woman should do no matter how old. She said she was with her co-workers, and staying out late was an American tradition she needed to follow. But enough was enough. He had not suffered and wandered war-torn Germany to bring his daughter to a place where all she did was drink and carouse. It was not right. Behaving in such a way was weak, and could lead to complacency. His family was not weak, and they would never be complacent. Not as long as he was alive.

Granted, the two years spent in Grantville had been the best in many years. It was comfortable, they had enough to eat, and he had steady employment building elegant wooden coffins which occasionally challenged his talents as a cabinetmaker. He was well paid. They had central heating in their tiny apartment. Plumbing from the twenty-first century. It was very comfortable.

They had no friends and only knew a few people, and he liked it that way. If you became too settled, you became weak, which led to being complacent, which inevitably led to tragedy. Always vigilant, always prepared to survive. That was the struggle of life in this time, and anyone who thought differently was a fool.

He heard the sounds of conversation at the door in the hallway. Quietly he picked up the sputtering candle and moved to the door. He put his head against it to listen.

"...nice time as usual, Ian. Thank you for walking me home again. You don't have to do it, though. I was walking home for two years before I met you."

"As always, it's my pleasure to do so." There was a pause.

Karol opened the door and looked at the two of them. Ian was holding his daughter's hand and was bending to kiss it. The candle held below Karol's countenance made it look as if his disembodied head was floating in the darkness. Both Ian and Ursula jumped back, Ian dropped her hand.

"Papa! This-this is a surprise."

He responded with a small grunt.

"Papa, have you ever met Ian? Ian, this is my Papa, Karol Volz. Papa, this is Ian. He is a-a friend."

Another small grunt. He looked at this Ian fellow, slowly, up and down. Karol didn't like the way he was dressed, the way he stood, or the way he smelled. He liked nothing about the man. He sounded foreign. Foreigners are never a good sign.

Ian tuned to Karol and extended his hand. "I'm very pleased

to meet you, Herr Volz. I've heard many things about you. Your daughter says you're a wonderful man, very intelligent."

Karol let the man's hand hang in the air, and raised his candle to the man's face to get a good look. He was handsome in a way. Which made it all the more improbable his intentions toward Ursula were honorable. Karol gave a slightly more definitive grunt which registered his displeasure, then looked at his daughter and tossed his head in the direction of the door. She immediately went in, leaving him and Ian alone in the doorway. Karol gestured for the Englishman to come closer, and he whispered a monotone into his ear.

"If you do anything to hurt her, you will pay."

Karol leaned back and again put the candle up to the face of the Englishman, and watched for a reaction. The fact there was none told Karol all he needed to know. *He's masking his reactions, his intentions are far from honorable. He is a skilled liar.* Karol kept his face passive as he read the man's reactions. As he brought the candle back to his face, he said simply and flatly. "Understand?"

"Perfectly." Ian then looked past Karol, into the darkness of the apartment where Ursula was waiting, out of sight. "I will see you on Monday night, Ursula. Thank you for a wonderful evening."

"Thank you," replied Ursula timidly from the darkness, as Ian retreated down the hallway.

Karol closed the door and grunted again, softly, with worry. He held the candle below his drooping face, and turned to seek out Ursula, who appeared out of the shadows. Without changing expression, he simply said, "I forbid you to see him."

Ursula whispered angrily. "You can't do that. Not here. Not in Grantville. Things are different here. *I* am different here."

"There is no discussion. I forbid you to see him."

"Papa. I am old enough to make these decisions for myself. It's important I keep seeing him; I'm enjoying life for a change, Papa. Can you understand?"

Karol stepped toward Ursula so quickly, she retreated a step. He whispered harshly. "That man is false. He will hurt you."

"So what? So what if he hurts me? That's my choice, not yours. You don't think I know he's full of... of—poop most of the time?"

"Keep your voice down. You'll wake your mother."

"Do you understand why this is important to me, Papa? I need to do this. I need to do this now. Here in this place. Grantville. This is our home now, Papa."

"Our home is where I say it will be!" His voice was barely contained. "We're staying here for now. It's comfortable. Too comfortable I think, for our own good. It has clouded your judgment. The evil world is still out there, Ursula. And it can come roaring down the street any time of the day or night, like the horsemen of the apocalypse. We need to be prepared to move on at a moment's notice, fleeing before whatever army or plague is coming next. There is always an army or a plague coming. Being involved with people only slows you down. It clouds your judgment. Stay separate from the community, and live off of it. You must not become attached."

"I don't want to be a parasite on where I live. I want to live here, not just exist. I want to be part of this community, to grow. This is a special place."

"Special? All you do is pick up people's trash in the evening."

"You just don't understand, Papa. You just don't understand."

"You are wrong, Ursula. I do understand. I understand perfectly well what you wish. It's you who fail to understand the consequences of what you wish for. You know I'm right. We've escaped from how many towns before they were destroyed? Three? That boy, back in Magdeburg. Is he alive now? No. He is dead in the ground. Rotting flesh, if there was any flesh left from the fires. What would have happened if we—or you—had stayed behind because of a feeling of fondness for him? Or his family? Or our neighbors?" He paused and looked at the candle, the single source of light in a very dark room. He took a breath and looked his daughter in the eyes. "There are two states of being. Life and death. Don't give me any religious crap. When you die, you go to the same place you were before you were born. Nothingness. So if we flee, if we live like parasites, it is because we must. To survive. To live."

He could see Ursula's eyes full of tears in the dim light, and she snuffled. "There's got to be more, Papa. There's got to be more…"

He placed the candle on the table, and put his strong arms around her. "There is no 'more.' Only family, and to survive. Stay away from him, and all the other entanglements and snares in this place. We must be able to think clearly."

"I can't, Papa."

"I will not leave you behind."

"You won't have to. When and if the time comes to leave, I

will be there with you and Mama. You have my word, Papa. My solemn oath. But I must keep seeing him. It is very important."

Karol broke the embrace, and looked at his daughter. Her features were difficult to make out in the light of the fading candle. "Is there something you are not telling me?"

"No, Papa."

"You are not with child?"

"NO, PAPA!" she gasped. "I would never. We would have to sue him for support for the child. That would be an entanglement."

"Go to sleep now. In the morning, in the light of day, this won't seem so bad. I have an errand I want you to run in the morning."

"Yes, Papa."

He grunted his goodnight.

Ursula squinted against the bright sunshine as she made her way into the heart of Grantville. Ollie Reardon's machine shop was easy to spot. It was one of the largest in town, near where the railroad tracks used to be, before they were torn up and used for the ironclads. The large metal-sided building was confusing, and she did not know where the office was located. There was a group of men outside one of the big roll-up doors, who looked to be taking a break. They all squatted on the ground, or perched on various pieces of scrap in the side yard of the shop. She timidly approached one of the men standing away from the others, reading.

"Excuse me. Can you tell me where to find the office? I have some hinges from my father . . ."

The man looked up from his reading, a thick book with very small printing. It looked to be some sort of a technical book, and he had been studying it closely. "Of course. It's right through the door here, and to the right, follow the path with the yellow lines, the office is just past the line boring machine and the old . . ." He stopped and looked at her expression. "Never mind, just follow me."

"Thank you, sir."

"No need to call me 'sir.' My name is Heinrich. Heinrich Fremd. Haven't seen you around town before."

They walked toward the door. "My name is Ursula. Ursula Volz. We have lived here for two years."

Heinrich got a twinkle in his eye. "That is a shocking name, Miss—it is 'Miss' isn't it—Volz?" She nodded, blushing slightly as they passed into the shop. "I guess you hear that joke all the time."

"What joke is that, Heinrich?"

"You know, Volts. Shocking? Volts can Hertz you? There have got to be a million of those up-timer jokes." The expression on her face must have given it away. "You have no idea what I am talking about, do you?"

"No, Heinrich, I don't."

"Seriously?"

Ursula felt mortified. If it had been two months ago, before she started going out after work, stretching herself, she would have fled this embarrassing encounter in tears. But today: "Heinrich. I—I . . . You are embarrassing me." The last part came out stronger than she meant it to, and poor Heinrich looked stunned.

Heinrich stopped and turned to her in the middle of the quiet shop. He was blushing. "I'm terribly sorry. I assumed you were an old Grantville hand after two years. Please forgive my forward behavior. I apologize, I'm not that sort of an oaf. Although I'm acting like it." He bowed at her briefly, as a courtier might, in the middle of the machine shop. "I must make it up to you. We need to start over. Could I buy you lunch tomorrow as an apology? Please?"

She saw the office door just ahead of her. "Thank you Herr Fremd. I appreciate the guidance. But I can make it to the office by myself now."

"And lunch? Tomorrow?"

She stopped with her hand on the doorknob to the office, and turned to him. "Why not? I'll meet you at Billy's Diner tomorrow at noon." She really liked the cute expression on his face, a combination of embarrassment, happiness, and now worry. What on earth could he be worried about? She went into the office and closed the door behind her, a quick glance told her he was still standing in the aisle, with the same dumb-cute look on his face.

The end-of-break bell rang, and men started going back to the machines. The bell shook Heinrich out of his trance. "What in the hell did you just do, Heinrich? You idiot." He started walking back to his machine, shaking his head slowly.

"Hey, hang on there a minute, Heinrich. You sure were nice to that young lady. Although she looked like she wanted to run away for a moment or two." His foreman, Grant Matowski, was flagging him down. "What did you say to her?"

"I made a stupid joke about her last name. It is Volz, so I made a very lame joke about volts and hertz—"

"Her name is Volz? Holy shit, it's true. Eeyore does have a daughter. Wait a second. You didn't ask her out did you?"

Heinrich shifted uncomfortably. "I had to, after I embarrassed her. Lunch is all. Billy's Diner tomorrow. And who is E-hore?"

Grant started laughing. "EE-Yore. You know, the melancholy donkey? Surely you know Eeyore Volz, the saddest man in town? Oh, I remember now. You don't go to funerals. Or church."

"Let's not start that again, Grant..."

Late August 1635, Grantville

Elsa Volz looked at her daughter across the kitchen table that doubled as a sewing table in their small apartment. The apartment, while very tiny, had one major advantage: the large south-facing window in the kitchen. The large window allowed Elsa and Ursula to sew from dawn to dusk. Elsa looked carefully at her daughter. She seemed very tired, her eyes were red, and there were circles under her eyes. He hands were steady, so Elsa knew it probably wasn't alcohol. She had lost weight. She came to bed late, and awoke before anyone else. Elsa leaned back from her work and looked out the window.

"You look tired, Ursula. Have you been feeling well?"

"I'm okay."

"Have you been sleeping well?"

"Enough."

"I see." Elsa went back to her sewing for several moments; the only sound was of rustling cloth. She put it aside again. This time she looked at her daughter, not out the window.

"Your father says you are 'dating' three men."

Ursula flinched. "Ouch. I stabbed myself with a needle. Silly me." She popped her thumb into her mouth, sucking on it to stop the small blood flow.

The room was very quiet now, and Elsa leaned forward toward her daughter. "Care to explain to me how you are dating three men? At the same time?"

"I am not 'dating' three men at the same time. Daddy is over-reacting. I have only seen two, and one of them only once. I don't know where he gets the third one."

"Go on."

"Well, you know about Ian. He's just a friend from work. He doesn't work there, but he hangs out at the place we go after work most of the time. We're just friends."

"Your father said he caught him kissing you?"

"That's silly. On the hand, yes. But he's English. They do that sort of thing."

"And what does this Englishman do to make a living?"

"Mother, it is not like I am planning on marrying him or anything. He's a student of sorts, and he does research about Grantville, and he corresponds with his home."

"So he has no normal job?"

"His job is not normal."

"And this mystery man from the south? The one who has a regular job at the machine shop? Who says his name is Fremd?"

"Has Daddy been following me?"

"He heard you went to lunch with him. Is this true?"

"Yes, Mama. It's true. But we met at a public place, and he just bought me lunch. He wanted to apologize to me for embarrassing me at the machine shop. He's really very sweet."

"Do you know he's not married, yet cares for three children? Three he 'adopted' after Magdeburg."

"He told me about it at lunch. He positively dotes on those children."

"Parents are known to do that now and again." Elsa trailed dry and loving humor through her last remark.

Ursula finally looked up and smiled. "I have heard that now and again, about parents."

They both went back to sewing for a while, and Elsa asked another question. This time there was no humor or kindness in her voice. "And the Jew?" Elsa watched her daughter's reaction. She seemed surprised, and yet frightened. Elsa's concern grew. "Your father says that you meet him right after work sometimes, but only for a while. What are you doing with a Jew in a dark alley? I have heard about them, and some of the things they do to good Christian women."

Her daughter sputtered. "I don't know what you are talking about. I know nothing about this Jew. Why would I do anything with one of them, mother? This is just silly."

Elsa leaned back in her chair and pushed a strand of graying hair out of her face. She sighed. "So you are not going to tell the truth about the Jew?"

"There's nothing to tell. You and Father are mistaken. So just drop it. Please, just drop it. Next you will have me as one of the emperor's concubines." Ursula stood up. "I will need to be at work soon. Tell Papa to stop following me. I gave him my word I would leave with you, if it came to it again. Isn't that enough?" Her voice started to rise, and Elsa's followed.

"No, that's not enough! Do not raise your voice to me."

"Then don't accuse me of meeting Jews in alleys!" She stopped, horrified she had yelled at her mother. She began to cry almost immediately. "I'm sorry, Mama. Please forgive me. Please. It's been hard these last few weeks for me. It's almost over. Please, do not be angry with me. I am a good and faithful daughter. You must understand. Please."

"But I don't understand. If you're in trouble, then you must talk to us. We can help."

"No. I can't. You can't. Please. Just leave me alone." With that, Ursula broke down and ran crying from the apartment, leaving Elsa frozen at the kitchen table.

Later, she spoke to Karol. He paced about the room after she related the story to him. "What's wrong with her? What's she doing?"

Karol stopped his pacing. "It's time to move again, away from here. If she's in trouble, then the best thing to do is to run away now, before whatever it is blows up. Gather up the money from the hiding places. We will change it to gold as soon as we get somewhere we can. I'm thinking Amsterdam. The lowlands are prospering with the peace. There are many opportunities. We'll do well, I am sure. We leave as soon as we can close accounts from the bank in the morning."

Elsa stood resignedly. "Very well. This was such a nice place."

"I liked it too. But we must survive. And to do so, we must move on. This is why we've no close ties. So we can pick up and move on without any encumbrances."

"Do we have to Karol? Do we have to leave? Let's wait until we see what happens. How bad can it be?"

"This isn't open for discussion. We leave tomorrow."

"Where's your partner tonight Ursula? She been having too much fun lately? Couldn't make it to work today?"

"She is just sick, Rolf. And that means more work for me. Let me be, so I can do my work."

"That's too bad." He pouted. "When are you going to make this old man happy? Will you ever say yes to me? A little smile? A quick peck on the cheek? I'm just a harmless old man. Come on, Ursula. When will it ever be?"

"Not tonight, Rolf, I have a lot to do. Please." She stepped past him and through the door, which he closed and locked behind her, as usual. She went in to the bathroom, flipped on the light, and started to clean it very quickly. While wiping off the mirror, her reflection caught her eye. Any other night, she would have ignored it. Tonight, she stopped and stared. The harsh fluorescent lighting in the white bathroom gave her face a hard and worn look. Her plain brown eyes had lines under them, and crow's feet at the edges. There were dark circles under her eyes, a too large jaw and a too large nose for her face. Her hair was pulled back with a scarf tied around the back of her head. It surprised her how old she looked. She spent several moments mesmerized by her face. Her expression then began to go from neutral to hardened. Her expression made her uncomfortable. Resolutely, she embraced the discomfort, turned, and headed out the door of the bathroom, flipping off the lights as she went.

She immediately went to the next to last office at the end of the hallway, and closed the door behind her. She then pulled up her dress, and began to bring objects out of the shift beneath. The first was a small flashlight, that she held in her mouth, the others she placed on the table. She then unwound two cables from beneath her shirt, a tiny one and a larger, thicker one. She crawled under the table where the tall box for the computer sat, then pulled the computer away from the wall to access the back. She unscrewed one of the thicker cables, and then inserted her own, routing it to the top of the table. The other cable, the extension cord, was plugged into a power strip, and into that cable, she inserted a fist-sized black box she knew was a power supply. That cord she quickly routed to the table top.

She scanned the tabletop with the small flashlight for the next items. A small flat blue box, with a slot in the front, and a small floppy disk. Into the blue box she plugged the cords. A light lit up on the blue box. She inserted the floppy into the computer on the floor, and turned on the power. The machine cranked slowly to life. She held her breath for a moment, and waited for the old one hundred megahertz machine to recognize the floppy, and start to boot from it.

It did. She started to breathe. She was focused, she had practiced long hours to understand all of the components, to be able to connect them in the dark.

She reached under her skirt again, and pulled four small square plastic boxes, removed the one hundred megabyte Zip disk (she remembered how she smiled at the funny name the first time she heard it) and placed it into the blue Zip drive where she had already connected the cables. She then removed the floppy from the computer, and restarted it.

While the machine slowly rebooted, she went to adjacent offices and began to quickly dump the trash cans into her cart. It would not do to not have the office at least partially clean, anything else she could blame on the fact Margit was not in tonight. She completed six offices by the time the computer was ready to be used. She glanced at the locked door, where Rolf sat outside. Up to this point, she had been too busy to be frightened. Now came the hard part. Sitting in front of the computer and copying files to the external Zip drive.

Since the security to the machine was bypassed with her floppy, she was able to access the files. But it took time. Time to locate the right files, time to copy the files to the discs, and time to remove any evidence of her being there. Sitting and looking at the screen, with little else to do than wait for the process, her nervousness began to build.

She scanned the file tree for the files labeled "NSICSH," and copied them to the zip drive. Nasi Cash, is what that stood for, she knew. It was a slow transfer. While other files were transferring, she dashed out and grabbed waste cans from three other offices and emptied them. She copied other files onto the disks, swapping them out until they were full. She knew it was taking too much time. She would be in the security area longer than normal. And that could raise suspicions if someone reviewed the logbook. But there was little she could do, except wait for the files to copy, excruciatingly slowly, to the external drive.

The contents of the computer looked like mostly spreadsheet files filled with financial data. When the last Zip disk filled, she began to disassemble the devices and reconnect the system to the original configuration. She placed the disks, power supply and the blue Zip drive into the pockets sewn into her shift. She shut the computer down, and then restarted it. She only had to wait for it to boot up again, and then shut it down for the last time, understanding this action would erase evidence of her presence.

While the machine was rebooting, she emptied the last of the trash cans, and was in the hallway on her way back to the open office, when Ursula heard the key turn in the lock of the hallway door. She suddenly stopped, halfway back to the computer, her back to the door. She heard the hallway door open, and Rolf called to her. "Ursula? Miss Volz? What are you doing in there tonight, my beautiful girl? You are ten minutes longer than usual."

Her heart, which was finally beginning to settle down, started beating wildly again. "I-I'm just about finished Rolf, I will be right there."

"You are done in here for tonight, and don't argue with me. You have been working too hard, young lady, and you need to go home." He walked into the hallway to her cart, and began to drag it out of the room. "Wait until Margit comes back here, I am going to give her a piece of my mind, leaving you to do all the work. Let's go. Now."

She stayed still, trying to figure out how to get back to the office where the computer was still on. She had to turn it off, and she had to do it without raising Rolf's suspicions. She turned to Rolf. "I just have the one office to finish, Rolf. Let me finish that one." She pointed to the open door.

"Okay, young lady. But hurry it up. If you are in here longer than normal, I need to write a report. And I hate paperwork."

"Oh. I d-didn't know!"

He grabbed her cart and began pushing it toward the door. "Close that door and come along."

She swallowed and rushed into the office, grabbed the computer mouse and clicked the on-screen buttons to start the minute-long shutdown sequence on the machine. She quickly turned and backed through the door, trying to make sure the computer was really going to shut down. It seemed to be. She turned around and bumped into Rolf.

"Ursula, is everything okay with you tonight? You don't seem like yourself."

Her heart started to race again, and she could feel herself

trembling. Rolf's eyes looked her over, and then went to the office door behind her. He got a questioning look in his eye, and moved her to the side. His hand went to the knob of the still open door.

"You are right Rolf, I haven't been feeling very well lately. Maybe I've got what Margit has. Not been sleeping well, either."

His hand still on the doorknob, he looked at her with a question in his eyes. She could see the light from the monitor inside the dark office, as the slow computer went through its shutdown sequence. Her mind was racing, and her tension was building to a panic. *Oh, God. He is going to see the computer on, and that will be the end of me.* She stepped back slightly and her knees felt weak.

"What is the matter Ursula? Are you ill?" Rolf stepped away from the door and went to her. She took another involuntary step back.

"I-I don't feel well, nervous or something, I guess. I think I need to sit—yes, sit down, and some water please?"

He took her hand. "Lord, girl. You are trembling. Come. Sit in my chair. Out there on the landing. Can you make it?"

"I think so." She glanced over her shoulder at the open door, where the computer was still shutting down. She could see the glowing light in the office from the monitor. "Yes. Let me sit in your chair." He led her down the hall to his chair behind the tiny desk. She eased herself into the chair, still trembling slightly, forcing herself to breathe normally.

Rolf looked at her with kindness. "You have been working way too hard. A pretty young lady like you should not have to work so hard. It leads to a shorter life, let me tell you. My brother worked very hard, and he didn't live to see fifty. Simply dropped dead in his shop one day. That's what his widow told me. Me, I don't plan to have that problem, and so far it's working." He chuckled and then smiled at her. "Can I get you something to drink? Water maybe? I have a little coffee left?"

She looked past him in the hall, trying to see if the glow from the monitor was still dully illuminating the office. "Yes. Water, please."

"Okay, coming right up." He went into the bathroom with an empty coffee mug. "I need to rinse this out..." He disappeared into the bathroom. She could hear the water running. She looked down the hallway and could tell the monitor was still on. The distance was too far for her to get up and close the door before Rolf returned. She tried to swallow, but her mouth was too dry. Rolf emerged with the mug of water. "Here, drink this."

She took the water from him with both hands and drank greedily, draining the mug. She gave it back to him with both hands, so he would not see her trembling. "Thank you, Rolf."

"You are welcome. Stay here, I will get your cart and close the doors." Ursula watched helplessly as he turned and strode down the hallway to the slightly open office door, looked briefly inside, and closed the door. Ursula gave an inward sigh of relief. The computer had shut off. Rolf then pushed her janitor cart with the trash out of the corridor, and locked the door behind him.

Rolf looked at her with a scornful expression. "Young lady, you are done working for tonight. I'll take the trash and the cart down later. Go home and get some rest. Old Rolf knows the dangers of working too hard. One uncle on my wife's side worked too hard, and he didn't even make it to forty. Of course, Tilly's army burning his village and killing him might have had something to do with it. But still—he worked too hard before that." He looked at her with a concerned expression.

Ursula acknowledged his concern, and managed to return a small friendly smile. "Thank you, Rolf. I think I will go home now."

"Do you need help going down the stairs? Don't worry about signing out, I'll take care of it. I can't leave the floor, but I can call Marcus up here to help."

"No. No. That's not necessary. I can make it down. The water and just sitting for a moment helped. Thanks, Rolf."

"And don't work so hard. When you're well and return, I will tell you about my cousin—"

"—Thank you, Rolf." Ursula turned and eased down the stairs, increasing her speed to a quiet scurry as she distanced herself from Rolf. She felt one of the cables around her waist working loose. She slowed to snug it under her clothes. At the top of the first floor landing, she nearly ran head long into Dennis Grady, while she was tugging at her shirt.

"Easy there, Ursula. It's Ursula, isn't it?"

Ursula's hand went to the top of her blouse and clenched the neck. She looked at the floor. "Y-yes, Mr. Grady." Her other hand went to her lower back, where she could feel the cable coming loose. Part of it was hanging out of the back of her shirt. "I am sorry, sir. I don't feel well tonight, and my partner did not show up for work." At least it was easier to take a deep breath without the tightness of the cables.

"I hate it when that happens. Is old Rolf awake up there? I don't want to scare him too much. I came to get some paperwork out of my office for a meeting tomorrow."

"Rolf, sir, is very conscientious. He doesn't sleep on the job."

"Ursula, look at me please." She slowly looked up to meet his eyes. She thought he must certainly hear her heart beating. His gaze was penetrating, his face was analytical.

"He knows!" her brain shouted. *He knows something is wrong. I can't keep looking at those eyes. They have to know. He must know.* She dropped her eyes to the floor to escape the scrutiny.

He looked at her in silence a moment longer. "You're right. I don't think you look at all well. Are you done for the night?"

"Yes, Mr. Grady, sir."

"Please call me Dennis."

"Yes, Mr. Dennis, sir."

He rolled his eyes and chuckled. "Just Dennis, Ursula. Just Dennis. Okay?"

"Okay. D-Dennis. I'm done mostly for this evening. I didn't do much on the second floor. That's Margit's."

"Then go home. Now." He put his hand to her forehead. "You're warm. And trembling. Get out of here before you infect all of us."

"Yes, sir. I was just going." She backed away from him on the stairs. "Thank you—Dennis." She continued backing away, and he continued to watch her. Still observing, still analytical. She smiled at him a last time as he abruptly broke his gaze. He then turned and trotted up the stairs.

She quickly adjusted the dangling cables under her shirt, and went down the last stairs to where Marcus sat with his logbook. She quickly signed out, noting the time, and left the building by the back door.

She had done it. She was out of the mansion. Free and clear. She felt pride about what she had just done, and at the same time ashamed. *I have lied to everyone who has been nice to me since I came here. I have lied to my parents, my friends.* She had reached the end of the sidewalk, and started down the street. Tears welled up in her, and she fought to keep the feelings under control. Pride. Grief. Passion. Betrayal. They all started to boil and conflict like a toxic soup, as she increased her distance from the mansion.

"URSULA! STOP! STOP RIGHT THERE!" It sounded like Marcus, the downstairs guard. She stopped in mid-stride. She fought with the emotions already there, as they mixed with the overwhelming reoccurrence of fear. She felt physically sick. She swallowed bile in her throat. She slowly turned around and could see Marcus and Dennis Grady walking quickly toward her. She involuntarily reached for her waist, to check the cables wrapped there. She felt one dangling out.

She felt an odd sense of relief sweeping over her, pushing every other emotion aside. *I am caught. Finally, it can be over.* She strangely welcomed the capture. They trotted up to her, and Marcus grabbed her by the upper arm. She drew away, but could not break away. She pulled her hands to her chest. She was unable to say anything.

"Hold on a moment, Ursula. You're not going anywhere." It was Dennis Grady, and he was—was smiling at her? "You're not going anywhere without this sweater. It's getting cold out here. Feels like fall. Take this, you are sick enough. Okay? It is too big for you I'm sure; it's mine."

Somehow, she wasn't sure how, she managed to say "Thank you, Dennis. This is very nice of you." She choked back a confused half sob. She saw the two men look at her, and then smile a "we-did-the-right-thing" smile at each other. She put the sweater on. It was almost the size of a nightshirt, and hid the dangling cable. She gave them a damp, teary smile. "I must go. Th-thank you."

When she was out of sight of the mansion, and alone on the dark street, she started to sob quietly to herself. To anyone walking by, it sounded like a cry of grief.

Ursula walked up to the door of the small house her three foreign friends were renting, and rapped on the door. Pitor, the one from Poland who was her computer "guru" as Ian called him, answered the door. She went into the living room where the curtains were drawn, and went to the table where Ian and Francois were already sitting. Ian's eyes were bright with anticipation. "Did you get them for me, my love?"

"Of course, I did. Did you doubt me?"

Ian turned to Pitor. "How did she do?"

Pitor smiled. "She was amazing. I thought she was going to be captured by the guards, they told her to stop outside the mansion. But she kept her cool, because they just gave her a sweater, didn't they Ursula?" She nodded. "This is a brave woman."

She smiled at Pitor. "Thank you. It was nice to know you were nearby."

"You're welcome. May I have the things? We need to look at them to know if they are valid or not."

"If you don't mind, I will excuse myself and remove all of this hardware." She went down a hallway, and quickly removed the cables, drives and the valuable disks from their hiding places in her clothing. She went next door to the bedroom, where a computer was set up on a desk. Pitor took the items from her, and started to reconnect it to the system.

"You were right, Pitor. The system there was very slow, compared to yours. It almost got me caught upstairs by old Rolf. But the boot disc worked perfectly. You really are amazing, Pitor."

"I have been doing little else than studying the technology for the last six months. It is complex, and I certainly don't know everything about how it works, but I have learned enough to get by."

Pitor was starting his computer, and he eagerly put in the first disc.

Ursula cleared her throat to get their attention. "How is Margit?"

"How is she, Francois?" asked Ian.

Francois looked and smelled like he had been drinking before he arrived. He rubbed his eyes and shook his head to clear it. "She'll be sleeping this one off for a while yet. We were drinking Haygood Redeye. She matched me shot for shot, until she passed out. Margit could never resist a drinking challenge. But one thing about that kind of alcohol. It can be cut with water, and you never know it." He smiled mischievously. "Mine was watered, hers wasn't. Still, I have a headache. And I'm not looking forward to riding hard in the morning. I will miss the little fireball, even though I never got into her knickers. Damn!"

Ian turned to the other two men. "Gentlemen. I believe we agreed once we had possession of the information, we would never be apart. Not that we are dishonest men, understand, but while we are together it removes any... temptation." He looked at his partners, and they looked back with smiles and nods.

Pitor grinned as his computer started. "It looks like it is here. This is amazing. We are rich! Here is the file, just as promised."

Both of the men stepped forward eagerly. "Open the file. Open it!" They waited as the computer buzzed and the file started to open. It then stopped.

"It requires a password to access the file," groaned Pitor. "This was not supposed to be there."

Ursula cleared her throat at the men. "Ahem." The three turned from the computer screen and looked at her. "Go to the last zip disc. There are a couple of text files I found, with lists of passwords in them. I think they are called 'PSSWRD dot txt.' Not very clever if you ask me." She smiled at Ian. He turned and embraced her.

"My love! You astound me."

She blushed and looked at the floor. "I just remembered what Pitor said about how up-time people were very careless with passwords and such. I checked around the office like we planned and I couldn't find any. But I found them on the hard drive. At least I think I did."

Pitor had his head down on the computer, and after a while, gave a little whoop. "That's it! We're into the file! I am making copies now. On floppies, zip discs and the hard drive. That should cover us."

Francois came out of the kitchen with four beers. "This calls for a toast. To Ursula. The brave, beautiful, and very smart lady to whom we owe it all. Cheers."

Ian embraced her, and gave her a gentle kiss. "Why do you look so sad, my dear?"

"Because you are all going to leave in the morning, and I will be very lonely. At least until you send for me, Ian."

Ian looked into her eyes. "I'm very proud of you, my love. I'm going to miss you. You know I'll send for you the moment I get back to my estates in England. There are many things I must do there before I bring you to me. You understand, don't you?"

Ursula sighed. "I'll wait for your letter, and leave my family in an instant. Do you have my traveling money, for when you send for me? You said I would have it now, Ian. Do you have it?"

He smiled the warm smile of his at Ursula, which certainly melted her heart, and reached for an envelope in his case below the table. He handed it to her. "This is your money for traveling, my dear."

She blushed and turned away, then quickly looked into his eyes and chewed on her lower lip with sadness. "The next time we walk arm in arm, it will be in London, at your estate. Please don't wait long to send for me."

"It will be as soon as humanly possible, my love." He released his embrace. His eyes were shining at her with pride. "May I have the pleasure of walking you home for one last time, my love? I am afraid we will have some company." He kissed her hand, and turned with a flourish. He proffered his hand, she accepted with a curtsy. He then took her hand and led her through the door. As they hit the outdoors, the air felt crisp. Fall was coming and there was a hint of it in the night air. They waited as Pitor and Francois locked the house. They each had a floppy disc in their pockets, just to be sure.

They joined arms and began walk toward town, with Francois and Pitor following them. Ursula looked up at the moon, and sighed again. "Will you send for me in the spring, Ian? Is that when?"

"Most likely, my love."

She touched the envelope tucked into her waist. "I hope I can wait that long."

He leaned over to her. "We English have a saying about such things. 'Good things come to those who wait patiently.' That will be you."

She giggled excitedly. "Yes! I am so looking forward to seeing London. The holes in the tower walls are quite a tourist attraction now, I hear."

"You are right, my dear."

"Oh, Ian." She put her arm around him, and felt the blade he sometimes carried inside his coat. She looked at him quizzically.

"It is a precaution, Ursula. Nothing more. We have all worked hard to get this information. We can't let anyone else have them, can we?"

"You are so wise. I knew the first time I saw your face in the pub. 'That is a wise and caring man,' I said to myself. Hard to believe it was only three months ago. It seems like a lifetime." She looked over her shoulder at the two men following at a respectful distance. "There is no chance of us to be alone tonight, then, is there, Ian? Not with them behind all the time."

Ian leaned to her again. "Sadly, my love, it's true. I rather wish you had said something earlier about being alone together, before tonight. There just isn't enough time, I'm afraid."

She shrugged. "I can wait until London. We will be together then."

"Over my dead body, you good for nothing piece of—" It was Eeyore Volz charging out of the blackness of night. His powerful arms took Ian down to the ground. There was not time for him to draw a blade. They began to struggle.

Ursula's first impulse was to scream. She cut off the impulse, and nearly crashed head-on into Pitor and Francois as they were coming to Ian's aid. She hissed at her father to stop. Francois and Pitor dove in on the side of Ian. Ian then stood and drew his blade.

"No!" hissed Ursula. "You can't do this. I will scream if you do. The entire neighborhood will hear us and we will all go to prison." Francois and Pitor had by now pinned her father to the ground. Ian knelt down with the blade in his hand.

"Ian!" she hissed again, "you mustn't!"

"Quiet, Ursula." He turned to the men struggling on the ground. "Stop it and get up. I have this blade, I will use it if I need to. You must be quiet." The struggling stopped and the three men got up, disheveled and dirty. Karol had his arms pinned behind him.

"If you hurt her, so help me . . ."

"If you make any more noise, I will hurt *you*. Let's all be quiet, and finish a nice walk home, shall we? It is only just around the corner." The little group formed up, and began to move toward Karol's home.

Francois and Pitor frog marched Karol, while Ian took Ursula's arm, still holding the knife. Her heart was racing again, as she tried to figure an angle.

Karol stage whispered to Ursula. "Didn't I tell you getting involved would lead to no good. Didn't I tell you this piece of shit is no good? Did you listen to me?"

She felt Ian go tense, and he turned toward her father. "Papa. Be quiet. Please, he has the knife."

They walked along in silence for a moment, until Ian lowered his head to her, and asked, "Why didn't you scream?"

Her knees went weak, and she almost stumbled. "I just didn't. I didn't want you or Papa hurt. Didn't want to go to prison."

He nodded, and they continued to walk. Their home was just around the corner.

"You are not going to hurt us, are you, Ian?" She felt him stiffen slightly.

"No." He stiffened some more, turned and growled. "It's right up here. Not a word, Eeyore."

They rounded the corner and headed for the building. They began to cross the street, when a Grantville police cruiser came slowly around the corner at the far end of the block. It headed toward them, met them halfway across the street and stopped, blocking their way to the little house.

"Evening, Officer," said Ian calmly. "Can we help you?"

Ursula noted the officer was a down-timer, and actually quite small for a policeman. He looked familiar. He was looking them over carefully from his seat behind the wheel. Ursula watched him look at each of them, and his eyes settled on Karol. "What's wrong with him? He looks pretty pissed off. What is going on here?"

"Actually this is my Papa, Karol Volz." The officer looked as though the name didn't register. "You know, Eeyore. He works at the funeral home, building caskets. You certainly have seen him at funerals. He's had a little too much to drink this morning, sir, and these gentlemen were helping me get him home." She turned away from the police car, and looked to her father with pleading eyes. "Isn't that right, Papa?"

When Ursula looked at him, she saw the rage that was building inside him. "He just needed a little persuasion to come home tonight, right, Papa?" She turned back to the policeman, and smiled at him.

The radio crackled in the police car. "Patrol Two, this is Dispatch. We have a report of a disturbance with property damage at Monroe and Washington. Sounds like the Scotsmen have been partying at the Flying Pig."

The officer picked up the microphone and spoke into it. "Copy, Dispatch. Roll patrol one for backup, please." He turned to the group. "You folks get home. Gotta go." The officer turned on his red lights and zoomed away. As the car left, Ursula thought she saw movement in the shadows of the doorway to their place, as if someone had slipped in and eased the door closed behind them.

Ian turned to Karol. "Well done, old man. You too, my love. Now, into the apartment. Time to wake up Mama."

They filed into the tiny apartment, and woke Elsa. Karol and Elsa were bound together, gagged, and placed on the kitchen floor. They used cloth from clothing under repair, bits of rope and a halter or two snagged from a nearby barn, trussing up the couple very securely. They could breathe, but that was it. Ursula bent down in front of them. "Please be quiet. This will all be over soon. Please." The expression of rage in her father's eyes had become frightening to Ursula. She could never remember seeing this much expression on his face at any time. It was a consuming expression, hard and violent. Her hand went to her mouth involuntarily. She tuned to Ian.

"You're not going to hurt them. You mustn't." She was still whispering so as to not raise any alarm.

Ian sighed. "As I see it, we have a couple of options. None of them great. We could take Ursula as a hostage, to guarantee the family silence, but from what she has told me of them, I don't think we could depend on that. Apparently the relationship is not good."

Ursula turned and looked at her parents on the floor; she could tell her mother was sobbing. She could still see her father's eyes. They were still on fire. His body was quivering. She had never seen him with this much rage. She wondered where it came from. He never showed this much intensity over anything.

"The other option is to just kill them." Pitor and Francois both looked at Ian, and then at Ursula. Ursula was staring at Ian, her mouth open and her hand in front of it. She reached back and steadied herself against the wall. She saw him finger his blade. Her father struggled against his bonds.

"You can't." Ursula felt her knees go weak, and she slid down the wall to the floor. The last six hours had driven her to the limit of her emotional endurance. She struggled to stand, and her legs failed to respond. She started to sob. "No, you cannot do it. Please."

He pulled out his blade and held it to her throat. "Shhh, my love. Quiet." He stood quickly. "Tie her up too." Pitor and Francois mumbled their apologies, and started to gag Ursula.

Her mind was racing. How did she get into this? All she wanted was a little excitement, a little fun. She was exhausted. There was nothing more she could do. She looked at her parents, and started to sob again. As the gag reached her face, somewhere she finally found the strength to plead. "You were going to send for me, Ian. I thought you loved me?"

"Did you really think I would send for you?" He smiled his smile, and all Ursula could do was hate it now. There was nothing charming about it. "I have met some naive girls—it is part of this line of work—but you, you fell for it hard. It's refreshing in a way. Gives one hope for humanity."

"I believed you."

"At times I did myself." He shrugged. "*C'est la vie.*"

Pitor looked at her sadly, and started once again to put the gag into her mouth. She shook back the sobs. She had to try something-anything. "Wh-wait. Y-you are forgetting. Something." Ursula choked back another sob.

He held up his had to pause Pitor. "What is that, my love?"

"If I tell anyone, I-I will go to prison. I'm not going to say anything to anyone about this. I can't. Think about that, Ian. I don't want to go to prison."

Pitor looked at Ian. "She has a point."

She looked at her parents again, bound with only their eyes watching her. She found more strength she did not know was there. "And if we are found dead, the police are not stupid. They will check the mansion right away. They will put it together with my extra time in the Department of Economic Affairs. Pitor said if they know what to look for; they will be able to tell the computer was on when I was there. They have radios. The police saw you take us here. You would never get away, no matter how many fast horses you have. Think about it, Ian."

Francois stepped forward in the small kitchen. "She has a point there, too."

Ian paused, put his hands on his hips and hung his head in thought. He looked at Ursula. Ursula looked at him, emotionally spent and exhausted, unable to move. He paced back and forth a couple of times in the small apartment. He began to nod his head.

"Okay. But, Ursula. If I ever hear about you mentioning this to anyone, I will return someday and end this. Do you understand?"

She sobbed again. "Of course. You have my word. Thank you. Thank you."

He turned to Elsa and Karol. "Do you understand?" Elsa nodded vigorously, and Karol just glared. "Eeyore, I think you need to understand what this means. You either go along with us, or I will have to kill you. Do you understand?"

After a brief pause that made Ursula's heart stop, Karol nodded yes.

"Are you going to call the police or turn in your daughter?"

Karol shook his head no.

"I have your word on this?"

Karol nodded again, and Ian stood up.

"Should we untie them?" asked Pitor.

Ian looked at the anger still boiling in Karol's eyes. He shook his head. "No. Go ahead and loosen up Mama, but keep this Eeyore tied up. He still looks too pissed off. He needs time to settle down." He knelt in front of Elsa. "Mrs. Volz, my apologies." He shifted to Eeyore. "And Mr. Volz. You need to be more pleasant. Be nice to people once in a while. Especially your daughter. Smile. It may do you good." He stood. "Is there anything we are forgetting?"

"The traveling money?" asked Pitor.

Ian looked at Ursula, lying on the floor. "Do you still have it?"

She nodded.

He quietly moved to her, and gently stroked some hair from her face. She recoiled slightly. "Keep it." In the darkness, she could see him smile. "You did good, kid." He looked at Pitor and Francois. "Any objections?"

They shook their heads.

With that, the three men left the room, and closed the door behind them. Ursula slowly collapsed onto the floor and lay at her parent's feet, for she did not know how long.

She awoke from her trance with a start, and sat up. Ursula could feel her father's anger was diminished. She was sure his discomfort was severe. She began to untie her mother first, when she heard a noise at the door. She could feel her father tense. For a moment she thought they had changed their minds, and were coming back to finish them. The door opened, and she could just make out a man with a knife. Her father saw him too, and started to struggle.

"Ursula, are you okay?" The voice had an unusual accent, Spanish and something else. Her heart leapt in joy, and she started to get to her feet, but fell back in exhaustion. Two more men entered the room, and more were out in the hall. She could tell they had up-time weapons. The first man knelt in front of her.

"Lorenzo! Am I glad to see you."

"And I'm glad you're okay as well. Are your parents okay?"

"A little shook up. Get Mama cut free, please." A gray dawn was starting to break over the hills. Several candles were brought in to lighten the room.

Someone pulled her father's gag out, about the time Lorenzo

was helping Ursula to her feet. The room was so small, they could only have a couple of people working in there at a time cutting them loose.

Elsa was not happy with the sharp knives cutting the bindings made from her customers' clothing. "Stop cutting the cloth! It is not mine, and I will have to repair it. Untie it, you idiot." She scolded the men in the dark clothing and was carried into the hallway to give them more room to work.

Ursula sat across from her father as Lorenzo went to untie him. She could see his eyes were still angry, but not furious as before. "First of all Papa, I want you to meet Lorenzo Nasi. He works for the government in counterintelligence. He is my handler."

"Nice to meet you, sir. I apologize for not coming earlier. We had to be sure they were headed out of town. They're gone, computer and all." Lorenzo did not smile much, as he was always so proper. He continued to work on the bindings.

"This is the Jew you met in the alley."

"Yes, Papa. But I first met him almost a year and a half ago, right after I started at the mansion."

"You have known this Jew for over a year and a half?"

Lorenzo Nasi raised his eyebrows at Karol, and slowed his cutting of the bindings.

Ursula felt her strength returning. "That's right. Very good. You are very clever. Tell me the rest of it. What do you think?" Ursula knew this mental puzzle would calm her father.

He shifted slightly as a rope was cut, and tension was relieved behind his back. "That's better. I don't understand why they let those men get away. What did they do?"

Lorenzo chimed in. "They stole some top secret lists of our agents, all around Europe. Your daughter helped to steal them. From a computer, I might add."

Karol looked confused. "Why would you do that, Ursula? You should not be involved in such things. You should not endanger your family in such a way."

"Papa, please. Think about the files."

He paused for a moment. "That would be disastrous. We will have to move right away..." His voice trailed off. "You let them steal those files, didn't you? Those aren't the real files, are they?"

Lorenzo looked impressed as he cut another binding. "You were right; he is smart!"

Ursula sat back with a smile. "Told you he was. Except you almost messed it up, Papa."

He looked puzzled, then nodded. "I see. That's why you didn't scream when I tackled that smarmy English bastard. If the police had gotten involved, the whole plot would have been discovered." He looked at his daughter as more ropes fell away. He frowned at her and nodded his head. "But why couldn't you tell us what was going on?"

Ursula looked over at Lorenzo. "What is it called again? Operational security?"

Lorenzo nodded. "Yes. People only know if they have a specific need to know. With this much riding on the outcome of the operation, we just couldn't extend the need to know."

"After you attacked Ian, Papa, w-we just improvised. I assumed Lorenzo and his men were nearby the whole time, and they were. I don't think I could have done it without knowing they were behind me—us, actually."

"How did you know they wouldn't kill us?" asked Karol.

Lorenzo shrugged. "That's one reason we asked the police car to delay you. To make sure they knew they could be identified. It gave us time we needed to get our team into the building. We also know Ian, whose real name is Maurice Rettanuer, and is originally from Alsace. Which is quite a way from England. He is a spy for hire, a 'freelancer' to use an up-time notion, but he has never killed anyone, as near as we can tell. No reason for him to start now."

Karol addressed Lorenzo. "If I ever get my hands on that son of a bitch, I am personally going to wring his neck." He shook his head so his droopy jowls swung back and forth.

"Well Mr. Volz, you will have to travel to France, or Spain, or wherever they sell those files. Although they may be dead before you get to them, if the files are found to be bogus too quickly." Lorenzo cut another rope, and Karol could move his legs.

"Much better. I have feeling back in my legs," he said, with his typical matter-of-fact monotone. Ursula grinned widely at him.

Karol turned to his daughter, with just a hint of pride in his eyes. "But why did you do this, honey? It was dangerous. Too dangerous. You have never done anything like this before. Not even remotely like this. What possessed you? You became involved!"

"Papa, I have told you before. I don't want to live on the outside of the world any more. I want to be a part of it. A part of a community, not a parasite. I wanted to grow, to put down some roots. This was an opportunity to do both, and do some good for this place at the same time. So, when Lorenzo contacted me last year, and asked me to watch for someone to approach me about something like this, I had to say yes."

Finally Lorenzo cut the last of the ropes holding Karol, and they both helped him to his feet. He shook his legs and arms to restore circulation. He held out his arms to his daughter, and they embraced.

"Papa. You frightened me with your anger. And when you attacked Ian, I did not know what to think. It didn't seem like you."

Elsa walked quietly into the room with mounds of fabric in her hand. Karol looked at her, and they both nodded.

"It *was* me, Ursula. When you were young, there was a village that was destroyed. I could do nothing about it. I was tied up, and your mother was..."

Elsa joined them in a quiet embrace. "Maybe, someday we will tell you more, Ursula. That is enough for today."

Ursula stifled a sob. "I never knew, Papa. But I don't want to leave here. It's safer here than it is anywhere. This can be our homc. Please."

"I like it too. I have said it to you before, Karol. This is a good place," Elsa added.

Ursula looked into his sad droopy face, and hoped. The anger in his eyes flared for a moment, and he hugged them harder.

Karol sighed. "I suppose we could stay a while longer. Just to see how things go."

Nobody Wants to be a Pirate in the Baltic

Anette Pedersen and Kerryn Offord

Kolberg, Pomerania, March 1635

"Viktor not have all day."

Hans Johansson jumped and nearly dropped the musket he gingerly held in his soft, white hands when the gravelly voice broke the silence. He'd been so busy examining the musket that he'd momentarily forgotten Viktor, though, as he glanced at the big brute of a man with his barrel chest, gray hair, and badly pockmarked, battle-scarred face, he had to wonder just how he'd managed to forget the man was waiting for him to accept the consignment of weapons. Even when he was just standing still, there was a brooding intensity about Viktor that was more intimidating than his physical presence warranted.

"I'm sorry. Is . . . is something wrong, Herr Viktor? These are very fine guns. I'm most impressed that you've managed to acquire so many of the new Russian AK3s. They only went into production last summer." To his annoyance Hans realized that he was babbling.

He wondered if he needed to make eye contact, if it would make him seem more sincere and trustworthy. He had forced himself to do so when this deal was set up and it hadn't been something he had enjoyed. On the surface Victor looked like any other thug, but there was something about the fire in Viktor's eyes that was scary. Something not quite right. No, eye contact wasn't necessary. Hans was sure he had Viktor convinced that he was just another harmless clerk handling his master's dirty transactions, and it wouldn't be a bad idea to let Viktor think that Hans was somewhat scared of his violent reputation. That Hans had spent the last three years looking for revenge against the powerful Vasa family for the loss of his heritage, and was now one of the duke of Courland's most trusted agents, was not something Viktor needed to know. Especially since the duke's new mission might bring Hans into more contact with Viktor and his men.

"Viktor's weapons is good. Why you take so long?" The big man folded his arms over his large chest, and frowned. Hans was acutely aware that he had his back to Viktor's henchman standing by the pile of gun crates, and that the two guards at the cellar door were now looking in his direction.

With an effort Hans returned his attention to the musket in his hands. It was, as Viktor had promised it would be, a used weapon, but in very good condition. That was something Viktor's reputation had promised. When you bought from him, you bought weapons you could rely on. He didn't deal in rubbish, and he didn't try to palm off damaged weapons as useful ones. On the other hand, he was also rumored to be willing to go to any length to get revenge for a betrayal, real or imagined, and Hans had no intention of telling Viktor all there was to know about the mission. Still, there was no one else capable of carrying it off who might also be willing to do it, so Hans knew he just had to out-smart the big man.

"They are very good, Herr Viktor. In fact they are exactly what you promised." Hans plastered an ingratiating smile on his face, and managed to look somewhat like the apple-cheeked Swedish boy he had once been.

"Viktor keeps his word, and others better keep theirs to Viktor." The scarred face looked even more evil twisted by a dark frown, and the thick Russian accent grated on Hans' ears.

"Surely no one would try to cheat someone as noto . . . eh, noted for fair dealings as your honorable self, Herr Viktor." Hans gave a slight bow, and handed Viktor a purse containing the exact number of gold coins as they had agreed upon.

"Not twice. No, not twice." Viktor bounced the purse in his hand a few times, and stuck it into his belt without counting the money.

"Surely not even once, Herr Viktor. Why even my illustrious master knows of your reputation. He has, in fact, empowered me to approach you concerning another deal."

"For what?"

"As you know, there are many new weapons being developed more or less secretly in various places, and it has come to my master's attention that a weapon of significant military value will be traveling from Wismar to Stockholm within the next couple of weeks. My master wishes to acquire this new weapon, but speed is essential."

"Why you need Viktor?"

"I lack your organization's sources of information and connections. The Doppels have intense security surrounding the transportation of the new weapon and I am at a loss as to how to obtain it." Hans tried another smile and a bow.

"Johann and Georg Doppel from Gothmund, Luebeck?" Viktor's speech was suddenly faster and smoother, making Hans wonder if he'd been playing games with him.

"Why, yes. Do you know them?"

"Viktor knows of them. For the right price Viktor will do it. From Wismar to Stockholm, you say? First Viktor will need a good ship and crew."

"I already have a ship and crew ready and waiting to take the weapon back to my master."

Viktor shook his head. "Viktor wants his own ship and crew."

"The captain is my cousin, and my master has already agreed," Hans insisted.

"Viktor has your word your men are to be trusted?"

"Of course," Hans answered.

"Then we discuss Viktor's price to get your master his weapon system."

The Vulgar Unicorn, Stralsund, a couple of days later

Tat'yana's nose twitched at the strong smell of sex in the air of Victor's room. She paused to examine the child, for child was what she most definitely was, that Viktor had been amusing himself with. She was standing there in her threadbare clothes, staring nervously back at Tat'yana, twisting the drawstring purse Viktor had thrown her. Tat'yana called over her shoulder. "Boris, get this girl a coat from the bag and see she's given something to eat before she leaves."

"No, Boris, you stay." Viktor waved towards the second man who had entered the room behind Tat'yana. "Grigori, do what Tat'yana said."

Tat'yana waited until the door was shut behind Grigori and the girl. "She looked young even for you, Viktor."

"Yes, the sweet little flower has barely started to bud," Viktor answered, "but I wanted to celebrate with a virgin." He looked over to Boris. "We have been given Johann and Georg Doppel on a platter."

The grim smile on Boris' face had Tat'yana wondering. "Who are Johann and Georg Doppel?"

"It's a long story," Viktor began.

Tat'yana settled herself comfortably on the bedside chair. "I've got plenty of time."

"It was back when me and Viktor first started dealing in arms. We thought we had a deal with honorable men..." Boris said.

"But we were wrong," Viktor interrupted. "The written contract they produced did not say what they claimed it had said."

This was news to Tat'yana, and it explained why Viktor and Boris had so readily accepted her into their inner circle six years ago. Not only could she read and write, but she also owed Viktor for rescuing her from the back streets of Paris. She was his way of ensuring he wasn't cheated on a bad contract again, which brought up another question. Viktor wasn't the kind of man to let a wrong go unpunished so long. "And you haven't done anything about them yet?"

Viktor snorted. "Not yet. We couldn't do anything ten years ago. We were short of money and the Doppels had powerful friends. Until now our paths haven't crossed." Viktor glanced over to Boris. "But now I will have justice."

"Don't they still have powerful friends?" Tat'yana asked.

"Yes, but they will be on board a ship. It will be a simple matter for them to be lost at sea."

"Murder on the high seas?" Tat'yana asked.

"Not murder, Tat'yana. We are not pirates. Nobody wants to be a pirate in the Baltic. There is nowhere to hide. No, I only seek justice," Viktor answered. "Do you know where to find Lasse?"

Tat'yana nodded. "He's working the docks here in Stralsund."

"Good. Bring him to me. I have a special job for him."

Viktor turned to Boris. "Hans Johansson says he has a ship and crew. Its name is the *Dunking Dolphin*. Learn what you can about them while I find out what I can about the Doppels' ship."

The Harbor, Stralsund

"Hello, Cookie. Wanna turn a trick?" Lasse turned around at the rough voice, and saw his old friend Tat'yana standing with her hands on her hips, and her head slightly tilted in a come hither pose.

"Tat'yana, what can I do for you?" Lasse rose gracefully from the bollard he had been sitting on.

"Viktor has a job that needs your special abilities."

"Horizontal or vertical?" Lasse's sweet smile never reached his eyes.

"Getting to be quite a fancy speaker, eh?" Tat'yana normally preferred to speak and dress as a respectable middle class German, but that would have made her a target for every predator on the Stralsund docks. Today she was a full-blown dockyard-doxy and, despite her small stature, someone even the most drunken sailor wouldn't harass.

"I've been keeping company with a priest lately." Lasse shrugged. "In between bemoaning his sins, and praying for his soul, he tries to convince himself that he is actually trying to save me by preaching to me and teaching me. I've lost most of my Swedish peasant accent, and learned quite a bit of Latin. Not quite enough to pass as a priest, but..." Lasse shrugged again.

"It's good to be as many persons as possible." Tat'yana looked across the pier to the sea. "Then you can afford to stop being those you don't want to be."

Lasse didn't answer. He had been happy and proud to have reached a position as second cook in Princess Kristina's household at the royal court in Stockholm, but being accused of trying to poison the princess had broken his dreams, and what he'd had to do to escape had broken more than that. Someday Lasse intended to find out if Jan Potocki had been the reason the queen had been so unwilling to accept that Lasse simply hadn't noticed the cracks in the tinned beaker he had used to serve the tisane to the princess. The queen's new favorite had certainly been quick enough to offer to arrange Lasse's freedom from jail in return for Lasse's "services."

"Viktor wants us to leave for Wismar today. We must be onboard a certain ship when it leaves the harbor there. You as a cook, me as a passenger. Are you in?"

"Sure." Lasse smiled. "Viktor pays much better than the priest, and he doesn't expect freebies."

The Vulgar Unicorn, Stralsund

"I have accepted a job," Viktor growled at Lasse as he and Tat'yana entered the suite of rooms that was his permanent base. "Tat'yana and Hans Johansson, our employer's man, will sail as a married couple on the *Martha of Wismar*. You will take the place of the cook. One morning Tat'yana will tell you to poison the food. Then I will come with a ship and a crew, and we will take what is on board."

"Piracy?" Lasse sat down and stretched his elegant legs out in front of him. "But nobody wants to be a pirate in the Baltic. It's much too cold."

"Not piracy. This is justice. Two men who cheated me many years ago will be traveling on this ship. It is their cargo we will take."

"Ah, and will the crew be Fritz Felix and his men?"

"No." A frown twisted Viktor's scarred face. "The crew and ship belong to our employer. They are not my choice."

"Hmm, pity. Working with unknown comrades is a dangerous undertaking." Lasse lifted a questioning eyebrow. "What arrangements have been made for getting me into place as cook?"

"Tat'yana and Hans Johansson will be visiting his brother in Wismar before going to Stockholm. You are the brother. You are a baker's apprentice who wants to run off from a bad master. When the cook goes missing, Hans Johansson will pay the captain of the ship to hire his brother."

"I don't like the idea of pretending to be somebody's wife," Tat'yana interrupted. "I can protect myself, but sticking a knife in our client might mean that we won't get paid."

"I'm not that concerned with payment, Tat'yana. What is more important is that the Doppel brothers feel my justice. Hans Johansson is a clerk and not brave. If he gives you problems, you nick him a little." Viktor smiled. "He is a man who would be henpecked if married."

"Well," said Tat'yana with a broad grin, "I can do that. Come, Cookie, my bags are packed and the tide waits for no man."

The Hairy Bird, Wismar

"The cook on the *Martha of Wismar* likes big-assed, blowsy barmaids," said Lasse as he closed the door to the private parlor behind him.

"Damn. That doesn't describe either you or me." Tat'yana rose from the window seat and walked to the solid oak table, choosing the chair as far as possible from the eating Hans Johansson. "On the other hand," she continued with a nasty smile, "Hansi here is a bit pudgy. Don't you think he would make a lovely barmaid with a wig, a padded corset and a dress?"

Hans looked alarmed and nearly choked trying to swallow and protest at the same time. "How... How dare you? I will not accept such insults from a sodomite and a whore!"

Lasse took out his knife and started cleaning the dough he had used in his disguise as a baker's apprentice from his fingernails. Tat'yana just looked at Hans until he started fidgeting.

"But, Hansi," said Lasse, keeping his voice especially sweet and mild, "we really need to get that cook separated from his friends, and the only other way would be to hire somebody with the right looks. Surely you would rather do a little playacting, than have to pay a real barmaid for the job."

"Such creatures are cheap."

"Yes, but their silence is not." Lasse noted that Tat'yana relaxed when she realized what he was doing. Or rather, part of what he was doing. Lasse didn't share Viktor's confidence that Hans Johansson was just another harmless clerk. Of course, the knife hidden inside the man's doublet, which Lasse had seen when they shared a room last night, could just be a sensible safety precaution, but it had been a stiletto. And of course the man's preference for very bland food could just be a sign of stomach troubles, but it was the same food Lasse ate himself, since it was difficult to hide any kind of poison in such food. Lasse also didn't like the fact that Viktor wasn't in control of all the aspects of the job, but had to depend on an unknown crew of men supplied by Hans, so this mild attempt at extortion might reveal more about what they were dealing with.

"Ah, I suppose such money might be well spent." Hans visibly tried to gather his dignity and looked down his prominent nose as he handed Lasse ten silver thalers. "After all it is important that I—and my supposed wife—stay in our roles. People will be watching us." He directed a patronizing smile towards Tat'yana. "Which reminds me, the way you were giving orders—even to me—when we arrived was quite unacceptable from a respectable woman. A respectable woman is meek and obedient toward her lord and master."

"Well, you better learn to accept it, Hansi, 'cause you would surely be dumb enough to marry a shrew." Tat'yana narrowed her eyes and continued. "And if you had any ideas about matrimonial rights, you can just forget them. If you try anything I'll cut off your balls and feed them to you. Viktor might have accepted the job, but he knows who you're working for and could just deliver the weapons to your master himself if you should suddenly come down with a bad case of death. You need us to get your weapons, we don't need you."

"How dare you! You're nothing but a thug's doxy—"

"I'm Viktor's secretary, you moron, and he..."

When the conversation deteriorated into a shouting match Lasse slipped quietly out the door. Tat'yana was obviously quite able to handle Hans Johansson on her own. The business with the thalers had shown that the man was open to extortion, and inclined to pay his way out of anything unpleasant. So, not a professional—or at least not a very good one.

The torches outside the tavern were smoking in the damp wind when the barmaid led the cook from the *Martha* out the door. For three thalers she had agreed to take her customer into the alley beside the tavern, rather than upstairs to her room, so that the pretty, young baker's apprentice could get his revenge for the unspecified harm the cook had done him. She probably intended to get a bit extra afterwards by threatening to tell the baker Lasse had named as his master, but that wasn't going to be a problem.

As the entwined couple passed the shadow where he was hiding, Lasse stepped out, put one hand over the man's mouth to silence him and swiftly slit his throat.

"Hey, you gone done kill him! That wasn't it." The barmaid let go and backed away.

"Wait!" Lasse reached into his purse and held out the rest of Hans' coins, carefully polished to make them shiny. "Here. I'll pay you more."

"But they saw me leave with him." She stopped and looked at the coins shining brightly even in the dank alley. "Okay. Give them to me." With her mouth twisted into a smile, she grabbed the coins and tried to run, only to have Lasse grab her and slit her throat as well.

Lasse waited a few moments to be sure they were both dead. Viktor wouldn't like that he had killed the woman, but it had been too dangerous to let her live. The town guard might not care about another dead sailor, but the *Martha* was based here in Wismar, and the Doppel family might demand inquiries when one of their employees was found murdered. Lasse squatted down to clean his knife on the woman's skirt before gathering the money and checking the bodies for any valuables. Viktor would probably insist that Lasse gave the loot to charity, but leaving it would tell even a half-wit that something more than an ordinary robbery had been going on, and there was no way Lasse would risk going to jail again.

"Did you have a good fight?" asked Lasse slipping silently into the parlor where Tat'yana waited.

"Only middling. But what's more important is the fat creep claims to have left a letter with a lawyer telling all that he knows of our plans, with orders to mail it to the Doppel family if he doesn't return for it within a month." Tat'yana spoke barely above a whisper and sat very still, though Lasse could see she longed to pace the floor.

Lasse sat calmly beside the agitated Tat'yana. "Do you think it's true or just a belated attempt to ensure his safety?"

"I don't know." Tat'yana shrugged. "But Viktor is going to be absolutely furious."

"Oh, I'm fairly furious myself." Lasse looked toward the bedroom, where he could hear Hans snoring, but then shook his head. "We can't contact Viktor before he leaves for Christiansø, so we'd better continue as planned, and deal with Hansi later. See you in the morning."

On board the Martha of Wismar *just east of the Ertholmene Islands*

Hans watched Lasse carry the bread-covered mug of poisoned soup to the captain at the helm. Having that skinny little bitch Tat'yana refuse to show him any respect at all, and even threaten to harm him, was bad enough, but the knowledge that Lasse the sodomite was the more accomplished poisoner really grated on his pride. Hans had removed a few people over the years for the duke of Courland, but since his poisons never seemed to work very well he had often had to resort to the far more messy and dangerous method of a knife in the back to actually kill them.

He really should have insisted on knowing the details of the plan before leaving for Wismar, but Viktor had insisted that he didn't need to know, and Hans hadn't felt like arguing. After learning that Lasse was to poison the crew but only drug the Doppel brothers, Hans had unbent enough to ask what and how much Lasse was going to use, and why the Doppels weren't to be poisoned, only to be told by Tat'yana to mind his own business. Stupid bitch and stupid sodomite, didn't they realize that since Hans held the purse-strings it was he who gave the orders? Well, they'd regret it when Hans *did* write the letter. A pity he hadn't done so already, but who would have thought a thug could be so creative? A smash and grab attack at sea with guns blazing and a quick escape was more in keeping with the stories he had heard about the man. This time, instead of fighting his way aboard, Viktor intended to step aboard unopposed. By sinking the ship with all hands afterwards he also concealed all traces of the crime. The *Martha* would be recorded as just another sorry loss at sea with nobody suspecting foul play or searching for the perpetrators. The thug had planned the perfect act of piracy. After all, nobody wanted to be a pirate in the Baltic. The prizes usually weren't worth the effort.

At least cousin Erland would be on his side. For a moment Hans considered having Erland and his crew dispose of Viktor and his team, but regretfully decided against it. Cousin Erland might not be above a bit of piracy if the risks were sufficiently low and the prize sufficiently large, but taking on Viktor and his bodyguards would simply be too dangerous.

Lasse had come up again to empty a couple of slop-buckets over the side and Hans was watching the diving seagulls when the captain cried out. The man let go of the helm, took a few steps, and fell flat on the deck. Without a hand to hold it the wheel started spinning. Shit! They were close to those small rocky islands, and who would steer the ship? Had those incompetent morons even thought about that?

Hans ran towards Tat'yana as she came up from the cabin holding a hand mirror. "There's nobody to steer! We'll be smashed against the rocks and killed!"

"Stupid!" She pushed past Hans and signaled with the mirror in direction of the islands. Hans turned in time to see Lasse calmly grab the helm.

How mortifying. For a moment Hans felt the blood rush to his cheeks, only to go faint at the sound of a desperate scream from below.

"Damn it! There's always one who can't hold down his dinner," Tat'yana shouted over her shoulder. "Lasse!"

"Just need to secure the helm, Tat'yana." Lasse tied the helm with a rope and walked toward the wild-eyed sailor who had just stumbled up from the mess, screaming and covered with vomit. Lasse led him to the gunwale, and with one quick movement slit the sailor's throat before tipping him over the side.

Christiansø, the Ertholmene islands, 12.5 miles northeast of Bornholm

Grigori kicked at the ashes of an old fire. "Probably from the Swedes when they based themselves here before trying to invade Bornholm last summer."

"And Viktor was most displeased at the Swedes for doing so. He'd been planning on selling the Bornholmers muskets so they could rise against their overlord. Instead the Swedes made a mess of their invasion and left a couple of thousand good muskets in the hands of the Bornholm militia. Bang goes that market," Boris said with a shrug. He was as dour as ever, but he seemed in a fairly talkative mood, so Grigori decided to see if he could get a bit more information about the man who had hired him.

"You and Viktor go back a long way, don't you?"

"Yes, more than ten years. We first met in Brazil when the Dutch West India Company took Bahia from the Portuguese. We were doing very well until Colonel Jan van Dorth died and the Schouten brothers took command. Then everything went to hell in a handbasket. When Bahia capitulated with barely a shot being fired, we were returned to the United Providences in prison ships with only that loot we could conceal within our bodies. Viktor decided that fighting was a mug's game and that the real money was in supplying the military. He asked me to join him as his bodyguard and I've been with him ever since."

"What about the clerk, Tat'yana? She doesn't seem Russian."

"She's not. Viktor discovered her on the back streets of Paris."

"The back streets of Paris? Then how did she learn to read and write?"

"I have my guesses on how she paid for lessons, but don't ask Tat'yana. Her past life in Paris is buried alongside Brigitte."

"Who's Brigitte?"

"That was Tat'yana's old name. If you want to die, just try calling her that."

"Die? But Tat'yana is such an inoffensive little thing."

"True, but Brigitte wasn't. She couldn't be and survive eighteen years on the streets of Paris."

Grigori swallowed and gazed off into the distance. He knew how his widowed mother had been forced to earn money to support him and his younger brothers and sisters before he was old enough to get this job with Viktor. That sort of thing changed a person. He could well imagine Tat'yana's desire to bury her past.

Out to the east he thought he could see something flashing. He pointed. "Boris, is that the signal?"

Boris looked. "It looks like it. Let's warn Viktor in case the lookout has missed it."

"He's over with the captain of the *Dunking Dolphin*," Grigori paused, "Boris, I don't trust Captain Erland and his crew."

"You're wise not to trust them. They are our employer's men, not some of Viktor's. Keep your gun ready at all times."

Grigori passed a hand under his jacket to fondle the butt of his automatic pistol. It was a beautiful weapon, inspired by the automatics from Grantville, and with its custom-made brass cartridges and high-capacity magazines it offered considerably more firepower than any revolver. If Boris wanted him to be ready, he would be.

Off the coast of Christiansø

Boris and Grigori boarded the *Martha of Wismar* before Viktor, and while they kept a lookout for possible threats Viktor walked over to Tat'yana. "Where is the clerk?"

"He's in the hold looking for his cargo. Captain Erland and his men have joined him to look for loot. Don't worry; Lasse is keeping an eye on the little creep."

Viktor sniggered at Tat'yana's description. "Did he try it on?"

"Yes, but I soon put him right."

"I'm sure you did, but I'm also surprised you let him live after so grievous an offense."

"I almost didn't, but he claims to have left a letter betraying your part in the theft of the Doppels' new weapon with his lawyer."

Viktor turned to stare at the cargo hatch. "Do you believe him?"

"I don't know. He might have. By the way, what is this weapon system that Hans Johansson's master wants?"

"I don't know. Whatever the cargo is, it isn't as important as getting the Doppels. By the way, what have you done with them?"

"Follow me. Lasse and I left them in their cabin."

Viktor and his bodyguards fell in behind Tat'yana as she guided them toward the Doppel brothers. "What condition are they in? I want them to know what is happening to them."

"They should be awake by now," Tat'yana reassured Viktor.

The sight of both Doppels lying hog-tied on the cabin floor pleased Viktor no end. "Johann and Georg Doppel, so we meet again."

"Who the hell are you, and why are we tied up? Untie us immediately. Do you have any idea who we are?" Johann demanded.

Viktor exchanged smiles with Boris and fell into his game of talking about himself in the third person whenever he wanted to intimidate someone. "They do not recognize Viktor."

"Maybe it's the bad light," Boris suggested taking the cabin lantern and holding it up close to Viktor's face.

Viktor waited hopefully, but neither brother recognized him. "You still don't recognize Viktor? You don't remember stealing from Viktor ten years ago?"

The brothers mutely shook their heads.

Boris held the lantern over them. "Maybe they make such a habit of changing contracts on people that they have forgotten something from so long ago."

"A pity. They will die not knowing why. But if they forget from who they steal, they are not owed that kindness."

"Look, if it's money you want we have plenty. In the strong box by the bed. Take what you want. Take it all, but don't kill us," Georg Doppel begged.

"Grigori, the strong box."

The looks of relief on the brothers' faces amused Viktor. They were such naive fools, worse even than he and Boris had been when they first did business with the Doppels. He used the key he found around Johann's neck to open the strong box. It held a number of heavy bags. He emptied one out on the lower bunk. "Boris, do you remember how much they owe Viktor?"

"Yes." Boris moved over to the bunk and rapidly counted out coins. "There, that covers what they stole."

Viktor scooped up the remaining coins and returned them to their sack before putting it back in the strong box. Then he picked up the strong box. "Tat'yana, see what is happening on deck."

Seconds later Tat'yana returned. "It's all clear. The creep and his followers are still in the hold."

"Very good. Grigori, Boris, if you'd be so good as to help our friends up on deck."

"Now just a minute! We gave you our money," Georg cried as he was carried out of the cabin and dumped on the deck.

"And Viktor is grateful for finally getting the money you owed him. But Viktor doesn't take more than he is owed." He opened the strong box and tossed money bags alternatively to Boris and Grigori until the box was empty. "Viktor is a man of honor. Viktor does not steal from the people he does business with. You value money above honor, so Viktor will let you keep your money." He turned to his men. "Tie the bags to their belts. We don't want them to lose any of their precious money."

The Doppels looked at each other in confusion as Boris and Grigori tied the drawstring purses to their belts. Georg was the first to realize what was coming. He started to struggle as Grigori picked him up and carried him towards the side.

Grigori paused at the gunwale, the struggling Georg held firmly in his arms, waiting for Viktor's instructions.

Viktor nodded and Grigori threw Georg over the side.

There was a high-pitched scream suddenly extinguished by the splash of Georg hitting the water.

Johann started to struggle in earnest. "No, please, I beg you. Don't kill me."

"Viktor is not going to kill you. He is leaving your life in God's hands. If you reach land Viktor will let you live in peace. Boris."

Johann screamed when he went over the side.

Viktor calmly watched the men struggling to keep their heads above the water. He didn't expect to have long to wait. The water was icy cold and, hog-tied as they were, the brothers would have difficulty saying afloat, while the copper, silver and gold coins tied to their belts would help counteract the buoyancy of their fat bodies.

It was barely five minutes before Georg sank for the last time. That brought out a renewed effort to stay afloat from Johann, but three minutes later he too succumbed to a combination of the cold water and fatigue.

Viktor pushed away from the gunwale and looked around the *Martha of Wismar*. "Where is Hans Johansson? It is time we discovered what this wondrous weapon is."

The four of them walked over to the hatch where Lasse was watching Hans and the crew of the *Dunking Dolphin* struggle to lift a crate from the cargo hold.

With Viktor, Boris and Grigori helping they soon had a number of crates and barrels stacked on the deck.

"What is it?" Viktor asked.

Hans, in the process of supervising the levering open of a crate looked up. "It should be a prototype of a new machine gun, a 'Gatling gun.'"

When Captain Erland's crew opened the crate Hans dived on it, pulling away the straw packing to expose the multibarreled machine gun. "Yes. Right, close this crate and check the others. There should be a second 'Gatling gun' and several thousand rounds of ammunition."

Viktor crouched down and passed an expert eye over the Gatling gun. He'd heard about the up-time weapon and had Tat'yana read out several articles about it. "That looks like it's twelve bore," he observed.

"Yes," Hans agreed. "It fires the same rifled ammunition as the American 'shotguns.' The Doppels claimed it could fire as many as six thousand rounds per minute."

"Nobody can afford to pay for that rate of consumption," the bookkeeper in Tat'yana cried out. "Shotgun slugs were selling at almost four dollars apiece last time I was in Grantville."

Captain Erland Mansson exchanged looks with his crew. Four Grantville dollars a round—and Hans said there were more than twenty thousand rounds in the barrels—added up to a considerable sum. He looked down at the pile of loot he and his men had collected. It had looked impressive, but that was before he learned how much the weapon system his nephew wanted was worth. Behind him he could hear the murmurings of his crew as they did the arithmetic. His cheapskate cousin was shortchanging him. Erland reached for the butt of one of the wheel-lock pistols in his belt. Drawing it to provide some authority to his complaints, he turned on his cousin. "You didn't tell me how much the cargo would be worth when you hired me."

He detected movement out of the corner of his eye and turned in time to see one of Viktor's men pulling his pistol out from under his jacket. Erland fired before the man could raise his gun, hitting Grigori in the gut and dropping him to the ground.

Erland looked at the fallen man. He'd had no choice but to shoot, but this changed things. He had only wanted to force his cousin to pay a fair price, now he had to think about killing Viktor and his men. Edging on panic he struggled to prioritize. First he needed to gain control of Viktor and his men's guns. Pointing his second wheel lock towards Viktor he called out, "You and your men, drop your weapons."

He watched the play of emotions between the men. The girl, Hans' doxy, seemed pale and shaken. She was no threat. Best to worry about Viktor and his men.

"Boris, Lasse, drop your weapons."

Lasse dropped a couple of knives while Boris dropped a large pistol just like the fallen man's. Erland looked pointedly at Viktor. "Your weapons."

"Viktor employs dogs and Viktor should bark?"

Erland was confused for a moment by Viktor's way of speaking, but he recognized the attitude. Which left the matter of gaining the guns without getting too close to Viktor and his men. He gestured toward the girl. "You, bring me the guns."

He was surprised when the girl turned to Viktor for permission. He'd thought she belonged to Hans. He took his attention from her to check what Viktor and his men were doing.

Tat'yana turned her head toward Viktor and silently asked for instructions.

"Do it, Brigitte."

For a moment the past threatened to flood the present. Then the iron gates of her will clamped down on her past life in Paris. Tat'yana knew what Viktor wanted her to do. Could she do it without calling upon Brigitte?

She walked over to the moaning Grigori and reached down for his pistol. She had to peel his fingers off the butt. Then she walked toward where Boris had dropped his pistol. She didn't know Grigori well enough to know if his pistol was ready to fire, but the slight nod from Boris was enough to let her know his was loaded and ready. She held the heavy steel pistols and walked toward Captain Erland. The man was looking beyond her, completely ignoring her. "Now," a voice in her head screamed. She dropped Grigori's pistol and grabbed the thick butt of Boris' pistol in both hands. Then she rushed the last couple of steps to Captain Erland, pushed the barrel into his gut, and squeezed the trigger as rapidly as she could.

After four shots the voice in her head ordered her to stop shooting and check what the rest of the crew were doing. She looked up to see the pale faces of the *Dunking Dolphin*'s crew staring at the mess that had been their captain. Her body was starting to shake as she aimed the pistol at the closest one. But she didn't have to fire. Boris had arrived. He took the pistol from her hands and dispatched the crew one by one.

Tat'yana slumped down against the foot of the mast, her shaking hands wrapped around her legs. She could see Boris picking up the spent brass cartridges while Viktor held Grigori in his arms. Lasse had retrieved Grigori's gun and was keeping an eye on Hans.

Viktor held Grigori in his arms, tears running down his face. "Grigori, silly boy, why did you have to go for your gun?"

Grigori struggled to talk. "My family. Who will look after my family?"

"I will care for family." Viktor stared into Grigori's pain-filled eyes, then he slipped a fine stiletto from under his sleeve and thrust it deeply just behind Grigori's left ear. Grigori's body slumped in his arms. He lowered the body to the deck and slowly stood. He knew who was to blame for Grigori's death. He turned toward Hans, the stiletto still in his hand. "This is your fault."

Hans blanched.

Tat'yana hurried over to Viktor and placed a restraining hand on his arm. "Remember the letter, Viktor," she whispered.

Viktor paused. He wanted to kill Hans just like his man had killed Grigori, but it seemed he couldn't do it, not as long as that letter existed. He had to settle for wiping the blood from his stiletto on Hans' lace collar. He glared down at Hans before turning and walking away.

Aboard the Dunking Dolphin

Viktor was fuming. He'd finally gotten even with the Doppel brothers for fooling him with the written word only to be screwed over by that ass-kissing little creep Hans Johansson and his letter. He slammed his fist down on the gunwale. "I won't have it. Tat'yana, when we land you will follow Hans. See if he goes to a lawyer. If he does you will visit the lawyer and look for Hans' letter. Bring me that letter. Do anything you have to do. Even call upon Brigitte. But get me that letter."

Viktor knew he was asking a lot of Tat'yana's loyalty to him by suggesting she call on Brigitte if necessary, but he wanted to be sure she understood how important that letter was. He reached out his arms and gave her a comforting hug. "I wouldn't ask this of you if it wasn't important, Tat'yana."

"I understand, Viktor."

Stralsund, two days later

Hans paid Viktor the full amount they had agreed on and got off the *Dunking Dolphin* as quickly as he could. He needed to secure passage to his master and the sooner the better. He was lucky to still be alive. Who'd have thought a man of Viktor's reputation would worry so much about a mere underling? But obviously he did, and he blamed Hans for the young man's death. He fingered the bloodstain on his collar where Viktor had cleaned his stiletto. He'd been sure Viktor intended to kill him then and there, but he hadn't. Hans could only assume the girl had told Viktor about the letter he'd claimed to have lodged with a lawyer and that had stayed his hand.

Hans knew that lie wouldn't protect him for long. He had to do something about Viktor before Viktor did something about him. A grim smile brightened his face. A letter. Not a letter left with a lawyer to be forwarded in a month's time. That wouldn't do him much good; he could well be dead by then. No, he needed something much more immediate. Like a letter to the Doppels' family implicating Viktor in Johann and Georg's disappearance... one they would receive soon after he left Stralsund.

☆ ☆ ☆

Tat'yana paid off the street kids she'd asked to follow Hans. Unfortunately the creep hadn't headed for a lawyer as soon as he'd arranged passage for himself and his cargo. That worried Tat'yana. Could he have really left a letter with his lawyer before going to Wismar? Such a letter could be anywhere.

She edged closer so she could see what Hans was doing. It looked like he was writing. Then he bought one of the new pre-paid postage stamps from the shopkeeper and stuck it onto the letter before handing it to the shopkeeper.

Tat'yana watched the woman toss the letter into a shallow basket on the counter. She had to get that letter, but she also had to keep an eye on Hans. Tat'yana looked around for someone to follow him. Then she smiled. The girl who had followed Hans before was still close by. A few hand signals and Tat'yana was ready.

When Hans left he had two shadows, a pair of girls walking along as if they didn't have a care in the world. With a tail on Hans' movements, Tat'yana could target the post basket. It wasn't very big. She doubted there would be more than a dozen letters a day posted at this dockside store, so Hans' letter should be easy to identify.

Tat'yana approached the counter. Yes, she could see the letter on top, and she recognized Hans' handwriting. She could just buy the letter, but that went against the grain. It would be much cheaper to lift it from the basket while the woman turned her back, and anyway, this shop stocked some of the best lemon drops in the city. Tat'yana reached under her skirt for her purse and smiled at the shopkeeper. "Two dozen lemon drops, please."

The woman turned and reached for the jar of sweets from the shelf behind the counter and opened it in front of Tat'yana. With Tat'yana paying close attention she counted out the sweets into a paper cone before screwing it tight and exchanging it for the money in Tat'yana's hand. "Haven't seen you for a couple of weeks, Tat'yana."

Tat'yana popped a lemon drop into her mouth. "I've been out of town."

"Well, don't eat your lemon drops all at once. They'll rot your teeth."

Tat'yana smiled and waved as she left. The shopkeeper said something similar every time Tat'yana bought sweets.

Once out of the store Tat'yana examined the letter she'd stolen. She swore when she saw the address. Viktor had to know about this.

The Vulgar Unicorn

"Read it again," Viktor demanded.

For the fourth time Tat'yana read out the letter Hans Johansson had written to the Doppel family. It wasn't that Viktor was hard of hearing, or that she had any trouble reading the letter. Tat'yana was sure Viktor's problem was accepting the magnitude of Hans' betrayal.

"I will kill him."

That, from Viktor, was entirely predictable. "What about the letter he said he left with his lawyer?"

Viktor snorted. "I doubt there is any such letter."

"But can you risk that Hans was telling the truth?" Tat'yana didn't think there was any such letter either, not with Hans having written the letter she'd been reading as soon as he landed in Stralsund, but it was her job to protect Viktor from the written word.

"I will employ agents to trace Hans and identify his lawyer. There is plenty of time. But Hans will be leaving Stralsund soon. We must act quickly."

"What do you plan to do?" Tat'yana asked.

"I will talk to Lasse and then we will take passage on the same ship as Hans."

Somewhere in the Baltic

Hans awoke with a feeling that there was something wrong. His watch said early morning, and daylight was visible through the dull glass in the small bull's eye, but his head felt heavy and sore. Drinking a full bottle of wine the night before had perhaps been a mistake, but finally leaving Viktor behind in Stralsund had certainly been cause for celebration. That he was also bringing the duke the wanted weapons was good, but getting away from Viktor was better.

Hans reached for the bottle of cold tisane he always drank when traveling—rather than chancing the dubious quality of the ship's beer—and took a deep drink. The seagulls. Their cries were filling the air, but that was all. He stopped drinking. There should have been sailors talking, people moving around, but all he could hear was the seagulls, the water, and the groaning of the ship's timbers.

Still in his nightshirt, Hans stumbled out of his cabin. A loud snoring sounded from the only other cabin, the captain's cabin, and after a pro forma knock Hans entered. The captain slept beyond waking. Now in full panic Hans rushed to the deck, and was greeted by the sight of Lasse feeding slop to the seagulls like he had onboard the *Martha*.

"Good morning, Hans Johansson." Hans swirled to see Viktor leaning against the gunwale behind him with Hans' crates and barrels by his side.

"What . . . What are you doing here?"

"Viktor has unfinished business," the big man growled, and showed Hans the letter in his hand.

"It . . . it's false. I know nothing about this." Hans recognized the letter and backed away, only to swirl again as Lasse came up behind him. "I didn't . . . It . . . It must be the woman. She claimed to be your secretary, but she got angry when I wouldn't screw her." Hans tried to force a smile. "You know how women are. Hell has no fury like a scorned woman, and all that."

Viktor growled again and walked towards Hans. "Nobody cheats Viktor twice." As Hans felt the big man's hands close around his neck he reached for the stiletto he normally carried hidden inside his doublet, only to realize too late that he was unarmed.

It could only have been minutes, but when Hans recovered consciousness he was tied up and had his feet secured to one of the gun crates. He watched in horror as Viktor and Lasse rolled the barrels of ammunition over the side and then they started to push over the crates.

He was screaming and thrashing about when they started to push his crate over the side. Then he was flying through the air. The crate slowly settled in the ice cold water as Hans looked up at Viktor for one last time. Silhouetted against the rising sun the bastard was waving good-bye.

"I still think we should have had Fritz Felix pick up both us and the guns. They were worth a small fortune." As the first sounds of stirring came from below, Lasse let go of the helm, and drank from the sleeping potion bottle before passing it to Viktor.

"No." Viktor drank and tossed the bottle over the side before settling down to sleep. "I won't steal a cargo I've been paid to acquire. That would be worse than piracy, and I am not a pirate. And certainly not a pirate in the Baltic."

An Irish Sitter

Terry Howard

Augsburg, September 1634

"Horatio Alger Burston, this is totally unlike you!" a rather exasperated Catharina said. She would very much have preferred for her new husband to leave the hiring of staff completely up to her as he always had before. Well, almost always, anyway. For some reason she never understood he had insisted that the head cook had to be French, and that he—yes, it had to be a man—was to be referred to as "the chief," like the Indian leader in the movie they saw at the Higgins Hotel in Grantville the one time he took her to his hometown.

Then again, when she chose the carriage driver he wanted an Englishman named James but he hadn't insisted on it like he was doing now. It was well and good that he hadn't insisted on it since there was nary a James to be found. He had nothing to say when she hired the chamber maids and her personal maid. When she hired his valet, his only comment was to laugh when he found out he now had a valet. When he quit chortling all he said was, "Well, that's service for you." She asked what he meant but he never did manage to explain. Sometimes up-timers could be so completely incomprehensible.

But, now, for some completely inexplicable reason, he was insisting on having his own way on the question of hiring a nurse for their youngest child. Little August was Horatio Alger's stepson and he was two and a half years old. She was expecting again so it was time and past to hire a nurse. With the third child coming she would have less time and the children would have completely different needs. She very much remembered the troubles she had when Casimir was jealous of his baby brother.

When she proposed bringing another member on staff Horatio muttered something about a live-in babysitter. Then he smiled that smile that he'd been known to call "a shit-eating grin," and said, "That's fine, dear, as long as she is Irish."

"Irish?" Catharina was truly puzzled. "Why do you want an Irish nurse?"

"Well, the Irish speak English with such a delightful accent."

"That is an absolutely ridiculous reason to choose a staff member. Besides, where will we find an Irish nurse? Now, there are any number of fine healthy young German girls to hand to choose from."

"Nope. If you want a nanny, she is going to be Irish," Horatio said.

"But, darling, be reasonable. Where will we find her?"

"I don't know. But, I'm sure you'll manage. If you don't then I guess August will just have to make do with the walking stick on hand instead of his own private nursemaid."

Catharina knew what he meant. This was one oddity he had managed to explain. A walking stick was a staff so the staff collectively was a walking stick. "But dear," Catharina said, "I've found this perfectly marvelous—"

"Nope."

"But—"

"Nope."

Well, that was the third time he said no and the soup was still on the table. Catharina knew when to back off. She waited for desert before she brought it up again. "Horatio, Chef Andre's paramour has a niece visiting from out of town and she is looking for a position for the girl. I've met her and she seems such a lov—"

Horatio cut her off. "We already have more staff than we need. I have no idea what the chamber maids do all day. Reclean already clean chambers, I guess. We aren't running a home for wayward girls here. I'm sorry, but tell her no."

"Well, we were thinking of her as the nurse."

"Is she Irish?"

"Of course not."

"Then the answer is still no. If you can't find an Irish nanny then you will just have to raise the kids yourself."

"Don't be ridiculous. That is simply impossible."

"My ma raised six kids, kept the house clean, did all the cooking and worked part time. I don't see what you're complaining about."

"I meant finding an Irish nurse, not raising the children."

"Well, impossible or not, if you get a nanny, she will be Irish. I gave in on an English driver named James because we had to have one right away since neither of us can handle a team of horses, much less harness them. But this is different. You've got all the time you need to look for what we want, so it's an Irish nanny or no nanny. Oh, and see to it that she has dark red hair."

"Horatio? Just what is this all about?"

"It's about hiring a nanny."

"No, it isn't. If it was, then any healthy, steady, lass would do."

"Well, maybe I want another somebody about the house who speaks English as a first language."

"Then you don't want an Irish. If they speak English, it's a second tongue."

"Really? Then what do they speak?"

"Irish."

"Is that a language?"

"Yes."

"Oh."

"So then, if she doesn't speak English as her mother's tongue it will be all right to hire a—"

"No!"

"No?" Catharina almost wailed in frustration. "Why not."

"Because I want an Irish nanny for my son."

A completely annoyed wife demanded of her absolutely irrational husband, "But why? Give me one good reason!"

"Well, an Irish nanny is romantic."

"*Oh!*" Catharina lost it and it showed in her slipping English grammar. "So the true comes at last. You want an Irish mistress."

Horatio laughed. Catharina shook with anger. Horatio laughed louder. When she realized it wasn't going to work she changed to a pout and Horatio laughed with renewed vigor.

At last he ran down. "No, my dear," he finally said. "But there is a toast my father taught me." At that he raised his wine glass and said, "Here's to the happiest days of my life, spent in the arms of another man's wife." He paused for her to blow up, which she did. As she took a deep breath the better to cuss him good and proper like, he concluded the toast with the words, "my mother."

As the meaning of what he said filtered through the red haze of fury, the power went out of the gale force wind that was lodged in her lungs.

"If my son is to have a love in his life to rival that of his mother, then it should be someone special, exotic, beautiful, unique, someone who has a chance of competing, not something he can see by the dozens passing in front of the house any hour of the day. Anything less is not fair to him, or her, or you."

Suddenly Catharina not only lost the steam she had for a good screaming fit, she also lost any momentum she had for the argument. Horatio's id quietly congratulated his ego on a very good save.

"But, where will we find such a person?" Catharina asked.

"I'm not sure you can, dear, but do your best."

"Horatio . . ." Catharina suspected that she was somehow being swindled. Still it might be as he presented it. After all, Americans had some really strange ideas. "Are you sure this is the reason?" She hadn't completely let go of the idea that he was the one who wanted a lover.

"Okay, I admit it," Horatio said, throwing his hands up in a theatrical gesture. "I've always wanted an Irish setter." Then he laughed.

"What is an Irish setter?" Catharina demanded.

The Irish Sitter Sings

Terry Howard

Late January 1635
Near the City of Nijmegen, Netherlands

"Innkeeper, we need a wet nurse."

One of Henrich's company—probably his daughter, the timing was right and she looked just like him—had a fever. The stout lass was down and likely would not be getting up. She had been no help with loading the mules for three days and then, unable to walk, she had to be carried the last half day to the inn. Now she was out of her head with fever and out of milk for her child. When she got pregnant Henrich cursed himself as a softheaded/softhearted fool. He never should have taken her on as hostler help. But she had gone ahead loading and unloading the mules through it all with nary a word of complaint or a hint of expecting things to be different. Indeed, when someone started to help her out when her belly was at its biggest, she cursed the lad roundly. Then she gave birth in the night after having done her full share of the work the evening before and she did her full share the morning after. Her boy was now a toddler and could have been weaned already but the mother thought breast-feeding would keep her from getting pregnant. They tried giving him solid food, but he would not eat and now he would not stop crying.

"Yes, there is a wet nurse." The innkeeper named a price.

"I want milk for a bastard," Henrich said. "I don't need a gold-plated tit." They haggled halfheartedly and settled.

The company sat for two days while Henrich's daughter finished dying.

"Innkeeper, can we leave the child with the nurse?"

"No!" The innkeeper was adamant. "But you can take the nurse with the child!" he added quickly.

"You would have her leave her home?"

"This is not her home. Her man died in that corner . . ." The innkeeper pointed with his chin at a spot in the front room. ". . . over there. We buried him in the churchyard. It is damned good the Irish are all Catholics. The priest was not about to let any but Catholics be buried there."

"Irish, you say?" Henrich's mind began to turn over, counting the cost, assigning probabilities and weighing the long- and short-term benefits against the liabilities. "What of her children?"

"None. She gave birth in that same corner and buried her man and babe on the same day. I need her gone. She hasn't enough language to wait tables, the regulars are fighting over who gets her, and the other girls are deathly jealous. Here, she's poison. You need a nurse, I need her gone. Take her."

"She will agree?"

The innkeeper snorted. *What an odd question*, he thought. Who did the merchant think he was dealing with? He had no intention of giving the girl a choice. "Oh, yes. She will be quite agreeable."

Once again Maire was off to where she knew not. That was the story of her life since leaving Dromiskin in County Louth with Tadhg. It was all a grand adventure until Tadhg didn't come back from his last battle. Maire found him on the field with his face blown away. She lost his child when it came too early into the world. Ruairi looked after her in her bereavement, but he failed to come back to camp before everyone fled when a battle became a rout. If he lived, he never did find her.

Alexander was next on hand to see to her needs but he caught the wound fever and wasted away. She stayed with him when he could not keep up and the rest of the band moved on. She was delivered of his child the day before he died. Father and son were laid to rest together in the churchyard.

Now a traveling merchant had taken her on. Oddly, he saw

to it that she slept alone, except for the babe. The merchant fed her often and well, much better than he needed to just to keep her in milk. He was buying meat daily and watching to see that she ate everything on her plate . . . almost as if he wanted to fatten her up. He also insisted that she learn English and a start on being able to read.

"Come, lass, walk with me," Henrich said the first day on the road.

"What did you say?" Maire asked.

Henrich smiled. "The language was English. You need to learn it. I said come walk with me."

"Why do I need to learn English? We are going southeast. England is west of here." After the band left Alexander and Maire, he decided to make for home so he could at least be buried in Eire. They got as far as Nijmegen in the Netherlands. There weren't enough Englishmen in County Louth to call the language at all common. She had heard it a few times in the inn as a child and young girl, but no more than that.

"We are going to Augsburg. When we arrive, there may be a good job for you there. If there is, you will need to speak English."

"They speak English in Augsburg?"

"No." Henrich laughed. "In Augsburg, they speak mostly German, and a miserable strain of German at that. But there is a man there who speaks English and his wife is due any day now. They will want a nurse. If we are lucky, that will be you. It will help if you speak English."

Maire asked no more questions. It did not matter. She was eating well and sleeping warm and dry, and she had a child to care for and love. What else could one ask for in this life?

One night at an inn there was a west-bound merchant with news.

"Henrich, I see you're importing Irish. You're too late. Dietrich passed me several days ago with two in tow."

"Damn!" Henrich said.

"Caspar," a voice called out, "you're peddling old news. Dietrich's Irish were turned down. Dietrich abandoned them at the first inn he came to when he left Augsburg. They were still there when I came through."

Caspar, annoyed at being upstaged, looked across the room. "You're Nicolas, aren't you? How is the dispatch business going?"

"I'm making a living."

"Join us for a beer," Caspar said. "My friend here is buying."

"Don't mind if I do."

"Do you have any idea why Dietrich's Irish were turned down?" Henrich asked.

"Yes, the tale was all over Augsburg. The American insisted that his wife could only hire an Irish nanny with red hair, but when he saw the two Dietrich brought to town he said to Dietrich, 'they look like they were rode hard and put away wet. What are they, camp followers?' Well, the way Dietrich tells it he was pissed at the man's snotty attitude. He claims he said, 'What did you expect, a virgin wet nurse?' Then he claims he walked out. The other version says the American told him to leave and to take his bedraggled guttersnipes with him."

The next day Henrich resolved to instruct Maire in behaving like a shy maiden, something she never had been. Shy, that is. After all, every girl was a maiden once upon a time. He began by instructing Maire on her backstory. "Your father was a returned mercenary. You were raised on a small farm."

Maire snorted and let off with a string of obscenities. "That is a load of crap. My mother had no idea who my father was. I was raised in the barnyard of an inn with the chickens and the pigs. A boy I knew wanted to follow the Wild Geese and asked me to go with him, or most likely I'd be there still." By Wild Geese she meant the many Irish bands who found themselves in the Catholic armies of Europe. The boy was a lad from the same barnyard, not much older than she. He was a gentle lover and a sweet lad As he was reaching a man's height there was no place for him in the staff.

"Lass, that time was free. The next time I hear you using language like that, I will slap you."

Maire paled but said not a word.

"Bite your lip and look down."

Her face stormed red in the way only a redhead can.

"No!" Henrich almost barked. "When you blush or go pale or get angry—especially if you get angry—bite your lip and look down. If you look up, you are ready to fight. Fight with me, girl, and you will lose. The only question is how badly you will hurt when we are done. But that is not the point. A sweet, young, blushing maid will not make eye contact; she will avoid confrontation. I can land you a good job as a sweet, young widow.

They will have no use for a loud, harsh wench out of some inn's barnyard with shit between her toes. They will not want a whore raising their child."

Maire blinked and thought about what he said. When the blink was over, her eyes were on her feet and she was pulling her lower lip into her teeth.

"Good. Very good. I almost believe it myself. And another thing, this boy was your husband. He was the only man you ever knew carnally. I doubt you have ever been married, but from now on you refer to any man you laid with as 'my husband.' He was a poor boy from another farm in the village and the two of you got married and ran away to the continent to win a fortune and return home to lease a farm and raise a family. Do you understand? No! Don't look up. Just nod your agreement while counting your toes."

At the next inn there was a troupe of wandering entertainers who had exhausted their welcome and were moving on. Since they were traveling in the same direction, Henrich arranged for someone to instruct Maire in singing as they walked. It turned out the lass had a good ear, as well as a clear, sweet voice, and clever hands.

The instructor convinced Henrich that she had promise as a lute player and just by chance the company had an extra lute they were willing to part with. "An innkeeper had it. Someone died or left it or couldn't pay? Who knows? He couldn't or wouldn't pay us but he offered me the lute instead. The strings were dead but I've restrung it." Thomas, the group's leader, did not mention the shape the wood was in. A little oil and a lot of rubbing made it look good. It would take a professional to know it had suffered from neglect. It had also been left with the strings taut so the neck was warped. Thomas strung it over the backside. After a month of careful adjustment the instrument was playable, at least enough to be passed off on some rank amateur. "I don't need two and I'm tired of carrying the thing around."

When they parted company, Maire had the basics for the lute down. Her teacher's parting words were, "Don't worry about speed. That will come with practice. Work on your chord changes and your rhythm. Play a little everyday you have a warm place, and remember to let the instrument warm and cool slowly."

Henrich saw to it she played every night, after dinner. He

even taught her a few songs he remembered from his visit to the theater in the Higgins Hotel in Grantville.

One night, after he had spent over an hour helping her get the tune and the words to an English song just right, Maire finally asked, "Why are you doing this?"

Henrich smiled. In a voice full of piety he answered, "It is an act of Christian charity, my child."

Marie looked down and counted her toes. She couldn't bite her lip because she was too busy gritting her teeth.

Henrich laughed. "Very good, Maire. If I didn't know better I would indeed believe it.

"Very well, lass, I will tell you why. It might make things go better if you know. There is a man in Augsburg, an American from Grantville. I'm sure you've heard of those. He is doing quite well. He is the merchant's agent in Augsburg for a great many concerns. The business that passes through his hands is worth several fortunes. I want a slice of that trade. If the man owes me a favor then I will turn a profit on it. You are that favor. For some reason, he has told his wife she may only hire a redheaded Irish lass as a nursemaid for his child. There isn't one to be had in all of Augsburg. I know at least three men who are racing to Ireland and back or scouring the army camps for such a lass. By chance, I stumbled over you. If they will take you on as part of the household, then every time I come to Augsburg, your uncle Henrich will look in on you to see how you are doing and he will leave you some small trifle he has found on his journeys that he thinks you will like.

"Of course, while I am about it I will brush past this rich American commercial agent and ask in passing if there is any freight he needs hauled or something he needs fetched. And perhaps they will let you keep . . ." Henrich looked to the toddler on Maire's hip. ". . . him below the stairs. If not then perhaps I can find someone near by to raise him where you can keep an eye on him. I would like it if I knew that someone who loved the boy was watching out for him. If not, then I need to find something else to do with my grandson. Is that enough reason for you?"

Maire counted her toes and nodded.

"Look at me, Maire." He waited for eye contact. "Is that enough of a reason?" he demanded.

Her hard, cold eyes said not a word. Her mouth said only, "Yes."

"Then you will do it?"

"Yes."

"Good."

By and by she found herself in the city of Augsburg, freshly bathed, in new and modest apparel, on her way with Henrich to a meeting with H.A. Burston and his wife Catharina.

"Horatio Alger Burston," Catharina said, "I don't know why you are wasting your time. This Henrich hasn't had time to go to Ireland and back. So this girl will have been through the wars like the last two you turned down. I do wish you would be sensible and just let me hire a local girl."

H.A. knew his young wife was annoyed with him when she addressed him by his full name. It was by way of being formal. He thought he had her, mostly, trained to his more comfortable, informal, West Virginian ways. "Catharina, Henrich is a man of business, in a small way, with a good reputation. It would be unthinkable to not even look at what he has to offer. Yes, the last two prospects were not what we wanted, but in time, if we are patient, what we want will walk through the door."

"Horatio Alger Burston, you are a most infuriating man. When it comes to business you have all the common sense in the world. Why can't you apply those same principles to a simple family matter?

"What you want does not exist. Any wet nurse will have a sad tale of misery and woe or she would not be hiring herself out while she is still in milk."

"Perhaps you are right, my dear," H.A. admitted. "Perhaps what I want is just a fantasy." He knew his dreams of how a rich man should live were, after all, a product of the twentieth-century entertainment media. The best cooks were French chefs, so he insisted they hire a Frenchman to cook for them. A rich man got into his car and said, "Home, James," in that upper class almost-British accent, so he wanted an English coachman named James. In the movies, the servants who knew how to have fun were Irish. It was okay to have straitlaced, stern German chambermaids keeping things clean, but his children should have fun growing up. He was rich. He should be able to have what he wanted. What he wanted was an Irish lass to raise his children.

"Horatio Alger, face reality. There is no perhaps about it. You are not being fair with me in this matter. At best, a wet nurse is a tragic woman who recently lost her child or she wouldn't be in milk. She probably just lost her husband as well, or she wouldn't need to be self-supporting. And that is if she ever had a husband. The truth is, most likely, her tale will be a sordid one. Or if she has been a wet nurse for a long time, and she is looking for a job, then you can be sure she has no personality or no skills. If she had either she would have been kept on in the household after the child was weaned and she would no longer be a wet nurse."

"You're probably right. It is just that . . . well . . . oh, never mind." H.A. sighed. "You are completely right about one thing though. Henrich said Maire recently buried her husband and her child."

Catharina didn't let her smile show. Horatio was on the verge of giving in. She was sure, when the coming interview was over, he would give up and let her hire whomever she wanted. There was no possible way any woman could look good after she got through questioning her. What she said next was carefully calculated to make her seem reasonable, to disarm her spouse and set him up for the next round, which she was now—finally—sure she would win. "Well, Tio Al, let's give this one a fair chance, shall we? After all, maybe she will be what you want." She knew using the shortened form of his first and second names would please him and make him feel like he was gaining ground in their clash of wills over cultural matters.

One of the maids showed Henrich and Maire into the room H.A. called the front parlor. He started to rise to greet his guests but Catharina's hand on his arm kept him in his seat. She had, after all, her own firm ideas on what was and wasn't proper, and she also was working on training her new spouse.

Catharina watched H.A. smile when he saw the lute Maire was carrying. She took one glance at her husband's face and sharpened her questions to be sure the girl came off looking bad lest Horatio should decide to *let* her hire this one.

The girl was young. She was clean and appeared demure or even shy. Her long, dark red hair framed a pretty face. Indeed, if Catharina did not already have someone picked out and waiting she might have wanted this girl as part of the household.

Horatio addressed the prospective employee and her escort. "Please be seated."

Catharina squeezed his arm. H.A. knew her thoughts on how

the help should be treated. He did not agree. Besides, if the lass played the lute she probably needed to be seated to do so. H.A. nodded at the instrument. "Are you any good with that thing?"

Maire looked down and bit her lip to smother a chuckle. She unwrapped the lute, risking the rapid change of temperature just this one time. She quickly tuned the stings and began to sing a slow song in her native Irish tongue in a soft, sweet voice. It was nice but H.A. steeled himself for the employment interview that would follow. Maire started a second song in charmingly accented English without a pause, "Dough is for the rising bread, ray is for the rising sun. Me is a name for my rising self—"

The words and the tune were almost, but not quite, familiar. It nagged H.A., while at the same time it set him at ease. At last he made the connection. The song was almost like one of the signature tunes from the Maria von Trump . . . or von Trap . . . well, von something, anyway . . . story, the one where the failed nun was sent to raise a family of children and ended up marrying the father. H.A. made up his mind with a smile.

When she finished the song H.A. said to Henrich, "She is exactly what we are looking for. We'll take her."

Catharina's mouth fell open and was as quickly closed. She was not given the chance to ask the new nursemaid a single question. What *could* her husband be thinking? She sighed the most exasperated sigh imaginable and said under her breath, "*Americans!* Who can understand them?" Still it was clear her husband was in a good mood. If she was going to get anything out of this other than the embarrassment of not getting to hire who she wanted, now was the time to get it. "Tio Al, we could use some new clothes for our baby daughter. And with the diapers to be washed the laundress will need some help. I was wondering if we might buy a sewing machine and hire a girl to help out for a bit."

"I don't see why not." H.A. replied.

Catharina smiled. It wasn't the job the girl was expecting but at least she wouldn't have to turn her away after letting her think she would have a place in the household. Horatio was a generous man when he wasn't being stubborn.

On November second, All Soul's Day, H.A. arrived home, as usual, about five minutes before noon for lunch, which would be on the table, piping hot, promptly at twelve o'clock. Catharina was sitting at the dining table, waiting for him. Her air of intense concentration clearly told H.A. that there was something on her mind and that this was not going to be an ordinary lunch.

"What's the matter?" H.A. asked.

"A doctor called this morning and just left. It seems one of the help brought a sick child into the house." Her tone made it clear. Heads would be rolling just as soon as she found out who did it, who knew about it and didn't say anything or who didn't know about it but should have. To H.A. it was obvious that if his wife had her way, all of the resident staff, and maybe the entire staff, would most likely find themselves in need of new jobs. Considering the history of plagues and epidemics and the high mortality rate of young children, her wrath was fueled as much or more by fear than anger. But, still, H.A. was glad he had made it plain that while she could hire mostly as she pleased, he would be reviewing the circumstances and making the final decision before anyone was dismissed from service. Catharina was a loving mother and a thoughtful, compassionate wife. Unfortunately, those traits did not seem to apply when she was dealing with servants.

"I know, dear. I quite agree. We can't have the servants bringing sick children into the house. That's why I sent the doctor around to see him."

H.A. could have grown a tail and horns without startling his wife any more than he did with his calm agreement that was not an agreement at all. "*You* sent the doctor? You knew about this?"

Briefly H.A. was worried about his own head rolling. Then he remembered that this was the 1600s, that the money was his, and that she really didn't have much of anywhere else to go if she wanted to continue living in the manner to which she was accustomed. "I've known for months that Maire was unhappy with the care Alois was getting."

"Maire?" While Catharina was satisfied with the care her children were receiving—she had to admit the children were clean, happy and well behaved—she had never gotten completely over not being allowed to hire her first choice. "Her child is supposed to be dead!" The implication was they had been lied to and that she should be dismissed.

"Alois is the grandson of the merchant Henrich. He hired Maire to care for the child and then he brought her here. When she took this job he made arrangements with his usual inn to look after the boy for him. That is where Maire goes when she has time off. As I said, I've known for some time that she was unhappy with how the boy was being looked after."

"I don't think I like our nanny being distracted with other children," Catharina said.

H.A.'s voice took on a firmer resonance. "I don't think I would want my children being raised by someone who could turn her back and let a child she once cared for die just because it was no longer convenient. If she cares for the last lot, then she will care for the next. I like knowing she cares."

"Well, she can't keep it here!"

"Why not? Now, I quite agree that we can't be having the help bring sick children to work, but this is the only home Maire has, so she sure couldn't leave the child with its grandmother, now could she? So I sent a doctor. That last girl you hired, Anna, can look after the boy and still get her work done. She's been unhappy and pining away over not having a child to care for since you hired her. That's the job she thought she was getting after all, wasn't it! Well, now she can quit sneaking upstairs to peek at our kids."

"And just how do you know all of this?" Catharina was suddenly very suspicious. Her husband seemed to know a lot more than he should about the nanny and one of the maids.

H.A. had enough sense not to chuckle. "I talk to Fred."

"Fred? Fredrick? You talk to your valet?"

"Yes, I talk to my valet. He is a very interesting character. He has a bottomless supply of dirty jokes. He's been through some rather incredible circumstances, and he keeps me posted on what is going on in the kitchen, in the stables and in the garrets."

Catharina was mollified on one point but still wound up on the other. "And you think it will be all right to just let the staff raise this merchant's bastard"—she made a correct assumption on the child's lineage—"grandson."

"I don't see why not. We've got way more staff than we need to get the work done. If the child is to hand, then Maire will know he's well and she can quit worrying about him so she will have one less distraction, and she can pay more attention to what she is supposed to be doing. Look, we've got a live-in Irish sitter. Think of Alois as a live-in playmate."

H.A. got that look on his face; the one Catharina was learning to associate with things her husband seemed unable or unwilling to explain, the look he sometimes described as a shit-eating grin. "No. I don't see any reason we can't keep an in-house playmate. But, I will definitely draw the line at keeping bunnies."

Arsenic and Old Italians

Iver P. Cooper

The liquid in the shallow dish ignited, releasing a burst of yellow-green fire. The audience, a curious mix of Tuscan scholars and glitterati, applauded.

Lewis Philip Bartolli acknowledged the applause with a briefly lifted hand. "This lovely green reveals the presence of the element boron, which was not known to the ancients. The liquid is distilled spirits, which burn nicely. To the spirits, I added what chemists call boric acid. This boric acid contains one atom of boron, three of oxygen, and three of hydrogen, and it was obtained from the volcanic emissions of the Maremma of southern Tuscany."

A servant in the livery of the reigning Grand Duke of Tuscany, Ferdinand de Medici, silently glided down the aisle, and whispered into the ear of Andrea di Giovanni Battista Cioli, the Tuscan Secretary of State. Cioli flinched, then muttered something to his companion, the teenaged Prince Leopold.

"The green color of the flame is the result of the excitation of the electrons of boron. Next, I would like to show you—"

Cioli rose abruptly. "On behalf of the Serenissime Grand Duke, of His Highness don Leopoldo, the learned fellows of the Academy, our guests, and myself, I would like to thank Dottore Bartolli for a fascinating presentation on chemistry. Unfortunately, we must excuse him, as he has a pressing engagement."

I do? But Lewis kept this thought to himself, and bowed.

The crowd filed out. The increased hubbub woke up Galileo

Galilei, who was snoring away in a front seat. Like Lewis, the great man was expected to entertain the court. Lewis gave chemistry demonstrations during the day, and Galileo set up his telescope and explained the wonders of the night sky. Since he was up half the night, and was more than twice Lewis' age, it was perhaps understandable that he couldn't always stay awake for Lewis' lecture.

"Um, what. Oh. Wonderful presentation, Lewis. Another nail in the coffin of the Aristotelians."

Cioli put his arm around Lewis. "Walk with me, dear chemist. You can take my coach to your pressing engagement." He turned to Leopold. "Your Highness, you are welcome to join us, I think you will find the matter of interest." Leopold was the grand duke's youngest brother.

In the privacy of the coach, Lewis finally could speak his mind. "For Christ's sake, what is this all about?"

"Grand Duke Ferdinando was dining with one of his leading noblemen. The man suddenly showed signs of severe gastric distress."

"I am not a physician—"

"You don't need to be; he is already dead."

"And you suspect—"

"Murder. Yes. By poison, we think. So we need your expertise."

Prince Leopold chimed in. "Surely your mentor, the great Sherlock Holmes, would expect you to assist us."

The grand duke and his brothers had not initially grasped the concept that the Sherlock Holmes Lewis had told them about was a fictional character, and Lewis' business associate in Tuscany, Niccolo Cavriani, had warned Lewis not to correct them. "In general, it is not a good idea to tell a ruler that he is wrong. Especially when the error is a harmless one" were his words. Hence, earlier that year, Lewis had not protested when Grand Duke Ferdinand proclaimed the young up-timer to be "Consulting Detective to the Grand Duchy of Tuscany."

They rode in silence for a few minutes.

Cioli cleared his throat. "During your investigation, Lewis, please keep in mind that the deceased lord might not have been the real target of the poisoner. The grand duke is not popular in all circles of power in Tuscany. Or beyond. Especially since he has shown favor to you, and thus, however obliquely, to your United States of Europe."

"So you think it was an assassination attempt gone amiss?"

Cioli shrugged. "Who can say? But you see that the investigation is of the greatest importance. You doubtless will be rewarded appropriately for proving the identity the poisoner." Cioli was too polite to mention the consequences of failure.

Or perhaps he thought it more effective to leave them to Lewis' imagination.

The coach stopped in front of a villa. The footman stepped down and open the door. Lewis was about to step out when he was stopped by a soldier. He aimed a lantern into the compartment. "Excuse me, Your Highness, Your Lordship, Dottore. I have my orders. Would you wait just a moment, please?" He closed the door.

"This is exciting, isn't it, Dottore?" asked Leopold.

Lewis reminded himself that Leopold was only sixteen. With the *gravitas* that came from being fully two years older, Lewis acknowledged that the case might have its interesting aspects.

When the door was opened once more, it was to reveal the familiar visage of the ruler of Tuscany. "A curious turn of events, eh, Lewis?"

"Yes, Your Grace."

"But with you here, the game is now afoot."

Lewis fought back a groan. "Indeed."

"Thank you for your assistance, Lord Cioli. Oh, and hi, Leopoldo. Try not to bother Lewis with too many questions."

Ferdinand beckoned to a tall fellow in an officer's uniform. "This is Lieutenant Cosimo Capponi. He and his men will help you conduct searches, question suspects, and so forth. I want to make sure that you encounter no difficulties on account of your being a foreigner."

Cosimo bowed. "I look forward to working with you, Dottore. I will make sure that you can go where you need to go, and that people answer your questions. And of course I can question witnesses on your behalf."

Cosimo pointed out two soldiers. "Carlo and Rocco. If you need a suspect watched, or a door broken in, they're your men.

"Also permit me to introduce Giovanni di Niccolo Ronconi, who is one of our family physicians. A Padua man."

"I'm a West Virginia man, myself," said Lewis. The Tuscans all nodded sagely.

"But please proceed with your investigations, Lewis."

"Your Grace, who was at the table besides yourself?"

"Pietro, the deceased. His wife Silvia, and their children Domenico and Olimpia. The Senator Francesco di Alessandro Arrighi, and his wife Lucrezia. The banker Alberto Spinelli, and his sister Isabella. *La Cecchina*—"

"I beg your pardon? *La Cecchina*? 'The Songbird,' who's that?"

"I perceive you are not a musician, Lewis," Ferdinand said. "Why not? Didn't Sherlock Holmes play the violin?"

Cioli intervened. "*La Cecchina* is the composer and singer Francesca Caccini. She sang for our court for at least two decades. Maria of Tuscany, the Queen of France, tried to steal her from us but her uncle, Ferdinando the First, forbade Francesca to leave."

"A wise move. She was, I think, the first woman to write an opera. Do you remember it, Cioli? It was *La liberazione di Ruggiero dall'isola d'Alcina*; it was performed at my villa in 1625."

"It was exquisite. She married a Luccan nobleman, he died, and she returned to Ferdinando's service last year."

"That's right. And then there was Lorenzo Pippi, the poet. Or perhaps I should say *Perlone Zipoli*, since that's his pen name."

"Would-be poet," muttered Cioli. "Wise of him to use a pen name. Should have stuck to painting."

Ferdinand laughed. "Perhaps a half-dozen others whose names slip my mind. Silvia can tell you who they were."

"So describe the dinner," Lewis prompted. "What was served, who ate what, that sort of thing. And when did Pietro show the first signs of distress?"

"Hmm . . . first course was prosciutto cooked in wine and Neapolitan spice cakes. Those were served off the sideboard, 'help yourself.' I did."

"No spit-roasted songbirds, this time?" asked Leopold.

Cioli shook his head minutely. "Now that wouldn't have been very polite, with Francesca Caccini in attendance."

Ferdinand chuckled. "Second course, several different roasts. I had the goat and the rabbit, I am not sure what else there was.

"For the third course, there was a stuffed goose, smothered with almonds, with cheese, sugar and cinnamon on the side. Also Turkish-style rice, in milk, with more sugar and cinnamon sprinkled over it. Cabbage soup with sausages half-submerged, like those submarines you once told me about, Lewis. And boiled calves' feet. How could I forget that?

"We saw, but never got to taste, the fourth course, the desserts. They were arranged on the sideboard. Quince pastries. Pear tarts. Leopoldo, do you remember the time—"

"Please, Brother, don't tell them."

"Oh, very well. More cheese. More almonds. Roast chestnuts. My, it's making me hungry just thinking about them. And it's barely an hour past sunset.

"Anyway, *La Cecchina* sang between the first and second courses."

"Paying for her supper," Leopold said.

Better than listening to restaurant muzak. Or worse, karaoke, thought Lewis.

"Lorenzo recited a few of his poems between the second and third courses. That's when Pietro started seeming out of sorts."

"And no wonder," grumbled Cioli.

"The remains of the third course had just been carried off and we were heading toward the sideboard, when Pietro clutched his stomach and claimed he was nauseous. We urged him to lie down, but he refused. Then he vomited.

"Silvia ordered the servants to carry him to the nearest couch and lay him down there. At that point of course, none of us were thinking about poison."

"Or dessert," Leopold said.

Ferdinand gave his brother a quelling look. "We assumed it was just a case of indigestion. At worst, that he ate something that was spoiled. Pietro complained that he was thirsty, and we brought him some wine. He seemed to have difficulty in swallowing, and he complained that his throat was sore. He soon vomited again.

"When Pietro was still in great distress an hour later, I sent a messenger to fetch Dottore Ronconi. Since the incident happened in my presence, I was insistent that Pietro be seen by the best doctor in Florence." Ronconi bowed.

"Ronconi will have to tell you what happened next."

Ronconi took a deep breath. "I came and questioned Pietro. He told me that he was of the opinion that there were people 'out to get him.'"

Lewis raised his eyebrows. "So he thought he was poisoned. Did he name any names?"

"He did not. He said that they must be in league with the Devil to get through his defenses."

"Defenses?"

"He has an armed guard at the door," Cioli said. "And I have heard that he has detailed servants to spy on each other, and that it is rare for a servant to stay more than a year or two before being dismissed on suspicion of wrongdoing. It is not a happy household."

"In any event, I examined him," said Ronconi. "Besides the obvious problem of the nausea and repeated vomiting, his stomach was very sensitive to pressure. He found even a light touch to be painful. I prescribed some medications, and departed.

"The following morning, I received a message from Silvia, urging my return. He had had an attack of diarrhea. Several in fact. By the time I arrived, he was in an advanced state of tenesmus."

"No medical gobbledygook, please," ordered Ferdinand.

"You feel you have to poop, and you can't. And it hurts." Ronconi shrugged. "It was at that point that I began to wonder whether there was some truth to Pietro's speculations, and I asked that the leftovers be gathered together for testing."

"I am surprised that the servants hadn't eaten them all by then," Leopold said. Since he was a sixteen-year-old boy, the concept of failing to eat any available food was no doubt alien to him.

"They had, indeed, eaten most of what had been left from the first and second courses, but naturally that tended to suggest that those courses were free of any taint. The servants had not disturbed the third course; no doubt Pietro's sufferings discouraged them from doing so.

"Hence, I was able to feed the remains of the third course to the family dog, and he seemed none the worse for the experience."

Clearly, thought Lewis, *animal rights have yet too make much headway in early modern Italy*.

"That quieted my concerns for a time. But the next day, Pietro's skin became cold and clammy, his pulse weakened, and at last he died."

"Were his wife and children present? How did they react to his death?" asked Ferdinand sharply.

"The wife and children seemed properly remorseful." He spread his hands. "There is not much left to say. He passed from my care to that of Our Lord and Savior."

Ferdinand gripped Lewis' shoulder, then released it. "In view of the allegations of poisoning, I thought it appropriate to call upon my 'Consulting Detective.' Don't disappoint me."

"Don't forget what I said about keeping your mind open as to whom the target might have been," Cioli added softly.

"Well, there are a few options. I can do a Marsh test for arsenic on the remaining food."

"I am sorry, Ispettore Bartolli," the doctor said, "but none remain. The dog ate it all."

"Well, then—I don't suppose you saved any of the vomit?"

"No, I'm sorry. The servants cleaned it up. There might be a little staining his clothing, but I can't make any promises."

"Doesn't matter. I will just have to ask you, in the grand duke's name, to perform an autopsy. You can examine the stomach lining for signs of damage, and I can test the contents for arsenic and anything else I can think of.

"I will need to interview the family. One by one, if you please. I'll need one of your men, Cosimo, to act as a witness."

"I'll give you Rocco, he has some letters."

"Good. And Cosimo, if you would interview all the servants. Again, one by one, so they can't influence each other."

"Right, but I can assure you that the servants are probably hoarse from all the gabbing they've done already."

"I am sorry for your loss," Lewis offered.

The widow, Silvia, dabbed at the corner of her eye with a small handkerchief. Suddenly Lewis was reminded of a scene in a *film noir* movie. He couldn't remember the name. He was pretty sure that the widow in that movie turned out to be guilty, though.

"Thank you."

"I regret that I must ask you some questions."

"I understand . . . the grand duke told me. . . ."

"Perhaps he also told you that I am a stranger to this city, even to this time. You can trust me to seek the truth."

"At least as long as that truth isn't politically inconvenient for the grand duke."

"Even then, I might surprise you." Lewis hoped so, at least.

"Ask your questions."

Lewis asked her everything a mystery reader or crime TV fan might expect him to ask. The poisonous substances that were kept in the house or its grounds, and whether they had shown signs of recent use. The names and duties of the servants, their term of service, their past employers, and their whereabouts on the day that Pietro was stricken. The medications which Pietro had taken over the past month or so. The names and business of any visitors within the same period, and the dates of their visits. Who might be expected to benefit from or take pleasure in Pietro's death.

"Is it true that he thought someone wanted to kill him?"

"Yes."

"When did he first form this belief?"

"Several years ago. First he was attacked by ruffians at night, and was saved by the chance appearance of a couple of young noblemen. And then he was standing by a building, and was grazed by a falling brick."

"He saw someone drop the brick on him?"

"No, he said it happened too quickly."

"And do you think he was right, that he was in danger?"

Silvia shrugged. "This is Florence, who can say? Politics can be vicious. And commerce, even more vicious."

You aren't being paranoid if people really are out to get you, Lewis mused.

Domenico was a sullen twenty-something of no clear occupation. Other, perhaps, than his former occupation of "Waiting for Pop to Die So I Can Make a Real Dent in the Family Fortune." He disavowed any knowledge of poisons or medicines, not that in the seventeenth century there was a big difference between the two.

Olimpia was equally irritating, in her own special way. While Domenico tried to answer every questions with a single word—and then, only after a long pause, Olimpia was obviously in training for the Run-On Sentence Olympic event.

Before leaving, Lewis took samples of Domenico's tonic, and Silvia and Olimpia's cosmetics. He also borrowed the household accounts book.

Lewis and Cosimo compared notes.

"I spoke to Pietro's manservant, Taddeo. He told me something peculiar. Seems that Pietro was in the habit of making trips by himself, perhaps once every other month. Went in disguise."

"That's interesting. Sounds like a Clue with a capital C."

"Frustrating, is what I'd call it. If he were alive, I could have him tailed. With him dead, I can't follow up on it."

"If he weren't dead, we wouldn't be talking about it in the first place."

"It's too bad. I would have looked forward to tailing him. Probably lead me through three or four taverns a night. Perhaps even a brothel or two. And I would have to buy drinks, and so forth, all at Medici expense. So I didn't look suspicious, you see."

"I do indeed."

"I feel cheated, I must say."

"Pietro ever say anything about why he made the trips?"

"Apparently not. As you heard, Pietro was secretive. Didn't trust his own servants. Might have been going to see a girl, but I rather think it was something political. If it was directed against the Medicis, perhaps it's just as well he's dead."

Cosimo cocked his head. "Any great insights? Has Sherlock Holmes spoken to you from beyond the Great Unknown?"

"Well, a detective looks for who has means, motive and opportunity. The family members, and the servants, of course have opportunity. And often motive, too. As to means—by God Almighty, there's arsenic everywhere! In Domenico's tonic, in Silvia and Olimpia's face powder, in the servants' storeroom. They use it to kill rats, they say.

"If my chemical tests show that Pietro was poisoned, it won't be a surprise to me. The surprise is that everyone else in the damn household is still alive!"

"Signorina Bartolli is waiting for you in the courtyard," the butler said.

Lewis nearly dropped the instruments he was carrying. "Who?"

"Your sister, Marina Bartolli." The servant gave him a reproving look. "You really should have warned us, sir."

Lewis ran down the hall. It was Marina all right, sitting on a stone bench, her back to him. "What the hell are you doing here?" he sputtered.

She turned her head. "It's good to see you, too, Brother. The roses here are lovely, don't you think? Not a variety we have in Grantville."

"I mean, how could you come without sending me word, giving me the chance to tell you whether conditions were safe?"

"I did send you word, a few weeks ago. But then I had the chance, thanks to Duchess Claudia, to snag a seat on the Monster." That was the world's first commercial airplane. "You can't begrudge me having chosen to cross the Alps in just a few hours, rather than a month by land, can you? And then it was just a coach ride from Venice to Florence." She added impishly, "I'm sure my letter will get here eventually."

"Claudia de Medici? The *arch*duchess and regent of Austria-Tyrol? How do you know her?"

"Why, she came into the store."

"Claudia de Medici visited Bartolli's Surplus and Outdoors Supplies?"

"No, she just pressed her face against the window glass, idiot. Yes, she came in. It was refreshing to have a visitor who asked questions about things that didn't go boom. We hit it off."

Lewis stared at the ceiling. "I don't suppose she asked about our family, too?"

"Oh, yes, I bragged a bit about our brother-in-law." Greg Ferrara, once Grantville's high school chemistry teacher, and now the USE's Grand Poo-Bah of Military R&D. "And I might have mentioned Toni Adducci, Senior." He was their first cousin, once removed, and the Secretary of the Treasury for the State of Thuringia-Franconia.

"Good God, Marina, you were talking to a Medici. For them, there is no boundary between family life and political life. I wouldn't be a bit surprised if she knew about Greg before you opened your mouth. She flew you to Venice—"

"And arranged for me to be escorted here. And I have a letter to her nephew Ferdinand, asking that he see to it that I am safely returned to her townhouse in Venice when I am done here."

"How nice. Given that 'nephew Ferdinand' is the grand duke of Tuscany, I am sure you'll travel in style. But what sort of favor do you think Claudia will expect from you? And what will she do if you can't deliver?"

"Oh, pooh," said Marina. "I can deliver. I already had cousin Greg and *Arch*duchess Claudia over for dinner, for example. It went fine, even if Mother nearly had a nervous breakdown. And I can ask my brother Lewis—" She winked. "—whether there might be any 'investment opportunities' in his boric acid operation. So, are there?"

"Given that the operation is backed by Medici money, and Claudia is a Medici, I think that's a safe assumption."

"Good. I also have a list of chemistry questions for you. Mind you, I think Claudia already put the same questions to cousin Greg, and just wants to see if your answers are the same. She's a smart cookie."

"I'm sure."

"She kinda hinted that she might be able to take me on as one of her ladies-in-waiting."

"You want to be a glorified servant to a noblewoman?"

"Oh, that's right. I could stay in Grantville and be a sales clerk in a sporting goods store. What was I thinking?"

"Still—"

"Okay." She held up her left hand, palm up. "Sales clerk in Grantville." She held up her right hand the same way, at the same height. "Lady-in-waiting and ornamental up-timer in Tyrolia." She jiggled the hands up and down, as if they were the pans of a balance, then suddenly raised the left and lowered the right, sharply. "Tyrol wins!

"Anyway, you're one to talk. Isn't 'nephew Ferdinand' your patron now?"

"Technically speaking, he, and his brother Leopold, are patrons of the Academy, not my personal patron. I am still an officer in the USE Army."

"Technically speaking, 'Mister Consulting Detective,' if he tells you to piss, you say, 'yes sir, how far, sir?' Because we want Tuscany to be a friendly neutral. At least, that's what the ambassadress told me when I passed through Venice."

Lewis winced. "As a matter of fact, he has given me a little assignment. A murder investigation."

"Ooh, tell me more."

"Well, the gruesome part is done," Lewis said. After the grand duke's physician had clucked-clucked over the corrosion of the stomach lining—typical of arsenic, antimony or mercury poisoning—Lewis had divided the stomach contents into two parts. One part he preserved intact, for study under the microscope, and the other part he homogenized, acidified, and heated. He let it cool back down, and ran it through a filter.

"Your Grace, if there is any arsenic in the filtrate, it is now sodium arsenate. We can now perform the Marsh test." Lewis pointed at a bottle. "That contains arsenic-free sulfuric acid." Lewis pulled some small rods of metal out of a chest. "And these are arsenic-free rods of zinc metal; what the alchemists call 'Malabar lead.'"

The World's Most Blue-Blooded Lab Assistant, otherwise known as Grand Duke Ferdinand, put the rods into a flask and poured the acid over the metal.

"Take it easy, Your Grace," warned Lewis. "We want to keep the temperature low, and the evolution of hydrogen slow." Lewis stuck his precious up-time thermometer into the flask. "Hmm... you were perhaps a little too enthusiastic. Let's cool things down a bit." He put the flask into a dish of cold water for a few minutes, then removed it.

"All right, next step." Lewis stoppered the flask, and inserted two tubes into it, one for adding the sample at the proper time, and the other to a U-shaped drying tube. This in turn he connected to an L-shaped tube with a long arm passing over a candle.

"Now we wait for all the air to be expelled."

The minutes passed.

Leopold fidgeted. Finally, he asked, "Why is it called the 'Marsh test'? That is your English word for a 'swamp,' *si*?"

"It's named after the English chemist, James Marsh. Marsh was called upon in a case in which a young man was accused of poisoning his grandfather with arsenic trioxide... that's what your apothecaries call 'arsenic.' He detected it by its reaction with hydrogen sulfide, but by the time of the trial, the yellow precipitate had deteriorated, and the jury refused to convict. Marsh was apoplectic over this miscarriage of justice, and worked long hours in his laboratory until he devised this test."

"Why the zinc?"

"The zinc reacts with the sulfuric acid to generate hydrogen, and the hydrogen reacts with the arsenic to form arsine gas."

"A gas? Like air?" Leopold, clearly, had attended Lewis' lecture on how air was a substance. "How will we see it?"

"When the gas is brought to a red heat here"—Lewis pointed to the part of the tube right above the alcohol burner—"it will decompose into metallic arsenic and hydrogen, and a shiny black deposit of arsenic will be deposited on the inside of the tube, just beyond. That's what we call the..." He paused for effect "... 'arsenic mirror.'

"It is time. Leopold, would you like to do the honors?" The World's Second Most Blue-Blooded Lab Assistant dropped the filtrate down the sample tube into the flask. And his older brother lit the burner.

"I can't believe you're letting them do everything," Marina complained.

"I thought you hated lab work when you took chemistry last year."

"I did. But you still should have *asked* me."

"I don't see anything yet," said Ferdinand.

"Let me see if this helps." Lewis held a white paper behind the tube.

"No. . . . Wait . . . yes! I see a brown stain."

"It's getting blacker," said Leopold.

"Black as sin," pronounced Ferdinand. "We have a poisoning, don't we, Lewis?"

"It looks that way, Your Grace. But let me confirm." Lewis brought the burner to the free end of the tube, and ignited the escaping gas. It produced a bluish white flame, with white fumes.

"So far so good. Or bad, depending on your point of view."

Lewis held a cold porcelain dish to the flame, then brought it away. There was a brownish black spot upon it. "And that, my friends, is the 'arsenic spot.'"

Marina walked into Lewis' house, followed by a servant trying to balance a large pile of goods.

Lewis eyed the pile warily. "I hope Archduchess Claudia gave you an expense account."

"Nothing to worry about, Brother. These are gifts from relatives."

"Relatives?"

"You didn't think that the Bartollis climbed out of the trees in West Virginia, did'ya? There are Bartollis right here in Florence. Cosimo, Lorenzo, Giovanni, Matteo, Niccolo, Piero . . ."

"And you think we're related, just because of the last name?"

"Well, they thought it was reasonable. Of course, they weren't sure of the blood connection until I mentioned that I had been in Ferdinand and Leopold's private laboratory, and flew to Venice with Archduchess Claudia."

"You impudent namedropper, you. Even if it's true, let me think . . . 370 years . . . twenty years a generation . . . you might be their cousin eighteenth removed, if I've got the terminology straight. You're probably more closely related to John F. Kennedy than you are to them."

"Whatever. So, who d'you think knocked off Pietro?" Marina said.

Lewis laughed. "Suspects? They are as common as mosquitoes in the Maremma. Silvia is sure it's some business or political rival. She gave me a list. Pietro was recently appointed to a salt magistracy, and she thinks that perhaps he discovered that one of his colleagues was embezzling funds, and threatened to inform the authorities if he didn't turn himself in."

"More likely asked for a cut in return for his silence, and got too greedy," said Cosimo.

"But were those rivals at the dinner?" asked Marina.

"Even if they weren't there, they could have suborned a servant," said Cosimo. "But actually, I think it's the wife. Wives have poisoned inconvenient husbands since time immemorial. A half-century ago, Bianca Cappello, the most beautiful woman in Tuscany, poisoned Pietro Bonaventuri, so she could marry her lover, Francesco de Medici."

"Yep, Silvia's a suspect, all right. Silvia would have much more financial independence as a widow, and she's still good looking. For that matter, perhaps there's some young fellow she already has her eyes on."

"We'll look into it," said Cosimo.

"Then there are the heirs," Lewis continued. "Domenico and Olimpia. You do know what they call arsenic in this day and age? 'Inheritance powder.' It can be added to food or drink without imparting a suspicious color or taste, and seventeenth-century alchemy is quite incapable of identifying it. That made it the ideal poison until chemistry caught up with the poisoners in the nineteenth century."

"Rocco got chummy with Taddeo, found out that Pietro's got a mistress. Had a mistress, I should say. Her name's Stella. Lives at a nice address, dresses well. Sin pays."

"Ah," said Lewis, "the plot thickens. Or, more precisely, the list of suspects increases."

Marina looked unconvinced. "Why would she kill the goose that lays the golden eggs? Surely she would be left with nothing if he died."

"Right," said Cosimo. "Usually the mistress gets rid of the wife, and marries the husband. Bianca Cappello did that, too. Remember her? She poisoned Giovanna, the Austrian princess, and married Francesco de Medici."

Lewis shrugged. "A mistress might murder a patron. Perhaps she found a fatter 'goose,' and Pietro wouldn't let her move on. Or perhaps he beats her, and she wanted revenge. Or he refused to divorce his wife, and she decided to poison Pietro and hope that the death would be blamed on Silvia."

Marina had a different idea. "Or perhaps some young fellow is madly in love with Stella and killed Pietro out of jealousy."

"You're quite a romantic," said Lewis.

"No, no, your sister's right," said Cosimo. "That sort of thing happens. I'll ask around."

"Perhaps I should interview this Stella myself."

"How very conscientious of you, dear brother."

Cosimo found Stella's boy toy. "His name's Fabio," Cosimo reported.

"Occupation?"

"Artist."

"Great, all I need," said Lewis.

"What's wrong with artists? Even artists named 'Fabio'?" asked Marina.

"The pigments they use. Which include realgar red and orpiment yellow. Realgar is arsenic (II) sulfide, and orpiment is arsenic (III) sulfide."

"While those are poisonous, you can't put them in food without anyone noticing," said Cosimo.

"But you can react them with natron, sodium carbonate, to get arsenic trioxide. And heat that in vegetable oil if you want pure arsenic. As I said, all I need."

Lewis started pacing, then stopped abruptly. "Although while this Fabio may have had the means, and the motive, I am not so sure he'd have the opportunity. When would he come into contact with Pietro?"

"Perhaps he gave the stuff to Stella to administer to Pietro. He might not even have told her it was poison. Perhaps that it was an aphrodisiac."

Lewis snorted. "We're making quite a mountain of accusations out of a molehill of evidence."

Lewis knew that Pietro's body contained a large dose of arsenic, the Marsh test on his stomach contents was ample proof of that. If the arsenic had been administered on the day of the infamous dinner, then the list of suspects could be trimmed down, to just the family, the guests and the servants present that day. Still a long list, of course.

But Pietro and Silvia thought that there had been a series of attempts on his life. And if that were the case, and they were all by the same party, then knowing when the attempts were made could help narrow down the list of suspects.

Unfortunately, the Marsh test didn't provide a timeline. The statements collected by the investigators, and even the household account book, hadn't been of much help, either. There were payments for medicines, but the responsible doctors and apothecaries swore that these didn't contain significant amounts of arsenic, and Lewis' testing of the remaining vials, ointments and whatnot confirmed that. In fact, it seemed that Pietro had the least chronic exposure to arsenic of anyone in the household.

Lewis had one last resort. Back in 1997, the high school had been the recipient of an extraordinary gift, a $300,000 atomic absorption spectrophotometer. The gift had come about because one of the high school teachers had led a statewide high school science club trip to Carnegie Science Center in Pittsburgh, and had run into some LaFarge executives there.

As the name suggested, the AAS atomized a sample and then analyzed its ability to absorb light of different wavelengths. It should be able to detect arsenic at a level of just one part per million. Perhaps less.

"It's been a month since Pietro died, Dottore," Ferdinand said. He and Lewis were sitting in Ferdinand's laboratory, a corner of which had been appropriated by Lewis. "Can this wondrous AAS of yours still find the poison?"

"That's the good thing about an elemental poison, like arsenic, or thallium, Your Grace. The body can kick it out, but it can't decompose as it can, oh, snake venom. Within an hour or two of ingestion, the arsenic is distributed all over the body, even in the hair roots. Within a few days, it can be detected in the hair above the skin. And if the victim died with arsenic there, it will be still be there a month, a year, a decade, even a century later. The arsenic atoms stick very well to the sulfur atoms in the hair."

"A century? Are you sure?"

"That's right. In the nineteenth century of the old time line, there was an emperor of France named Napoleon. He got defeated by the Brits and sent into exile on an island. He died there, and some people thought he had been poisoned. Over a century after his death, someone took a lock of hair that Napoleon had given to one of his aides, and had it tested with modern equipment for arsenic.

"Sure enough, he had way more than normal levels of arsenic."

"Wow!" said Marina, who had been invited to look at Ferdinand's chamber of curiosities. "Napoleon was poisoned!"

"Well, not necessarily deliberately," Lewis admitted. "There was a green wallpaper used at that time, which contained an arsenical dye. They didn't know that it could be decomposed by bacteria to release arsine gas, which is really nasty stuff."

"A hundred years..." muttered Ferdinand.

"I beg your pardon, Your Grace. What did you say?"

"Never mind that for now. You already know that he was poisoned, from the contents of his stomach, so why look at his hair?"

"Because the hair would chronicle his arsenic exposure. Hair grows from the root outward, at a rate of a centimeter a month. So if his hair were twelve centimeters long, we could cut into sections and know when he ingested arsenic over the past year or so."

"Marvelous. And so you could eliminate any suspects who were absent when he had an arsenic peak," said Ferdinand.

"Exactly."

"Would you know the very days of each poisoning attempt?"

"I wish. To narrow down the time, you need to test shorter segments of hair, and there is more of a chance of contamination of the segment with arsenic from other sources. And that one centimeter a month is an average, it varies from person to person, and even from one part of the head to another. But we should be able to pin it down to a particular month, maybe even a particular fortnight.

"While I'm at it, Your Grace, I would like to send Grantville some additional hair samples for testing. My hair, Marina's, Cosimo's and your own, perhaps. We'll make sure that no one is putting arsenic in your soup, that way, and the rest of us will act as controls."

"See to it. Tomorrow morning I will have a courier take it to Venice. It can be there in two days, and then catch the next flight to Grantville. And your colleagues can radio the results to Venice to save time. All I ask is that the communications not reveal anyone's names."

"I wouldn't want them to. I will number the hair samples, so the testers won't be influenced in any way."

☆ ☆ ☆

"These results... are very strange."

"How so?" asked Marina.

"Okay. Look at the report. Sample 1 is your hair, that was the main control."

"Why not your hair?"

"Well, since I've been in Italy for a few months, and I have made few enemies, I couldn't be sure that no one was poisoning *me*."

"Oh."

"Anyway, your levels are low. About one part per million. So are mine, and Cosimo's, and even the grand duke's, for that matter. All under five parts per million. But now look at Sample 5."

Marina stared at the graph. "That's weird. They're up and down, on a regular basis. But... the peaks get higher and higher. And then the last peak is way up. So what does it mean?"

"First of all, these peaks are way above what a seventeenth-century Italian would naturally be exposed to. So Pietro was being poisoned all right."

"Which I thought we knew already, from the Marsh test on his tummy-wummy."

"Yes, Marina, but it was nice to get that confirmed by a more sensitive test.

"Second, Pietro suffered both chronic and acute arsenic poisoning. Which means that either our poisoner kept notching up the dose, and finally got impatient for some reason and hit him with the chemical equivalent of a two by four..."

Marina finished his thought. "Or we have two poisoners, working independently."

"Cosimo, I need to construct a plan of the house," Lewis said.

"What good will that do?"

"When a general is planning a battle, he consults a map of the terrain, does he not? When a detective investigates a crime in a house, he needs a house plan."

Cosimo shrugged. "All right, that makes sense. Perhaps I can borrow an assistant from one of the grand duke's architects; he'll do a better job than we could."

"Fine, Cosimo, but I need exact dimensions, not just a general layout. I want the length and height of every wall measured, and every corner checked to make sure that it's a right angle. I want to know the apparent thickness of every wall, beginning to end."

"You're looking for secret rooms?"

"Yes, like the priest's holes the Catholics in England have. Or even just a little hiding place."

"There, Cosimo, just as I thought. The dimensions of the study aren't right. This wall should be a foot farther away from the windows, to match the next room over."

"So what does that mean?"

"A false wall, and something behind it." Lewis put his ear against the wall, and tapped it.

He then did the same for one of the other walls.

"I believe the far wall is hollow. You try it."

Cosimo did just that. "I guess we need to go get some axes," he said cheerfully. The thought of a little authorized mayhem, even directed against the inanimate, was apparently pleasing to his martial spirit.

Lewis rubbed his chin. "Let's not be hasty. If the secret compartment, or whatever, was accessed frequently, his lordship certainly wasn't bashing in the wall each time. Start feeling around for a hidden panel."

They found it eventually, just below the ceiling. It had been superbly designed; it was no wonder they hadn't found it the first time they searched the house. The compartment it concealed wasn't that big, but it was big enough to hold some oddly marked vials, and a journal. Lewis handed them down to Cosimo, then stepped off the chair.

One of the vials contained a white powder. Lewis pointed to it, and Cosimo handed it over. Lewis pulled out the cork, and waved his hand over the top, wafting the released air toward him. "I'll have to test it, but I think it's arsenic. I wonder what the book says."

Cosimo had already started leafing through it. "Makes no sense to me."

"Here, let me. After reading the Latin mumbo-jumbo the alchemists write, I am pretty good at understanding esoterica. Not to mention reading really bad handwriting."

Cosimo handed the book over, with a slight smile.

"Why are you smirking, Captain? Oh." The text was clearly encrypted. "I guess I'll save that for later."

☆ ☆ ☆

Lewis had taken the first steps to solving the secret text. First, he tabulated all the symbols used on the first few pages. There were twenty-six different ones, which implied that each stood for a letter of the Renaissance Latin alphabet. It was just what Sherlock Holmes had done in "The Adventure of the Dancing Men."

However, Lewis couldn't be sure whether the cipher was in Latin or Italian, and in any event, Lewis didn't have frequency tables for either language. That problem was easy enough to solve; he gave Cosimo and Marina a few texts in each language, and had them compile tables for him.

In the meantime, he made a frequency table for the cipher. He was relieved to discover that it seemed to have the characteristic look, in terms of variation in frequency among the letters, of a monoalphabetic substitution cipher. That is, one in which each letter of the plaintext was replaced with a single cipher letter, and always that letter. Lewis had read that polyalphabetics had been invented in the fifteenth century, and wasn't at all sure that his deciphering skills were up to tackling one.

"Here you go," said Marina. "I hope this is based on enough data. I'll go blind if I look at any more Latin gobbledegook today."

Lewis looked it over. From most to least, it ran E A I T U . . . English would be E T A O N . . . Fortunately, with so much cipher text to work from, it would be easier to solve than even a newspaper cryptogram. Assuming that Lewis hadn't made any mistakes in converting the symbols into letters, and that Pietro, or whoever, hadn't thrown in too many nulls, abbreviations, code names or mistakes.

Marina looked over her shoulder. "I can tell you what it says. 'Dear Diary . . . '"

"You're right, Maria, it *is* a diary. Although each entry begins with a date. So I will decipher the first few entries, and then switch to the last ones."

"Fine. I am going out."

"Okay, you know the drill. Summon the coach, have them wait for you, don't go off with any strange men. Actually, with any men."

"Yeah, yeah." She gave him a vague wave and went looking for a footman.

Lewis went back to work. He was still working when she returned, late in the evening. But he was able to tell her something important. The text wasn't a diary, exactly. It was a journal. An experimental journal.

The next morning, when Cosimo arrived at the door, Lewis was waiting for him. "Cosimo, we need to visit a few apothecaries," said Lewis. "Oh, tell Carlo and Rocco I would like them to dress as servants, not soldiers. We are going to collect information, not to make arrests. I'll explain along the way."

"I understand you have solved the mystery," the grand duke declared.

"I think so, Your Grace. Pietro poisoned himself."

"Suicide? That is a serious charge—"

Lewis held up his hand. "Forgive the interruption, but while the poisoning was deliberate, the result was accidental."

"Explain."

"You will recall the testimony of the Lady Silvia that Pietro thought that someone was poisoning him. He questioned and fired a few servants, but of course he then had to hire new ones, who he soon suspected in turn. In desperation, he began his experiments."

"Oho," said Leopold, "he emulated Mithradates."

"Who's Mithradates?" asked Marina. "The name sounds Greek, not Italian."

Leopold smiled at her. "Mithradates of Pontus. He fought three wars with Rome. He was afraid of assassination, and he protected himself from poisoners by taking tiny doses of many different poisons. Then when he was about to be captured by the Romans, he tried to poison himself, without success. Had to ask a friend to run him through with a sword. See, Brother, I wasn't sleeping during my history lessons."

Ferdinand pretended to yawn. "That's what you did at least once a lesson, and you sure looked like you were sleeping. I guess you came awake if you heard the words 'poison' or 'sword.'"

"The infamous 'auditory echo,'" Marina muttered.

Lewis coughed, and Ferdinand motioned for him to continue. "Pietro took arsenic in small doses. Probably every other month, which is why the arsenic level in his hair fluctuated the same way. And he kept increasing the dose, as his tolerance increased, which is why the peaks got higher and higher."

"But the big peak at the end—surely that was something different? A poisoner got through his defenses?"

"That's what I thought, at first. And I suppose I can't rule it out, completely. But his secret journal records where he bought his arsenic. On those mysterious solitary trips in disguise that Cosimo told us, I believe. Pietro usually went to Cinelli's. But this last bottle, he got it from Rossi. I'm not sure why; perhaps Cinelli was out of town."

"What difference would that have made?"

"A crime was committed all right, but it wasn't murder. I made tests on the arsenic in the secret compartment, and also bought arsenic from both Cinelli and Rossi directly.

"Rossi's arsenic was fine. Cinelli's, on the other hand, was, excuse my French, crap. I think Cinelli was adulterating his arsenic all these years, and Pietro never realized it. Rossi, on the other hand, was an honest man. When Pietro bought arsenic from him, it was pure stuff. Consequently, Pietro received a much greater dose than he was expecting."

"Deliberate, yet accidental," murmured Ferdinand.

"Exactly."

"Captain Cosimo, see to it that Cinelli is arrested for criminal adulteration. I will tell Silvia that she and her son are now free of suspicion, and there will be no interference with the disposition of the estate."

Cosimo saluted, and left the room.

"Oh, Dottore Bartolli. I am most gratified with your work on this matter. But please, while you are welcome to mention your Marsh test in your lectures, please say nothing about the ability of this atomic absorption spectrophotometer in Grantville to detect arsenic in even a hundred-year-old corpse. At least, not to anyone other than a member of my family."

"Yes, Your Grace."

"There is going to be a party at the palace, I hope you and your sister can come," said Ferdinand.

"Yes, please come, Marina," said Leopold. "You can tell me more about Grantville. Do you know how to dance the *gagliarda*?"

"No, but I can teach the *macarena*."

Sometime later, on a flight from Venice to Magdeburg…

"It sounds like you had a most interesting visit to Florence," said Archduchess Claudia de Medici.

"Indeed I did, Your Grace," said Marina. "But, why didn't your nephew Ferdinand want Lewis to talk about the AAS? Wouldn't he want to discourage future would-be poisoners from practicing their art in his realm?"

Claudia laughed. "Oh, yes. But it's the past he was worried about."

Marina looked blank.

The archduchess leaned over, and whispered her explanation. "You haven't heard the story? In 1587, my Uncle Francesco and *Step*-Aunt Bianca"—she carefully enunciated the "step"—"both suffered a sudden illness. Francesco was the grand duke at the time, Papa being his younger brother. Fortunately, Papa had arrived at the villa a few days earlier. He took charge, seeing to it they had the best possible care.

"Alas, they died eleven days later. The grand duke's death was, according to Papa and his physicians, because of Francesco's terrible eating habits. And Bianca's grief was too great for any mortal to bear, so she died the same day. From the stress of watching Francesco's decline, no doubt. The autopsies confirmed that the deaths were completely natural, and Papa bowed to the inevitable and became the next grand duke. Ferdinando the First. His first son was my older brother Cosimo, who fathered Ferdinando the Second.

"Anyway, certain rash and unprincipled people have nonetheless suggested that the deaths came at a too convenient time for Papa, Bianca having been maneuvering to have her bastard Don Antonio declared the heir. The word 'poison' was trotted out. It is really annoying, the way people think 'poison' as soon as you say 'Medici.' We aren't the Borgias, after all.

"It is possible that someone unhappy with my brother's rule might agitate for this AAS test to be performed on the bodies of Francesco and Bianca. If the results were anything but unambiguously negative, then they could be used to question the legitimacy of Ferdinando's rule."

"But wouldn't your nephew want to know whether they were poisoned?"

"God knows already, dear Marina. Just God. And it's better that it stay that way."

Which Way is Up?

John F. Harvell

Kudzu Scientific Instruments
Grantville, September 1634

Helmut Strauss pounded the table in frustration. "I don't care what you do, you have got to get this thing working. Der Adler has about reached the end of his patience, and so have I!"

"But Herr Strauss," Betha Klepsch protested, "we've tried everything we could think of to make it work. Followed every suggestion we've been given! Everything we do just seems to make it worse. At this point we simply don't know what else to do."

"You were able to repair the up-time gyro instrument for Herr Smith. I do not understand why you cannot make the new unit work. Der Adler is very anxious to be able to install these gyro instruments in all of his aircraft. Do something! Use stronger springs! Lubricate the bearings! Do *something*!"

Strauss stood abruptly and stalked out of the shop. He headed back to the procurement office at the air base.

Hans Richter Field
Grantville, October 1634

"You know, Woody, I'd never even heard of a graveyard spiral before," Kevin Clements said.

"Yeah, well, I'd just barely heard of it," Woody Woodsill replied. "They mentioned it in AFROTC when we were getting ready for the instrument familiarization. It makes a difference when it kills a buddy, doesn't it?"

"It sure does. Poor Rudy. He never had a chance. Haze can be as bad as fog when it gets thick." Kevin hesitated. "The boss sure seems to be taking it hard."

"That's the truth. I worry about him. He keeps trying to do everything himself, at least when he's here. He blames himself every time we lose a pilot and it really frustrates him that we don't have any decent instruments or navaids yet."

Woody got a thoughtful look on his face. "Navaids . . . navigational aids. Up-time we had VOR, TACAN, and GPS. What I wouldn't give for GPS now. I know VOR and TACAN were just radio stuff, but pretty sophisticated by our current standards."

"Jesse mentioned something about radio ranges and low freq homers, once, but we didn't have time, then, for him to explain about them. He just said that they were pretty basic and that some of the old heads had talked about them, but he'd never used them himself."

"We could sure use something like that," Woody continued, "we need *something* bad."

Hans Richter Field
Grantville, Late October 1634

Traditionally, at least back up-time, the graduating cadet class was supposed to pass in review for all of the assembled dignitaries and family members. In the USE Air Force, the graduating cadet class would barely have constituted a squad, hardly enough people to provide a reasonable review.

Instead, the ceremony held in the new hangar was pretty low-key and relatively brief. Colonel Wood had returned just in time to make the traditional remarks, the chaplain provided a nondenominational blessing, the cadets received a commission and a training certificate, and the sweethearts and mothers pinned the new gold bars of a second lieutenant on their shoulders and a pilot's wings on their chests.

Major Woodsill was circulating among the new lieutenants, congratulating them on their achievement, and wishing them well for the future. When he came to the newly-minted Lieutenant Joseph Glazer he grinned and said, "Congratulations, Joe. You did a great job, and you really earned those wings and bars. Good luck to you!" He turned away, then turned back. "Oh, before I forget, the boss has a job for you. Why don't you stop by the colonel's office before you take off and let him tell you what he has in mind."

"Hi there, Joe. Congratulations on winning your wings. If you're like me, you'll remember today for a long time." Colonel Wood looked exhausted.

"You wanted to see me, sir?"

"Yes, I did." He stared into space for a moment or two while he gathered his thoughts. "Joe, you know what happened to Rudy in the weather. What you may not know is that last summer I almost busted *my* ass by going out and trying to fly in marginal weather, too." Jesse stopped for a moment.

Joe was startled. This was *The Colonel, Der Adler*, the man who knew more about flying than anybody! He just didn't *do* things like that!

Jesse smiled grimly. "Yeah, it really happened. Mother Nature is, indeed, a bitch. I had forgotten just how fast you can get yourself in trouble without gauges.

"We've been trying to fix that, but so far we haven't gotten the damned thing to work. I've had KSI working on a turn needle for about a year, and it certainly looks almost identical to the one usable one we've got, but somehow it just doesn't work right. I'd like for you to help out and try to see if you can get it to work."

Again, Joe was startled. "Me, sir? What . . . ?"

"We really need to be able to fly in bad weather, which means we really need gyro instruments and radio navigation aids. In fact, we're already damn late, considering Rudy." Lines furrowed the colonel's forehead.

"Major Woodsill tells me that you've done some gyro work. Is that true?"

"Well yes sir, I did try to make a gyro autopilot for a model back before the Ring of Fire, but I don't know if that really qualifies in this case. It didn't work too well, either."

"Joe, that gives you a hell of a lot more experience than anybody else I know down-time. I need to leverage that experience to try to get this thing going. I've got an old manual, *Instrument*

Flying, and it gives you a pretty good introduction to the things we need and how they're used, but it only gives us principles, not designs.

"What I'm hoping *you* can do is figure out how to translate those principles into something we can build and use." He held up his hand before Joe could protest. "We've gone over everybody's records and you seem to be the only one in our bunch who might have a chance to do this."

Joe started to say something, then he closed his mouth and sat back, his mind racing through the implications of what he had just heard. He recognized that his modeling work did give him just a little bit of a leg up for a job like this, and probably no one else had even done that. But it was certainly a big step to go from there to any kind of gyro instrument. He didn't know anything about navaids! "I don't know whether I can figure out how to fix the turn needle or not, but I'm willing to give it a try. I know we really need them. I don't know anything about navigation aids, though."

"I'd have been surprised if you did." Jesse tapped the manual lying on the desk. "Read through this and see if it makes any sense to you. If you have questions, come see me and I'll try to help. I don't expect you to make this stuff on your own, but you need to be able to talk intelligently to somebody like GE and get them to make something we can use. I think I can carve out a budget for you."

"I'm sure willing to give it a try, sir."

"All right, Joe, why don't I take you and introduce you to Helmut Strauss? He's my chief of procurement, and he does a good job getting supplies and services for the air force. Do you know him by any chance?"

"I think I've seen him around, sir, but we haven't been introduced."

"Well, let me warn you that he is a pretty crusty sort of guy and he's really frustrated that he hasn't been able to get this gyro delivered. He may not take it too well if he thinks I'm replacing him with you, which I guess I really am, to some extent. Just remember, he's the procurement officer and you're his technical advisor. I want to make it clear that you're working *with* him, not *for* him. You'll be working directly for me as a coequal technical assistant to Helmut. Notwithstanding all that, it would be a big help if you could be as diplomatic as possible with him. The last thing I need is to have my folks fighting with each other."

"Yessir, I'll do my best."

Strauss was rather stiff and formal when he found out what Joe was going to be doing, but he agreed to introduce Joe to the people at KSI who were working on the turn needle, on the following afternoon.

Same Evening, Glazer Residence

Sophia Glotz opened the front door in response to Joe's knock. "Why, good evening Herr . . . no, I guess I should say *Lieutenant* Glazer, now. What brings you here this evening?"

About that time a young woman in a sweater and jeans came down the stairs. "Ah! I thought I heard strange voices. Hi, Joe. What are you doing here tonight?"

Joe and Maria Glotz had been classmates in high school for the years since the Glotzes had arrived in Grantville in 1631, and shared a lot of classes because both of their family names began with "G." Neither Joe nor Maria had realized that the other had applied for Cadets until they found themselves standing next to each other in formation at their first muster.

"Hi, Maria. Oh, and congratulations, *Lieutenant* Glotz! I was just about to tell your mother that the colonel has given me a project that means I'll probably have to make use of my workshop in the basement. I hope that won't be too much of a bother for you folks."

"And congratulations to you, too, *Lieutenant* Glazer!" Maria made a mock curtsey. "I don't think there'd be any problem unless you got particularly noisy or smelly down there."

Maria's mother said, "We really shouldn't stand here in the door. Please, Joe, why don't you come into the living room and sit down?"

It was an odd sensation for Joe. This was the house he'd lived in for most of his life. Even most of the furniture remained, except for some small pieces that his parents had taken to Badenburg. And yet, it felt different. It even smelled different.

When they were seated, Joe shook off the feeling of strangeness and turned to Maria, who was more likely to understand. "The colonel wants me to see if I can help get some instruments made that we can use to fly in weather. They will have to be gyro instruments, so I may need to use my shop to do some machine work."

"I think I remember a little about gyros from science class," Maria said. "Are you a good enough machinist to make something like that?"

"Well, I don't have to make a complete gyro. KSI has been working on a prototype for some time. The colonel hopes that I can help sort out the problems they're having. I have a little experience building a gyro autopilot for a model airplane, but that was just before the Ring of Fire, so I never finished it. I'm not real sure I can do what the colonel wants, but I can at least give it a try. Maybe I can help.

"The other thing we need is more difficult, at least for me. The colonel wants me to get some navigational aids, navaids, started. They're radios that allow you to figure out where you are in flight. I just barely got through the electrical stuff in school, and I don't know anything about radios. I wouldn't even try to make something like that on my own, but GE should be able do it. Anyway, I need to use the shop."

"Ooo! Can I come along and see your secret laboratory, Doctor Frankenstein?"

Joe shook his head in mock disgust. Shy and retiring she was not. "You might as well come along," he said, and headed for the basement stairs.

His shop looked smaller than he remembered it, and messier, which was not helped by the dust that had accumulated in the time since he'd been there last. Joe turned on the two lights over his workbench, then pulled off the dust cover that covered his modeler's lathe.

"What's that?" asked Maria.

"Hmm?" responded Joe absentmindedly as he examined the machine minutely. "Oh, this is the combination lathe/milling machine. Compared to what you'd see in a machine shop this looks like a toy, but if you're careful, you can do pretty good work with these little things. I've already used it a lot to make things for my models. One of them was the small gyro that I mentioned." He searched through the clutter on the bench for a few moments and then held up the gyro.

Maria didn't know what a gyro should look like, but she could see that what he was holding was neat, smooth and gave the appearance of good workmanship. She was impressed. He blew most of the dust off and spun the wheel experimentally. She noticed that it spun very smoothly, and continued spinning for some time.

When it finally stopped, Joe wrinkled his nose. "Not too good. It used to spin much longer than that. I guess the dust has gotten into the bearings." He put it back and wandered along the bench sorting through the clutter to see what was buried there. He opened the drawers one at a time and shoved stuff around till he could get a good idea what was in each one. He walked over to the set of shelves along the other wall and inventoried the odds and ends on them. Finally he pawed through some boxes that were under the bench.

He stood back and ran his hand through his shock of short, unruly brown hair. "Well, are you properly impressed by my secret laboratory? Is there anything more you'd like to see? I'm sorry, Igor has the day off so I can't fire up the lightning machine."

Maria laughed.

The next day

While everyone was stiffly correct, it was obvious to Joe that the relationship between Herr Strauss and the artisans at KSI was not the best. After Herr Strauss had made the somewhat stilted introductions and left, Joe tried to ease the tensions.

"Look guys, I'm no expert, no *master* as you might say. I'm just a fellow who had a little bit of experience with gyros back up-time. I know they can be tricky to work with, and it may be that I can see something that's causing your difficulty when it's not obvious to you. Why don't we sit down and get a good look at this thing and see if there's something that sticks out."

When they brought over the covered tray and pulled the dust cover off, Joe was immediately impressed with the appearance of the assembly. Whatever their problem might be, it was not lack of craftsmanship. Joe praised their workmanship, which caused a noticeable lessening of tension around the table.

Joe looked up. "Do you have an air or vacuum source we can use to power this up?"

"Yes, of course. Just a few minutes," Elise responded.

When the air source was connected the rotor spun up handily, but to Joe it did not sound quite right. He put a finger very lightly on the gimbal. He could feel just the faintest evidence of a tremor. He sat back and thought for a moment. "Do you know how fast the rotor is turning?"

"Yes," Jakob answered. "The rotor is spinning at almost 12,000 rpm. We could go even faster if it were not for the vibration."

Joe thought *That's too slow, and it needs to be balanced better.* He sat back and signaled for them to turn it off. "Tell me about how you got started in this."

"Yes, of course. Herr Smith loaned us the only available up-time unit to study last year," Betha explained. "He apologized that it was not performing properly, but said we could use it as a pattern. We disassembled it, making note of every screw and every adjustment so we could restore it accurately. Drawings were made of every piece, and each process and procedure was written up. In doing that we cleaned every part thoroughly so we could make precise measurements. When the unit was reassembled and returned to Herr Smith he discovered that it was once more functioning properly, and later installed it into one of his airplanes. That gave us a great deal of confidence that we would be able to produce new units. Unfortunately, we seem to have been mistaken, at least so far."

"And did you make your new unit *exactly* like the up-time unit?"

Jakob, Betha and Elise exchanged looks. Elise took up the explanation. "It is as close as we can make it. We could not obtain the jeweled bearings, so we had to substitute bronze. Because of vibration we couldn't spin the rotor quite as fast, plus the nozzle would have to be opened up to get a little more air. It was Herr Strauss' opinion that this would not make any difference, so we did not try to run it faster."

Joe stared at his steepled fingers for several moments. "Have you ever done anything with gyros before? Do you understand how they work?"

Jakob looked embarrassed. He shrugged and replied, "Unfortunately, no. None of us have ever worked with gyros before, and I've found no one who can explain them more than the most basic theory. All of us have had problems grasping the principles behind this device."

"That's because you don't think at right angles." Joe grinned at him. "You shouldn't be embarrassed. Gyro instruments were not invented until the late nineteenth century in the old time line, about two hundred and fifty years from now. If you can be available tomorrow, why don't I come back and provide a little introduction to how gyros work?"

Betha spoke up quickly. "If you could do that, we would be forever in your debt. Do you have any idea how difficult, how frustrating it is to work with something you don't understand?"

The next day Joe came back with the toy gyro his father had found in a flea market when he was a kid, and with the manual that the colonel had given him. After a half hour or so of demonstrating the basic principles of the gyro, Joe then went through the illustrations of each of the basic gyro instruments in the manual and showed how the principles were applied. Joe had never thought of himself as a teacher, but it was actually thrilling to see the light of understanding dawn in the eyes of his new friends.

Flight Line, Hans Richter Field
Early January 1635

Joe and Maria were headed back to the briefing room to debrief after their afternoon training mission. A cold north wind was blowing, and it cut like a knife after the relative warmth of the Gustav cockpits. They were both huddled down in their winter flying gear.

Maria raised her voice to be heard over the wind. "You goin' over to the Club for a brew after we debrief?"

"Naw, I got to hurry back to the shop. KSI has done some more things to clean up their gyro and I want to run some turntable tests on it tonight," responded Joe.

"You sure spend a lot of time on that stuff. How's the work going?"

"Tell you about it after debrief," Joe said as he turned up his fur-lined collar and pulled his chin down into its protection.

Later, Joe spent a few minutes trying to explain to Maria just how a turn needle worked. She was having a hard time grasping the ideas.

"But I don't understand! Why do you need this gyro thing? Couldn't you just use a plumb bob, or something like that?"

"A plumb bob can't tell when you're turning. It only tells you whether you're coordinated. That's the kind of thing that killed Rudy Hocheim."

"I'm still confused, and I still don't understand what you're telling me."

"Okay, tell you what. Come down to the shop tonight and I'll try to show you how this thing is supposed to work."

"Gee," she teased, "a date?"

"Nope," he responded, straight faced, "a training session."

"Ah well, too bad."

Joe hung up his coat and headed back to the kitchen where the basement door was. Sophia Glotz was busily getting dinner ready for her husband, Hubert, and Maria.

Joe stopped for a moment. "Hi, Missus G. How are you this cold, chilly evening?"

"Good evening, Joe. It certainly is cold. I almost froze walking home after work." Sophia worked as a housekeeper at the Higgins Hotel. Her husband had been a farmer, but now he had worked his way up to foreman at one of the large firms that had sprung up in the area around Grantville.

"Have you had any supper yet, Joe? Should I set another place?" Joe had been spending so many afternoons and evenings in his shop that the Glotzes had taken to inviting him regularly for dinner. Joe had finally accepted with the condition that he be allowed to contribute some money toward the food budget.

The same circumstance had led to Joe frequently spending the night in what had been his old room instead of at the air base. Joe found his old room comfortably familiar, although it was not nearly as cluttered as it had been when he had lived there. He did discover that he had to be a little more circumspect about using the bathroom. He'd never had a sister, so dealing with two females in the house took some adjustment.

Joe had grown up in the old foursquare and knew most of its quirks. He knew how to stop the toilet from running, how to relight the pilot light in the furnace when it blew out, and which gland nut to tighten under the kitchen sink when the drain started to leak. It didn't take too long for Joe to begin to seem like one of the Glotz family.

They heard the thumpety-thump of someone coming down the stairs, and shortly Maria breezed into the kitchen. "Well, are you ready for the training session, oh lord-and-master instructor!"

Joe made a face at her and then looked helplessly at Sophia.

Sophia grinned at the two of them. It was obvious to her that Maria was "interested" in Joe. It was equally obvious that Joe hadn't a clue.

"Come on," Joe said and led the way downstairs with Maria following closely behind. Early on, Maria had followed Joe down to his shop every visit, but she soon found that, for her, things got pretty dull in a hurry. Once Joe started working he became very absorbed in what he was doing, and Maria discovered it wasn't very exciting to watch someone else work. She quickly became bored with that and went back to doing whatever it was that girls did, while Joe toiled away. About the only time they saw each other at the house was over the dinner table on the days when Joe ate there.

Joe switched on the lights and pulled the dust cover off of a stand in front of the bench. He started his guided tour. "I salvaged an old phonograph to make the turntable." Joe pointed to the middle of the assemblage of things on the stand. "Of course, I had to change the gearing with these belts and pulleys so I could run it at either a half rpm, or a quarter rpm. The motor is a synchronous motor, so that it stays phase-locked to the commercial power."

Maria rolled her eyes.

Joe saw it and grinned ruefully. "Okay, okay, okay. I guess I need to start another way. Let's see . . . all right, the first instrument we're trying to build is what's called a turn needle." Joe launched into a detailed discussion of what a pilot would see and how he would use the instrument.

"That seems easy enough," she said, "but what does the rest of this stuff do?"

"Those are the guts that make the turn needle work, just like *those* are the guts that make you work." He poked her in the midsection.

"Hands off the bod!" she shot back.

Embarrassed, Joe felt his ears turning red. "Sorry," he mumbled. He changed the subject.

"I guess you need to get some idea how gyros work." He rummaged around in one of the drawers for a minute or so, then held up the object of his search. "Okay, this is a toy gyro I got as a kid. Gyros do two things: they stand still, or they turn over."

"Huh?"

Joe demonstrated the basic gyro principles again with his old toy gyro and then explained how they were used in the prototype, ending up with "What I want to do is power up the latest version and then start the turntable to see if it works. Assuming it does, then I'll try to calibrate it. They got everything put together yesterday, so if it doesn't blow up when we power everything up we should be able to run the test tonight."

"Blow up?" exclaimed Maria, sounding alarmed.

"Well, no. It's just a figure of speech."

"I'm certainly glad of that! You never know what to expect in a secret laboratory," Maria said with mock severity.

Joe laughed, and then Sophia called down the stairs. "Joe, Maria, dinner is ready and Papa is at the table, please come up to eat."

The tests that night were, at best, partially successful, which was still far better than before. The turn needle sort of worked, but it had a tendency to hang up sometimes and then jump. Joe thought that part of the problem was the need for better bearings, and it seemed like the speed was still vibration-limited, too. Joe knew that KSI had about reached the limit of their high speed balance capability. He knew that jeweled bearings would work, but he didn't have any experience with those, and he didn't know where they might find such a thing down-time, anyhow. The only other thing he'd heard about that might have lower friction was air bearings, but they required finer tolerances than either KSI or Joe could achieve. Then too, he'd need to figure out how to get the air to the bearings through the gimbals. In addition, he figured that he would have to get the services of an up-time machine shop to balance the rotor to reach 20,000 rpm.

The testing finished up fairly late, and Joe spent the night in his old room. The next morning Joe and Maria caught the bus out to the air field. Joe owed the colonel a progress report, so he brought along the latest version for show and tell.

The colonel sat quietly while Joe pointed out the changes they'd made since the last status report and then discussed the results of last night's testing. He asked a few technical questions, which Joe was able to answer readily. Then he commented, "Joe, you're making much more progress than I had hoped. I think you're on the right track with the air bearing idea. Why don't you go down to Marcantonio's and see if they can provide any help? Hal Smith says they do pretty good work. Do you have any drawings of these bits and pieces?"

"Yes, sir, I do. KSI made up drawings and I've copied them to my computer. Do you want me to bypass Herr Strauss on this?"

The colonel shuffled some papers on his desk and came up with that day's flying schedule. After perusing it for a moment he said, "Okay, Joe. Looks like you're not on the flying schedule today. Helmut is all wrapped up in trying to negotiate a big buy right now, and I don't want to wait. Why don't you go ahead and take this down to Marcantonio's and explain what you're trying to do." Then he rummaged through a desk drawer and found a piece of paper with project numbers on it, copied one of them to one of the requisition forms and handed it to Joe. "They can charge any work on this project to this number. I shouldn't have to tell you to be sparing in its use."

"Yes, sir."

When Joe and Dave Marcantonio got down to talking about the purpose of his visit, Dave asked a lot of penetrating questions, most of which Joe was able to answer. He'd brought along his archive of drawings and he and Dave pored over them, talking about how they might be modified for air bearings and for easier machine work. The price Dave quoted seemed astronomical, but Joe swallowed hard and told him they'd go ahead with it. On the other hand, when Joe reported the price to the colonel, it didn't seem to faze him.

The hardest part was waiting for his project to come up in the queue at the machine shop. Joe went in a couple of times, mostly to discuss proposed changes for various reasons, and most of which he agreed with.

Early February 1635

It was almost a let down to go into Marcantonio's to pick up the turn needle to take to his shop for testing, along with some auxiliary stuff. After setting things up and mounting the latest example on the turntable Joe and Maria headed upstairs to dinner.

After dinner they headed back down to the basement, fired up the system, and found that it performed just exactly like it was supposed to. The only thing needed was calibration of the needle in each direction. Joe timed the rotation of the turntable each way to be sure that the rate was correct, and then adjusted the tension on the tiny springs inside the unit to get the needle in exactly the right position. It looked like the air bearings had done the trick.

Joe had carefully avoided touching Maria after that one night, so he was a little startled when she threw her arms around him and hugged him after the test was seen to be a clear success.

The next step was to get the instrument into an airplane. After reporting to the colonel the next morning, Joe went over to see Hal Smith. Some time earlier they had agreed to use Belle 01 as the test bed. Hal had stayed abreast of the progress on the turn needle, so he was ready when Joe showed up and announced he was ready to put it in the airplane. It took the better part of two days to get the prototype installed in the airplane and all of the checks completed.

Since it was Joe's project, he had the job of conducting the first test flight. The flight itself was an anticlimax. He spent about a half hour, first checking that the turn needle functioned in the airplane like it did on the turntable, and then practicing standard rate and half-standard rate turns.

When Joe landed, Colonel Wood was waiting in the parking area. Joe climbed out, the colonel climbed in, then the whole system got a second shakedown.

"That's really great," Colonel Wood said after he landed. "Maybe there's a little light at the end of this tunnel. Maybe we can actually do this!"

Jesse invited Joe to his office and sent someone to get Major Woodsill. When Woody arrived Jesse got right down to business. "Okay, what do you think? Can we build this thing now and start an instrument training program pretty soon?"

"We already had a decent set of drawings and Marcantonio's has updated the drawings for the precision parts and the air bearings, so we have a good set of technical data. Air bearings don't wear out like others do because there's not normally contact between the bearing surfaces. As long as we keep the bearings from being contaminated by dust or dirt they should last for a long time. Other than that, I can't think of anything that we'd need to worry about," Joe said.

Jesse looked at Major Woodsill. "What do you think, Woody?"

"I've got a simpleminded partial panel training program blocked out in my head. It's really not very involved. It's just giving the students practice under the hood until they can fly straight and level with just needle, ball, airspeed, and whiskey compass, and do it fairly reliably, then learn to make timed turns, and finally have them fly a series of three-cornered round-robin cross countries under the hood. Until we have some navaids, there's not a lot more we can do."

The colonel stared at Woody, thinking. After what seemed like a long time he returned from wherever he had been. "Okay. Joe, I'll call Marcantonio's and get a price for twenty-five units. You work with Major Woodsill to schedule airplanes into the shop for modification. I'll set up with Hal to do the mods. We'll start with the Gustavs first, but I want all of the birds modified before we get through. Woody, let's get that training program down on paper and start breaking it down into training sorties. Any questions?"

Joe stuck up his hand. "Sir, one of the reasons the price was so high was that Dave Marcantonio doesn't really like to do the fiddly little assembly work. Mostly he just likes to make things out of metal. It might make sense to have KSI be a prime contractor and have them hire Marcantonio's as a sub for the high precision stuff. I think they'd both be happier and we might end up with a better price."

The colonel thought for a moment. "Okay, Joe, you've been working with both those guys more than I have. I'll buy going that way. Rather than me getting involved, why don't you work with Helmut to get them on contract ASAP. Try to be diplomatic in how you approach it with him. Anything else?"

Neither Joe nor Woody could think of anything.

"Okay, you guys better get at it... No, wait! Joe, stick around for a minute."

After Woody had left Jesse asked Joe, "Have you done anything yet with the navaid problem?"

"Well, sir, not a heck of a lot. Early on, I did go down to GE and spent an afternoon talking to them about the project, but I haven't been back since. They seemed to think that there were no fundamental stumbling blocks, and the only thing they were concerned about was getting the radios small enough and light enough to fit in the airplanes. Now that my time is freed up a bit, I'll get down there and see what's going on."

"You do that. Let me know how they're doing."

"Yes, sir. Is there anything else?"

"No . . . Yes. Damn fine job so far, Joe. Keep up the good work."

Since Joe hadn't heard anything from GE, he just assumed that they'd either forgotten about the project, or not made any progress. When he got there, they led him back to one of the labs and showed him some equipment on the bench. He saw what he took to be a loop antenna on a stand, and what looked like a car radio nearby. Sitting on the bench not too far away was a wooden board with some electrical stuff on it and a wire connected to it that Joe realized was a makeshift antenna.

"Actually, we've been looking for a use for old car radios," Jennifer Hanson told him. "They don't have any components that we use for our other radio requirements, so they're just sitting around. This operates in the regular broadcast band, where VOA operates. That means that it's susceptible to electronic noise, like lightning. While it's not as good as citizen's band, at least there are lots of them available. We've cobbled it together with a simple loop antenna so that we have a basic system of the type you and I were talking about before." Joe was flabbergasted, but Jennifer wasn't through.

"Now that," she said, pointing to the varnished wooden board with a few electronic components mounted on it, "is a signal generator Rolf put together for a class assignment in high school electronics shop. It's only meant for lab work, but Else did some back-of-the-envelope figuring, and she thinks if we give it a good antenna, an airplane could pick it up at least twenty miles away. Rolf rigged it with a tone generator so you can identify it on the AM receiver. I'll show you how to take bearings on it, and if it works out for you, we'll build one that'll stand up in the field. It'll run a few months on a car battery, so you don't need to fool with windmills and stuff.

"So, over there you have your radio direction finder for your airplane, and here you have a low frequency homer to put at a ground station. They've both held up fairly well during testing, here, but of course that's not the same as service use."

"I'm really surprised that you have been able to put this together so fast," Joe said.

"These were really pretty simple stuff that didn't use resources we needed elsewhere. It wasn't a big deal to adapt them to meet your needs."

Joe thanked Jennifer profusely and made his way back to the base and headed for the O'Club. It was a Friday, and Happy Hour, and he ran into Maria and bent her ear mercilessly while they put away a few more than the usual number of beers. Finally she suggested, "Look, why don't you go change into something besides a uniform and go home with me? I'll change into some glad rags and we'll go out and celebrate, my treat." That sounded good to Joe, and the result was their first real date, even if she did end up inviting him, *and* paying for it.

On Monday Joe brought the colonel up to date and laid out his plans for the test program. The colonel gave his go ahead.

The mod to install the radio in the airplane was rather more involved than the instrument mod since they had to modify the aircraft structure to mount the loop.

Altogether they gave up about twenty pounds of useful load capacity, assuming they stayed within the established max gross weight limits. The whole process took all of fifteen days. The additional weight was barely noticeable the first time Joe flew Belle 01 after the mod.

Siting the homer was not the problem they had feared and they were able to get it up on battery power while they waited for commercial power to get out to the site.

Happy Hour at the O'Club
First Friday in March 1635

"Hey! Look! It's the Bobbsey Twins!" Dev Martin yelled over the usual hubbub.

"Oh, buzz off Dev!" responded Maria, grinning.

Joe and Maria picked up mugs of beer and headed for a more or less quiet corner where they could talk.

"Well, wha'd'ya think? Are we getting any better?" Joe had been working to develop an instrument approach for the base.

Maria studied Joe's earnest face for a few moments. "You split the runway three times out of four. The fourth time you could have corrected, no sweat, if you'd broken out at minimums. I'd say that was pretty damn good."

"I don't know. I was having so much trouble switching back and forth between the RDF and the turn needle/compass that it just felt all wrong. I didn't feel like I really had the airplane under control."

Maria took a deep breath. "Joe, you were a little rough, sure. But you still ended up in the right place at the right time. That's what counts. Don't keep beating yourself up over it. I don't think there's anyone here . . ." Maria gestured at the rest of the room ". . . who could do as well, let alone better. I know I couldn't, and I'm pretty good." She smirked.

"Actually, that's one thing I'm worried about," Joe said. "I think I screwed up the human factors on this setup. I've got to find some way to get the antenna indication on the instrument panel. Every time you have to move your head the way you need to now, the vertigo gets really bad."

"Yeah! I know that time you put me in the left seat I had a lot of trouble with that. Do you think there's some way we can fix that?"

"I really don't know. We could do it up-time, no sweat, but down-time . . . I don't know."

The next flying day was something of a bust. It was miserably cold, and a plane coming back from the south reported snow moving north. Joe's flight in the Gustav that afternoon was already canceled because of the impending snow. He flew 01 on his usual practice flight that morning, but Maria had been detailed to take a passenger to Magdeburg, so he flew with Major Woodsill, instead. For whatever reason, Major Woodsill was crotchety that morning, so it hadn't been a pleasant flight. As far as Joe could tell, it was nothing that he was doing that caused it. In fact, it seemed to Joe that he was finally getting tolerable on the approaches.

It was about time to land when they heard a faint call on the radio.

"Mayday! Mayday! Mayday! This is Belle 03. I have a fuel leak and I'm down to just the header tank remaining. I've only got a few minutes of fuel left. I'm somewhere northwest of Halle, close to the west bank of the Saale River. I'm going to try to set her down while I have some power." Maria's voice was remarkably calm and businesslike.

"Shit!" Major Woodsill's voice was not calm and businesslike. "Let's get this thing on the ground so I can talk to the boss!"

The colonel was waiting as they taxied into their parking spot. Major Woodsill jumped out of the airplane and headed over to the colonel.

"You heard?" Jesse nodded. "Do we have any way to get hold of Halle?" Jesse shook his head. His face was a mask. "No, the phone lines are still down after that mess yesterday in Grantville."

Joe climbed out of the airplane and headed over to the line chief. "Sarge, let's get this thing fueled up right now."

"Yes, sir. We'll get on it right away." The sergeant hurried off to get some help getting the fuel bowser dragged over to the airplane.

"Colonel, if I leave as soon as 01 is refueled I can get to the search area before the snow moves in," Joe said.

The colonel's head jerked around. "Forget it, Joe! I'm not putting any more lives at risk today." His eyes had a haunted look. "I'm sorry, but I've already lost too many people. I just can't send anyone out with that snow moving in."

"But, Colonel, if you insist on that and she's not dead already, she'll freeze to death tonight. Even if somebody helps her, what if she's hurt bad? It might be important to get her back here right away. You could be killing her!"

"I know that, Joe," the colonel said in a more reasonable tone. "Maybe *I'll* go, but I just can't send anyone else out in this stuff. I have more experience than anybody here, so if anybody goes it'll be me."

Woody chimed in, "Sir, let me go instead. You're needed here."

A humorless smile passed over Jesse's face. "Thanks, Woody, but if anybody goes, it's me."

"Begging your pardons, sirs, but neither of you is as experienced in flying *this* airplane with *this* set up as I am." A brief, crooked grin passed over Joe's face. "Besides, if it comes to that, I'm more expendable than either one of you."

He turned to look very intently at the colonel. "Respectfully, sir, if you don't have someone hold me down, I'm going as soon as I can get 01 turned around. You can have me court-martialed when I get back." Joe turned to walk to the airplane.

"Joe!" called Jesse. Joe stopped. "You're right." He sighed. "God help me, I won't try to stop you. Look, I know that you and Maria have a sort of 'special relationship.' Don't let that special relationship make you do anything stupid. Up until now you've shown pretty good judgment. Don't let this become an exception."

A look of surprise on Joe's face was followed by a slow smile. "You know, sir, that 'special relationship' actually never occurred to me. I think you're right, though. I can't guarantee I won't do something stupid, but I'll really try not to. After all, I may be the only hope she has." Joe smiled briefly, went into base ops and took their first aid kit, and headed for the airplane.

"Grantville Tower, this is Belle 01 for takeoff. Did you get a bearing on Belle 03's last transmission?"

"Belle 01, Grantville, you are cleared for takeoff at your discretion. Belle 03 was weak but we got a bearing of approximately 027 degrees."

"Roger, 027, Belle 01 rolling now."

Once in the air, Joe turned left to a heading of 027 and looked around. There was a solid overcast, but the visibility underneath seemed to be holding up. He settled down and tried to fly the heading as closely as he could.

When he got near Halle, Joe dropped down to about a thousand feet and tried to fly right up the middle of the Saale River. Maria had said she was near the west bank, so if he flew up the middle, she'd be where he had the best chance of seeing her from the left seat. He scanned every field he came across anxiously. Nothing there, next one . . . nope, nothing there either. After what seemed like an eternity he caught a glimpse of something orange. He turned left and pulled the power back a little to slow down.

There it was! Thank goodness for the orange tail and wingtips. He dropped down to get a closer look. Belle 03 was lying on its back. No sign of life. He let down even more and anxiously scanned the area around the airplane. No footsteps in the snow around it. He climbed back up and surveyed the area around the wreckage. It was actually two fields with what looked like a road dividing them. He could see that there were snow drifts up to two feet deep in the fields. That was probably what had flipped 03 on her back. It was clear he couldn't land in one of the fields.

He dropped down to take a good close look at the road. It was fairly straight where it ran across the fields. Like many down-time roads, there were low stone walls on either side where the farmers had cleared their fields of rocks, but they looked far enough apart to clear the landing gear with a little to spare, and low enough to be below the wing struts. On the road the snow seemed to be packed down pretty well. Must get a lot of traffic.

He turned around and flew back the other way, checking the other side. There were some ruts, so it could be tricky trying to keep her straight, but if he could do that there was room, just barely, to land on the road. His mind made up, Joe climbed back up to a thousand feet.

"Grantville Tower, this is Belle 01, over."

"Belle 01, Grantville reads you weak but clear, over."

"Grantville, please pass the following message to Colonel Wood: I have found Belle 03 in a field. She's pretty much intact but on her back. There are no footprints in the snow around the airplane. My intention is to land on a nearby road and investigate. I will call when I am airborne again."

"Belle 01, Grantville, Roger. The colonel is right here, so he has your message."

"Roger, Grantville. Belle 01 going below your horizon for a while."

Joe dragged the road one more time, right down at the tops of the rock walls. There was no turbulence, and no wind that he could detect. Just as he reached the end he saw that there was a local headed down the road. He pulled up and came around to land before the villager could walk far enough to obstruct his landing. He slowed it down as much as he dared, and dropped it in on the first straight stretch of road. Belle 01 wallowed and darted on the packed, rutted, snow but Joe managed a tap dance on the rudder pedals that kept her clear of the rocks. It seemed like forever, but he actually stopped rather quickly. He just sat there for a minute, and remembered to breathe again. He wiped a hand across his forehead and grinned wryly. Imagine sweating at 25°F!

Joe wormed his way out of the airplane and looked around. The villager had stopped, and was watching from a distance, then he waved and walked back the way he had come. *Must have decided I had things under control,* mused Joe. *I hope he's right.* Belle 03 was about forty yards away. He grabbed the first aid kit from behind the seat and walked back down the road to the nearest point to the airplane, and then climbed over the pile of rocks that was the wall. As he plowed his way through the snow he tried to tramp down a trail for the return trip. He came up on the right side of the airplane. Heedless of the wing fabric under foot he worked his way to the right door. It stuck a little bit, but his exasperated heave got it open. He knelt down and looked inside.

Maria was still in her seat on the left side, hanging from her seat belt. Her arms were hanging down, her face and head were swollen, and there was a slow drip of blood from her scalp. Joe's heart fell in a cold lump into the pit of his stomach.

Then she turned her head slowly and looked at him through slitted eyes that were almost swollen shut. She worked her mouth a couple of times and then whispered, "Took you long enough."

"I came as fast as I could," he protested.

"I know," she whispered back and then turned her face forward again. "Damn seatbelt buckle wouldn't release. Not my preferred kind of hanging out."

"Okay," he said, "how are you otherwise?"

"Left arm hurts like hell, may be broken. I have this cut on my forehead. Legs and feet have gone to sleep from hanging upside down. Other than that, everything's just hunky dory." She'd picked up a lot of American slang in school.

He looked around the inside of the cockpit, then he ripped the seat cushions out of the right seat and slid them in below Maria on top of the puddle of blood, the splintered wood, and the broken glass from the windshield. "Now," he said, "I'm going to try to lift you up to take the strain off the buckle and see if it will unlatch."

It was awkward trying to do that in the restricted confines of the cockpit, but after a struggle he was able to lift her a little bit. Didn't help, the buckle stayed securely latched.

"I guess I'll have to cut it." He pulled out his knife and began sawing away on the tough fabric of the belt. After a few minutes he said to Maria, "Okay, I've cut most of the way through. I won't be able to catch you, so when it lets go you're going to fall on your head without any warning. It's probably going to hurt, but I can't think of any way to avoid that."

Maria pulled her left arm up against her chest with her right hand and nodded. Joe started sawing away again and in a moment the belt parted and Maria crumpled onto the seat cushions with a sharp cry. She lay there in a fetal position, eyes tightly closed, cradling her left arm with her right. Joe let her just lie there for a few moments.

Then, "Maria, I've got to get you out of here and into 01. We need to get back to the base. It's probably going to hurt, again, for me to drag you out, but there's no other way."

Again she nodded. He repositioned himself on his knees and

caught her under her arms. As gently as possible he dragged her out of the airplane and onto the wing. She moaned just a little bit.

He grabbed the first aid kit and said, "I guess we'd better get you patched up. Can't have you bleeding all over *my* airplane." She stuck out her tongue at him, but didn't open her eyes. "Let's start with the arm. I'll be as gentle as I can but it'll probably hurt some. Once I get it splinted and in a sling, it should help." Again she nodded. Working as quickly as he could, he secured her arm to the splint. He helped her to an upright sitting position, cradled her arm in the sling and tied the sling around her neck.

He dug around in the kit and found a bandage and a flask of alcohol. He saturated the bandage and used it to clean up her hair and face around the cut as best he could. It looked nasty and was certainly bloody, but he remembered from first aid class that scalp wounds were usually bloody and looked worse than they were. He hoped they were right. He put a clean bandage over the cut and began to wrap bandages around her head to hold it in place. "You're beginning to look like the Spirit of '76," he commented.

She opened one eye and looked at him. "Huh?"

"Tell you about it later. Do you think you could walk?" he asked.

She shifted around a little, testing her various body parts. She shook her head. "Nope, I'm still pretty numb and shaky."

"Guess I'll have to carry you then. Good luck to me!"

She opened both eyes and glared at him. "I'm not *that* heavy."

"I wouldn't know," he shot back. "Well, we'd better get going. Not much more we can do here. If you can stand up, it'll help."

Hanging onto his shoulder, with his arm around her back, she managed to stand up. She swayed a little bit, but then stood by herself, leaning against the side of the fuselage. Joe tramped out a path around the wing to his entry path so he wouldn't need to break trail while he was carrying her.

"Okay, here we go." He turned her so she could get her good arm around his neck, then bent over and scooped her up. He stood there a moment testing his balance and footing. The thought passed through his mind that it was kind of nice, holding her like this, but then he went on to more practical matters. She was solid, but not as heavy as he had feared. He was young and reasonably fit, but he was no muscle man. This was still going to be a challenge, particularly in the snow.

He stopped a couple of times to catch his breath, but they got to the wall in fairly short order, slipping and sliding at spots along the way. No way he was going to carry her across that wall. He set her on her feet and swept the snow off a moderate size rock so she could sit down. "I'll have to go drag the airplane back here so we'll have enough room to take off. After I do that, I'll help you across the wall and we can load you up and get out of here."

Joe clambered back over the wall and walked down the road to the airplane. Going to the tail, he picked the tail up by the handle placed there for the ground crew, and tugged. Nothing happened. He stopped and looked carefully at the airplane. Again he picked up the tail and this time rocked it from side to side, finally breaking the main wheels loose. Once more he pulled, slipping some on the packed snow, but it did start moving, and when he finally had it rolling, it continued rolling relatively easily. Soon he was back where Maria was sitting on the stone. By now some of the swelling had gone out of her face, and she was giving him an impish grin.

"Boy, am I glad to see you! My butt's about to freeze to this rock."

He shook his head sadly. "Jeez! Nothing but complaints. Next time I'll just leave you here."

He helped her get over the wall and up into the right seat.

She looked out the windshield at the road. "You know, that's pretty narrow up there ahead. Are you sure you can get us off okay?"

"Well, I got it down, so maybe I can get it off. It won't be easy, though, so a few prayers wouldn't hurt."

There were a few scary moments until he could get the tail up and get some rudder effectiveness, but after that, even though the heavy airplane took a while to get off the ground, he kept her right down the groove. As the heavily laden airplane slowly climbed out, both Joe and Maria started breathing again. Joe looked over at Maria. "Now, the only thing we have to worry about is the snow."

"Snow? What snow?"

"After you left this morning one of the guys came back from a round-robin cross country to the south and reported there was snow moving north. In fact, looks like it's starting here, now. I had to risk a court-martial to come and get you. We may have to use our instrument approach." Maria looked out. Sure enough random flakes were beginning to filter down.

Maria sighed. "You really do like to live dangerously, don't you? Do you think you can do it?"

"Well, I may *have to*, but, yes, I think I can do it. Practice went pretty well this morning."

"Oh great. Just when I was starting to feel safe, you have to go play Superman with X-Ray vision that can see through snowstorms."

They had reached 1000 feet and Joe fired up the radio.

"Grantville Tower, Belle 01, over."

"Belle 01, Grantville, go."

"Roger, Grantville. Belle 01 is southbound with Lieutenant Glotz on board. She has a possible broken arm and a scalp wound, but otherwise she's her usual snotty self so she can't be too badly hurt. I guess we should have the meat wagon standing by. We're estimating Grantville in about thirty minutes. How's the weather there? Over."

There was silence for a moment, then "Belle 01, Grantville, light snow started about twenty-five minutes ago. What are your intentions?"

Joe looked over at Maria. She made a face at him. "Grantville, Belle 01. We should be high station at GTV in about thirty minutes. If necessary we will use the provisional instrument approach to Runway 07, over."

"Roger, Belle 01. Call high station. Grantville, standing by."

Joe looked over at Maria. "I suppose we could have tried for Halle or Magdeburg, but this stuff seems to be moving fast. We'd be screwed if we went to either of those places and they were socked in when we got there. At least at Grantville we have the homer and an approach that I know."

As they got closer to Grantville the snow got heavier and Joe found that he had to stay on the instruments. If he looked out at the swirling snow he got vertigo in a hurry.

The colonel was pacing back and forth in the tower. Suddenly his head jerked up and he looked at Woody.

"Woody, go get some help and build some bonfires at the approach end of the field, on either side of the threshold. Use some gas if you need to, to get them started. We need them going before they start their approach."

"I'm on it!" Woody flung over his shoulder as he ran down the stairs. Woody raced through the briefing room, grabbing anyone there to help. Then he went up to Smith's and recruited more help there. They took scraps from the shops, old furniture, anything that would burn, and piled them in heaps at the corners of the field. A couple of crew chiefs brought jerry cans of gasoline and doused the piles. Somebody handed Woody an old, lit, Zippo. He lit a torch and flung it on the pile, which lit with a whoosh. Someone else went through a batch of kitchen matches before they got the other pile lit. He lost some hair and eyebrows in the process, but now both piles were blazing fiercely.

"Grantville, Belle 01 is stabilized on the back course approaching high station at 1500 feet. Estimating high station momentarily."

"Belle 01, Grantville. Past high station cleared to descend to 500 feet and execute a GTV 1 approach to Grantville, Runway 07. Over."

"Grantville, Zero One. Copy cleared for a GTV 1 to 07. Zero One is high station now, departing 1500 feet for 500 feet."

"Roger, Zero One, cleared for approach. Call low station, inbound."

"Zero One, WILCO."

Joe had hacked his watch at high station. He was flying with his left hand and furiously working the RDF with his right. Back and forth, back and forth with the loop, adjust the null, check the time, bring the turn needle into the scan, watch the altitude as they descended.

Time! Joe rolled into a right turn and checked the watch. Now he concentrated on the turn needle. He dropped his hand from the RDF and handed the CB radio to Maria. "Call at low station. I'm going to be pretty busy."

"Rog," responded Maria briskly.

Time! Roll from a right turn into a left turn. Check altitude... coming up on 500 feet, shift hands, add a little power, level at 500 feet, check the watch, set the RDF straight ahead, coming up on rollout, watch the altitude.

Time! Joe rolled her upright and centered the turn needle, then he checked the mag compass. Over-turned slightly, half needle right, roll out again, check the compass, okay, work the loop, left, right, left, right, adjust the null, watch your altitude. Add a little power, adjust the null, left, right, left, right.

Joe was concentrating so hard that he was startled when Maria reported "Low station inbound" as he swung the loop around to the rear.

"Roger Zero One, cleared for approach." A different voice. "Joe, we have bonfires on both sides of the threshold. It may help."

Maria rogered the message.

Joe risked a glance outside. Nothing but snow. He pulled the power back slightly and started a slow descent. He sensed Maria looking at him. He was going below minimums. Left, right, left, right, adjust the null, watch the turn needle, check the altitude... 300 feet, left, right, left, right, check the compass, check the altitude... 250 feet, airspeed good.

"Joe," said Maria quietly, fearful of breaking his concentration, "I see some lights ahead on either side. Must be the bonfires. Looks good as far as I can tell."

Joe just grunted. Left, right, left, right, 200 feet, 071 on the compass, left, right, left, right.

"Joe, we're way below minimums," Maria said quietly.

Joe grunted acknowledgment. He glanced outside again, saw the light from the fires ahead and a few streaks from the terrain below. Now he gradually began to bring the outside into his scan. Slowly, he transitioned from the gauges in the cockpit to what he could see outside. It was still murky, but now he had a pretty good view down. He let down to 100 feet, searching ahead for the rocky outcrop at the threshold. There! "Maria, tell them 'field in sight.'"

It was not his best landing, but at least it was in the right place, and the landing gear didn't collapse.

Joe took the radio from Maria and took a deep breath. "Grantville, Belle 01 on rollout. Where do you want us to park?"

"Belle 01, Grantville." There seemed to be more emotion than usual in the tower operator's voice. He started over, "Belle 01, you can park at Hangar Two. The ambulance is waiting for your passenger there."

Joe cut the switches. They looked at each other for a long moment. It seemed like the most natural thing in the world for Joe to put his arm around Maria and hug her tightly to him.

The Hair of the Dog, or the Continuing Adventures of Harry Lefferts

David Carrico

Late December 1633
Near the border between France and Spanish Netherlands

Sieur Chretien de la Roche awoke in misery. The bolster under his throbbing head seemed particularly hard this morning, and for some reason it was damp. A timeless interval passed, and it came to his attention that the entire bed was hard, much harder than he remembered it being. More eternity passed and, against great resistance, he managed to force open his eyes. It slowly dawned on him that he was not in his bed in the family hôtel. In fact, he was not in bed at all. He appeared to be sprawled on a floor—and a not particularly clean one at that—with his cheek resting in what seemed to be a puddle of drool.

The sieur contemplated moving for an age, and finally mustered the energy to drag his hands up level with his shoulders and place the palms on the floor. At long last, he exerted himself to arise from his hard bed, but no sooner had he raised himself from the floor than a white-hot spike of pain shot through his head, and he collapsed back to the floor, on his back now.

"*Mon Dieu*," he gasped hoarsely, "if I must be crucified, could it not have been done through my hands and feet, like normal?"

More moments passed, and suddenly de la Roche became aware

of pressure, of waves, of mounting rebellion in his body. Head forgotten, he rolled back to his hands and knees and scrabbled for the chamber pot. Reeling, he noted that apparently he had used it for its normal purpose sometime during the night, then his mouth locked rigidly open and it seemed like everything that had ever passed through his mouth during his entire life now spewed forth. Finished—at least for the moment—he huddled on the floor, misery compounded; head feeling like that of Sisera when Jael pounded the tent stake through it, cold, sweating, shivering, mouth tasting of hot sulfur.

Finally, he managed to sit up, back on his heels. He wiped the splatter drops off of his face with a sleeve that, in keeping with his surroundings, was also noticeably less than clean. The agony in his head had dwindled to a dull throbbing, although it still felt as if his eyeballs were being pushed out of their sockets. Looking around at the unfamiliar room, de la Roche deduced that he was in an inn, and a remarkably unprepossessing inn at that. For an instant, he was puzzled as to why he was here, but then the memories came cascading back: gambling with his friends and a couple of strangers; one of the strangers accusing him of cheating with dice (he didn't think of it as cheating, simply as an unusual skill); his perforce challenging the stranger to a duel, only to discover that the stranger was the son of the comte de Rochefort, one of the deadliest swordsmen in Paris, nay, all of France.

The remaining memories were a jumble—fleeing to the family hôtel in a panic, gathering together what clothes and funds he could find, telling one of the stable boys to saddle two horses and fleeing Paris as fast as he could with Luc, the stable boy, riding right behind him as a servant. In his mind he thought to go to Antwerp. Surely he could persuade (or bribe) the Spaniards to let him pass through their lines. He didn't remember how long they had ridden before they found this small insignificant inn in a small insignificant village. He did have a vague recollection of drinking a great quantity of appallingly bad brandy last night, however.

Looking down at the chamber pot that sat in front of his knees, he determined that its current contents were even more noisome in composition than that had been before he deposited what remained of his dinner and the brandy. His stomach lurched again, and he looked away hurriedly.

Luc—why wasn't Luc here, tending to him? Angry, de la Roche

tried to call out, but all that issued from his throat was a sound reminiscent of the caw of a crow. Crawling over to the bed, he laboriously climbed up it and managed to gain his feet. Leaning heavily on the walls, he lurched around the room until he found the door and almost fell through it.

Harry Lefferts and the members of what everyone in Grantville now called "The Wrecking Crew" looked up from their mugs to see an apparition stumble down the stairs from the second floor of the small inn. They had paused in their trip to the Channel long enough to grab a meal and make sure they were still on the right road. *If I didn't know better,* Harry mused, *I'd swear that one of the actors from those awful Grade B zombie movies me and Darryl used to watch when we were in high school just materialized.* He snickered. *In fact, this guy looks more like the real thing than any of the movie characters ever did.*

The haggard figure stood wavering at the foot of the stairs, until one of the serving wenches approached him. His thin, bony face creased in a snarl, and he took a swing at her and shouted in French that he wanted to see Luc, before his knees gave way and he dropped into a chair at a nearby table. Harry frowned. He didn't much like folks that abused women, but when the wretch remained seated he turned back to his mug.

"*Mein Gott*," Paul Maczka muttered, "I've seen three-day corpses that looked better than him. Mind you, I've been hung over enough before that I felt like he looks."

A thought fluttered at the edge of Harry's mind, but it wouldn't settle yet. He looked up as the zombie began to shout again.

De la Roche was still concentrating on keeping his stomach in place when Luc appeared from the rear door of the common room and hurried over to stand before him. "I am here, master." The zombie started to berate the boy for not addressing him properly, but just at that moment his aching head gave up the fogged memory wherein he had told the stable boy to not call him sieur or lord. So instead he began to rant at the boy for abandoning him in the room.

"...and you left me lying on the floor!" he ended with a final snarl, nose to nose with the lad and watching the boy wince away from the breath he knew all too well was foul.

"But master, I could not move you. First you hit me, then you grabbed me and called me Madeline." Luc was cringing now. De la Roche's temper flared, and he slapped the boy across the face.

Harry broke off his conversation with Paul in mid-word as the boy sprawled on the floor. His muscles tensed as he started to rise, only to stop as the boy scurried upstairs and the zombie collapsed back at the table with a moan audible across the room. He waved the serving girl over as she came by.

"What's with the walking corpse?" He nodded in the zombie's direction.

"Him?" She sniffed. "No one knows. He arrived from the south late last night, complained about everything, wanted the best room for the price of sleeping on the floor in the common room, and insisted on brandy. Our wine . . ." She spread her hands in a balance scales movement. "Eh, not so bad. Our brandy . . ." The *moue* of distaste on her face was expressive. "He drank enough to kill a Spaniard."

"Is he anyone important?" Harry fingered the lapel of his coat, where the other man had a bit of lace showing.

"Him? *Non,* only in his own mind. We see nobles on this road from time to time. He is at best a court hanger-on, or someone's second cousin who drifts around the fringes of the court hoping to receive a plum."

Harry waved the woman away with an order for another ale. As he observed the Frenchman, the fluttering thought settled and a slow smile crossed his face. The crew ostentatiously moved away from him slightly, as that particular evil smile usually didn't bode well for someone within arm's reach.

"What are you planning, Harry?" Gerd asked. "Need a boom toy?"

"Not this time," Harry said. "I'm just thinking that poor soul over there needs a helping hand."

"Low profile, Harry," Paul interjected amidst the laughter of the rest of the crew. "We're supposed to be low profile."

"I can do low profile," Harry replied as he pulled a couple of items out of his saddlebags. He showed one of them to his friends. "But I do think he needs a bit of the hair of the dog that bit him." Grins blossomed all around. Harry handed his bags to Paul. "Go get the horses ready. I'll be out in a minute or two." Still grinning, they finished their ale and followed the orders.

Walking across the room, Harry could hear the Frenchman muttering curses to himself, most of them invoking doom on some son of a whore, but more than a few of them dragging up every French obscenity Harry knew, and a few words that he didn't know but from their context must have been very vulgar. Harry made careful note of those. He dropped into the chair opposite the man, jarring the table as he did so. This caused the monologue to be interrupted by a heartfelt moan.

"Sorry," Harry said. "You look like you've seen better days." The Frenchman's head rolled up from staring down at the table top. Harry got a glimpse of eyes that were more red than white, and a whiff of breath that was truly foul.

"Who are you?" the zombie creaked out. "You are not French, or even Spanish. Where are you from?"

Harry grinned cheerfully back at the baleful gaze. "I'm from way east of here. A little town you've never heard of."

The zombie's head lowered back down. "Go away," he said in a tone that would have been a snarl if it hadn't been so pained.

"Looks to me like you need some of *die alte Katerheilung*," Harry said. "Guaranteed to fix you up. After you drink it, you won't even remember how you feel right now."

Harry was now the focus of the bleary-eyed Frenchman's attention. It took several tries for the word to come out, but eventually he said, "Truly? You can produce this . . . ancient hangover cure?"

"Oh, sure." Harry patted his pockets. "I've got the ingredients right here."

"And it works?"

Harry looked affronted. "I use it myself all the time. Great stuff."

The Frenchman took in Harry's size and obvious good health, eyes widening just a little. "How much?"

"Today, nothing," As the Frenchman's face began to cloud with suspicion, Harry leaned over and said softly, in the manner of one imparting a confidence, "The old Hungarian wit . . . wise woman I got it from said that as long as I gave it away I would have good fortune, but if I tried to make coin from it the fortune would turn evil." The Frenchman's expression cleared, and Harry smiled to himself—got him. That little bit of superstition just absolutely hooked him.

"As you will. I confess that I feel as if I have already died and missed Purgatory. I would willingly bargain with the Devil to be free of this."

Harry had to bite the inside of his cheeks to keep from laughing, but after a moment he could speak with a straight face. "Bear with me a moment, I just need a little wine to mix this with." He went to the bar, and collected a cup with an inch or so of wine in it, tossing a silver piece to the innkeeper ". . . For your troubles."

De la Roche watched as the very jovial stranger returned to the table. After he sat down, he took a silver flask from one of his coat pockets and poured a clear liquid from it into the cup. "First, we add some special water." The now-empty flask was returned to the pocket from whence it came. Then a small glass vial was produced from inside his coat. "Next, the herbal mixture." The stranger very carefully removed the cap from it and just as carefully poured the contents into the cup. Restoring the cap to the vial, he picked up the cup and swirled it around. "Now we blend the wine, the water and the herbs."

"There are no words to speak, no incantations to utter?" De la Roche was getting a little queasy as he watched the cup go around and around.

"None." The cup was set before him. "Just drink it all, and drink it quickly."

He reached out his shaking hands, managed to grasp the cup, brought it to his lips, and swiftly drank the contents. As the cup fell from his suddenly nerveless fingers and a red haze covered his vision, he remembered his rash statement earlier, and it somehow didn't surprise him that the stranger was gone.

The screaming began as Harry closed the door. Chuckling, he made sure his empty flask was back in place—last of the moonshine, he'd have to make do with brandy from here on out—and jogged across to his horse. He gathered the reins and mounted up. *Time to get out of here.* He started to slip the glass bottle back into a pocket, when Gerd asked, "Well?"

Harry grinned that same evil grin. "Like I said, just a little hair of the dog." He showed them the now-empty bottle. They began laughing uproariously, as they had all either been had with the same trick or had seen it done before. Harry slipped the empty bottle of his beloved habanero sauce into a pocket and put his horse in motion. "'Course, it was a junkyard dog."

If I Had a Hammer

Kevin H. and Karen C. Evans

April 1635
East of Arpke village

Dieter Schwarzkopf crouched on one knee and looked up at his partner, Finn Kelley O'Donnell.

"Ah, there you are." The huge Irishman raised his hammer with both hands. "Hold still, my lovely." He swung the hammer down and smashed his target in the head.

Dieter jumped back out of the way. "You didn't have to hit it so hard, you know. Halfway with one blow. You're making the rest of the crew look like slackers. Besides, you'll wear yourself out in an hour doing that."

Finn raised his hammer to his shoulder and took a couple of steps down the line, with Dieter following. "No, Dieter, it's like smashing clods in the field. My brothers and I did that all day every day; and picked up rocks, and planted, and hoed. Much easier working as a mercenary, if you ask me. As for this small job, I'm just here to pass the time away."

Finn and Dieter were no longer mercenaries. They were now working for the Grantville Central Railroad. When Dieter Schwarzkopf was released from his mercenary company, he heard from a cousin that there were jobs building roads. This road they were building was unlike any other road they had ever seen, though. Instead of packed dirt or cobblestones, this one was made of steel.

So he and his good friend, Finn Kelley O'Donnell, originally of Ireland, now worked as a spike team. Finn was the driver, and Dieter was the setter. To be sure, hauling steel rails and swinging a hammer was hard work. But it put silver in their pockets, and no one was shooting at them.

Another swing, and another spike was snug up against the rail. Before Dieter could set another spike, the blast of a horn shattered the air. Finn wiped his face with his kerchief, and glanced at the sun. "Looks to be lunchtime. I wonder if she'll talk to me today?"

Dieter frowned. Finn talked of nothing else lately. "She didn't talk to you yesterday, or the day before. What's so special about today? Do you think she will notice you among the four hundred men on this site?"

Finn's face spread into a huge grin. "Dieter, my lad, Wednesday has always been lucky for me."

As they stacked their tools, Dieter worried. That look on Finn's face always meant trouble. But he said nothing as they hurried into line at the cook tent.

They stepped up to the serving tables and Dieter started complaining. He was always more comfortable when he was complaining. "You be careful, Finn. Your Wednesday luck has only gotten me into trouble so far."

He was served a pile of boiled turnips and cabbage from the first pot. "I heard that the Dutchman has an eye for her. He's told anyone who will listen that she is his. And he's the captain of this job site. If you want to keep your job, you'll stay out of his way. They say he killed a man last month for speaking to her."

Finn was just ahead. "I'm not worried about the Dutchman." He grinned. "You didn't see the way she looked at me yesterday. I think she loves me already."

The woman filling the steins was the subject of Finn's obsession. Her red hair and green eyes were not the only things that held everyone's attention, there was also her smile. Roselynde was truly a beauty.

She was aware of her effect on the men, but tried to ignore their attention. Roz wanted neither their puppylike adoration, nor their lascivious attentions.

Today, as Dieter and Finn approached, she hardly even looked up. She smiled at the man ahead of them. "You must have really worked up a thirst out there this morning. Careful, now, or you'll slop it all out of the stein."

The man ducked his head, blushing, then gingerly picked up his tray and his beer, and hurried off out of her sight.

Roselynde filled two more steins. "Well, come along, then. Who's next? You're holding up the line." She smiled most of the time. But it was a kind of impersonal smile that didn't quite touch her eyes. She was determined to avoid attachments at this point in her life, so she was a little surprised when one of the men addressed her directly.

"Mistress, you're as lovely as this warm spring day." He stepped up and treated her to a winning smile.

It kind of reminded Roz of a hungry wolf. It was huge, and had lots of white shiny teeth. "My, aren't you the largest creature I've seen today."

He swelled a little larger at her compliment. "And you the bright ray of sunshine that lights our way."

Roselynde smiled as she always did. But she turned around quickly toward the tun. She could feel the heat on her face and didn't want anyone to see her blush. *What am I doing blushing? I can't let any of these rough men think they can have their way with me!* "Don't you be thinking that I'm fooled by your silliness, now."

He reached for one of the steins. "Silly it's not, mistress. I'm blinded by your loveliness."

Roselynde watched as he and his friend started to walk away from the serving line. She couldn't take her eyes off of the big one. He truly was a sight. He stood at least a head and a half over most of the men around him. Few were as broad of shoulder, either. And his dark hair and blue eyes drew her attention more than she wanted to admit. Why hadn't she noticed this man before?

The sounds of a disturbance across the track from the mess tent drew her back into reality. Crashes and oaths rattled out of the shanty housing the company office. The Dutchman, captain of the work crew, stepped out into the sunshine, still shouting. The office was a small shed on skids so it could be dragged to the next site every time the road crew moved.

Roz hurried to pick up some dirty steins, but the Dutchman plowed through the crowd toward the food line. "You there, that big Irish oaf. You've no right to speak to Roselynde. She is a lady, and above the likes of you."

All the sounds of laughter and conversation around the mess

tent dropped into silence as deep as a snowy morning. Roz turned and saw the big man carefully set down his tray and stein. He smiled, but this time the wolf look was a little more prominent.

The Dutchman was not as large, but his anger seemed to make him almost as tall. His speed increased as he stepped forward, and his beard bristled as he glared into the icy blue eyes of the Irishman.

"Roz, is this man bothering you?" He tried to put his hand protectively on her arm.

Roselynde avoided his touch. "Now that's quite enough. This young man wasn't bothering me, but you are. Go back into the office and pick up the mess you made of your lunch. If you want any more, you'll have to come and get it yourself. I'm busy."

His mouth opened and closed as he tried to think of something else to say.

Roselynde turned her back. "Get out of my sight, all of you." She carefully didn't look at him or anyone else.

Dieter watched the whole confrontation from the hillside where he ate his lunch. Finn finally joined him and threw himself down, but didn't eat. Dieter let him fume for a moment, then said, "I told you to be careful. Did you see how much the Dutchman wanted to kill you?"

Finn wasn't listening. As usual.

"Ah, Dieter, it was wonderful. I was right, she already loves me. I knew it the first moment ever I laid eyes on her. And now—"

Dieter interrupted. "And now what? She stopped the Dutchman from killing you because it would shut down the road crew for the rest of the day. She doesn't care a pfennig for you."

Dieter watched Finn pick at his food, and worried again. "Finn, you're really going to get us in trouble this time, I can just feel it."

West of Arpke village
After midnight

Gijsbert Keese watched a man in a black cloak appear from the trees and slip across the meadow in the moonlight. Then the man blended back into shadow.

He was nervous, and when he didn't see the cloaked man for a moment, he whispered, "Are you alone?"

The cloaked man edged into the moonlight, and pushed off his hood. "Of course, you fool. I know that we can't be found out. After all, we are conducting illegal activities."

Gijsbert said, "It's always good to check. I have the shipment for you. But I couldn't get it all—"

The man in the cloak exploded. "What? I told you I needed it all. The war continues on the coast, and we have men to feed. And they're paying a pretty penny." He started pacing.

Gijsbert kept silent. He was afraid of the man in the cloak. And he knew from experience that it was better to wait out the temper than to try to explain.

Finally the pacing stopped. The cloaked man's eyes were piercing in the pale moonlight. "I guess I'll have to take what I can get. How much do you have?"

"I was saying that I couldn't get it all because the woman who runs the kitchen was counting everything. And I've been unsuccessful convincing her to cooperate. But I brought everything I got before she started inventory. There are several barrels of flour, salt pork, and wine. I didn't get the beer."

"Yes, yes. That will have to do. Let's get it loaded on the carts and out of here. I don't like meeting you so close to the village. It's too likely that we'll be seen."

With a good deal of grunting and struggle, they rolled the barrels over to a waiting cart. Without another word, the man in the cloak climbed up to the seat, and gathered the reins. "I expect to see you next week with the full order. Don't disappoint me again."

Dieter's week went from bad to worse. Finn worked as hard as ever, but all he could talk about was Roselynde. "She has the sweetest voice. Wouldn't she sing like a whole choir of angels?" Even worse, "Never have I seen such eyes. Dieter, have you ever seen anything as beautiful as Mistress Roselynde's eyes?"

Dieter worried more and more. Should he push Finn into action, or was it better to endure the constant talk?

One evening when Finn began washing up for dinner, he was telling Dieter in great detail everything he had noticed about Roselynde from her small feet to the wispy hair that slipped out of the pins.

The more Finn talked, the more a frown threatened to pull

Dieter's brows together into one great dark brow. Finally, he could stand it no more. "Finn, I've listened to you talk about that woman for days now. Are you just going to talk me to death, or are you going to do something about it?"

Finn stood up straight, and wiped the water streaming in his eyes. "Well, I've been talking very politely to her each day. Isn't that enough?"

"You clod, of course not. All the men in the lunch line speak politely with Roselynde. In fact, I greeted her myself this morning. But you've been too busy acting like a mooncalf to know that. Finn, do you hear me?"

There was a pause. "Yes, Dieter, I do. You're saying that I need a plan. I need to do more than enjoy speaking to her at lunch."

Finn was silent for the rest of the evening. And that night Dieter was surprised when Finn went right to sleep.

Friday afternoon, Dieter was still worried. Finn still wasn't talking. Not a word as they placed spikes in the long rail.

Finally, the horn blew for quitting time. Dieter watched Finn washing up, and decided he needed to know what was going on in his head. So he threw a wet towel at him.

Finn pulled the wet towel off his face, and whirled. There was mayhem in his icy blue eyes. "Dieter, what's the matter with you?"

"Are you all right? Not a word about Roselynde, or anything else for that matter. Have you decided that you don't love her after all?"

Finn smiled sadly. "Of course not. I love her still. But you were right to tell me to make a plan. And I think I have one."

If Dieter had been worried before, he was downright fearful now. "What sort of plan, Finn? You aren't going to do anything that I'll have to save you from, are you? Remember that time in Rothenberg when you found . . ."

Finn laughed. "This is nothing like that time. And those two girls were really exaggerating when they—"

"Whether they were exaggerating or not is not the issue. What I need to know is how much trouble I'm going to get into trying to save your worthless neck this time."

Finn said nothing.

"Okay, Finn, what is this amazing plan? Does it involve killing anyone, because the company frowns on that."

"Of course not. It's really very simple. I'm going to get some flowers, go over to the women's tent, and tell Mistress Roselynde that I want to marry her."

He was inordinately pleased with himself. Dieter could tell that Finn thought this was the perfect and flawless plan. "That's your plan? Give her flowers and propose marriage? You know nothing about her. What if she's married already? What are you going to do then?"

It was obvious that Finn had never thought such a thing. "Why would a married woman be working in a place like this, I ask you?"

"Because, you lummox. Maybe her husband is working here too. Or maybe she really is the Dutchman's intended."

"Bite your tongue, Dieter Schwarzkopf. She would never consent to marrying a man like that. She's a much better sort."

Dieter plowed on, ignoring all objections. "You like Roselynde because she is a very good woman. Isn't it possible that someone of this high caliber will already be spoken for?"

Finn sounded a little deflated. "Yes, I suppose you're right. She is a quality woman. And why wouldn't a good woman like that be already married? She probably even has babies at home."

Keeping an eye on Finn was a day and night job. No wonder Dieter felt so dour all the time. "Sorry, Finn. I guess you'll have to come up with a new plan tonight. Don't worry, we'll be working on this stretch of road for a least another week or two. You have time for a really good plan."

Dieter watched his partner carefully through the weekend. Finn spent a lot more time listening than he did talking, something very unusual for him. He and Dieter sat in the tavern, listening to all the gossip. Dieter found him under a tree outside the latrine, listening. One night when Finn didn't come home, Dieter went to search for him, and found him asleep outside the woman's tent.

Sunday afternoon, Dieter was trying to nap when Finn suddenly appeared and sat on his cot. Finn sighed, but didn't say anything. He definitely didn't look like someone who was happy. "So, Finn. Have you devised another plan?"

Finn shook his head. "I have no plan. I haven't found out if she is married, or even if any of the working women are married. Sometimes I've heard them talking about men and husbands. But I never could tell if they were talking about real husbands, or imaginary ones. I really don't understand women at all."

"I've been thinking. Maybe your first plan was the best. Maybe it *would* be a good idea to take her flowers and strike up a conversation. But I would suggest that you ask her if she wants to go to the tavern for some beer or go for a walk. Don't just come out and ask her to marry you. That'll scare her away right off."

Finn brightened. "Do you really think that will work?"

"I don't see why not."

Sunday afternoon was a good time for some rest. Most of the girls in the women's tent were sleeping or reading letters. Roz was finishing a letter to her father. She wrote one every Sunday, and put it in the post on Monday morning.

Just as she had sealed the letter and set it aside, she heard a deep voice say, "Hello?"

Elsa went to the door and Roz could still hear the man's voice. "Good afternoon, Elsa. Is Mistress Roselynde in?"

"Roz, someone's here to see you."

"Well, if it's the Dutchman, tell him my last answer still stands. I am not available. I'm washing my hair."

Elsa's smile became a full-blown grin. "It's not the Dutchman. Come see for yourself. I think it's precious."

Elsa held the flap a little wider.

"Elsa, I swear, if you're playing some kind of joke on me, I'll..."

Then she saw Finn. He reminded her of a huge forest troll, standing in the doorway with a bunch of flowers. Not that he was ugly like a troll, but he was so huge.

"Good afternoon, Mistress Roselynde. How are you this fine day?" Finn smiled, and Roselynde remembered the day at the beer tun, when she saw all of those teeth for the first time.

Elsa grinned again. "If you throw him back, let me know. I think he's cute."

Roz didn't really know what else to do, so she stepped past Elsa and shooed her away, then reached back and closed the tent flap. Finn looked up from the ground, and held out a bouquet of flowers. It was a little mussed and starting to wilt. "Mistress, these are for you. But they pale next to your beauty."

"How nice. Thank you very much. I need to get these in water. Can you wait here?" When Finn nodded, she stepped back and handed the flowers to Elsa. "Take care of these for me, please? I'm going to be busy the rest of the afternoon. You're in charge of dinner."

Before Elsa could object, or even comment, Roz was back outside the tent, talking to Finn. "Why don't we walk for a little while? What was your name again?"

Finn fell into step beside her. "I'm Finn Kelley O'Donnell, named after my grandfather's younger brother. My mother's one of the Kelleys, so I carry her name myself. My father's from the O'Donnells of Limerick, if you've ever heard of them. Not too well known in these parts, but everyone at home knows what sort of workers the O'Donnells are."

Something in his voice reminded Roz of her own hometown. They fell into conversation as if they had known each other all their lives.

Late that night, when Finn returned to the crew tent, Dieter was waiting. He wanted to be ready in case someone showed up with a drunken Irishman in hand. But when the tent opened and Finn entered, Dieter could tell that he had not been drinking.

"How did it go? Did you get to talk to her? She didn't slap you, or anything, did she?"

Finn moved across the tent as if he were floating on air. He drifted over, and lay down on his bunk. "Dieter, it was wonderful. She is a fine and beautiful woman."

"Yes, I know that. But what happened. Did you go to the tavern? Did she like the flowers? What did she say?"

Finn sighed, still occupied in his gossamer dreams. "Say? Oh, she said a lot of things. I found out that she was born in Scotland, so she and I are almost kin, the Scots and the Irish being cousins after all. We talked for a long time. We didn't go to the tavern; we sat on the hill behind the cook tent until after dark. And then we walked out by the lake to see the moonlight. She liked the flowers."

There was a moment of silence. Finn relived his encounter, and Dieter imagined what it would have been like. "And Dieter, you're wrong. She's not married. She's working here to support her old, sick father. He was crippled in an accident at the mill, and as she has no brother, she is doing her best for her family. Her father's living in a village near Magdeburg now. She has no fortune, but is an honest working woman."

Dieter was drawn into his partner's recount of his romance. "What about the Dutchman? Is it true that they are engaged to marry?"

Finn sat up at that, looking angry. "It is not. The Dutchman started showing up at her door and pestering her since the day he got here. She doesn't even understand his interest in her. There are a lot of girls who would follow his money anywhere. He waves it around, and tries to convince her that she should be seen with him. And he spreads wicked rumors about her."

As Finn spoke, he became more and more agitated. Dieter could see that he might have created a monster. It was time to get a handle on the situation before Finn threw himself out into the night to beat down the Dutchman's door and call him out in some sort of duel.

"You're right, Finn. He's a dirt clod compared to Roselynde. But if you want to keep this job and continue to see her, you need to calm yourself. Morning is coming soon, and the horn will be blowing. You need to get some sleep."

Finn deflated a little, and then yawned. "You're right. Can't get fired now, when I almost have her convinced that marrying me would be the best thing in the world."

Dieter was a little disappointed that Finn was asleep so quickly. He would have liked to listen to more gossip, but he didn't want to get fired either.

Before lunchtime on Monday, Roz looked up to see a group of five men entering the kitchen tent. "We're not ready for lunch yet. You'll have to go out with everyone else and wait your turn."

The group of men stopped and whispered among themselves for a moment. Then one of them stepped forward and bowed. "My name is Carl, ma'am. We're a delegation of the crew, and we've come to file a complaint. We've noticed that for the past several days, the quality of the food we've been served has not been up to company standards, if you understand my meaning."

He stopped a moment. Roselynde had nothing to say that would help.

"What I mean, ma'am, is that we aren't getting very much to eat compared to what we had before. There's still stew and bread, but the bread runs out before everyone gets some, and the soup's too thin. If we wanted to eat this kind of rations, we'd just go back to our mercenary companies."

Roselynde listened until he seemed to have run down. She forced herself to be calm. "I understand your concerns, but the supply train should have been here day before yesterday. I bought all the supplies I can from the village, but it's spring, and they have as little as we do right now. If you all want something to eat for the rest of the week, we have to stretch everything."

Carl glared at her. He seemed to be trying to decide whether or not to argue, but his politeness won out. He turned on his heel and stomped back to the men's tent, with his "delegation" fluttering behind him.

Dieter was still worried. Not about Finn this time. What he worried about most was the morale of the camp. There was more grumbling, more boasting and threats. And the worst of it was that if violence broke out, it could very well be Dieter and Finn defending Roselynde against the rest of the camp. The odds were not in their favor.

Saturday night, Finn and Roselynde were walking along the finished railroad. She was brooding so deeply that she didn't notice that Finn wasn't really talking.

He finally broke the silence. "What is worrying you so?"

Roz looked up into Finn's eyes, and saw the concern there. "Oh, it's nothing I want you to get involved in. It's just that things have gotten very complicated."

Finn nodded, but said nothing.

"You know about the supply problem. I've been cutting back on things so that I have enough until the next supply train shows up. I'm not in dire straits yet. I have the chickens out back, and they are laying lots of eggs this spring. They're finding a lot of bugs and worms and the fresh grass is helping. So even though I'm out of any fresh meat and we don't have any more sausages, I can still serve something."

Roz picked up her apron, and pressed it against her face. "I don't want to alarm anyone else, but we're not waiting for one shipment, we're waiting for two. When the supply trains come out here to the end of the line, they've been carrying steel and ties for the road, but not one barrel of food for the men."

She was sniffling hard now, and there was a catch in her voice. "And now I have almost nothing. Only one flour barrel, and we only have enough salt pork left for three more days. Arpke village has no more flour to spare without starving their children. It takes almost a ton of food to feed all four hundred of you every week. I don't know what to do." She began to sob in earnest, then turned and buried her face in his chest.

"Have you heard at all from the company? Have they said why everything is late?" Finn asked.

Roselynde's voice was muffled in his shirt. "I've only spoken to the Dutchman about it. He says that bandits are stealing things before they can get loaded on the train. I pointed out that the men cannot work without food, but he says it's not my place to worry."

Finn could feel her shudder. "That's not all he said to you, is it?"

Roselynde gulped, and got herself under control. She stepped away from Finn, and started walking again. "No, it's not. He grabbed my hand, and told me that if I really wanted to support my family, all I had to do was consent to marry him. He yelled that if I didn't, I would get what I deserved. And when I tried to pull my hand away, he became angry, and looked as if he would strike me."

She stopped walking, and turned back toward Finn. "I didn't want to tell you, as it always seems to upset you so."

Before he could say anything, she planted her hand squarely on his chest. "Now you listen to me, Finn Kelley O'Donnell. Don't even think about confronting the Dutchman. He's a wicked man and doesn't believe in a fair fight. He'll do his best to kill you."

"Don't worry about that. The Dutchman never fought in the wars, as I have. He's nothing but a back alley scrabbler. I wouldn't even need my pike to deal with him."

Roselynde whirled around suddenly, and started walking again. She was speaking as she moved. "I don't know why we're even talking about all this. Odds are that food supplies will arrive on the morning train. I'm just worrying for nothing. I worry like this all the time, with no reason at all. Don't pay any attention to me."

Her voice sped on and on, and her feet kept rhythm. "And, you know, it's not like we are really out of things. Why, for lunch tomorrow, I've found some fresh greens. That will be so wonderful after a winter of dried fruit and salted pork. It's not like either of us has to—"

Finn caught her hand, and stopped her headlong rush. "Don't take on so. I promise not to speak to the Dutchman about this if it will make you happy. Everything's going to be all right, I promise."

☆ ☆ ☆

Roselynde looked up into Finn's blue eyes. Her heart fluttered as she realized for the first time how important he had become to her. "Yes, you're right. Everything *will* be all right. And you just remember your promise, Finn. You're not to talk to the Dutchman at all."

That evening, Finn recounted the conversation to Dieter. This had become something of a ritual. Finn enjoyed telling the events of the day, and Dieter enjoyed the romance by proxy.

When Finn came to the end of his tale, he said, "And I had to promise her again at her doorstep not to talk to the Dutchman. She knows that if I promise it, I won't talk to him. I've given my word."

Dieter sighed in relief. If Finn didn't talk to the captain, it was much more unlikely that trouble would erupt.

Unfortunately, it was a little too soon for him to be relieved. Finn swung his feet off the bunk. "Dieter, going out tonight and looking around his office isn't talking to him, is it?"

"What exactly are you planning?"

Finn picked up the candle and smiled like a wolf. "Well, now. The Dutchman's up to something, I can feel it in my bones. His office would be an interesting study, and since I promised not to talk to him, I have to look at it when he isn't there, like right now."

Dieter felt as if he were trying to hold onto moonlight. Finn dodged around him, then stopped outside the door of the tent. "You're coming, aren't you? Just to keep me out of trouble, as it were?"

The moon was dark, and the clouds were thick. It was difficult to see anything except in the open spaces. The blackness of the empty buildings was deeper than the darkness of the landscape around it. Dieter knew that appearing to sneak called attention to you, so he strolled across the yard as if he owned it.

Finn was already at the office door when Dieter arrived. "Quick, Finn. Someone will see us. Can you get it open?" Finn examined the lock, handed Dieter the unlit candle, then took a step back as if to throw himself at the offending object.

Dieter hissed. "We don't want to be heard either, you big oaf. Be quiet."

Finn nodded, then reexamined the doorknob. "This won't take but a minute." He braced himself on one side of the door jamb, and put his boot on the other side, next to the latch. He leaned back, and pushed with his foot. The building creaked and groaned like an old miser faced with the tax collector. Then the door quietly swung open. "Is that what you wanted?"

"I promised myself that I wouldn't allow you to drag me into any more trouble. How come I always find myself with you, outside an open door in the dead of night ?" Dieter asked.

"Because you're just luckier than most." Finn closed the door, then lit the candle.

"What are we looking for, do you think?"

"I'm not sure, exactly. Why don't you keep watch while I look for it?" Finn walked around to the chair, where the captain would sit to work. The Dutchman was by no means a neat accountant. Everything was strewn in heaps and piles.

When he started methodically sifting through the paperwork and books, Dieter turned his attention back to the window, and kept nervous watch.

Fifteen minutes passed by, and the search was taking longer than Dieter had planned. "Finn, aren't you done yet? Someone's going to see the candlelight, and we'll get fired for sure . . . if not worse."

Finn said, "Mmm." He wasn't really listening. "Dieter, this is very interesting. It seems that our Dutchman is part of a larger group of bandits. They smuggle the supplies off the train, and sell them to the black market. He's already gotten paid for one of the missing loads, and is arranging to sell the other this week. He seems to have it stashed somewhere in the woods nearby. I knew he was up to something."

"What does that . . . Wait, someone's coming!" Dieter dived behind the door, and Finn blew out his candle as he slipped under the desk.

The door came open, and the Dutchman entered, carrying a shrouded lantern. He turned back to speak into the darkness. "You can't just show up here now and demand the shipment. I've got to feed these men something."

A voice sounded outside in the darkness. "That's not really my problem. I just know how many barrels of flour and salt pork are needed by my associates on the coast. And that's how many I'm taking."

There were footsteps coming toward the desk. Finn made sure that he wasn't visible and held very still. No one had seen him or Dieter yet.

The Dutchman walked over to the desk, looking for something in the mess of papers. "Give me the money now, and I'll meet you at the rendezvous before dawn."

The laugh was an evil thing. "Do you truly think I trust you that much? You'll get your silver as soon as I've counted every one of the barrels and crates you promised. Until then, you can just dangle for your money."

The Dutchman was silent for a moment. "My pipe. Where did I leave it?" He opened a drawer on the desk, and brought out his pipe and tobacco, then stomped out the door.

Dieter was just letting out his breath when they heard the key in the lock.

"Why don't we just go get my hammer and beat some sense into the Dutchman's head?" Finn asked.

Dieter peered out a window, hoping that no one else was outside. "Who knows how far up the conspiracy goes? Shouldn't we send a message to headquarters?"

"Dieter, my lad, who are we going to get to send the message? The Dutchman? We're going to have to wait until the company sends out inspectors and auditors. I think they're due some time before summer. But it's not summer yet. That's why I want to express my opinions on the Dutchman's skull tonight."

"No time for that now. It's well past the middle of the night. I think it's a miracle that we haven't been caught in here yet. We need to get back to the crew tent before we're missed. I would prefer that no one ever knew that we were here. You've got to do the thing to the door again."

Monday seemed to drag for Dieter. He had not slept well for two nights, worrying. What if somebody had seen them? Still, there hadn't been any rumor of a break-in, maybe they weren't in for it after all.

This morning breakfast had been a little thin. The men had always been provided with bread and beer to break their fast before work. Today, there was only enough bread for each man to have one thin slice, and the beer was watered to tastelessness. At lunchtime, there was not much more than some bread, boiled eggs and thin soup. The men were beginning to grumble more loudly.

After lunch, Dieter saw the Dutchman came out of his office, and walk down the rail to examine their work. As he approached, the grumbling faded into silence, only to well up behind him as he passed. He seemed oblivious to the smoldering glares and icy silence directed at his back.

Dieter turned his head slightly as the Dutchman came near. He was half afraid that his guilty conscience was reflected in his eyes.

Finn didn't seem to have that problem. He was able to look at the Dutchman. As he approached, Finn rose to his full height, and rested his hammer on his shoulder. Dieter placed another spike in the fish plate to keep busy and not look like he was watching. Finn looked directly into the Dutchman's eyes, and grinned slightly. Then he straightened, lifted the sledge off his shoulder, and brought it down with a grunt. Another blow, and he stepped forward to the next tie.

The Dutchman looked nervous. "What is it, then, you idiot? Do you have something to say to me?"

Finn glanced at the Dutchman again, then turned to Dieter. "Are you ready? Let's see how many more of these spikes we can set before dinner." He knocked Dieter's placed spike into the tie with two solid blows.

The Dutchman watched for a moment, then continued the rest of his inspection round. After he left, Dieter took a step forward, and placed a spike on the next tie. As they continued down the length of their rail, the work blended into a graceful dance of set and swing and step and tap. The afternoon slid into the background as they concentrated on their movements.

As the week progressed, the mood at the camp worsened. The rain didn't help, either. It began Tuesday afternoon before the end of lunch. There was no lightning or wind, just the steady rainfall. It came in gentle waves, but there were very few moments that the work crew didn't have water dripping from their hair, making their grip on the tools difficult.

Late Friday afternoon, Finn was about the only crewman remaining cheerful. He was standing with his hammer on his shoulder as if nothing was wrong.

Dieter began to dislike him intensely for his cheerful smile. "My mother told me that if I were wicked, something like this would happen. Do you think it rains like this in hell?"

Finn's smile was maddeningly happy. "No. But it rains like this in Ireland. I grew up working in the thicker air." Finn waited for

Dieter to place another spike. "It's nothing but a little water. And since you're not made of salt, you've nothing to fear from it."

"I like water fine when I'm washing up, but not when it's running in my eyes. I'm just as likely to drop a spike and have you drive *me* into the tie instead."

Finn laughed. "Well, set up that spike, and we'll see if I hit you or it, why don't we?"

Dieter was grateful when the horn blew for the end of the day.

Some effort had been made to provide a shelter for dinner. Tarps and cloths had been stretched between trees. But the grass was still wet, and the pathways treacherous with mud.

Finn and Dieter were not at the head of the line, but they were close enough to hear the words exchanged by the man in front and the girl at the table. "What do ye mean this is all we have?"

The girl couldn't have been more than sixteen, and was frightened by the shouting crewman. She was from a nearby village, and had only been working for the company for a couple of weeks. She listened to the shouting man for just a moment, then turned and ran sobbing into the cook tent.

After a moment, Roselynde came out with a rolling pin in hand like a destroying angel. "You great lump, were you raised in the barn with the pigs? What do you think, making Marie cry like that? I'm even thinking that you don't deserve any dinner at all, if you would treat the girls that way."

The man who had done the shouting didn't back down. "See here, I was told we'd be fed properly for working here. Not just a bit of bread and watery soup."

Roselynde didn't back down either. "If you want more than that, you have my permission to catch a fish from the lake over there. But I better not see you yelling at these girls anymore. You'll go cool your head a little before I'll serve you any dinner."

The man stomped away. She turned to the other men in line. "And what about the rest of you? Are you wanting to shout at any more of my girls?"

The other men ducked their heads, not wanting to look at her. Roselynde turned and went back into the tent, and the line began to move again. Dieter thought a lot about that. He decided that it was just best never to get on Roz's bad side.

Dinner wasn't as bad as it could have been. The soup was

mostly cabbage, but it had been stewed with some beef bones, and there were fresh greens in it, too. There was bread as well. The men picked up bowls from the table, and shuffled forward, careful to not complain too loudly. Nobody wanted to see what Mistress Roselynde would do if she got really angry.

Saturday morning dawned bright and lively. It promised to be a beautiful day. The little bit of mist that wafted between the trees melted as the sun touched it. There were still puddles and mud, but it was the model of a beautiful spring day.

Before the horn blew for breakfast, the whole crew was out and about. Word spread that an inspection team had arrived.

It was something of a holiday on the line. Well, almost. The work was halted while the safety inspectors went over each rail and tie, looking for sloppy work. The men weren't allowed to leave the job, but the break from work was like a holiday anyway.

While the inspectors worked their way down the railroad, most of the crew found their entertainment by sitting on barrels and rocks along the sides of the right of way.

But Finn and Dieter weren't found among the other workmen. They were hurrying along the path toward the mess tent. "Finn, I don't understand exactly what we're doing."

Finn gestured with his hand as he hurried toward the cook tent. "Ah, Dieter. It's as clear as glass. The inspectors are going to want to see all the records as well as the rail work. Roselynde is quite certain that the Dutchman will try to throw the guilt onto her lovely shoulders. We just need to make sure that the auditors catch him at his shenanigans and keep her out of trouble."

Dieter was a little winded trying to keep up with his partner's long strides. "And how are we going to do that?"

"Well, if I know Mistress Roselynde, she'll jump into trouble with both feet. We need to be there to pull her out."

Finn was right. Roselynde had already jumped in feet first. She just didn't know how much trouble was heading in her direction.

As soon as the auditors started at the mess tent, she slipped out the back. This was the opportunity she was looking for. She opened the door to the empty office, and hurried inside. She became engrossed in her search for evidence, and didn't pay attention to anything else.

Then the door flew open, and the Dutchman stood framed against the bright sunlight. He saw Roselynde behind his desk, papers in her hand, then quickly closed the door. "Here, what's this? What are you doing in here?"

Before she could hide the letter she held, he caught her by the throat. "Roselynde, we can make it through this inspection together, if you cooperate. If not, I'll claim you were robbing my office and turn you over to the authorities. We'll see how long after that you have a job, let alone a protector in that Irishman. You're better off with me, anyway. What do you say? I'll cut you in for two hundred silver, up front."

Roselynde's heart was rattling in her chest like a captive finch, and she could hardly breathe with the Dutchman's hand on her throat. Her fear was so strong that it tasted like acid.

His fingers began to squeeze slightly, and his eyes began to burn. "Answer me now or you'll regret it. I'll have to tie you up and hide you away somewhere until the inspection is over. Answer!"

Roselynde wasn't afraid now. She was angry and getting more so. "You fool. I see nothing in you that's worthwhile. I'd never throw in with you, a liar, a thief and a bully." She pulled his hand off her throat with both hands. He still held her elbow with his other hand, but her anger seemed to give her superhuman strength. She gripped his left hand, sinking in her fingernails.

He kept glaring at her as he struggled to release his hand and bend her to his will.

Roz began to realize that she had more control over his hand than he had over her. In fact, she actually started enjoying the thought that he was in pain. Her anger overflowed, and everything around turned red. She bent and sank her teeth into his thumb.

Finn and Dieter searched the cook tent, the women's quarters, and the open areas in between. Finn scowled. "This isn't good at all. I'm sure she's gone to the office to try and prove her innocence." He broke into a run.

They were just outside the office when they heard a scream and a thud. They both recognized the voice. Finn kicked the door open.

Finn caught the Dutchman with a left hook. Not to be defeated so easily, the Dutchman came up and drove his head directly into Finn's torso. The momentum threw them both out of the cabin.

☆ ☆ ☆

Roselynde came to the door of the office and saw him on top of Finn, the anger still burning bright in her heart. She launched herself onto the Dutchman's shoulders, screaming like a banshee and tearing at his neck and head with her fingernails. She was truly a frightening sight to behold.

When he got a chance, Finn reached out and pried her off the Dutchman.

Roselynde was spitting like a rabid cat. "Put me down, you great clod of a man. Couldn't you see that I was helping?"

Finn kept an eye on the Dutchman while he struggled to hold the raging and wiggling Roselynde. "Dieter, now I know how you feel trying to keep me out of trouble. Give me a hand here."

Roselynde was trying to break Finn's hold. "Oh, I see now. Only the men can take care of business. You want me to step aside, and let you take care of everything. Well, I'm done with that! I can take care of myself, you know."

The Dutchman stepped back out of range of Roselynde's kicks. He dabbed at the blood on his mouth. "Hold her just like that until the inspector arrives, O'Donnell, and I'll not press charges against you for attacking a superior."

Finn placed Roselynde on her feet next to Dieter. "Hold her."

Now Roselynde had a new victim. She screamed and clawed at Dieter's heavy coat, but just couldn't get to anything she could hurt.

While Roselynde spouted threats, Dieter eased her away from the fistfight that had ensued the moment she was separated from it. "Roselynde, we have other things we can do to protect Finn. The inspectors are here now. They are the ones to deal with the Dutchman. You need to search for evidence to show them. It's up to you to find whatever you can before the fight breaks up. Finn's distracting the Dutchman now, but it can't go on forever."

She stopped struggling. "All right, Dieter. I'll look for the paper I had before the Dutchman found me. It can't have gone far. You go get Finn's hammer." She frowned. "And make sure he doesn't kill Finn. I'm holding you responsible!"

"Yes, ma'am, it's what I'm best at. I've kept that Irishman alive up till now, and I don't intend for him to be killed today."

As he reached the sidelines, Dieter could see that there were very few of the crew who had any sympathy at all for the Dutchman. Some were even moving among the rest, taking bets.

The crew were not the only ones interested in the proceedings. The inspection team came out of the kitchen tent. One caught Dieter by the arm. "See here, man. What is all of this? Why is that man attacking Herr Keese?"

Dieter paused to explain. "I think the captain gave an illegal order, and the other man is expressing his opinion of that order." One inspector stayed to observe the fray, and the other hurried off to find their guards. Dieter let him go. Time enough later to worry about legal complications. Now he needed to be get Finn's hammer and stay nearby in case Finn needed him.

The Dutchman caught Finn in the side of the head with a roundhouse blow. Finn saw the movement from the corner of his eye, and ducked. He jerked his head sideways, rolling backward to get his feet underneath him, coming up facing the Dutchman, hands in front, protecting his face.

The Dutchman charged in again. They were trading blow for blow, like titans in the battle at the end of the world. After a little while, the Dutchman took a step or two back, and stood with his hands on his knees, sucking in great breaths, letting his sweat and blood drip onto the ground. Finn stepped back also, and stood observing for a moment.

"Here, now. Are you surrendering?" Finn called.

The Dutchman straightened and glared, then brought his fists up again. "I'm more of a man than you, you uneducated ogre. I'll not surrender."

Finn stood up with his fists at the ready. "Ogre am I? Well, you little weasel, take your best shot."

The Dutchman charged again. He stepped up and delivered a two punch combination, left and right. Finn caught one of the blows on his forearm, but the second came past, and slammed onto his cheek. The Dutchman rolled back and turned, just as Finn's fist came hurtling toward him. He tried to duck, but his feet found one of the many mud puddles in the area and he slid into the mud.

Finn started to laugh. The spectators pushed their way forward, and Finn was shoved into the mud as well. Laughter scattered across the entire meadow.

When the Dutchman fought his way to his feet, he was almost knee deep in the muck. Mud clung to every part of him, sticks and leaves as well. There was a low rumble through the crowd, as he resembled nothing so much as the ogre he'd just invoked.

Finn stood, covered in the same glorious muck. He went at the Dutchman, throwing punches, plowing through the slippery slime as though he were a locomotive. By the time they reached the bank of the mud hole, the Dutchman was standing more from stubbornness than anything else.

The edge of the puddle met the back of the Dutchman's knees, so suddenly he was sitting. When Finn saw his opponent collapse, he backed up to see what was happening. The Dutchman blinked like a rabbit blinded by a bright light.

Finn leaned forward, and rested his hand on his knee. His breath was blowing like a warhorse after a sprint. He heard a groan from the crowd.

So Dieter spoke for everyone. "Hey there, Finn. You're not finished yet, are you?"

Finn straightened. "No, Dieter. We're not near finished yet. My friend here was only taking a small breather. Any of you fellows got some water for us?"

It was only moments before a wooden bucket appeared. The Dutchman stood to get a drink, and was a little surprised to have the water poured over his head instead. Finn, watching from the other side of the mud hole, burst out laughing until a similar bucket was emptied over him.

"Here, now. What's the idea?" Finn shook out his hair like an dog after a bath. "Wasn't I wet enough already?"

Finn made his way out of the mud hole while the Dutchman cleared enough muck out of his eyes to see. Finn turned and offered his hand to pull him up out of the mire. The Dutchman took Finn's hand and finally reached solid ground. Then, keeping hold of Finn's hand, he pulled Finn close and swung his fist at his head.

Finn tried to duck the blow, but caught some of it. He stumbled, but didn't let loose of the Dutchman. He tumbled to the ground, taking his adversary with him. They rolled across the grass, causing the crowd to back up.

Then Finn got his feet under him, stood up with the Dutchman's lapels firmly in each hand. He swung the lowlander around, flinging him against the wall of the nearby office, then he put his head down and rammed it into the Dutchman's gut.

☆ ☆ ☆

Roselynde was startled when the walls shook and the crowd roared. Dust shook out of the rafters, and she coughed a little. Then, looking down, she finally found a crumpled letter under the edge of the desk. She stooped to retrieve it. Yes, this was important, a list of shipments that she had never received.

Then she noticed a wooden box under the desk. The box was locked, but Roselynde wasn't even slowed down. It didn't look very sophisticated. A few moments work with a letter opener, and the box was open.

Inside, there were a couple of money pouches, and several papers. It was the letter underneath that was exactly what she was looking for.

Outside, the Dutchman snapped a punch into Finn's chest. The big Irishman's arms windmilled and he stumbled back. Before he could recover, the Dutchman was on him, throwing a hail of body blows. They broke apart, and rolled slowly to their feet. This time Finn was ready. The Dutchman charged, Finn swung hard and he bounced backward, the momentum carrying him into the kitchen area of the camp, knocking over pots and pans, stumbling into crates and barrels.

Finn followed him. His face no longer carried a look of laughter or fun. The crowd drew back from him as they would from a bear in the forest.

The Dutchman scrambled to his feet as if to make a break for it. Then he spotted something that had been thrown from an overturned table. He picked up the butcher knife, holding it like a bully from the docks.

Now that the Dutchman had a weapon, one that he obviously knew how to use, a hush fell over the crowd. The only sounds were the fire hissing nearby, and a few bookmakers at the back of the mob.

"Finn, I fetched this for you," Dieter called. "Thought it might come in handy." He threw Finn's huge hammer. Finn held out his hand and caught it.

Finn raised his voice. "Are ye sure you want to do this? It will not go well for you."

The Dutchman crouched slightly, and held his knife like a dagger. "I've heard bluster like yours before. You don't want to come against this knife. You should just let me leave in peace."

Finn crouched slightly as well, and took a couple of steps to the left. The two men circled for a moment, then charged.

It was difficult for Dieter to tell what was happening. He saw the butcher knife glitter, and the hammer swing, almost too fast for the eye to follow.

Finn stepped back, blood dripping from his left forearm. The Dutchman was lying on the grass, unmoving. Dieter moved cautiously next to Finn. "What did you do, Finn? Is he dead?"

Finn lowered his hammer and looked down. His voice sounded distant, as if he were coming back from a far place. "No, I don't think so. When he came at me, I aimed at his elbow. I think I heard it crack. Then I threw a blow right into his knee. I decided not to kill him, just tapped him lightly on the back of the head. Not hardly a blow at all, really."

Finn kicked the knife away into the tall grass. "I guess his head wasn't as hard as he thought it was."

Dieter heard a disturbance at the back of the crowd. He turned and saw Roselynde come out of the office, letters in hand. She was shouting and waving them over her head. Her red hair streamed behind her like a bright flag.

"Where are the inspectors? I have proof the Dutchman was stealing from the railroad company, and I have the name of his accomplice."

As she shouted and ran, the crowd parted in front of her, and she found herself next to Dieter and Finn. "What happened here?"

Finn's smile was like the sun after a cold March rainstorm. He seemed to come back to himself with Roselynde next to him. "Nothing at all. We were just dancing a little. And then he tripped and fell, right there."

Roselynde put her hands on her hips. "And, pray tell me, how did you get that bloody wound on your arm? Is it a bug bite, perhaps?"

Their conversation was cut short when the inspectors appeared with guards in tow. Ten men with six foot staffs followed their commander, who was armed with a shotgun.

The men surrounded Finn and the Dutchman, and held their staves at the ready. Roz stepped next to Finn.

"Here now. What is all this?" the head inspector asked. "We don't need a riot. What did you do to Herr Keese?"

Finn put his right hand on his chest, and grinned a little. "Herr Inspector, I'm afraid that the captain can't speak to you right now. He's napping."

The guard commander knelt and felt the Dutchman's throat. "He's alive all right. Where's your medic? I think he needs to look after this man."

The inspector frowned up at Finn. "What's the meaning of this? Assault on a supervisor is not tolerated by the Grantville Central Railroad."

Before Finn could answer, Roselynde stepped between him and the inspector. "My name is Roselynde, and I'm in charge of the kitchens. We've been having difficulty finding enough to feed these men. He's been selling the food to bandits." She gestured with her evidence. "I found these letters that prove it." She pointed. "And when he tried to kidnap me, why, Finn only stepped up to protect me. And that's the whole story."

The inspectors remained on the site for three days more, examining the books and all the papers in the office. Gijsbert Keese had been carted off to lockup by the guards, and Finn and the other men had been sent back to work. The fully-stocked supply train showed up bright and early Monday morning, and Roselynde was able to feed the crew as much food as they wanted.

On the final day of his business, the head inspector summoned Finn into the captain's office. He was sitting behind the desk, shuffling papers when Finn tapped on the door frame. "Ah. Finn. Come in, come in."

Finn was a little nervous. It was very possible that he would still be reprimanded for striking a superior.

The inspector stood, and offered Finn his hand. "Have a seat. As we're planning to move on tomorrow, there are a couple of things that you and I have to talk about. This worksite is in need of a competent captain, and I'm ready to offer you the job."

"Me? You want me as the captain?" Finn was having a little trouble following the discussion. There was a roaring in his ears, and the room seemed to tip dangerously to the side. He eased himself into the chair in front of the desk.

The man sat down in the other chair. "Why, yes, we do. We've had reports from many of the men that you're a good leader and an honest man. That's exactly what we need. Your pay will increase accordingly, of course. You'll be expected to keep track of the records, as well."

Still, Finn couldn't find his voice. It was all like a dream.

The inspector looked at him, then continued. "You'll need an assistant, as well, I think. There's really a lot to do here. You can hire anyone you feel fit for the position. As a matter of fact, it's the first task you'll have as captain. So what do you say, O'Donnell? Can we depend on you?"

Suddenly, everything was clear as glass. This would finally give him the opportunity and standing to marry Roselynde. "Yes, I'll do it. You can certainly depend on me."

April 1636
Farther down the line

Dieter was sitting at the desk, shuffling paper. There was a knock, and the door opened. A very pompous man stepped into the office. "I'm Schmidt, the civil engineer for this project. Are you the captain?"

Dieter stood, and shook the engineer's hand. "Have a seat, Herr Schmidt. The captain isn't available today. I'm his assistant. What can I do for you?"

The heavy man settled carefully in the small chair, and looked disgruntled. "This is very disturbing. Where is Herr O'Donnell, the captain? I was told he was always on site."

Dieter leaned back in his chair and smiled. "I'm afraid that this week I'm all you'll get. Don't worry, I know everything you need. But Captain O'Donnell and his wife aren't available. They took some time off to celebrate the birth of their first son."

A Great Drowning of Men

Walt Boyes

28 August 1627 (old style)

The hooves of the cavalry horses thundered as the lifeguards of Friedrich, third of the name, duke of the Danish province Schleswig-Holstein-Gottorp, rode for their lives with the duke safely in their midst.

Behind them was the carnage of the battle of Lutter. There, twenty thousand Imperial troops under the command of Jan Tzerclaes, Count Tilly, had managed to rout an equal number of Danish troops under the direct command of Christian IV, King of Denmark.

Most of Christian's army holed up in Stade, but Friedrich headed for Nordstrand Island, off the west coast of Schleswig.

Tired, hungry, and somewhat fearful for his life, the duke of Gottorp hauled his horse to a stop in the town square of the little town of Husum. It was just dawn, and he and his men had been riding all night.

"Find somebody who knows what is going on around here," Friedrich ordered. One of his troopers saluted and turned his horse off toward the *Rathaus*. Well, it would have been a *Rathaus* if the town had been really big enough for a city hall.

"I want to get to Nordstrand by nightfall," Friedrich said to his aide de camp. The aide, probably wisely, said nothing.

The trooper returned. "Lord Duke," he reported, "the burgomaster says that he thinks there are Imperialists on Nordstrand."

"Nonsense!" Friedrich glared, moustaches quivering. He slapped his leather riding coat. "We will go. If there are Imperials, we'll just have to beat them!"

The troop remounted, dressed their lines, and started for the dock. There was a decent sized sailing ferry there.

The ferry captain was sitting on a wooden bollard on the dock. He had a piece of wood that he was whittling into something nondescript. His mate stood next to him, smoking a long clay pipe. They watched the cavalry troop ride down the road and out onto the dock.

"Well, Hubertus," the captain said to the mate, "I guess we're going for a sail."

It took less time to sail to Sudhaven on Nordstrand Island than it took for Friedrich's small troop to load themselves and their horses on the ferry. It was a beautiful day, with light wind, and the sea was running fast between the mainland and the island. Soon, the jetty at Sudhaven came into sight, and with it, the ranks of Imperial troops standing on the pier. There was a small group of burghers standing with the soldiers.

Without being told, the ferry captain brought the boat to a stop about fifty feet off the jetty. The ferry rocked in the light chop.

Friedrich went to the rail. "What is this?" he shouted. "And who in the Devil's Hell are you?"

"I am Pieter Karstense van Nortstrant, the burgomaster," one of the civilian burghers shouted back, "We have joined the Imperials, my lord."

Nordstrand was home to a small Catholic population surrounded by Lutherans. As they were an island, and they were small, Friedrich had never bothered about them.

"If you come ashore, my lord," van Nortstrant, who was standing beside the obvious commander of the Imperial troops, shouted, "you must be taken prisoner."

Friedrich stood by the rail, his blood pounding in his ears. After being beaten badly the day before at Lutter, and riding cold and hungry through the night to what he thought was going to be his safe haven, only to be repulsed! It could not be, it would not be borne. Friedrich gave a wordless shout of anger, tore off his hat, threw it to the deck and stamped on it.

"With God's help, this island should sink into the sea!" he shouted.

Friedrich turned to the ferry captain. "Prepare to take me back to Husum."

22 October 1634 (old style)

It was very early. The sun had just come up, and there was Jan Adriaanszoon walking the dike near Dagebüll for cracks and damage during the previous night, just as he did every morning including Sundays. When ministers remonstrated with him for working on the Sabbath, Jan had always told them, "The sea works on Sundays, so must the engineer."

Jan was born in the Low Countries, and he called himself Leeghwater, "low water" because, as he told his son Adriaan, "we engineers drain the polders and make the water low." He always laughed as he said it. Now in his late fifties, Leeghwater had grown corpulent and his big belly shook as he laughed.

There was a wooden footpath laid on top of the dike, and he navigated his ponderous bulk up it to the stairs that led to the top of the sluice. Jan grunted as he knelt to inspect the gaskets on the sluice gate. The leather gaskets were well greased, and looked to be in good shape. Jan levered himself upright and huffed through his mustachios from the exertion. There were wooden stairs leading down from the sluice gate platform. Jan made sure it was easy to get to every gate he'd ever designed.

He'd been working in the Low Countries on trying to make a polder, a reclaimed field, from a low-lying saltmarsh called Beemster. That project was nearly complete but with the unsettled political situation in Holland, he'd agreed to go to Denmark for a while to work on a project to build dikes at Bottschoter in western Schleswig, or northern Frisia, depending on who you talked to.

Before he came to Denmark, Jan had bought from a bookseller in Amsterdam some up-time books. They'd been written by a man called George, with the unpronounceable surname of Tchobanoglous and another man called Takashi Asano. While the first name sounded maybe Turkish, and the second sounded like somebody from far Nippon, the men apparently were up-time professors in someplace called the University of California. Their books on water and wastewater treatment and design, said to be from the library of the water treatment plant in Grantville, had some new techniques that Jan was eager to try, if the cursed war would ever end, but the fundamentals were still what Jan knew. Since he'd read the books, he'd taken to calling himself by the up-time title, "hydraulic engineer."

Jan clattered down the wooden steps from the sluice gate, and walked briskly down the raised earthen dike. This dike was old, and only a few feet tall, which was why Jan had been hired to replace it with a bigger, stouter, taller dike. After the storm surge in 1632, the Nordfrieslanders decided that they'd have to come up with the money to rebuild and renew the barrier that kept them from the North Sea.

Even though the 1632 storm had been much less severe than the up-timers' histories described it in the original time line, the Nordfrieslanders didn't trust the butterfly effect. So they went ahead with the project, despite the very high taxes they were paying because of the war between the Swedes and the Imperials. Jan, with his experience based on a thousand years of dike building in the North Sea and his new up-time knowledge sounded to the burghers like just the ticket.

Jan stood on the dike, looking out to sea. The water was as calm as the North Sea got, at least in the channel between Dagebüll and the big island of Strand, or Nordstrand. There were few clouds. It was a beautiful October day.

After he finished his inspection, it was almost noon, and Jan headed to a tavern. Like nearly all the small towns in Nordfriesland, Dagebüll was built on a raised mound that had been added to for as long as the inhabitants could remember. It was as if Dagebüll had one long street, raised above the fields where crops grew and cattle grazed.

The inn was old, as buildings went, but still had the huge beams exposed in the ceiling that made the building stout. That was important when the winds blew in off the North Sea, and the weather turned.

Jan joined a group of men sitting at a long table under the window, reading newspapers and drinking small beer.

"And what is news today?" he asked his master carpenter, Pieter Jansz, who was reading a broadsheet.

"Work on the Union of Kalmar moves apace. Apparently we are all to be Swedes now."

"Well, I am Dutch, and not likely to wake up Swedish one day," Jan said, tugging on his VanDyke beard. "It appears, however that I may be Spanish now." He sat and picked up another paper from the small pile on the table and nodded thanks when the server brought him a mug of beer.

"Prost!" he said, raising his mug.

He settled down to read. The paper was full of news about the dashing rescue of the Princess Maria Anna by the new "king in the Netherlands," the former cardinal-infante Don Fernando. Jan wasn't sure he approved of the treaty between the House of Orange and the House of Habsburg ending the Netherlands war. But he was sure that the situation for engineers was going to improve tremendously, especially since the Swede was building docks and a fortified harbor so he could cut off traffic through the Zuider Zee if he wanted to.

There was even talk about draining the whole Zee . . . just like the up-time Hollanders did in the twentieth century. Jan had read about the project in another book that claimed to be "faithfully republished" based on a book in the library of Grantville itself. He was as excited as he could let himself be thinking about working on that project.

The newspaper also had an article about the aftermath of the Galileo business in Italy. Jan sipped his beer and continued to read.

A hand dropped on his shoulder. He looked up to find Jansz standing over him.

"Master," Jansz said, "we are having some people over for dinner tonight. Will you join us?"

"I would like that," Jans said.

"Good. We will be seeing you at dinnertime tonight then."

Jansz went out the door of the inn. Jan ordered some lunch and decided to eat it out in the inn yard. There were some trestle tables there for outdoor eating in good weather. Even though it was October, it wasn't very cold. There were more scudding clouds in the sky, but the sky was blue and the wind was dying down. Jan ate a nice chunk of ham and a piece of Gouda cheese that reminded him of the Netherlands and home.

After he ate, Jan walked back up to the outer dike and walked along it, looking out to sea. The wind, he noticed, was coming up. The sea had bigger swells and was raising whitecaps. He could see the rip current in the channel between Dagebüll harbor and Nordstrand off in the distance. There was definitely a change in the weather. He thought he'd best do another inspection before he went to Jansz's house for dinner. He walked from sluice gate to sluice gate, checking the great wheels and chains that could raise the gates and the pawls that kept the gates closed. He checked the dry wells that were installed every few hundred yards to make sure there was no seepage or at least no more than normal.

When he finished, Jan went back to the inn and finished reading the news broadsides. About seven or eight o'clock, he walked down the inner dike from the inn to the house that Pieter Jansz and his family were living in.

All through dinner, Jan and Jansz discussed the state of the big new sluice that Jansz was building. It was more or less on schedule, which was certainly a wonder, Jan thought. They hardly noticed the wind picking up.

After dinner, they lit their long clay pipes and talked about politics. Jansz was from Friesland, and he supposed, he said, that he was Danish. "I don't really know. We speak the dialect here," he said, "and we pay our taxes to the Duke of Gottorp, but this new idea that we are citizens of a country . . . that takes some thinking about. Especially when our country has gotten beaten in a war by the Swedes and the Americans."

"Yes," said Jan. "I can see that. But it looks like the king came out pretty well, with his son betrothed to the Swede's daughter."

They laughed. Suddenly a shutter blew in. One of Jansz's older children ran to close it. Jan and Jansz went to the door. They opened the half-door and quickly closed it, struggling against the wind.

"This sounds like it may get nasty," Jan said. "I think I ought to be getting on home."

"Well why don't you stay with us here tonight, master?" Jansz said. "It is getting foul out and by the time you get home, you're likely to be drenched."

"Ah," Jan said, "it isn't so far as all that. Besides, you have a full house. Where would I sleep?"

"On the floor," Jansz said.

"No, Pieter Jansz," Jan replied. "What if the water rises? Your house is only five to six feet above ground level. Mine is on the dike, at least at eleven feet."

"As you wish, master," Jansz said, and brought Jan his coat.

Jan headed for his own house. The wind was high and swirling, and it was beginning to rain with big heavy drops. He wrapped his coat around himself, his long hair whipping around his face and his mustachios bristling.

It was getting bitter and cold. Up ahead, Jan saw the house of another one of his crew, Pauwels Harmensz, with all the lights still on. Jan realized he was freezing.

He fought his way through the wind and rain to the Harmensz's door. He banged on it, and Harmensz opened it. Jan almost fell through the doorway, but managed to stay upright.

"Pauwels," Jan said, "I need to warm up before I go on home. It is incredibly cold out there. The wind is high and the water is rising."

Harmensz sat Jan before the fire, and as Jan warmed up, they talked about the storm.

"It came up very suddenly," Harmensz said. "I hope we don't have another surge like we did two years ago."

"Well, the dike is taller now," Jan said. "If we get a surge we'll see how well we've built, that's for sure."

Jan stood and began to put on his coat.

"It is dark as pitch," Harmensz said. "Why don't you let me send one of my men along with you? He can carry a lantern and make sure you get home safe and sound."

"The lantern sounds good," Jan said.

When they reached Jan's house, Jan's son was waiting for him.

"I was beginning to be worried, Father," Adriaan said.

"Nothing to worry about," Jan replied, "just a storm."

Jan had Harmensz's man stay. Adriaan helped him get a hot drink and warm up, and then sent him with his lantern back home.

Even with a fire, it was very cold in the house. It was also quite late, being close to midnight.

"Tired, boy?" Jan asked his son.

"Yes, Father. Can we go to bed soon?"

"Probably we should. And since it is so cold, we should probably sleep with our clothes on as well."

The wind was coming from the west now, and the house shook and rattled with each gust. The rain hammered on the roof and the western wall of the house like buckshot. Even though the house wasn't right at the shore, the sound of the waves grew louder and louder.

"I can't sleep, Father," Adriaan said.

"Come here, boy," Jan said, "you can sleep with me in my bed. You'll be safe then." Adriaan climbed into bed. Jan hugged the boy hard.

They lay there dozing for about an hour as the wind grew even more harsh and blustery.

"Father, I think the roof is leaking."

Jan rolled off the bed. There was a steady drip of water from the ceiling. As Jan watched, the leak got bigger and bigger.

The waves were smashing on the sea wall. Every sixth or seventh wave was so large that it would crash over the sea wall, and smash against the roof of the house. There was a flash of lightning, a clap of thunder, and one of the shakes on the roof blew off with a bang. There was a sudden gush of water through the hole onto the mattress.

Suddenly there were shouts from outside the house. "Leeghwater! Leeghwater! It's time to get up!" Jan pulled the door open and found his boss, Supervisor Siewert Meynerts with a small group of people. "We have to get to the mansion," Meynerts shouted.

Jan and Adriaan collected what they could and went up the dike to the mansion, which was close by but built on substantially higher ground.

Meynerts and his people were right behind. "I'll be glad if we reach the mansion alive," he shouted.

There was quite a lot of flying debris. All the planks and slats were blown from the stockpiles where they'd been waiting to be used in the construction of the new sluice. They were flying around like feathers and straw.

Looking back from the doorway of the mansion, Jan could see that the water was almost at the top of the dike. Adriaan clung to his leg, sobbing.

Meynert was counting heads. "Eighteen, nineteen, twenty . . ." Then the door opened again and a large number of people rushed in, soaked and panting with exertion from fighting the wind and the rain. "I make us about thirty-eight souls, all told," Meinert told Jan.

The wind turned a little to the northeast, and the waves pounded harder on the dike. Suddenly, one of the big doors on the west wall of the house blew open and water came pouring into the house. The fire was extinguished by the wave rolling into the room and Jan's boots were instantly filled with seawater.

One of Meynerts' men, a carpenter, took his axe and made a hole in the lower part of the wall so that the water could run off. Jan looked out the window.

"The water is above the dike now!"

"How high is the surge?" Meynerts asked.

"That would be at least thirteen feet," Jan said.

"Oh my God, what will become of us?" the carpenter's wife moaned.

"Well, God has seen to it that we are all equally rich now," Meynerts said. The joke fell flat.

Adriaan had taken refuge in the scullery. "Oh, Father, are we going to die?" he asked. Jan grimaced as the cry was taken up by several others.

"We just have to hope that the Almighty will have mercy on us." Jan said.

The storm went on for hours. Jan tried to see if the water was rising even more or if the height of the surge had passed, but he couldn't tell.

There was a loud noise from the northern side of the house. The wall on that side started to fall apart. Through the hole that appeared suddenly, Jan could see a huge eroded channel like a gutter that was about six feet deep and at least ten feet wide. The wall started to fall into the gutter, and the flow of water broke it into kindling and washed it away.

The house itself started to collapse. The refugees huddled together in the center of the house under the groaning rooftree. The water kept pouring through the house. A large money box broke loose from its fastenings and before anybody could grab it, it came open and its contents, money and jewelry, was washed away by the water and swallowed by the earth. The entire mansion was being washed away.

Jan, Adriaan, Supervisor Meynerts and the rest of the refugees held on for dear life. It seemed to Jan like time was standing still. He thought that he was looking into the maw of Hell.

15 November 1634 (old style)

"The storm went on for hours, Majesty," Jan said to King Christian IV of Denmark. Enthusiastically adopting up-time habits, the king had called for a Grantville-style meeting, instead of a throne room audience. "The next morning, when it was safe to come out, I saw that the ruins of the reeve's mansion were the only house still standing on the dike. All thirty-seven of the workers' houses lower down toward the sea had been washed away. I had to take a boat to Dagebüll because the dike had been washed away and the sea had covered the fields. There were bodies of men and animals floating everywhere."

"Do we know how many dead?" Prince Ulrick spoke up.

"No," Duke Friedrich said. "We are still burying the men, and also the cows. My men estimate somewhere between eight and twelve thousand persons perished."

"It was like Noah's Flood," Jan said. "The priest in Dagebüll said that the water had reached almost five feet high inside the church, which is built on its own hill in the town. Jansz and Harmensz's houses, where I had been before the storm had vanished, and they and their families were all dead. Big sea ships were stranded up on the dikes, and several ships were aground in the higher streets of Husum. I've been on the beaches, where I have seen horrible things, Majesty."

"We have been checking the up-timers' books, Father," Ulrick said. "It seems that the storm was in the books, but on a different date . . . October 11th. In the original time line, though, the area was never really rebuilt, and the only thing that you, Duke Friedrich, would say was, 'God is just. My wish has come true.'"

Friedrich said, "That's not going to happen here. I have learned . . . I think we have all learned something from the events of the past few years. We will begin rebuilding the dikes immediately and draining the fields. We will need the farms and dairies. So, Leeghwater, how fast can you get back to work?"

"I can raise men in Holland, and begin ordering the materials immediately, my prince," Jan said, "but it will take time. We should have things back to normal in five or six years."

The king had been sitting quietly through all of this. He was staring at the end of the table, where another man sat silent.

"So," the king said. "You, Cantrell. Tell me how it is that my new allies didn't warn me of this horrible event. Since, as we have found, it is in your books that you brought with you in the Ring of Fire. Why didn't you tell us?"

The room grew silent. Everyone in the room stared at Cantrell. He swallowed convulsively.

"I think . . . well, Majesty," Cantrell said, "we believed that it wouldn't happen because of the butterfly effect. At worst, we thought it would be much less severe than the storm in the history books that they called 'a great drowning of men.' And the dikes were being rebuilt, so we just didn't think to say anything."

A king's anger is not safe to see. Especially if you are on the receiving end. Eddie Cantrell thought back to the night he became betrothed to the king's daughter. How he felt when he was told to kneel and King Gustav pulled out his sword. Beheadings could still happen. King Christian's face could have been carved from granite. His eyes, however, burned.

Ulrick intervened. "Father, what this has shown us is that we must carefully read the up-timers' histories. Yes, there is what they call the 'butterfly effect.' But some things will happen, and we must prepare for them. That is the awful lesson we must learn from this."

"Then learn it!" the king roared. "You and Cantrell must read and learn so we can plan. See to it.

"And you, Jan Leeghwater, build as fast as you can. We have had two of these devastating floods in two years now, the one in 1632 and now this one. We will not, we must not, ever, suffer another one, as I am the king!" King Christian slammed down his ever-present wine cup on the table. "Why are you still standing here? Do it!"

Blaise Pascal and the Adders of Apraphul

Tim Roesch

Grantville Power Plant, November 11, 1634

Bill Porter staggered out of the staff lunchroom in the Grantville Power Plant as if he'd been cast out against his will or was in fear for his life . . . or possibly both. He caught sight of Julie Drahuta walking serenely down the corridor and held up his hands as if surrendering to her.

"Julie," Bill whispered, "Julie, just wait a second, okay? Wait a second. Jesus Christ, don't go in there. It's crazy. I can't believe it and I was there."

"What did the boy do now?" Julie smiled.

"The boy? Blaise? Nothing. Everything. It started with that damn pressure flutter in boiler number two. It was there before the Ring of Fire. Blaise is pumping out solutions to electrical engineering math problems faster than he can read the damn book and, right in the middle of everything, he's figuring out the harmonics of the flutter in boiler two like it was nothing and now he's in the staff cafeteria . . ."

"Hey, Bill." Nissa Pritchard walked up to her boss with a smile as bold as brass on her face. "Is it true? In the cafeteria? Is it really him?"

"Yes, Jesus Christ, yes," Bill gasped. "Don't piss him off."

"No need to get huffy." Nissa shook her head and walked past, entering the door leading to the cafeteria.

"What's wrong?" Julie asked.

"Wrong? Blaise is figuring out how to make a computer. Hell, tell the kid we can't go to the moon and we'll be there a week after Thanksgiving. I am afraid to ask the kid to solve problems because he'll do it. He's got an idea for a hydraulic adder but he really wants it to be pneumatic. He thinks water is too messy. Rod was playing a joke on the boy—"

"A joke? You know what happens when people mess with the kid? He doesn't understand it and he ends up hanging from church steeples or trying to electrify cats or trying to make his own hydroelectric plant."

"I talked to Rod about what he did, Julie. Look, it was an April Fool's joke from a *Scientific American* issue about this analog computer supposedly dug up at a site on a South Pacific Island called Apraphul and used by Pacific Islanders to navigate with. It was all hogwash, I mean look at the name of the island and the month the magazine was printed, April, but the kid tried to make one, well, a dozen, okay, forty-nine and he's all ticked. . . . Right, but that leads him to a hydraulic computer. Jesus, why didn't I think about that? Anyway, he needs more room so I get some old chalkboards rigged up in the cafeteria. Easier to watch him with a pot of fresh coffee, right? Anyway, he's in there creating hydraulic computers amongst the microwave ovens and coffee machines."

"You let Blaise near a microwave! Jesus Christ, Bill! I wouldn't let him near a picture of microwave in a book after what he did!"

"Easy, Julie. He's being watched and he is following directions. He passed the safety course and he walks around in the main generator room like a priest in the Vatican . . . always under supervision. He's cool. I even punished Rod for jerking the kid's chain by making Rod personally responsible for escorting the kid. Rod is running himself ragged trying to keep up."

"But a microwave? Matheny is still pissed about that one." Julie sighed.

"Hey, he fixed it right? Anyway, Blaise almost has an Adder working!"

"An Adder?"

"Yes, Julie, it's a fundamental unit of a computer. We could have a computer up and running in no time. To hell with Silicon Valley. We could make a working computer out of stuff he got here. We don't need photolithography and silicon disks. Hell, we could get the Europeans to understand this. Sure, it would be bigger and slower but it would work. Then, I go in this morning and—"

"Hey Boss!" Rod Shackleton rushed up to them both, holding a box. "I got these pastries. Think he'll like 'em?"

"Who knows what he likes? Take 'em in! And find out what Blaise is doing in there. You left him alone too long." Bill waved at Rod to hurry up. Rod rushed to the open door and hurried inside. There was a loud burst of French, then a more quiet discussion ensued.

"They're writing on the walls now, Julie." Bill shook his head.

"Blaise knows better than that." Julie made to go around Bill but Bill held up his hand.

"Do you know who's in there? He just shows up as if it ain't a thing. Poof! Allan Sebastian is just following along as if he's lost or something."

"You mean he's here already?" Julie frowned. "I thought he'd settle in first. It's a long way from Toulouse. He just got in like what, twenty hours ago?"

"You knew!"

"Of course I did. Someone comes into town asking about Blaise, I get curious." Julie shrugged. "For all we know, Blaise *is* a secret weapon. All by himself. It could have been Richelieu's secret plan to blow the place up by giving the kid all the electricity he could want."

"You knew that Pierre damn Fermat was coming and you didn't tell me?" Bill almost shouted. Bill Porter was not a man to shout without reason and this was almost a reason.

"He's Pierre Fermat, not the pope," Julie smiled. "Besides, Allan knew. Allan is a math teacher."

"Blaise Pascal and Pierre de Fermat are in my staff lunchroom," Bill gasped.

"I think you can drop the 'de' thing. My guess is Richelieu isn't going to let him keep it after this little escapade gets out. I've been reading up—"

"Pierre. Fermat."

"I. Know. Bill. I am going to put them up at my place for now until they get settled. She's pregnant. They have this incredibly incompetent maidservant with them. God, my son Joseph could do better."

"She?"

"Mrs. Fermat. You know he was, well, is married. Finally, some famous person who isn't eleven and hanging by his neck from the church steeple. Thankfully, the 'False Messiah' thing worked out. Shabbethai Zebi is in there with Blaise, right? You realize how hard this is? I got a False Messiah in the power plant and Mary Timm in a basement cutting glass. And Blaise Pascal in a room with a microwave. God, who's gonna die first?"

"Shabbethai is in the corner reading a scroll." Bill shook his head. "Jesus Christ, Julie, it's like an episode of *Laugh In*! Who the hell is going to show up next? Descartes?"

"He's too old to move out of Amsterdam. Besides, I don't think—"

"Excuse," Jacqueline Pascal said politely as she led Logan Sebastian by the hand past them both. "In here?"

"Yes, Jackie, Blaise is in there and busy. I'll be in in a minute." Julie waved. "Don't start without me. And keep your brother away from the microwave!"

"Start?" Bill shook his head, almost whimpering. "What's Blaise going to start?"

"Logan didn't want to wait any longer for Blaise to ask her to the Thanksgiving Dance so Jacqueline decided to act *in loco mommy* and bring the two together," Julie said. "Jacqueline treats her brother like he's a lost puppy."

"I hope Allan knows, because he's in there." Bill pointed and, as if on cue, Allan Sebastian, Blaise Pascal's second mathematics teacher, poked his head out of the crowded staff cafeteria.

"Hey, Bill, you're needed." Allan waved then hurried back inside.

"Jesus, Julie," Bill whispered, "I'm needed in a room with Blaise Pascal and Pierre de Fermat."

"Pierre was very adamant about the 'de' thing. I think he's interested in teaching in Grantville," Julie told Bill.

"We don't have a college here yet." Bill shook his head.

"I think he wants to teach middle school," Julie said.

"Middle school!" Bill shouted. "Pierre de Fermat teaching middle school? Are you out of your cotton picking—"

"That would be grand, just grand," a voice from behind them stated joyously. "Pierre Fermat teaching. What could be better? Is the man within, my good man?" John Pell bustled past Julie and Bill. "What could be better for the children of Grantville than Pierre Fermat teaching mathematics? Have you read his history? Is the man here? Ahh, I hear French!"

Bill snatched the radio from his belt. “Whoever is watching the front gate, would you warn me when civilians come traipsing onto the power plant grounds? Who is on guard duty?”

“Calm down, Bill.” Julie watched John Pell enter the staff lunch room. “I brought them.”

“You . . .”

“*Pardonnez-moi*, Monsieur Porter.” A well-dressed man walked out of the staff cafeteria, glanced once up at the overhead lights then held a book open under the light. Jacqueline Pascal was right behind him.

“I don’t know all those big math words and Blaise is under the sink trying to take apart the drain,” Jacqueline grumped, her small arms crossed over her chest.

“Jackie! You promised!” Logan shouted from the door.

“In a minute! My brother is not going anywhere. That is his lucky wrench. Just take it away from him if he tries to leave,” Jacqueline shouted back then smiled up at Pierre Fermat. There was an exchange of very polite and fluid French at the end of which Jacqueline, looking very polite and very put upon, looked up at Bill. “He wants to know what these ‘S’ things are and why there are three of them.”

Bill peered at the open textbook as if it were one of the original, extant copies of the Bible and he was a bishop asked to explain an obscure passage to Jesus.

“Tell him it is a triple integral. You integrate three times,” Bill began softly. Julie waited politely as Bill Porter made a few more comments which Jacqueline translated as if under firm but polite duress.

“Be nice, Jackie,” Julie told the girl.

“I am, but mathematics is not my ‘thing.’” Jackie sighed. “I am under a lot of stress right now.”

There was another polite exchange and Pierre Fermat bowed slightly and thanked Bill, in French.

“He said thank you,” Jacqueline told Bill then turned to follow Pierre Fermat into the staff cafeteria.

“Julie,” Bill whispered, “I just taught Pierre Fermat integral calculus.”

“Now I think you’re full of it. Hell, Blaise needed at least a week to teach himself calculus and he’s a genius. I don’t think even you could teach Pierre Fermat this integral calculus stuff in a few sentences, even with Jackie’s help.”

"You don't understand," Bill shook his head sadly. "A whole new computer is being created in there. We're going to have functioning computers, not some kludge or the last laptop. We can make a fax machine, for Christ's sake. Low speed internet . . . It's like being in the garage with Steve Jobs, Steve Wozniak and the other guy when they invented the Apple."

"Bill!" Allan stuck his head out into the hallway. "We need you." Allan Sebastian was distracted by something happening in the lunch room. "Blaise! Put the wrench down! You're making a mess! And answer Mr. Pell's question. Bill! It's been a little while since I did triple integrals. I could use some help. Pierre is a little insistent and he's being distracted by Shabbethai who's translating the Torah. In Greek. Out loud. We need to keep everything on track, Bill. This is going to be big!"

"That other guy wasn't Bill Porter, was he?" Julie smiled.

"Logan!" Allan went back inside the staff lunchroom. "Stop kicking Blaise! Why? Because I'm your father and I said so, that's why!"

With that there was a huge, shattering crash.

"My Adder!" a very recognizable voice screeched in the midst of the sounds of disaster.

"You splashed muck on my best Winnie the Pooh sweatshirt!" came the girlish reply followed by a flurry of loud, angry French.

"I better get in there," Julie muttered. "God alone knows what will happen next."

Bill stood in the corridor, outside the staff cafeteria in the Grantville Power Station and wondered, himself, if God knew what would happen next.

The Sebastian House, November 24, 1634

"I should kill you right now, Blaise Pascal! Right here!" Logan Sebastian could be quite loud but not nearly as loud as the boy standing in the doorway. The green silk pants he wore fairly screamed their wavelength into the room. The red lace that flowed at his throat was lost in the garish incredibility of the waistcoat. "God! He looks like someone ate a whole paint store and threw up!"

"Logan Sebastian! You apologize right now!" Mrs. Sebastian shouted back at her daughter. Mr. Sebastian had to leave the room for the perceived safety of the kitchen. He just couldn't look at his former student and maintain an appropriate, fatherly bearing.

"I brought you my first Adder." Blaise Pascal held out a large boxlike object with as motley a collection of tubes dangling from it as could be imagined.

"Why don't you get some water for his bouquet, Mom! I am certainly not wearing that on my dress!" Logan shouted back at her mother.

"No water." Blaise looked sadly down at the device. "It still leaks but less now. Monsieur Porter was right. I should use air instead. It changes the parameters . . . not even up-time Americans solved equations of the turbulence. It is that many times cursed 'chaos' again. Fah!"

"Ahhh!" Logan screamed as she ran for the safety of her room. "All he cares about is math! I'll kill him!"

"Logan tells me she would murder me if I didn't come with her to the dance and now she wants to murder me because I am taking her. Solving the synch parameters of a gang of generators is easier than figuring out girls. I would rather try to integrate a chaotic equation, triple integrate even, than this."

There was a burst of laughter from the kitchen. It ended quickly.

"Boys!" Jacqueline pushed in past her brother with a small bouquet of flowers. "I told you she would want flowers. Your Adder looks like something flattened in the road, then thrown away."

Blaise watched his sister head for Logan's room with the flowers, his Adder still clutched in his hand. Compared to the peach-colored lace at his cuffs, the Adder appeared conservative.

"Blaise," Mrs. Sebastian began carefully, "where did you get those clothes?"

"Father sent me here with some formal clothes, but I outgrew them. I had some extra funds so I ordered a new outfit. Do you like it? I liked all the new colors so I had my clothing made with one of each of my favorite colors."

"It is . . ." Mitzi wondered if Madame Delfault had to be locked into a closet. Mitzi couldn't imagine how the boy's governess allowed him out of the apartment dressed like this. "Well, do young men dress like this in France?"

"Most normal people have one favorite color, Blaise!" Jacqueline shouted from the hallway leading to Logan's room. "They don't like the whole spectrum! They would throw you into the Seine if you showed your face at a ball dressed like that. And they would do it from a closed window!"

"I wish I had a camera," came the comment from the kitchen.

"Allan? Shush! While your sister gives Logan your flowers, tell me about Adders," Mrs. Sebastian inquired politely of Blaise Pascal, the boy who was taking her daughter to the Thanksgiving Dance; assuming Logan didn't kill her erstwhile "date" first.

"Mom! We'll be here all night talking about math!" Logan charged out of the hallway, holding the bouquet Jacqueline had brought to her. "We are ready to go, Dad! Blaise, can you wear a cloak or something? Halloween is long past. Dad? Where are you?"

"Allan? Are you up to this?" Mitzi called toward her husband, who was still hiding in the kitchen.

There was no answer from the kitchen other than odd, strangling noises.

Allan Sebastian, to his credit, could accept that his daughter was going to a dance with *the* Blaise Pascal and that Blaise had taken precious time from his dreams of working in the power plant and building a working computer to go with her; regardless of the threats. Blaise would have seen no hardship in hiding in the power plant.

What Allan was having trouble accepting was the clash of preteen, West Virginia couture with a seventeenth-century French genius who believed in an utter and total desegregation of colors. His outfit would have had Liberace running for the safety of a plain brown monk's robe and a life of religious contemplation in an undecorated stone cell.

All Allan could think of, standing in the kitchen, was the term "File Type Mismatch."

A Study in Redheads

Bradley H. Sinor and Tracy S. Morris

"Paul, we need to talk!" Paul Kindred, managing editor of the *Grantville Times*, stifled a groan when he heard that voice. Betsy Springer came toward him at a dead run, her red ponytail bouncing like an excited rooster's tail, and would have collided with him had he not stepped aside at the last minute.

"Hello, Betsy." He sighed. Paul had been hoping for a quiet day. The political hijinks that fed both the front page and the dull ache just behind his eyes had been running at high tide lately, getting hotter as summer approached.

"Hello, Paul! Look, this is important: Rosebud and Watergate all wrapped up in one! We need to talk, but not in the street."

Paul couldn't count the number of times he had heard that phrase. Like the common cold germ, it would get under his skin, make his pulse race and leave him in a cold sweat, and before long he would have a major headache.

He gave Betsy a pleading look, hoping she would at least wait until he got into his office to pitch another harebrained conspiracy theory story idea. But as Betsy hopped from one foot to another in excitement, he knew that there was little chance for peace.

"Indeed." Paul consoled himself with the thought that if this story turned out to be too wild for the *Grantville Times*, at least Betsy wasn't opposed to letting him "redirect" it into the pages of *The Inquisitor*.

Paul also knew it would only be a matter of time before Betsy would start in on the movie quotes that were her trademark. It seemed like she could remember every detail of every movie she had ever seen.

One of these days he really needed to convince his father, the publisher of the *Times*, to send Betsy on a "Nellie Bly" style tour of the USE and surrounding areas, just to get her out of his hair. If sending her around the world were practical, he might have considered that.

As they neared the paper's offices, Paul could see Denis Sesma's gangly frame leaned against the front door. Denis was one of the artists he kept on staff to do woodcuts, one of the few who turned his work in on time, if not early. He should have expected that Denis would not be far when Betsy was around. They were a couple, though neither would admit it.

"Good morning, Mr. Kindred," said Denis, doffing his cap the moment he spotted his employer.

"Hi, Denis. Come on inside," Paul unlocked the door and gestured for the two of them to follow him. Betsy whispered something to Denis, who nodded and sprinted away. A few moments later he returned, followed by a skinny boy dressed in a typesetter's apron and a square paper hat.

"If you want to stop the presses, you need to hijack more backshop people than that, Betsy," Paul said. "So what's the story?"

In response, Betsy snaked her arm around the kid and pulled him forward. The boy seemed reluctant, like he would have preferred to hide behind Denis.

"This is Alessandrio . . . Alessandrio?" Betsy looked to the boy with a quizzical expression. "Alexandrio." She said firmly. The boy made a noise of protest but Betsy waved it away with a dismissive gesture. "I like that better. It's more American. Paul this is Alexandria, actually." Betsy began again. "She's from Venice." Hearing Betsy's words, Paul looked at the young typesetter again and realized this wasn't a scrawny young boy, but a girl.

She wore her red-blond hair in a close-cropped, masculine style, but her overly large, blue eyes made her seem more like one of those Precious Moments figurines of a street urchin rather than an actual person.

"Alex here found something important," Denis said. The younger girl nodded and began to speak quietly in a string of broken English mixed with German, Venetian and Italian. Paul thought he heard the words *reading* and *murder*, and the name of a town not that far from Grantville: Hildburghausen.

"Okay, you've got my attention," Paul said. "Let's go in the office."

If it were possible for Alexandria's eyes to get bigger, they did at the prospect of going into Paul's office. Most of the time when an employee went in there it was to be fired.

"Come on, he won't bite," said Betsy, and then turned to Paul. "You better not!"

"Yes, ma'am." He led them into his office and slid into the high-backed chair that had been a gift from his father when he took over as managing editor. "Now, what the hell are you three talking about?"

"I read." Alexandria blurted out.

"Alexandria's father was a printer in Venice. His chief apprentice, Vito, turned out to be a lazy lout; unfortunately he couldn't get rid of him, because of the boy's family's political connections, so Alex had to help in the shop to take up the slack," said Betsy.

"Small fingers." Alex held her ink-smeared hands out so that they could see that she had the nimble fingers that were perfect for setting type. "Typesetting for Papa, that's how I learned to read English and German, besides Italian."

"Unfortunately, her father was killed in an accident a year or so ago and the family business was seized by creditors," said Denis.

Paul could almost finish the story himself. Even though she was trained as a printer and typesetter, there was no way any other printer would take on a girl, no matter how good she might be.

"Alexandria had two choices," said Betsy, waving away the girl's protest about the Americanizing of her name "Become a prostitute or hope she could find a convent that would accept her; neither idea was to her liking; so she found a third choice. She sort of reminds me of me in that way."

"I heard about USE and how women have rights to work here," she said slowly, picking her English words carefully. "Only way I could travel was disguised as boy. Took me four months, walking mostly. I had gotten used to having my hair like this, wearing pants and even answering to the name Alexandro, so when you hire me I didn't bother tell you I was girl."

"I only found it out by accident," said Denis. "We were taking a wagon of supplies and the wheel broke. It threw Alex off and knocked him, er . . . her out. When I tried to see if he . . . she, was all right I opened his shirt and . . ."

"I get the picture," Paul said. "But how does this lead to murder?" Paul could feel his right eye start to tic. Betsy often had that effect on him.

"I read!" Alexandria cut in. "Always I read, books, pamphlets, even the type that I set. In library I find books about—what you call them?" She snapped her fingers as she searched for the correct words. Then her eyes lit up and she pointed at Paul. "Serial killers!" She said triumphantly.

"Wait!" Paul sat up straight. "Back up! Serial killers?"

"Yes, I see it in the type! I'm sorry my English not as good as I would like. I read it in the stories I set. I even read the other newspapers we get in here."

Betsy nodded and gave Paul an apologetic smile. "I guess she was reading about criminal profiling at the library, how she got on that I still haven't figured out. But she's been setting stories about a series of strange deaths in Hildburghausen, and began to notice things that look like deliberate arsenic poisoning to her."

As Betsy said this, Denis pulled out tear sheets of the stories and pointed to the pertinent passages. "The victims seem healthy. They eat enough to get fat—there's a clue right there. How many people do you see who are actually overweight anymore? And the poison stays locked up in the body fat. When the poison stops, they lose their appetite and as they get skinny—the poison works its way back into their body and kills them. By the time they die, the poisoner has gotten away."

"And she knows about poisons how?" Paul asked, a number of possibilities running through his head.

"Her uncle was an alchemist," Denis said. "But he was murdered by a client so that he couldn't give testimony before the tribunal."

Alexandria sniffed. "Typesetting is better. Nobody gets pissed at you, at least not that much."

"I saw this in a movie once," Betsy said. "I think it was about the Borgias and how they used poison."

Alexandria pointed to the article on top of the stack that Paul held. "Sickness in Hildburghausen. And here." She pulled a third article out of the stack. "Again and again."

Paul looked from the articles to the two reporters and the typesetter. "You think it was murder?"

"Yes," proclaimed Betsy. "The three of us spent a good while at the library. The symptomology matches."

"Some of them could have been accidental," Paul pointed out, though as he glanced over the articles there was something in the back of his mind that said there might actually be a story. "How do you intend to prove your theory?"

"We read up on a couple of tests, and scrounged what equipment we could. Alexandria thinks she can perform what's called a Marsh test if we can find tissue samples and bring them here to her."

"What tissue samples?" Paul asked pointedly.

Betsy gave him a blank look. "Swabs from dishes, or maybe leftover meals?"

Paul rubbed the bridge of his nose as he realized that the young redhead hadn't thought this through. "To prove anything, you need tissue samples from the actual victims. You do realize that the authorities, not to mention the families, would not be pleased to have you digging up their relatives?"

"That is just gross," said Betsy, "And I wouldn't even think about it unless it were absolutely necessary."

"You may be on to something here." Paul said slowly, "But I think that you three are going to have to be very careful, very circumspect in what you do and what you say. Do you hear me, Betsy?"

"Right!" Betsy grinned. "We won't let you down, Paul!"

"Excuse me, sir," said Alexandria. "You say 'you three'?"

"Yep, you're going with them," he said.

"B-b-but I'm supposed to work," she stuttered. "Mr. Kinkelly will fire me if I not there!" Kinkelly ran the newspaper's back shop and ruled it with an iron hand, though Paul knew that the man actually had a very soft heart.

"Don't worry about Kinkelly; his bark is worse than his bite. You're on full salary for as long as it takes to get this matter settled. No matter what happens, you will definitely have a job to come back to. On that you have my promise."

"Oh," she said in a little girl's voice and looked uncertainly at Betsy and Denis.

"You may have to be both a boy and a girl," said Betsy.

Alexandria looked up at Betsy with a start. "Pardon me?"

They had arrived in Hilburghausen that morning and gotten rooms at a small inn on the south side of town. It was the sort of place where strangers were the norm, so no one looked at them twice when Betsy, Denis and their "younger sister" checked in.

"It's just a matter of letting people see one thing while something else is going on," said Betsy. "It's a kind of magic."

Alexandria jerked back at the mention of magic, crossing herself and muttering something in Italian as she looked back and forth between Denis and Betsy.

Denis laughed and tore the corner off a piece of paper from the edge of the copy of *The Inquisitor* that lay on the table. He rolled it up in a ball, showed it to her, then holding it between two fingers, he passed his hand in front of it and the ball was gone. Alexandria's eyes grew even wider than they normally were. Denis smiled then reached across the table, touched her ear with one hand and seemingly produced the paper ball from her ear.

"How?" she stuttered.

Denis didn't say anything, he repeated the move, making the ball disappear, but then held his hand up and turned it around to where Alexandria could see the piece of paper hidden between two of his fingers.

"I let you see one thing, when something else was going on. That's what Betsy's talking about. It's just a little misdirection; you're expecting one thing while I'm doing another. Like they do it in the movies." Denis looked over at Betsy, smiled and ran his finger down the side of his nose; hoping that was the gesture she had talked about in that movie *The Sting*.

Alexandria laughed and picked up the paper ball, rolling it over and over in her hands.

"The fact is that everyone saw us check in with a young girl, so. I doubt anyone else will be paying attention if a young boy is seen wandering around town, listening and maybe asking the occasional question," said Betsy.

"I see," Alexandria said with a mischievous smile as she waved the crumpled paper around. "I sneak around, quiet as mouse, and listen in dark alleys and back corners." She folded her hand over the paper ball, hiding it from sight.

"Exactly," Betsy said. "Do you think you could sneak into one of the victim's homes and get a look at the dishes?"

"It's probably been too long to even try," Denis said. "The first case was three months ago, and the second was a month later. Whatever possessions were left would have been distributed to their heirs."

"You don't suppose that's the connection, do you?" Betsy tapped her upper lip with her forefinger. "The people in the second case. The Fuchs, yes?" she looked to Alexandria for confirmation. "Maybe they bought something that had been in the first home."

"The home of Zedler," Denis said. "That may be the case, but we won't be able to find the connection that way."

"I'm just afraid that the trail, as they say in detective movies, has gone cold."

"They always made this look so easy on the detective shows," Betsy muttered. "Paul may be right. We may have to dig up the bodies, no matter what he said or how gross it might be. We could find out for certain that way."

"And even if this is the USE, our German hosts take a dim view on grave desecration," Denis shuddered. "I have no desire to face a hangman for the sake of a story."

"All right," Betsy said reluctantly.

"I hope Alexandria had better luck than we did," Betsy said moodily as she dug into her bratwurst. There were hardly any other people in the common room of the tavern. It was still relatively early; even the tavern girl had disappeared into the kitchen after dropping their plates in front of them. "Do you believe that those guys actually thought that breathing onions would stop the spread of illness? The thing is, in a couple of hundred years this area will be one of the first places to regulate food. They already regulate beer."

"Not everyone believes the CoC when they talk about germs," Denis said. "Knowing what may be going on makes me reluctant to eat anything in this town."

"Don't be silly," Betsy said around a forkful of food. "Dad always told me that if I go anywhere, I should try and eat like a local. That way I learn more about the culture." She smiled a little in recollection; it was a sad smile nonetheless. "We always did stuff like that on family vacations. Sometimes I wasn't sure just exactly what cultural experience I was supposed to get, but I suppose it didn't matter as long as it was an experience and it was cultural and it was with my dad."

Denis nodded; he reached over and patted her hand. Betsy didn't often let herself slip into melancholy, but thoughts of her dad always caused her eyes to water. "What would he want us to do?"

"Go get the bad guys, pilgrim," she said.

"Pilgrim?" Denis shook his head. He was used to most of her movie references, but not all of them.

"Time to watch some John Wayne movies, then." She squeezed his hand.

Just then, Alexandria slid into the seat across from them. Her wide, dark eyes looked serious. "Others have fallen sick." She folded her hands and rested her chin on them. "So far, no one has died. But many are ill." She looked at Betsy's plate. "I spoke with both Herr Zedler's neighbors and those of Herr Fuchs, along with a number of their servants; it's always the servants who know more about what is going on in a house than the family that lives there. Herr Zedler bought a cow for slaughter days before he died. Frau Fuchs was known for her cooking, especially beef sausages. The cook here at this inn is her cousin."

Betsy's eyes bulged. She looked down at her plate, her stomach rolling. "I . . ." She set the sausage down. "Suddenly I don't feel so good."

Denis held Betsy's hair back as she threw the contents of her stomach up into the chamber pot.

"I think I just threw up my toenails." She wiped at her mouth, and then flopped onto her side on the floor. "Wurst food I ever ate. Pun intended."

Denis patted her shoulder in sympathy. "You're fortunate," he said to her. "You're only suffering from your own overactive imagination. But you must be feeling better if you're making bad puns like that."

Betsy lifted her head from the floor and looked at him weakly. "Are you telling me that there wasn't any arsenic in my dinner?"

"Alexandria checked your sausage." He smoothed her hair back. "It was poison free. Now that you're okay, she'll start testing samples of meat from the families who are ill. I think we may have found the connection there."

"She's getting the samples how?" asked Betsy.

"She said 'Don't ask,' so I didn't. There probably are things that it is better for us not to know."

"So I guess this means the butcher did it. Although, that doesn't quite have the ring of saying the butler did it." Betsy grimaced as she sat up, a little pale, but the color rapidly coming back into her face. She gave Denis a sheepish smile. "Now I feel silly."

Denis extended his hand to help her to her feet. "You say that like it's a new feeling? There is someone I know here in town that I think we should talk to."

Betsy looked surprised at that. "Who?"

"His name is Calvin Norcross," Denis said. "We were apprenticed to Master Ribalta at the same time. If anyone knows things that are going on in this town, it will be him."

"You ought to take up investigative journalism yourself," Betsy said. "Everywhere we go you seem to have connections from the old days."

"I can't write with your flair," Denis said, noncommittally. "Besides, don't you always say a picture is worth a thousand words?"

"I figured that you would either be dead or in the army by now," laughed Calvin Norcross.

The air in the studio was heavy with the smell of turpentine and paint. Half finished paintings and sketches filled every nook and cranny. Norcross stood just an inch shorter than Betsy and was thin enough that it looked like a good stiff wind would blow him away. The studio was bigger than Denis had expected, but still little more than a closet. The accumulated work showed him that Calvin was doing well and *that* fanned a tiny bit of jealousy in Denis. Calvin had obviously found another painter to take him on after Master Ribalta died.

"I figured you would have been beaten to death by some jealous husband or boyfriend," returned Denis, taking his old friend's outstretched hand.

"It helps to always know where the exit is and to be able to get your pants on while you are running," laughed Calvin. His laugh cut off abruptly as Betsy stepped through the doorway around Denis. "And who is this stunning beauty?"

"This is Betsy Springer." Denis took her hand protectively. "She's a reporter for the *Grantville Times*."

Calvin looked at Denis and Betsy's clasped hands, and then smiled at his old friend. "And what does the *Times* want in Hildburghausen? Obviously something that is very important to send someone as lovely and talented as you. If you have the time, I hope you would consider modeling for me; with that beautiful face and red hair I would call it A Study in Red."

"Well, now aren't you just the one? Perhaps I might consider posing for you once our business here is completed," said Betsy. Denis heard a familiar tone in her voice and knew that she didn't buy into Calvin's flattery. "We're here investigating some mysterious deaths. There's a chance they may have been from deliberate arsenic poisoning."

Calvin looked from Denis to Betsy and back. Then let out a low whistle. "That's a very serious matter," he said. "If someone has been doing so, they would very quickly be hanged."

"We hoped that you might be able to tell us if you had heard anything suspicious? As I recall, when we were studying with Master Ribalta you were always aware of what was going on around town," Denis said.

"It never hurts to listen to what people are saying, Denis. I suppose you could say that it is only common courtesy. As for suspicious, I'm not sure what you're looking for. I did lose a commission a while back. Herr Fleischer wanted me to do a portrait of his daughter, but then canceled it at the last minute."

"That would cost a lot of money, yes?" Betsy looked to Denis, who nodded in confirmation.

Calvin walked across the studio and pointed to a half finished canvas where a figure had been sketched out. "I haven't had a chance to reuse the canvas; there's always a chance he'll change his mind. Although the man actually had the audacity to ask for deposit back."

"Shameful," said Denis.

"Sounds to me like Herr Fleischer ran into money problems," said Betsy. "We need to follow the money, just like Woodward and Bernstein in *All The President's Men*."

"Woodward and Bernstein?" Calvin whispered to Denis.

"Don't ask so loudly," warned Denis.

"Strange." Calvin said, staring at his old friend.

"Tell me about it," Denis said, shrugging.

Their room looked like something out of a mad scientist's lab when Denis and Betsy returned to the tavern. Alex stood over a burner with an odd array of glass flasks, copper tubing and bent beakers. A copy of the Grantville library's *Fun with Chemistry!* book was propped before her like a cookbook. A number of tissue samples arrayed in bowls across the table reminded Betsy of the time in Charleston that she'd tried sushi on a dare.

Alex looked up from the burner and waved them over to her. "If I no make mistake, then it's arsenic in all samples."

Denis and Betsy looked at one another in trepidation.

"Ordinarily, I would say that we should go to the authorities, but…" Denis rolled his hand in the direction of the table. "What evidence do we show them? I barely understand this and I have my doubts the Burghers in this town will."

"We could try," said Betsy. "Combined with what we know from your friend, Calvin, we can at least set the authorities on Herr Fleischer."

"I'm not sure just how much I trust Calvin. He was always out for himself. Something doesn't feel right about him; I just can't put my finger on it. We've got to force Fleischer into a corner, but under circumstances that we control, not him. There is no one quite as dangerous as a man in that position. Besides, we still don't know why he's killing these people."

"Maybe we should just ask him? Sometimes you have to just march right up to Jabba the Hutt's palace and knock on the front door," said Betsy.

"Hello?" Betsy called out as she looked around the stables behind Herr Fleischer's home and shop. "Herr Fleischer?"

"He doesn't appear to be here," Denis said as he stepped around Betsy and into the stable.

"And he looks like he left in a hurry," Betsy replied as she pointed to the floor. Tack and slightly tarnished coins lay scattered across the ground. "I wonder if his daughter knows that he's gone on the lam?"

"The dropping here is still warm," Denis said as he held his hands over the steaming animal leavings in the stall. "Maybe we can catch him if we hurry." He grasped Betsy's hand and the two of them ran out of the stables and toward the river, in the opposite direction from whence they came.

"What did your sources at the Committee of Correspondence have to say about Herr Fleischer?" Betsy asked.

"They said to be careful," Denis replied. "Dieter Fleischer used to be a Feldwebel in the army. He curses like a soldier and kicks like an angry mule."

Betsy stopped abruptly, just over a mile beyond the city limits, pointing toward a shape lying just off the path ahead of them. "I don't think we have to worry about that anymore."

Denis followed her outstretched hand to see a man lying there in a rapidly spreading pool of blood. Half his head had been blown away. Judging by the mule grazing at the roadside with saddle bags filled to bursting, not to mention the physical description, the dead man was Dieter Fleischer.

"Definitely, gross," said Betsy. Even so, she knelt close to the body and began examining it. "He's still warm, so this has happened recently."

"So much for getting a confession out of him," said Denis.

Denis touched the side of Fleischer's head and rubbed a drop of blood between his fingers. The smell of gunpowder hung in the air, but there was something else, something familiar that Denis couldn't place. He began to pace back and forth along the bank, looking down at the ground, wishing he could do something like that fellow in the movies and books that Betsy talked about, Sherlock Holmes. The idea that he was starting to think in terms of movie characters scared Denis just a little.

"I'm thinking that we don't have a lot of options now. This was murder and we should report it to the authorities," said Denis as he passed close to some low bushes and trees. He had taken a few steps beyond them when he thought he heard the rustling of an animal within. Denis was about to investigate when Calvin Norcross charged out toward him, swinging a stout, jagged branch. The blow from his attacker's cudgel was enough to put Denis on the ground.

"What the hell?" Betsy stepped backward in shock. Before she could charge to Denis' rescue, Calvin dropped his club and produced a flintlock pistol.

"Old friend, I would not advise you, nor your rather well-endowed companion, to move. I won't hesitate to shoot either of you," he said.

Betsy scoffed. "It figures; even in the seventeenth century, men only notice one thing."

"Why, Calvin?" asked Denis as he raised himself up to a sitting position.

"Money," said the little painter. "That idiot cheated me out of my earnings! He was trying to get away with a fortune. I simply intercepted him as he left town. If you hadn't interrupted me, everyone would have assumed that bandits took his ill-gotten gains." He looked regretful, as if trying to convince himself that he had no other choice in what was about to happen. "Now I'm going to have to eliminate you, old friend, and your rather attractive traveling companion, to avoid a hangman's noose myself. I would much prefer to have had her posing for me."

"I think not." Alex came from behind a nearby tree, her two small hands around the grip of a rather large and outrageous looking pistol.

Denis gaped at the device. It looked futuristic and frightening: wrapped with pieces of bent copper tubing and bits of glass on it. If he hadn't seen the component parts in Alex's lab, he would have believed it to be yet another frightening and wondrous up-time device.

Alex pulled a lever as if underscoring that she meant business. "You will drop your pistol or I use this and it will make what happened to Herr Fleischer seem like a nice thing. Do it now! You will drop your weapon and get down on your knees."

Calvin looked at her and then the weapon. He seemed to be weighing his options.

"I wouldn't," Betsy said. "That's a .44 Magnum, the most powerful handgun in the world. It would blow your head clean off. So you've got to ask yourself one question: Do you feel lucky? Well, do ya, punk?"

Calvin swallowed, and dropped his own weapon. Then he slowly dropped to his knees.

Denis scrambled over and picked up the gun while Betsy pulled rope off the mule's saddle and tied Calvin's hands behind his back.

"He would have gotten away with it if it hadn't been for us meddling kids. But this still doesn't explain the tainted meat." Betsy threw her hands in the air. "If I can't explain that, then I don't have much of a story. I'll have to invent something for *The Inquisitor* and I would prefer to avoid that."

"There is an old horse trader's trick," Denis said. "You give a little bit of arsenic to a nag to fatten it up. The poison makes the coat glossy and soon the nag looks like a respectable mount. It's possible that Herr Fleischer purchased some very poor cattle at a very good price. Herr Zedlar purchased a cow and took it to Herr Fleischer. Herr Fleischer may have substituted his own poor quality meat for Herr Zedlar's good meat, without realizing that it was tainted."

"And Frau Fuchs purchased sausages from Herr Fleischer. Who

pays attention to the quality of meat in sausages?" Betsy concluded with a grin. "This is going to make an incredible story. But what do we do with him?" she waved a hand at Calvin.

"I think we had better take this man to the authorities," Denis said slowly. "With the three of us as witnesses I think that should be enough."

"How did you know he was in the bushes?" asked Betsy as they walked.

"The blood was still tacky, so I knew it hadn't been that long since Fleischer was killed, plus I caught a whiff of turpentine. It's hard as hell to get out of your clothes and most painters get to the point they don't even notice it," he said. "I almost didn't."

He pointed up the path to indicate that Calvin should lead the way. Alex backed up his motion by gesturing with her improvised weapon.

As the four of them walked down the street in a bizarre parade, Betsy leaned over to speak to Alex. "I meant to ask you earlier, were did you get the idea for the ray gun?"

In response, Alex reached inside her jacket and pulled out a rolled up comic book that she passed to Betsy. On the cover, Ming the Merciless threatened Flash Gordon with a ray gun that looked remarkably similar to Alex's creation.

"I read," she said.

Game, Set and Match

Kim Mackay

London

When George Goring entered the study, his father-in-law was seated behind his desk and focused on the paperwork in front of him.

George waited a few seconds and then cleared his throat.

Richard Boyle, Earl of Corke, and now the king's chief minister in all but name, looked up and smiled at him.

"George, so good of you to come on such short notice. How is Lettice?"

George cleared his throat again. *Damn it, stop being nervous. Yes, Richard Boyle has power now to go along with his riches. But you've treated Lettice well. Mostly.* "As well as can be expected, Your Lordship, given her health. She is off to Bath again with her cousin, Joan Gwyn."

"Ah," Boyle said. "And Grey Brown?"

George winced. In 1631, he had become bored with life on the Boyle estates in Ireland and had borrowed two thousand pounds. Then ridden off to seek adventure in Scotland and England, leaving his new wife in her father's care. The choice gray gelding he left with had been called Grey Brown.

"Very well, Your Lordship. I have him quartered here in London."

"Excellent!"

Boyle's look turned speculative.

"You know, George, my new secretary, Edward Hyde, speaks very highly of you."

"He does?"

Boyle smiled. "Oh yes. He says you have wit, courage, understanding... and ambition uncontrolled by fear of God or man." Boyle picked up the letter opener on his desk and began to twirl it on his fingers. "He also thinks you excel in dissimulation."

"I assure you, my lord..."

Boyle sliced the letter opener through the air.

George's throat constricted.

Boyle laughed. "Relax, George. I didn't ask you here to make an example of you. Instead, I have a proposition for you." Boyle motioned Goring to sit.

George sat down heavily. "A proposition, Your Lordship?"

"Indeed," Boyle said. "You've met Arthur Jones, the new Viscount Ranelagh?"

George nodded. "Of course, sir."

Arthur Jones, Viscount Ranelagh since his father's death by the outbreak of plague that had struck the city of London in 1633, was the husband of Boyle's fifth daughter, Katherine. Jones had become the butt of many jokes when his wife had gone on an extended trip to Grantville in 1632 with friends she had made among the Acontian society in London.

Without him, and without his permission.

Few blamed Katherine herself. As John Leek had told George, Jones was considered one of the foulest churls in Christendom whose best point for Katherine would have been that he was dead drunk every night and thus not awake to beat or abuse her.

"I've met him, Your Lordship, but we do not, uh, move in the same circles."

"Tactfully put, George. Tactfully put." Boyle considered George for a moment, then sat back in his chair. "George, have you ever read Fenton's translation of Guicciardini's *History of Italy*?"

"No, sir, I can't say that I have."

"You should, George. You should. He makes some very astute observations about political conditions that are relevant to England. For example, Fortune is a very fickle goddess, George. But men of virtue, such as myself, can always find ways to turn her intervention to advantage."

George shook his head. Where was Boyle going with this?

"Arthur, Viscount Ranelagh, has decided to attempt a reconciliation with Katherine."

"Really, Your Lordship? Arthur is going to Grantville?"

Boyle shook his head. "Not Grantville, Brussels. That is where my Katy is now. Assisting the Secretary of State of the Republic of Essen in negotiating a treaty with Fernando's Netherlands." Boyle begin playing with the letter opener again. "Katy and I have been in contact for some time. In fact, my youngest son, Robert, is visiting her right now. Although I believe he is still in Essen at the moment."

"Brussels," George said. "I have a number of contacts in Brussels."

Boyle smiled. "Exactly!"

"You want me to accompany Arthur to Brussels? Assist him in his attempt to reconcile with Katherine?"

Boyle's smile broadened. "Indeed. And I would be grateful, George. Are you still interested in one of Lord Tilbury's regiments? I think I can get you a troop of horse cavalry. Should be worth at least three thousand pounds a year."

George nodded. "That is very generous, Your Lordship."

"Worth it to me, George, especially if you can act as a mediator between Katy and Arthur. Not that I hold out that much hope for a reconciliation, you understand. Kate seems happy with her position, and Arthur seemed somewhat rigid in his own thoughts on the matter."

"I understand, sir. I will do my best to persuade Katherine to return to England with Arthur."

Boyle's smile turned grim, and he shook his head. "Oh no, George, that would not do, not at all."

George cocked his head. "Sir?"

"England, George, think of England. Kate has made many excellent contacts in Essen. She knows the governor general, Louis de Geer, who is a personal friend of the emperor, Gustavus Adolphus. Her closest friend, the up-timer Nicki Jo Prickett, is the principal research scientist for the Essen chemical company. And the Prickett woman has taken an interest in educating my son, Robert."

"Why is that, sir?"

"Apparently, in the other universe from which God delivered Grantville, Robert was the most well known of any of my children. In fact, he was considered the father of modern chemistry there."

"So what do you want me to do in Brussels, Your Lordship?"

"Try to keep Arthur from making an ass of himself—and a fool of me—if you can. If Arthur agrees to join Katy in Essen, that would be best. But in the end, if necessary, it would be much better if Katy was a widow." Boyle looked into Goring's face. "Don't you agree?"

George nodded. Now the light was finally dawning. "Of course, sir. I agree completely."

Coudenberg Palace, Brussels

It was only after their second bout of lovemaking that Fernando and Maria Anna began their usual pillow talk.

"I missed you," Maria Anna said.

"And I missed you, my love," Fernando said. "But it was only eight days, after all."

"Only eight . . ." Maria Anna's head came off Fernando's chest. "Why, I'll—"

Fernando laughed. "Just kidding, my dear, just kidding."

"You better be," Maria Anna said. She pinched him and Fernando yelped.

"So tell me about your trip," she said, settling her head back down on Fernando's chest. "Were the Portuguese bankers in Antwerp more accommodating this time?"

"Oh, yes, much more accommodating," Fernando said. "They also seemed interested in sounding out our position on Brazil. A number of the merchants want to start mining gold in the Minas Gerais area."

"Gold? In Brazil? I thought rubber and sugar were the most important products in Brazil."

"They probably are," Fernando said. "But once again, it's information from Grantville that is driving up interest. The merchants in Antwerp have discovered that a thousand tons of gold were taken out of Brazil in the late seventeenth and on into the eighteen century in the up-time universe. Many of them want us to mount an expedition as soon as possible."

"Wonderful." Maria Anna sighed.

"And you?" Fernando said. "What did you do while I was away?"

"Meetings, meetings and more meetings," Maria Anna said. "At least the treaty with the Republic of Essen seems almost complete. Hainhoffer's assistant for technical matters, Katherine Boyle, has been very helpful. We've actually become quite close. I'm looking forward to meeting her friend."

"Friend?"

Maria Anna nodded. "Nicki Jo Prickett. An American. She's more our own age, unlike the women I was with on my trip across Germany. It will be interesting to see how her perspective differs from theirs. She's also bringing some up-time tennis racquets and tennis balls. I've had the court in the Warande garden redone to the same measurements as an up-time court." She smiled. "It's been fun to see how the sport evolved."

Fernando laughed. "You've been practicing, haven't you?"

"As well as I can. But the cork balls we use just don't give the same bounce as an up-time ball, according to Katherine. And you don't use the walls at all. But another reason I want to talk to Prickett is the company that she and Katherine want to establish in Brussels, with my help."

Fernando began stroking Maria Anna's hair. "What kind of company?"

"A cheese and chocolate factory."

"Cheese I can understand, I know you love cheese. But chocolate? I thought you hated chocolate."

"Only the kind I tasted in Vienna. It was very bitter. But Katherine assures me that the chocolate I tasted will bear very little resemblance to what Royal Maria Anna's Cheese and Chocolate Factory will produce here in Brussels. After our tennis match on Thursday we will go to Essen House to sample some of their products. I'm looking forward to it."

"Perhaps I should come along."

Maria Anna laughed. "I don't think you'll have time. You'll be spending your hours soothing the feelings of the Brussels guilds about the Essen treaty."

Fernando growled. "They seem to have forgotten what Isabella and Albert did to them in 1619."

"I don't think you'll need to go that far. But they certainly don't feel the same way about us as they did the archdukes."

"Hmm... 'Royal Maria Anna's Cheese and Chocolate Factory.' It does have a certain ring to it." Fernando's hand moved lower on her body. "But all this talk of food has made me hungry for something else."

"Fernando! Come here, you beast!"

Inn of the Silver Swine, Brussels

"Bitch! Harlot! Have you read this?" Arthur Jones thrust the letter across the table.

George shook his head, then pretended to read. "No, of course not." *Ha! Not only have I read it, I helped compose it, you sniveling twit.*

Three weeks in the company of Arthur Jones had been the most trying of George Goring's life. It wasn't just that Jones was a drunk. He was a talkative drunk. A whiny drunk. One who demanded the attention of all those around him (especially his new best friend, George Goring) so he could itemize in enormous and nauseating detail the endless wrongs done to him by his enemies. The list of which seemed to extend from his own father to his wife to nearly every human he had ever come in contact with.

Boyle is going to owe me a brigade for this. George looked up from the letter. "So, she offers a judicial separation I see."

"Judicial separation!" Arthur sneered. He tilted the tankard of beer and swallowed three times before slamming it back on the table. "And won't that make me a laughing stock at court." Arthur poked the letter in George's hands. "The whoresome bitch even refuses to see me. She'll deal only with you."

Arthur belched. Then smiled. "We'll see about that, my friend. Indeed we will."

"Careful, Arthur," George said. "You're not in England here. And Katherine has some powerful friends who dote on her. I think it best if you let me handle the negotiations."

"Negotiations!" Arthur spat contemptuously. "What is there to negotiate? Either she comes back with me to England or I'll beat her bloody, I swear I will. And as for that American friend who is poisoning her mind . . . I'll kill that little conniving strumpet."

George had to sigh. "Arthur, that's why she left you in the first place." Although, truthfully, it was probably the mental abuse that drove Katherine away. God knew, George was sick of Arthur's company after only three weeks. And Katherine had endured him for over a year.

"Ridiculous!" Arthur said, taking another three swallows of beer. "I never used a cudgel on the trollop. Just my hands. Not even a fist. Slaps only. Nothing but light chastisement, George, I swear it."

Then, like a torch being thrust into a river, the anger and hate in Arthur's eyes went out.

Oh God, here comes the self-pity again.

"Please, George, please. Help me? I love her, George, truly I do. Help me convince her to go back to England with me. Please?"

George sighed again. "All right Arthur, let's work on your next letter."

A brigade? Even that was insufficient. Perhaps a barony as well.

"Let's start by you professing your undying love and devotion, Arthur."

Essen House

Nicki Jo Prickett was just beginning to climb down from the first wagon when Katherine Boyle emerged from the doorway and threw her arms around her.

"Nicki!"

Nicki laughed and hugged her friend. For a second her eyes watered. *God, how I've missed you, my love.*

Katherine squeezed her tighter, taking her breath. "Whoa! Careful there Katy. I'm a bit fragile after this trip."

A young boy jumped down from the second wagon and ran over to them. "Katy!" Robert Boyle jumped into his sister's arms.

Nicki laughed again. "Think he missed you?"

Katy kissed her brother on the cheek and then lowered him to the street. "I missed you both terribly. But we have to get the wagons unloaded as quickly as we can. The Brussels city council is strictly enforcing its ordinances against blocking the streets the next two weeks, what with all the visitors coming to see the festival."

"Festival?"

Katy nodded. "The Joyous Entry of Fernando and Maria Anna as the new King and Queen in the Netherlands. Very Burgundian. And very useful in terms of its political utility. Isabella and Albert did it when they became the archdukes. Lots of theater, pageantry, triumphal arches, *tableaux vivant*, and so on. You'll love it."

"I'm sure." Nicki said. She sighed to herself. She loved her life in the seventeenth century, but there were times...

Even with the help of the servants at Essen House the unloading of the wagons took almost an hour.

Finally Nicki and Katherine found themselves alone in the large kitchen.

"So, did you bring the tennis racquets like I asked you?"

"Of course," Nicki said, "and my last can of up-time tennis balls. But what's the story? I know you couldn't say much in your radio transmission given the limited time Hainhoffer allows for personal messages, but still..."

"The story is, my dear, that you have a match tomorrow with the queen in the Netherlands. And she and I have been practicing."

Nicki couldn't help but roll her eyes. "Oh, great. You know I hate playing down-time tennis. Yuck."

"Oh, no. She wants to play it by up-time rules. She's even had the court behind the Coudenberg palace laid out according to up-time dimensions."

"Now that's different. Do I have to throw the game for political reasons?"

"Not at all. Maria Anna seems pretty reasonable, for a royal. In fact, I think she'd probably resent it if you didn't play your best."

Katy's face clouded. "But we have other problems, I'm afraid. Arthur is here in Brussels."

"Arthur?" Nicki tried not to frown. "Your husband, Arthur? What the hell is he doing here?"

"Attempting to get me to come back to England with him. He has my brother-in-law, George, the one who married Lettice, with him."

"So what are you going to do?"

"Stall," Katy said, "until we leave for Essen. I don't think he'll follow us there. George is clearly helping in that regard. He hasn't said so, but I think he has instructions from my father to keep Arthur away from me. He is acting as the go-between during the negotiations." She grimaced. "So-called negotiations. I even offered to admit to adultery so he could get a judicial separation. He was not inclined to accept, according to George."

Nicki reached for Katy's hand, worried. "Any second thoughts?"

Katy shuddered. "None. I know I've told you about Arthur, at least a little. But if you really met him..." Katy shook her head. "No, I don't want you to meet him. And I certainly don't want to see him ever again. He was horrid. Truly, utterly horrid."

Women up-time had been abused. But from Katy's stories, Nicki had learned that physical and mental abuse of women in seventeenth-century England was much more the norm than it had been up-time. Unlike many Protestant states in Europe, women in England couldn't even get a legal separation unless they could prove the physical abuse was life-threatening, which was difficult to do. And of course, there were no shelters for battered women as there were up-time. So women just suffered. And endured. A few—a lucky few—with sympathetic relatives and enough money were able to escape their abusive relationships. But most didn't.

"That's fine." Nicki patted the up-time revolver on her hip. It had been a present from her father when she had moved to Essen. "But if he shows up here, he better be on his best behavior. Or he'll find out what Sam Colt said."

Katy raised an eyebrow. "Sam Colt?"

"Yeah," Nicki said. "Inventor of the colt revolver. Like this thing here. 'God made men and women. But Sam Colt made them equal.'"

Katy laughed. "Now I remember! The wild west!" Katy hugged her. "Would you really shoot him?"

"If he tried to hurt you? Without a second thought."

For a minute they said nothing, just held each other.

"So, when is this tennis match?" Nicki asked.

"Tomorrow."

"Tomorrow!"

Katy smiled. "Yes. I was afraid you wouldn't make it in time. And afterward, Maria Anna is coming here to sample some of the products for the cheese and chocolate factory."

"Cheese and chocolate factory? What the hell..."

"Didn't I tell you? We're starting a cheese and chocolate factory here in Brussels under Queen Maria Anna's patronage. Herr Hainhoffer's cook, Barbara, has been preparing for it for a week. She even has a new recipe for those cookies you like."

"The ones with chipotle?" Nicki felt her mouth begin to water.

"The very ones."

"So what gave you this idea? About the factory, I mean."

"It was something that evolved over the weeks we've been here. Josh and Colette Modi are willing to back it. But when Queen Maria Anna brings it up, you need to pretend you know all about it."

"Great. A tennis match with royalty. Your husband is in town. A new business I knew nothing about. Anything else you want to tell me?"

Katy grinned mischievously. "Well, the fitting for your gown for the Joyous Entry ceremony next week is on Saturday."

"What!?"

"You certainly can't wear those clothes to one of the most important festivals in the Netherlands, can you?"

Nicki looked at her skort and jacket. "What's wrong with my clothes?" She held up her hand when she saw Katy stomp her foot. "Never mind. I don't want to know. I'll submit to your superior knowledge of seventeenth-century fashion. Grudgingly."

Nicki liked the seventeenth century. She really did. But too many of the womens' clothes, especially the ones worn by "high" society were a pain. Literally.

"Okay, Katy, tell me more about this chocolate and cheese factory."

"Cheese and chocolate."

"Whatever."

Warande Gardens, Coudenberg Palace

"We're not supposed to be watching, Corporal. We're supposed to be guarding."

Corporal Sanchez jerked away from the doorway. "Sorry, Sergeant."

Sergeant Jorge Rodriguez motioned with his hand. "Make your rounds, Corporal, make your rounds. I'll guard the doorway."

Sanchez moved off down the wall.

Rodriguez looked around and then peered in at the court. *Come on, Your Majesty, you can beat the American!*

It was infuriating. Even more infuriating was the fact she had no right to be infuriated. But at least the woman wasn't calling her "Your Majesty" every five seconds.

"You asked for this match, Maria Anna," she muttered. "You oh so wanted to play up-time tennis. So stop being so petty."

"Ready?" came from the other side of the court.

Maria Anna nodded. Once again Nicki Jo Prickett's serve came rocketing across the net.

Nicki had turned out to be a young woman of Maria Anna's height and build. At first Maria Anna thought that might give her an advantage, since her opponent wouldn't be a quick little bunny running down every shot like Katherine Boyle did. Unfortunately, Nicki had a much more powerful serve. As the match progressed Nicki's double faults had diminished and Maria Anna found herself time and again hitting empty air in her attempt to answer serve.

But this time Maria Anna was able to get her racquet on the ball and the rally was a good one, only ending when Nicki hit a backhand passing shot on the left side.

"Game, set and match, Your Maj—Maria Anna! Nice rally. You want to go again?"

Maria Anna shook her head as she approached the net and reached to shake Nicki's hand. "I think not, at least today." She pointed the up-time racquet at Nicki. "But Saturday, late afternoon, if you are willing? And were you serious about giving me this racquet? It really is a marvel."

"You bet I was serious. I really don't have much time to play in Essen, so one racquet is good enough for me. You can keep the tennis balls, too. They should keep their bounce for at least a few months."

Katherine approached from the sidelines. Nicki asked, "Is Saturday afternoon okay? Will I be done with the torture session?"

Katherine laughed. "Yes, the fitting should be done by then." She looked at Maria Anna. "Nicki has a difficult time accepting the fashions of nobility."

"I can certainly understand that." Maria Anna said. She pointed at Nicki's legs. "Those look so much more comfortable for tennis. What did you call them again? I adore that color."

"Sweat pants. Yeah, I love emerald green, too. Unfortunately, they're a cotton and polyester blend, so we probably won't have something like them any time soon. But we're working on the color at Essen Chemical. Dyes are a big business."

"That was a very nice match, Maria Anna," Katherine said. She hugged Nicki. "Nicki played tennis on her high school team and in college. You adapted very well to the up-time tennis balls."

"Well, it didn't feel like I was adapting," Maria Anna said. "I kept missing the serves. It was infuriating. Will you work with me on that, Nicki? I'd love to have that kind of serve the next time I play my sister. I can just see her jaw dropping and rolling around on the court."

Nicki smiled. "It will be my pleasure, Your Majesty."

"But now," Katherine said, "I think it's time for refreshments. I know that Barbara is probably waiting anxiously for us at Essen House. Back to the palace, Maria Anna?"

"Definitely," Maria Anna said. The best thing about living in Mary of Hungary's rooms in the Coudenberg Palace was the fact that they faced the garden rather than the courtyard. They would be able to enter directly from the Warande without having to pass through dozens of courtiers and palace servants.

"But I think we'll leave by way of the side entrance to the gardens through the Domus Isabella. We'll attract less attention that way and I can travel incognito." She scowled. "Well, as incognito as my husband and guards will let me. It is very different now compared to my time after the escape from Munich."

"Katy mentioned your travels across Bavaria. Was that exciting?"

The women continued their conversation as they approached the entrance to the Warande.

Inn of the Silver Swine

"Where's Arthur?"

James Fallows, the Catholic Englishman and veteran of the Army of Flanders, whom George had hired to babysit Arthur Jones, nodded toward the back stairs of the inn. "Said he was feeling ill and was going to his room. He's been up there at least an hour."

Well, if the illness is serious enough, perhaps we can end this charade and go home, George thought, climbing the stairs. He knocked on the door to Arthur's room. "Arthur? How are you feeling? You awake?"

No one answered.

No, please no. George opened the door. Jones was not in the room, and the bed was in the same disarray that George remembered from the morning.

Bloody hell! He's gone to find Katy.

Essen House

Arthur Jones was fifty yards from Essen House when he saw the carriage and its guard detail of half-a-dozen cavalry pull up in front. He stopped and squinted as three women, including one who had to be his Katherine, climbed out of the carriage and entered Essen House. The carriage then moved off along with its escort and parked in the square further down the street.

Now or wait? There was no telling how many people might be in the house. Better to wait.

"Oh, this is very, very good. Chocolate covered strawberries!" Maria Anna took a second bite. "You were right, Katy. This chocolate is nothing like I tasted in Vienna. You say you have two different kinds?"

Nicki nodded. "Dark chocolate, which is semi-sweet. That's what's on the strawberries. And milk chocolate, with more sugar. That is what these were made with." She offered Maria Anna a cookie.

Maria Anna took a bite and her eyes opened wide. "Spicy? I love spicy! Hungarian dishes with paprika were always my favorite in Vienna."

Nicki laughed. "So do I. These don't have real chipotle, which would mean smoked jalapeños, but they're close. They're made from a chili pepper grown in a town in the Basque area of Spain called Espellete. Imported from America a century or so ago, of course."

"Fernando must taste these. Really he must."

Katy smiled and pointed at the basket on the table. "We thought you might like to take some samples with you. We'll put more cookies in the basket." She laughed when she saw Nicki's face droop. "And don't worry Nicki, Barbara will make more for you tonight."

Sergeant Rodriguez never took his eyes off the front door of Essen House. It didn't matter that the queen had ordered him to wait for her here in the square. It didn't matter that the square was less than seventy yards from Essen House. What mattered was that if anything went wrong, if anything happened to the queen, the king was sure to blame him, not Her Majesty.

"Sergeant, that man is acting suspicious."

"What man?" Rodriguez asked.

Sanchez pointed with his chin. "That one. The one across the street with his arms crossed. He's been standing there since we've been in the square, I'm sure of it. He never seems to take his eyes off Essen House."

It was at that moment that the front door to Essen House opened.

☆ ☆ ☆

"You two go ahead, I'll catch up at the carriage. I forgot something." Nicki turned away as Katy and Maria Anna opened the door. Yes, she felt guilty about palming the cookie from Maria Anna's basket. But they were just so good!

She was taking her second bite when she heard Katy scream.

Pistol. Bedroom. Shit! No time. She grabbed the tennis racquet off the table and charged out the door.

"Shut up, you whore!" Arthur said. "And stop struggling. You're coming back to England with me!" He turned to the woman with the basket in her arms. "And as for you, you American bitch..." He raised his wheel-lock pistol. A blur from the doorway made him turn and a woman with a cookie in her mouth and some kind of club in her hand came at him. He fired just as the club came down on his arm.

It took less than ten seconds for Sergeant Rodriguez to run from the square, but he was still out of breath when he arrived. "Are you all right, Your Majesty?"

The queen watched the large American woman chase the man down the street. "I'm fine, Sergeant. I don't think the man really intended to attack me. A case of mistaken identity, apparently. And his shot seems to have hit nothing but air."

She looked at the Englishwoman. What was her name? Ah, Boyle, Rogriguez thought.

"Was that your husband, Arthur, you mentioned?"

The Boyle woman nodded.

"Do you wish us to pursue him, Your Majesty?" Rodriguez asked. "I am sure the Brussels militia can find him."

The queen looked at Boyle, who shook her head. "I don't think that will be necessary, Sergeant."

Everyone turned as the American woman came back up the street. She had half a cookie in one hand and a tennis racquet in the other.

"I hit him at least three times, but he just kept running. Damn coward!"

The Boyle woman's eyes narrowed. "Nicki Jo Prickett, where did you get that cookie?"

"Cookie?" The American woman stuffed the remains of the cookie in her mouth. "What cookie?" she mumbled.

☆ ☆ ☆

Three days. Three days they'd had to wait for the hue and cry to die down before George felt safe to walk the streets of Brussels with Arthur again.

Even a brigade and barony weren't enough to put up with this, as far as George was concerned.

"Over here, Arthur." In the twilight the fog was just beginning to make its way down the streets of Brussels. George pulled Arthur into the alley.

"We've got to get you out of Brussels, Arthur. The militia may not be after you, but there are a lot of people who think very highly of their new queen. Given the stories circulating right now, you'll be much safer in Antwerp."

Arthur hugged his right arm to his chest and nodded. "The damn bitch hit me! Three times! It still hurts like hell."

George covered his smile with his hand. "You're lucky she hit you, Arthur. If you'd shot the queen . . ." Boyle would have roasted me alive, that's for sure. As it is, there's only one way to make amends with him now.

"Here's enough silver for a month in Antwerp," George said. "I'll follow you there as soon as I can. Now head for the docks. Remember, you're looking for the boat named *Santiago's Curse*. Your belongings are already on board."

Arthur nodded. "*Santiago's Curse*. Thank you, George. I'll repay you, I promise."

George pushed him out into the street. "Now, go." He watched Arthur disappear into the fog toward the city's docks. Two shadows detached themselves from the wall as he stumbled past. One followed him.

The other turned toward George Goring. "This will cost you extra," James Fallows said.

"I know," Goring said. "Part payment Arthur has with him. A purse with silver coin. Just make it look like an accident."

"That will be no problem. Plenty of drunks fall in the river during festivals. Especially when we have a fog at night."

Fallows disappeared down the street.

George began to walk back towards the Inn of the Silver Swine.

"Now what is that supposed to mean?" Nicki asked, pointing towards the *tableau vivant* on their left.

Their carriage had stopped once again and Katherine Boyle

waved to the crowds around them. The Joyous Entry of King Fernando and Queen Maria Anna into Brussels had so far been a slow but wonderful pageant and Katherine figured they had only an hour left to go before the procession ended. As usual, the carriages of the higher orders of Brussels society, including the foreign guests like themselves, brought up the rear.

"Oh come on, Nicki. Even you can figure that one out!"

Nicki nodded. "Okay, okay. The big guy in the center has to represent King Fernando. But what's with the hole in the tongue and all the gold chains attached to the women below? Looks pretty kinky if you ask me."

Katy repressed a sigh. She loved Nicki. She loved most of the Americans she had met in Grantville. But for a society built on the foundations of western civilization, their lack of knowledge was truly appalling.

"*Typus Herculis Gallici*," Katy said. "The man represents Hercules. So Fernando is being depicted as a new Hercules both in terms of mental agility and physical strength. But if you count the number of women, you'll see there are seventeen."

She waited for Nicki to remember, then prompted. "Seventeen?"

Nicki smiled. "Oh! The seventeen provinces of the Netherlands. So the chains represent..." Her forehead creased.

"The need for Fernando to win the loyalty of his new subjects with gentleness and kind words, and not force of arms," Katy said.

"*Righhhht*." Nicki sat back in the carriage as it lurched forward. "Did you get a chance to speak with Maria Anna about Arthur before the procession?"

"Of course. As far as they can determine, Arthur was drunk. He slipped and fell into the river down by the docks during the night fog two days ago. No evidence of foul play. So George's story checks out."

"Miss him?"

"Oh no. Just... he wasn't a evil man, really. Just a weak one."

Nicki patted her hand. "Well, don't think bad of me, but I'm glad he's dead. If that had been me carrying the basket instead of Maria Anna, I'd probably have died, since there would have been no one to smack him with a tennis racquet. Hey, does this mean you keep your title? You're still Viscountess Ranelagh?"

"And I will inherit his estate," Katy said, "according to George. It's not much, but there are several houses in London that are mine now. And with Arthur dead it will be much easier to make amends with my family. Oh, and before I forget, Maria Anna has agreed to give us a royal patent for the factory, with two stipulations."

Katherine began waving again to the crowd. "First, we have to name it 'Royal Maria Anna's Cheese, Chocolate and Cookie Factory.' Both she and Fernando think the cookies will be a big seller. Second—and this comes directly from Fernando himself—we have to name the cookie with chipotle 'Ring of Fire.'"

Nicki laughed. "'Ring of Fire' cookies? Oh my God, we're going to sell millions of them!"

Homecoming

Karen Bergstralh

January 1636, Dover, England

Four large bay mares walked quietly down the gangplank and on to the quay. Their heads lifted, nostrils widened, and ears swiveled taking in the new sights, odors, and sounds but they showed no signs of distress. Wilfram Jones smiled in relief. The mares were his gift to his family and the last of his group's horses to be offloaded. The English Channel had been choppy and not all of the horses had been as phlegmatic.

"That's it, Wilf," Reichard Blucher said, coming up behind him. "All our gear and animals are off that miserable excuse for a ship."

"It got us here without charging a king's ransom," Wilf answered, "and the captain didn't overcharge us for what your horse did to his ship." He glanced up at the clouds and frowned. "We need to get on our way. It's a long ride to our destination and yon clouds look like they hold snow."

Wilf directed Christian du Champ, Dieter Wiesskamp, and Reichard to manage the packsaddles and packs. Mike Tyler joined him in saddling the riding animals. In less than an hour all five men were mounted and each held the lead of a packhorse.

"Okay, let's go," Wilf called out and started his horses off through Dover.

"You should say 'Move 'em out,' Wilf," Christian said with a wicked grin.

"No, no!" Dieter chimed in. "It's 'Head 'em up! Move 'em out!' but only if you're leading a cattle drive or a wagon train. Ask Mike."

"Don't look at me," Mike Tyler replied. "Westerns never were my favorites. You guys are the ones who spend all your spare time watching Rob's old tapes."

Wilf ignored the banter and concentrated on winding through the crowded streets. Once clear of the town he led them off the Dover to London road and onto a smaller lane leading west. He kept them moving for half an hour before calling a halt to check cinches and give the horses a rest.

Dismounting, Wilf drew in a deep breath of cold, damp air.

"Ah, the smell of England. As we're upwind of the town, the worst stink is cow dung."

"How long has it been," Christian asked, "since you've had a lungful of English air?"

"Years. I came back once, but never made it past the docks." Wilf frowned at the memory. "I was just turned twenty and thought to show my father and grandfather that I'd survived and even had money in my pockets." His memories of that aborted visit stirred up a number of other unpleasant memories.

"What happened to stop you?" Christian asked softly.

"At a dockside inn a whore reminded me that mercenaries are the scum of the earth. She did find my money as good as any other's, though." Wilf faced his old friend and lifted an eyebrow. "No doubt, someone similarly informed you."

"None so kind as a whore. My grandfather ordered me out. Ordered that my name be removed from family records. He told me that I wasn't even fit to beg on the streets so that left becoming a mercenary."

The quick smile that crossed Christian's lips didn't fool Wilf. His own memories still festered and he suspected that Christian's did so, also. Movement among the horses drew his attention.

Reichard's gelding had his head up, a clump of grass hanging forgotten from his mouth. The horse's attention focused on the road behind them. One by one the other horses lifted their heads and subtly tensed.

"Get mounted," Wilf ordered, "someone's coming." Before he was fully settled in his saddle his right hand had moved his up-time pistol from its holster to his coat pocket. "Michael, take the packhorses and stay behind us. If a fight starts, ride off down the road as fast as you can manage. We'll catch up."

"Are you expecting a fight?" Tyler asked calmly. Wilf smiled at the sight of the pistol ready in Michael's hand. The young man had come a long way from the shy, nervous boy he'd first met. Briefly Wilf wished that Rob Parker was with them. Rob had several times proved capable of handling a pitched battle. Michael was still green when it came to a life-or-death fight.

"No, but I picked this road because there shouldn't be much traffic." He paused, listening. "Our visitors are mounted. That could mean soldiers or an organized band of thieves. Not that there's always a difference between the two." When Tyler nodded thoughtfully, Wilf turned away and moved to the front of his little band. He noted that Christian held an up-time style shotgun instead of his usual blade. Dieter had his pistol out, but held it down along his leg, hidden from a casual glance. Reichard's pistol looked like a toy in his big hand and it, too, was held out of sight.

Satisfied, Wilf reined his horse to a spot ahead and to the right of Reichard. The first of the approaching group came around a bend in the road and Wilf allowed himself a smile. They were soldiers and he recognized the man in the lead.

"Ho, there!" the leader called out. His eyes went wide when he saw Reichard and he broke into a grin. "God's Blood! If it isn't Wilfram Jones! I should have known when the city guard reported a giant and a dwarf rode through." The soldier turned to the man beside him. "Sergeant, hold the men here. These villains are old friends of mine, dangerous only to beer and wine kegs." He rode forward and shook hands with Wilf.

"Robert Masters, you pox-ridden, out of luck whoreson! What are you doing here and who is the idiot that put you in charge of more than a pike?"

"Good to see you, too, Wilf," Masters replied genially. "And it's Lieutenant Masters now. Captain Bryce put together a company and, being a man with vast military knowledge, he begged me to join him."

"Your Captain Bryce wouldn't be Thomas Bryce, would he?" Wilf asked innocently. When Masters nodded, he added, "Then your band is lead by a drunken fool who's named the village idiot as his second. What are you doing in England?"

"Aye," Masters sighed dramatically, "that sums us up. Now that jobs are scarce on the Continent we'd have been more fools to not take the King's coin." Masters paused and looked back at his troopers. Lowering his voice he continued. "It's said that King Charles is pissing himself in fear over those supposed histories from the future. He's hired a number of mercenary companies, our amongst them, to keep what happened—what is going to happen . . ."

"What happened in another universe," Wilf finished for him. "We all get tangled dealing with four hundred years of future history." Scratching his chin, Wilf regarded Masters. "Hasn't anyone explained that just because it happened in that other universe doesn't mean that it will happen in this one?"

Masters shrugged. "There are those who say that speaking sweet reason to the king is a waste of one's breath. Such talk may be moot. Rumors have the king at death's door. Whoever it is giving orders, be it the king or some other, he's as vicious as Satan. I've seen people gaoled on the slightest suspicion. God's Blood! What were we to think when Archbishop Laud ended up in the Tower?" Shaking his head, Masters smiled and gave Wilf a speculative look.

"Still, a job is a job. We're waiting for the last of our company to come across before heading up to London next week. Most of the company is green as grass. Thomas and I could use some dependable old hands."

"Sorry, Robert," Wilf said, returning the smile, "but we aren't mercenaries anymore. No, now we're respectable horse traders. Christian's become so respectable that he's married and has children. Dieter and I are courting a pair of widows. He's made more progress with his suit than I, but I have hopes."

"So that rumor is true," Masters mused. "You are living in the town from the future. Do they know that you were mercenaries?"

"Aye, we live in Grantville. They know very well that we were mercenaries considering that they captured us on the field of battle. Among their strange ideas is that a man's past shouldn't be held against him if he wants to change. When you tire of the mercenary life come look us up."

"I may do that. What, pray tell, brings you to England in these troublesome times?"

"I've a client who thinks that a certain stud farm has some

interesting stock. The client is paying for us to come and fetch a few choice animals. As the stud is near my family's village, I intend to see if any of my family still lives."

"Walk softly, Wilf, and keep your thoughts to yourself," Masters counseled. "Especially if they are about the king. Stay well clear of London, too. It sounds like your new friends made a right mess of the Tower. Some of the rumors have Satan sending the Angel of Death to strike men down with an invisible sword and then five hundred fiery demons emerging from the very gates of Hell to pull down the walls. Impossible, of course, but how else could they bring down even part of the walls without siege cannon?"

"Ah, yes." Wilf grinned wolfishly. "But then, you've never met Harry Lefferts and his wrecking crew." He hesitated for a moment. Considering all the talk and wild tales he'd heard across Europe, it was certain that Robert had heard about Julie Sims. Wilf didn't know where Julie was but, should she be in England, it wouldn't hurt to polish up her reputation. He lowered his voice and, in a solemn tone, cautioned the mercenary. "The 'Angel' is a slip of a girl with the eyes of an eagle and a rifle from the future. Her targets never see her. Pray that you never, ever give her cause to hunt you. I helped bury dozens of Croats she killed when they attacked the school at Grantville."

Robert Masters blanched. "May God preserve us! I'd thought those tales were wild exaggerations."

Wilf shook his head. "When you come to Grantville you can see the grave for yourself." He waved a hand at the rest of his group. "Neither you nor the king have any reason to worry about us. Our destination lies well away from London. We're no more than a company of simple horse traders."

"That should do for anyone who doesn't know you." Masters nodded and smiled grimly. He glanced back at his men. The sergeant was haranguing a pair of troopers over loose girths. Judging from their faces neither man understood what the sergeant was saying. "Given what I've seen and heard, you may find me at your doorstep within the year."

"You'll be welcome, Robert." Wilf said.

"I'll be off, then. That is, if Sergeant Donaldson can get yonder whoresons mounted and whip them into some kind of order." He motioned to the sergeant and turned his mount back down the road.

The horse traders waited in silence until the soldiers disappeared.

"What now, Wilf?" Reichard asked mildly.

"We change roads. I hadn't planned on going by the London road." He shrugged. "But now I think that we'll join it for a bit and swing west north of where I'd planned."

"Why change roads?" Michael asked, his face showing nothing more than curiosity.

"Ah, well, not to put it too nicely, I don't completely trust our old friends Robert and Thomas. They may feel the need to prove themselves to their new paymaster. It could cross their minds that an easy way to do so is by arresting us. We'll change roads to avoid them. By the time we return to Dover they'll be in London." Wilf sighed. England was the land of his birth, his home. Perhaps it was just the perspective of his years as a mercenary, or perhaps because he'd left England at sixteen, but England now felt like a foreign land.

"The regular Dover authorities shouldn't be a problem. We landed legally and carry all the right papers. From the look on the customs clerk's face, we are probably the only people ever to pay our fees without arguing." He stared down the road before continuing. "When chaos stalks the land, strangers are easy targets. We might appear suspicious to those who don't know us."

"Actually," Michael replied with a wide grin, "those who know you guys best have no trouble considering you suspicious."

"Ah, Young Michael," Wilf replied lightly, "You wound me! Come on, daylight is burning." He ran a critical eye over the group as they started up the road. God help anyone fool enough to tangle with them, even with young Tyler.

"Nine days, given our detour, the state of the roads, and the weather, isn't bad time for the distance we've come." He peered at the map in front of them. "Wylye lies here. Stonehenge lies there, north and a bit east of it. Avebury is another twenty, twenty-five miles from Stonehenge. The stud farm we want is just north of Avebury." Wilf traced the route on the map. "We're twenty miles or so from Wylye tonight, about here. My family's farm is just outside a village about here." His forefinger thumped the map. "Too small to appear on Rob's map. Or, mayhap, long gone to plague or war by the time this map was drawn." He settled back and lit his pipe. Reichard and Christian looked at the map and nodded. Michael leaned forward, peering closely at it in the dim light the inn's candles offered.

After a moment Wilf took pity on the young man. "You'll get to see Stonehenge and Avebury, Michael. While neither are presently a tourist destination, people do visit them to gawk at the stones. One more band of awestruck yokels won't stand out. Unfortunately, the same doesn't hold for these other piles of stones we've passed. Dolmens, I think you called them. Many consider such stones cursed or the Devil's altars, and poking about them would draw the kind of attention you don't want."

Things had indeed changed since he'd left England. The villagers had been always been a bit wary of strangers but now suspicions ran dark and deep. Even the innkeepers greeted travelers warily. Foreigners were watched closely.

Since they'd left the Dover-London road Wilf had insisted that everyone speak only English. People were used to travelers from elsewhere in England having odd accents. After four years in Grantville even Dieter's English could pass for "not from around here but not foreign."

Wild statements about the king's health and mental state floated on every breeze. Each new rumor seemed to bring a spasm of activity by military patrols. The group had been stopped and questioned half a dozen times.

After knocking the dottle out of his pipe Wilf reached out and carefully folded the up-time map. He got up from the table and pointed to the stairs. "Enjoy your sleep tonight. There's no inn where we're going so tomorrow night we may end up sleeping in my grandfather's barn."

"Who be ye?" the voice trickled out from behind a solid oak door.

"Wilfram Jones. Second son of William Jones, grandson of Paul Jones, the horse breaker."

"Wilfram Jones be long dead," the voice muttered. "Dead and gone in some foreign land."

"I've been a long time in foreign lands but I'm most certainly not dead." Wilf stated firmly. He couldn't puzzle out if it was a man or woman behind the door. The voice and phrasing sounded elderly. It had been too many years since he'd heard his family's voices and he had no idea if the voice was family or a servant.

"Be ye Wilfram, ye must be a foul specter." The sound of the door's bar dropping into place signaled the end of the conversation.

Wilf looked around in frustration. The day had started out cold and dark and damp. By midmorning a light snow began falling. Now, with dusk upon them, they found his family's house shut tightly against them.

"That barn you spoke of last night," Christian's voice broke the silence. "Perhaps your grandfather's cattle will give us a kinder greeting. It'll get us out of this wind."

"Aye, though we'll need to watch out if he's got a stallion or two in there." After a last look at his family's front door Wilf led the group to the barn. He was dismayed to find it empty save for a single cow and half a dozen sheep. Snow sifted through a hole in the roof. What had happened here? Grandpa never allowed repairs to go undone. Da was swift with a cuff and words when Wilf or his brothers skimped on their chores. Were all his family dead?

"It appears that hard times have overtaken your family." Christian remarked. "That might explain the barred door."

"Someone's kept the stalls in good repair." Reichard's tenor came out of the dimness. "There are enough for our animals and, if we double up, for us, too."

"There's fresh hay in the loft. Straw, too." Michael's voice came from overhead. Wilf could see the beam of his up-time flashlight sweeping the loft. "I'd guess that there's enough hay to see a dozen cows or horses through until spring. There's a tin grain bin up here. It's only about a third full and the grain's musty. Jo Ann would not approve."

Dieter joined in, slapping Wilf on the shoulder. "It's fine, Wilf. We've slept in far worse places."

A flash of shame surprised Wilf. He'd come home at last and his family barred the door in his face. That was bad enough, but to have it happen in front of his friends... What was the quote Rob Clark had tossed off before they left? Something about never really being able to go home again?

"Are you a ghost?" a child's voice woke Wilf. A boy of five or six squatted beside him, peering intently at his face. "You look like Papa."

"Is Papa's name Andrew?"

"No," the little boy shook his head, "his name is Papa."

"Ah, your Papa is called Robert or Robin?"

The boy stared at him and nodded solemnly. This boy was the son of his youngest brother, then. It didn't seem possible. Robin had been scarcely older when Wilf had last seen him. There was the look of hunger in the boy's face.

"Reichard, is that bacon I smell?" Wilf called softly, not wishing to wake any of the others that might still be asleep.

"Bacon, a bit of salt pork, and the bread we bought yesterday. There's also half a wheel of cheese and a few onions."

"Do you think that there might be enough to spare for my nephew, here?" Wilf watched joy spread across the boy's face when Reichard agreed that there was enough for their visitor, too.

"Don't eat too fast," Wilf cautioned the boy a few minutes later. "Or you'll get sick."

"You have a lot of horses. Are you very, very, very rich men?" The question was mumbled around the cheese and bacon sandwich Michael had handed the boy.

"Nope, not rich at all." Michael answered. He flipped open his folding knife and sliced an onion to add to his own cheese and bacon sandwich. The boy watched closely, reaching out to touch the knife. Michael pulled out his flashlight and showed him how to crank the handle. A squeal of delight greeted its illumination in the dim barn.

"No, Nephew." Wilf added. "We're not poor, but we aren't rich. We've so many horses because we're horse traders. When we find good horses we buy them and then sell them to other people."

"You aren't a ghost." The boy made it not quite a question.

"I'm not a ghost." Wilf agreed. "Ghosts don't break their fast by eating bacon, cheese and bread." He took several big bites and chewed vigorously to prove the point.

"Your Papa is Robert Jones, youngest son of William Jones," Wilf stated after taking a sip of beer.

The boy nodded. "Momma calls him Robin. Granny Digby calls him Robert."

Relief washed over Wilf. From the way that the boy spoke of him, Robin was alive.

"Robin is my brother. That makes you my nephew and me your Uncle Wilfram."

"Uncle Wilfram is dead." The boy's voice wavered a bit and he looked uncertain.

"Touch my hand." Wilf extended his right hand toward the boy. Hesitating, the child finally reached out and poked Wilf's hand with a finger.

"Now, put your hand on top of mine. I'm no ghost, but solid flesh."

The boy inched closer and placed his small, grubby hand on top of Wilf's.

"See? Flesh and bone."

"Will? Where are you, boy? You better have watered the cow . . ." A woman slid the barn's door open and stepped in. She halted, taking in the presence of the five men. Her eyes widened when Wilf stood up.

"Andrew? It *was* you at the door last night. Your drunken jokes go too far. What have brought upon us now?"

"No, mistress, I'm Wilfram, Robin and Andrew's brother."

"He's not a ghost, Mamma." Little Will piped up. He reached up and poked Wilf's arm. "We're having a feast."

"Will, come here, now." Cold or fear made her voice tremble but she held her ground. No one moved and she took a few steps toward the men. She faced Wilf and looked him over carefully.

"You have the look. Enough like Andrew to be him when he's sober." Her eyes swept the interior of the barn, taking in the filled stalls and the cooking fire. That last held her attention. "I suppose I should thank you for cleaning out the old forge instead of burning down the barn."

"Give us a day," Dieter gave her his most charming smile, "and we'll set the roof right, ma'am."

"Why bother?" She said bitterly. "It won't be ours much longer."

"Because the Hampfords have demanded that it be fixed." A man's voice answered. A younger, taller version of Wilf maneuvered through the door. He leaned on a crutch, his free hand holding a pistol. His left leg was heavily bandaged and his face lined with pain. "Blessed Lord, this has to be Wilf!"

"Robin! Grown a bit haven't you, boy?" Wilf embraced his brother gingerly. "What's happened to you?"

"That thrice damned roof." Robin winced. "I fear that my attempts at repair only enlarged it and put the seal of death on me."

This close, Wilf could smell the infection in his brother's leg and his heart sank. He'd seen more soldiers die from infected wounds than in battle. By the time you could smell the wound there was nothing to be done save start digging a grave. Except... He glanced at Dieter. Dieter had medical skills and he'd taken some additional training in Grantville. The group's first aid kit held several up-time style medicines, too. Together they might be enough.

"Mayhap not, little brother. Dieter?"

"I'll do my best," Dieter agreed. "As long as he's still alive there's hope. The kitchen is probably the best place. I'll want boiled cloths for bandages and he'll need to be kept warm. Michael, you've had the advanced first aid course?"

"Yup. Should I break out my first aid kit?"

"Yes, and I'll need your assistance, too." Dieter turned back to Wilf. "Don't just stand there. Get your brother to the house."

Wilf picked Robin up, dismayed to find how thin and light he was. When Robin protested, Wilf scolded him.

"Save your strength. You'll need it to curse Dieter while he cleans up your leg."

"What happened here, Robin?" Wilf asked. He was pleased to see the change in his brother this morning. The pain in the younger man's face was less, the fever flush replaced by a healthy pink.

"Do you remember how it was when you left? Grandpa and Da constantly yelling at each other?"

"Aye, and at everyone else. It's one reason I left."

"The fighting continued until Grandpa died two or three years later. Then everything started to go to pieces." Robin's eyes lost focus and his voice sounded very young. "Why did they fight? I was too young to understand why they fought so."

Sighing, Wilf stared at the fire. He'd been old enough to understand and the memories were painful.

"Our great grandfather trained horses for battle and tournament. He was very good at it. So good that he had a reputation throughout England. People paid him well to have him train their warhorses."

Wilf paused, gathering his thoughts. "He was the one who built this farm. Grandpa told stories of it needing ten stable hands to care for the barn when Great Grandpa was alive."

"I remember some of those stories." Robin said. "What happened to change things? Da never told the old stories after Grandpa died."

"What happened was that war and fashions changed. Muskets

put an end to armored knights on the battlefield. Tourneys went out of fashion. A fully trained destrier no longer has a place on the battlefield. Some officers still ride warhorses but few of those are fully trained in the old style. It's too expensive and takes too long. Our great grandfather was a trainer of destriers. He couldn't bring himself to train lesser breeds."

"But Grandpa trained all kinds of horses."

"Aye, Grandpa did indeed. He would train any horse for any man who had the coin. He had the reputation for succeeding with horses others deemed impossible. The income wasn't as great but it was enough." Several memories surfaced and Wilf continued. "Great Grandfather taught Grandpa his training methods. Before I left, Grandpa hadn't passed his knowledge on to Da. Said Da wasn't ready yet. That was one of the things they fought about."

"I think I remember that part. When Grandpa died Da didn't have Grandpa's secrets. He tried so hard to do what Grandpa had done but it never worked for him. It was a horse that killed him."

Robin paused and Wilf offered him a sip of broth. The hand that grasped the mug didn't shake today and there was some strength in its grip.

"How did Da come to die?"

"Geoffrey Hampford had a vicious mare. She'd killed three men. Because she was out of the king's stud, gifted to the Hampfords, they dared not put her down. Pa boasted that he could train her." His eyes closed and tears leaked out from under the lids.

"Andrew and I got ropes on her and pulled her away from Da but it was too late." Robin's eyes opened and he stared up at his brother. "If Andrew had just slit her throat and been done with it, things might not have gone so wrong. He went mad and tortured that horse for hours."

"I think I can guess the rest. The Hampfords demanded recompense." Wilf dredged up what he could remember about them. Some service to Queen Elizabeth had made their fortunes. There'd never been a title, but some of the family took on noble airs. Geoffrey, he vaguely remembered, was one such.

"Yes. Jane and I were newly married." Robin picked at his blanket, sadness filling his face. "Mamma took sick and died that fall. Andrew lost himself in drink. What could be sold was, but each time we thought to have paid in full, Geoffrey's added another charge. Come next month's end the farm will be his."

"Vindictive, is he?"

"Oh, yes. He's told us that we must indenture Will to him. Others have heard him brag that he'll make my son a stable drudge. He says that it's all any of our family is fit for. I'd rather see Will dead than in his hands."

"Nay, that'll not happen. I will see to that. You rest now. Let me worry about things."

Wilf left his brother's side and sought out Dieter. He found him in what had been his grandfather's room. The room was bare, stripped of the furniture that Wilf remembered. Robin's wife, Jane and Granny Digby were making up pallets along the walls.

"The wound is clean," Dieter smiled confidently, "and we got all of the splinters out. He's responded well to the antibiotic. It should be just a matter of time and care. If I could find the right kind of maggots it might help keep the wound clean and let it heal a bit faster."

"How long before he can be moved?"

"A couple of weeks would be best, but if need presses he'll be able to bear riding in a cart or on a quiet horse in a couple of days. Given the state of the roads we've seen, I'd suggest a horse."

"Good. I'm thinking we can spare a few days for him to heal."

Jane came over and grasped Wilf's hands. "Thank God that you came when you did. If Robert died . . ." She looked away, tears flowing. "Granny Digby—" She looked over at the ancient woman fussing with a blanket. "—has a grandson in the village. He's offered her a place. I know not where we will go. My mother is dead and my father remarried. His new wife has made clear that we aren't welcome under her roof. If Robin lives he will be able to find work on one of the farms."

"I've an idea to take you back to Grantville with us. My present home isn't palatial but you'd all be safe there." Wilf watched hope flood his sister-in-law's face.

"There's plenty of room at Herr Parker's." Dieter suggested. "Or we can build ourselves new homes along with proper stables on that land below New Hope. Rob's gotten the land leases to the last of it. That's were he's intending to build his riding school and Michael's museum. Strelow's been dickering to use some of the land to extend New Hope. He figures it will become a good sized town someday."

"Aye, that's a thought. Marta has hinted that a converted milking shed isn't her idea of a proper house." Wilf grinned at the thought.

Jane stood silently, her eyes large and an expression of wonderment on her face. "You must be angels sent by Our Lord in answer to my prayers. You've brought healing for Robin and hope for our future."

Both ex-mercenaries broke out in laughter. In the far corner Granny Digby muttered about foul specters sent by Satan.

"So, what's the plan?" Michael asked at dinner that night.

"Tomorrow Christian and I will go into the village and look for Andrew. We'll go on to Wylye, too, if needs be." Wilf mopped the last of the stew in his bowl with an end of bread. "We need to buy more supplies in any case. Past that, Dieter stays here to keep an eye on Robin's leg and Reichard to watch over the place."

Wilf paused, calculating distances and travel times. "The day after, you, Christian, and I will find this horse breeder and see what stock he has. I rather we not stop in Avebury." He saw the disappointment on the young man's face and added, "You will get to spend time at Stonehenge, that I'll promise."

"Just the chance to take some pictures for my lectures will be fine." Michael agreed. "I didn't expect to do any archaeology."

"We should be back here in four or five days. Then we pack up everyone and head back home. If the weather holds we could be in Grantville by mid-March. How soon you get back to the University depends on your family and Jo Ann." Wilf grinned at the young man's blush. He gave Michael a bland look.

"I'd considered buying a cart but we've no harness and Robin would do better on a soft-gaited horse."

"Okay!" Michael smiled and held up his hands in surrender. "Macho's the softest gaited horse we've got. I'm assuming that the mares will go back with us, so I'd be willing to trade his services in return for Sasha." He smirked before adding, "Jo Ann was really upset when you wouldn't sell Sasha to her. Will we have enough horses and saddles?"

"Ah! We'll make a horse trader out of you, yet! Agreed. Sasha goes back to Grantville and Jo Ann. Between the horses we have and what we pick up for Rob, we should do fine. If not, we can pick up extras along the way. There are three or four saddles in the barn. Dieter and Reichard can check them over while we're gone. I would like to find another couple of packsaddles—maybe in Wylye or at the stud farm."

Wilf leaned back in his chair. He'd walked around the farm earlier in the day. There had never been enough land to support the family by farming. The fields were small and enclosed. They'd been laid out as paddocks for horses, not for crops. That hadn't stopped his great grandfather and grandfather from hiring men to harvest hay from any paddock not being used as pastures. In his own youth, with money tight, he'd scythed and forked hay alongside the hired laborers.

The barn was ridiculously big. His great grandfather had built it to withstand temperamental warhorses and impress their owners. The house been built to impress, too. Thinking back he realized that half the rooms had stood unused and empty when he'd lived there. The servants' rooms up under the rafters had been filled with odds and ends of broken furniture when he was Will's age. The two house servants had slept in a room used by family during his great grandfather's time.

He did know Granny Digby, but as Mistress Digby. She'd run the household and served as his mother's maid. A large room at the end of the second floor hall had been hers. Now, she and what remained of the family huddled in the three rooms nearest the kitchen.

It took a lot of wood to heat those rooms and that went far to explain why so few trees still stood on the farm's land. After looking at the woodpile he and Christian had cut one of those remaining down that afternoon.

"I'd not thought to ever set eyes on you again." Toby Beresford rumbled thoughtfully. "Heard tell you'd died someplace foreign."

"Fortunately, the rumors of my death have been greatly exaggerated." Wilf smiled, carefully keeping his voice neutral. There was no point in arguing with the man. After the Hampfords, Toby Beresford was probably the richest and most influential man in the area. Wilf vaguely remembered that Toby Beresford and his father had not been friendly. Some long past dispute had put the men at odds. The only reasons Wilf had come to the Beresford farm were the four hams and three slabs of bacon Christian was loading on his horse. In Wylye they'd come across Toby's oldest son, John, who had offered the hams for sale.

"Heard tell that you went for a soldier."

"Aye, I did so for a bit. I trade in horses now." What did the man want? The dispute should have died with his father but there was an odd edge to the man's voice.

"They say that there's a town filled with witches that appeared somewhere in German lands. Know ye about it?" Beresford looked Wilf in the eyes.

"Aye, if you mean Grantville. It isn't full of witches, though, just ordinary people."

"No witches, you say." Beresford looked doubtful. "Mayhap the Devil has deceived you. Vicar Wheatly has information directly from . . ." He paused and an odd look came across his face. He shut his mouth firmly and looked away.

Wilf shook his head. No doubt that Vicar Wheatly's informant had been Archbishop Laud. Given that Laud was now an enemy of the king, Beresford was afraid to say his name.

"I've been in the town and spoken to a number the people. Up-timers they're called," Wilf said quietly. "They are ordinary people. The extra centuries of knowledge they brought back with them allows them to craft things we've not learned to yet. They openly share the knowledge behind their work."

"Mayhap you've been deceived by Satan's minions," Toby Beresford replied. "We are good Christians. Best you not tarry hereabout, least some of Satan's taint clings to you."

"I came to England to buy horses and to see my family. I found my family in distress." When Beresford started to speak Wilf held up a hand to stop him. "I hold no one to blame for their state and pass no judgment on the level of Christian charity shown them. Robin, his wife, and son are under my care now. They will go with me when I leave England."

"You've another brother. What do you intend for him?"

"Can I find him, he goes, too. So far none I've spoken with know his whereabouts."

The elder Beresford turned away and walked off stiffly. Wilf watched him go, wondering what to make of the strange conversation.

"Best your family leaves quickly, Wilf," John Beresford spoke. He didn't speak again until his father walked around the corner of the house and out of sight. "There's been much talk of magic and witches from the vicar." He paused and looked around. In a low voice he asked, "Have you really been in Grantville? Do they have carts pulled by magic?"

"Aye, I've been there. The carts are called cars or automobiles and there's no magic to the way that they work. No more magic than there is in the way water, a wheel, and the gears of a mill move its millstones."

John looked doubtful and Wilf pulled out his folding knife. "This was made four hundred years in the future. Or so the man I got it from said. It could have been made last year to an up-time pattern. The only magic in it is good steel. Once a blacksmith has one to use as a pattern he can make copies as good as the original."

"Is the town as strange as rumors paint it?"

"Yes and no. Some of the houses look strange at first. Some customs seem strange. Perhaps the strangest is that each man is free to worship as he wishes be he Catholic, Lutheran, Calvinist, or Jew."

"I would that I could see such a place."

"Mayhap someday you will." Wilf took the reins Christian handed him and mounted his horse. Remembering some long ago conversations, he added, "Grantville has a library with more books than you can imagine in it. Anyone is free to come and read them. S'truth, John."

Christian remained silent until they were well away from the farm.

"I saw the look on his face. Your last shot was tossing a bone in front of a starving dog."

"I liked John when we were boys. Then he wanted nothing greater than to go to a university. All he could talk of was the great libraries at Cambridge and Oxford. His father forbade it, wanting John to run the farm."

"The talk of witches and witchcraft bothers me. Such can make the best of men do things . . ."

"Aye," Wilf agreed grimly. "We leave at first light tomorrow. I'll not begrudge Michael time at Stonehenge but we can't tarry in Avebury. If the stud has them, I'm of a mind to buy two or three extra animals."

Michael ran his hands along the massive stone. Above him a capstone connected the one he touched to its neighbor. Stonehenge had seemed awesome as they approached. Here, touching the stones, he understood the fascination people had with them.

Stepping back, he took out Rob's camera and started taking pictures. For an hour he stalked about, trying to capture details as well as the over-all scene, stopping only to change the memory chip in the camera.

Christian, sitting on one of the fallen stones, watched their horses graze. Wilf fussed fitting a newly bought packsaddle to one of the new horses. Both men covertly watched the area around them.

"The camera still works, then." Christian commented as Michael approached.

"Yeah, it works great. I really owe Rob for letting me use it." Michael sighed contentedly and brushed snow off a corner of Christian's stone before sitting beside him.

"Don't you need a computer? When I've seen Rob and Lannie use that camera they've always had it fastened to a computer."

"Sure, that's when they're taking pictures of horses. Rob's got it rigged to dump the pictures directly to his breeding database. He's also got it rigged to a converter so he doesn't need batteries." Michael checked the camera's display. "When we get back, Rob will download these pictures for me." He snapped off a shot. When the flash went off he frowned. "I didn't realize how dark it was getting."

Christian tapped the hand holding the camera and pointed. "The clouds are lowering. We'll have snow by nightfall."

Michael glanced up. "Looks like it. Think we can make it to Wilf's home by tomorrow?"

"We'll need to leave soon."

Wilf stalked up, frowning. "Can you keep from making that flash of light?" His voice was low and he sounded worried.

"Ah, I think that there is a way. I just don't know if I can figure it out. Is there a problem?"

"Out there, just behind those two bushes, there are men watching us. I've spotted at least two more creeping along behind us. If they are horse thieves, we can handle them. What I fear is that they might be witch-hunters. A witch hunt is the last thing my family needs."

"There are two or three or more to our right," Christian said casually. "Do you think that your neighbor Beresford set them on us?"

"I don't know, not after so many years away. When I was a boy Beresford was known for taking time to study a problem before coming to a decision. Unless he's changed greatly he'd not have made up his mind this soon. Yon men are more likely to be thieves attracted to our horses." Wilf sighed. "Or they may be local men watching us simply because we're strangers. The horses are ready. We'll leave now and if they are thieves we'll know shortly." He looked around and turned back to Michael. "Should we be attacked, don't bother aiming, just point your gun at anyone close and shoot."

"Ah, why not aim? I'm a pretty good shot."

"No one is atop a moving horse. With luck you might hit one. The fact that we're better armed than we should be might give them pause. The new horses may spook at gunfire, so be ready for that."

Michael turned the camera off and stowed it in his pack. His pulse began to race as their situation sank in. He walked to his horse and carefully tied his pack behind his saddle. Wilf had already tied the extra animals into strings of three. He quickly tied the lead rope Wilf handed him to his saddle horn, then mounted and reached under his coat for his pistol.

Wilf and Christian mounted quickly.

"We ride out quietly," Wilf said in a low voice. "Christian first. Michael, you stay close behind him. Whatever happens, keep moving. Should they be honest men and want to talk, I'll do the talking. If an attack comes, Christian targets anyone in front. Michael, shoot only at those to your right. I'll handle any on the left or behind us."

They started off and Michael didn't see any signs that they weren't alone. That lasted until Christian's horses slowed to pass over a trickle of water. Two men rose from the ground and stood. Three more appeared to Michael's right. None of the watchers said a word.

Christian shifted his shotgun subtly as he passed the first two men. Michael's back and shoulders tensed. His own hand and the pistol in it rested openly on his thigh.

Once past the men, Christian set a fast pace. Michael found himself profoundly thankful for both Rob and Jo Ann's riding lessons. Jo Ann's especially, as hell-bent-for-leather was her favorite way of riding. Finally Christian slowed his horses to a walk. Relieved, Michael slowed his and looked around.

"Thieves, I think," Wilf answered his unasked question. "Honest men don't walk about armed with clubs. When they saw we had guns and were ready for a fight they decided not to attack."

Michael nodded thoughtfully and holstered his pistol. He hoped that Wilf would think that the tremor in his hand was from the cold.

☆ ☆ ☆

Late the following day the three approached Wilf's family home. Wilf stiffened and cursed. A horse blanket fluttered on the tree near the barn.

"Arm yourselves. Something's not right down there. Reichard's left us a signal."

Christian pulled his shotgun from its scabbard and Michael drew his pistol.

When they entered the stable yard, Reichard stepped out of the barn and waved them to him.

"What's happened?" Wilf asked, trying to keep the worry out of his voice.

"We've had a couple of visitors. Nothing Dieter and I couldn't handle, but one of them did threaten to return with help. I thought it prudent to give you some warning in case we were busy when you arrived."

"Who where they?"

"First was your neighbor, Beresford. He came with his son. They questioned your brother, his wife, and the servant woman at length about us. Beresford seems troubled by rumors of witchcraft."

"Aye, such he addressed to me."

"You'll be glad to hear that he heard nothing to support such rumors from your brother and his wife. The old woman did keep calling you a 'foul specter from Hell.' Once it became clear that she refuses to believe that you aren't years dead and thus you and the rest of us must be ghosts, Beresford ignored her. He and his son were much taken by Dieter's explanation of the proper cleaning and care of an infected wound. He cleaned and redressed Robin's leg in front of them and afterwards bored them with descriptions of the best ways to make and use willow bark tea. They seemed satisfied that there was nothing and no one unnatural here."

"That's a relief. Toby Beresford has always been influential around here. If he turned the authorities against us we might well be hard pressed to get to Dover." Wilf drew in a deep breath. "Who were the other visitors?"

"Ah, they arrived this morning and were a bit less open-minded. Five men, led by a man who fancies himself a noble."

"Geoffrey Hampford, then."

"So he informed us." Reichard grinned wryly. "I fear that we failed to show the proper deference toward his most august personage. We also refused to hand the boy over to him and handled his four stout men a bit roughly when they attempted to seize the boy."

"Good for you. I take it he's the one threatening to return?"

"We had help. Your sister-in-law swings a mean milking stool. The man she hit was carried off by two of his friends. Little Will did his share. The lad can bite something fierce." Reichard's grin widened. "Our gentleman visitor was rude enough to draw first a pistol and, when I relieved him of that, a sword." The big man pointed to the roof of the barn.

"If he wants them back he'll have to find a ladder."

"That must have put him in a foul mood." They entered the kitchen. Robin was dressed and sitting in a chair beside the fire. Jane tended a pot hanging over the fire and Will kept watch on the doorway, fire poker in hand. Dieter was tending a man stretched out on Robin's pallet.

"If you are speaking of Geoffrey Hampford, then yes, he was cursing wildly when he rode off," Robin Jones replied to his brother's statement. "I've never seen him so furious. Not even when Andrew killed his horse." Robin's eyes were focused on the man on the pallet.

Wilf walked across the kitchen and found himself looking at his older brother. His breath hissed between his lips and he felt the hair on his neck rising. The man on the pallet had been severely beaten. Welts crossed his chest and arms and one lay across where his left eye had been. There was barely an inch of flesh without a welt or bruise or abraded patch. His ears had been cropped and his lips were cut and battered.

"Dieter?" it was all Wilf could manage between his rage and fears.

Dieter shook his head. "I've given him some opiates to ease the pain. They must have dragged him after beating him. Half of his ribs are cracked or broken and he's got internal injuries. He was both pissing and coughing blood. Dr. Nichols couldn't save him were we in the hospital in Grantville."

"Why now? Was it because I came back?"

"No, from the state of the bruising I'd say that most of this was done well before we arrived."

"How long does he have?"

Shrugging, Dieter looked at his patient. "Not long. He was awake enough to know he was with his family and safe."

"Geoffrey brought him," Robin spit out. "He said he'd exchange Andrew for Will."

Red rage rose in Wilf. He stood still, forcing it back down. Now was not the time for blind rage.

Dieter placed a hand on his shoulder. "This had nothing to do with your decision to come here. It would have happened without our presence. Something else provoked it."

From the hearth Jane spoke. "It's not just revenge for the mare. James Hampford is the oldest brother. When the father dies it will be James who inherits, leaving Geoffrey with all his ambitions and no land. He's a bride in mind but 'tis said that her father won't agree to the marriage without Geoffrey having his own property. This farm borders on Hampford lands. The land may not be much but this house is as large and once was as fine as any in the county. So it could be again, given money." She sighed and looked Wilf in the eye. "Envy is indeed a sin. This house, this farm, stirs envy in the breasts of others than the Hampfords. Your da turned down half a dozen offers. Offers that could have bought a place better suited to farming."

"Jane has the right of it, Wilf." Robin said. "Da and Andrew talked about selling. Andrew even had a place picked out, one where Da could still train horses and Andrew and I could farm. Then Da was killed and everything went bad."

Wilf nodded, acknowledging their words. He didn't trust himself to speak. The fires of his rage died back a bit and his mind began to work again. He dragged a chair next to Andrew's pallet and sat down heavily. He took his brother's hand and stared at his smashed face. Memories churned in his head.

Reichard, Christian, and Michael came in, knocking snow from their coats. Dieter took them aside and brought them up to date with events. Jane offered the men stew and bread.

An hour or so later, Wilf gently placed his brother's hand back on the blanket and stood up.

"Where's Mistress Digby?" he asked.

"Gone," Jane replied. "Her grandson came and fetched her the day before yesterday." She hesitated and Wilf saw a flash of fear cross her face as she glanced at Robin. "We . . . I, I gave her your grandfather's bed."

"As payment for the grandson taking her? No," Wilf half laughed. "That bed always fascinated her. I suspect that she'd often shared it with Grandpa."

Robin laughed. "Surely not such a crone as her?"

"She's younger than our mother would be. And, from comments I heard, was as good looking in her youth. Nay, Jane, I've no objection to her having it. We've no cart to haul such away." He looked around the kitchen and noticed the neatly tied bundles stacked in a corner.

"We packed what we want," Robin said, "and are ready. Dieter said that you would want to leave quickly."

"Aye, Robin. I've a mind to get you and yours out of harm's way at first light. How early might we expect Geoffrey and his helpers?"

Dieter and Reichard exchanged looks. It was Dieter who spoke.

"He arrived just before noon today. The four men he had with him seemed farm laborers, not bully boys. Your brother may have a better idea who his help could be."

"I'm not certain. Those with him today I've not seen before. It's possible he found them in Wylye. I know of four indentured male servants, three stable hands, and five farm laborers on the Hampford farm. If James comes along there could be eighteen here in the morning."

"The one your brave wife struck won't be in any shape to go visiting." Dieter smiled and bowed to Jane. "The other three may not be inclined to come back, either. They seemed rather scared when Reichard tossed them bodily out of the barn. So we're left with fourteen to seventeen men. I'd not expect them until an hour or so after daybreak."

"Take Jane and Will and ride out tonight. Get them safely away. I'll stay with Andrew." Robin said.

"Nay, Brother, I'll not leave you to face them alone." Wilf smiled. "There's no need." His smile and his tone gained an edge. "Four mercenaries and an archaeologist can handle five to one odds. Especially when none of our foes have experience beyond a few drunken brawls. Get some sleep now. Tomorrow will be tiring."

Reichard tapped Michael's shoulder. "Christian says that you handled yourself well. As your reward you can help me watch the barn."

"Thanks, I think." Michael answered, gathering up his coat and gloves.

"Thank him you will, Young Michael." Wilf rumbled. "If you ask politely maybe he'll teach you some of his tricks. Someday, one or more of them might save your life. We'll start saddling and packing two hours before dawn." With that he sat down beside his dying brother.

Jane handed him a bowl of stew and a hunk of bread. He thanked her absently. Dieter waited until the rest had left. He checked his patient before seating himself at the table.

"You should sleep, Dieter."

"Keep watch over your brother. Christian and I will watch the house."

"Thank you."

The hearth fire flickered and popped as silence settled on the house. Wilf watched Andrew, listening with a soldier's ear for death's approach. Some time later his head jerked up and his eyes opened. Christian was kneeling in front of the hearth, adding a log. Ashamed to have dozed off, Wilf peered down at Andrew. His breathing was shallow but he still lived.

Christian stood beside them, crossed himself and muttered a prayer. Wilf looked up in surprise.

"Some habits never die. On Sundays I go to church with my wife and children."

"I'm not sure that I still believe God exists. Besides, I've forgotten how to pray."

"I'll say one for you."

A rattling sound brought Wilf's attention fully back to his brother. After a half-gasp and a last sighing breath there was silence. Wilf found himself crying.

"He's at peace now."

Wilf nodded, unable to speak. Christian pulled the blanket over Andrew's battered face.

"You should get some sleep, Wilf."

"What time is it?"

"Just after midnight."

"I'll sit here with him a bit longer. It's been so long since we last were together."

Christian patted him awkwardly on the shoulder and left him alone in the kitchen.

Lanterns hung about the open space in the barn, illuminating an assembly line of horses, saddles, and packs. Little Will bounced about, asking questions. His mother, exasperated, sent him to join his father in watching for the Hampfords.

"This is the last one," Reichard said. "Rob is getting some nice stock."

"Aye," Wilf answered. "Here about they're known as good packhorses, being both steady and sure-footed."

"But why did you buy the mule?"

"I couldn't resist." Wilf's mood lightened at the thought of the look on Ev Parker's face when presented with a sixteen-hand-high mule. "According to Herr Parker mules this size don't exist at this time. It takes a big jack donkey and a big mare to produce them. That's why he wants a couple more of those French donkeys and a Spanish jack or two."

Jane passed around bread and cheese. Reichard took some for himself and left the barn to relieve Robin and Will. When the father and son joined those in the barn, Wilf called everyone together.

"Dieter, Christian, and Michael—you'll take Robin, Jane, Will, and all of the horses save Reichard's and mine. Make for that inn we stayed at. Reichard and I will hang back and take care of anyone inclined to follow us. Once we're sure no one is following we'll catch up with you. If, by some chance, we aren't at the inn by sunrise tomorrow, ride on toward Dover."

Christian stirred. "It would be better if I remained with you, Wilf. Reichard's size makes him easily identified if a hunt gets up."

Wilf shook his head. "You are the best to get everyone across France without delays. Dieter." He held up a hand, stopping Dieter's comment. "Robin's leg still needs care. And Michael needs to be back at Jena, or, at least to Jo Ann." That last brought a blush from Michael and grins from the others.

Robin limped forward and confronted Wilf. "What about Andrew? Where will you bury him?"

"I won't. For now this land, house, and barn still belong to our family. The papers you showed me say nothing about their condition."

"What do you mean to do, Wilf?"

"I'm going to give Andrew a magnificent funeral pyre. The Hampfords can have the land but the house and barn will be naught but piles of ashes."

Robin stared at him and then nodded grimly. "Andrew would appreciate that, I think. Be careful, Wilf. I don't want to lose you again."

"Reichard is a master at field and woodcraft. We'll not be seen except when we want to be."

The horses were led from the barn and everyone mounted. Jane, Wilf was glad to see, made no fuss about riding astride. Little Will sat behind his father on a pad Reichard had made for him. It had hooded stirrups and a strap for his waist. Gray lightened the eastern horizon as the train of horses started off.

Wilf and Reichard busied themselves in the house. They worked in silence, piling wood and tinder in strategic places. Finishing up, Wilf took a candle and lit the tinder under his brother's body.

"Fare thee well, Andrew. I know not if we'll meet again in Heaven or Hell." He watched until satisfied that the fire was well established. When the trail of tinder leading out of the kitchen lit, he went to the barn.

Reichard had turned the cow and sheep out into the farthest paddock. The horses stood patiently in the yard while the men lit hay and straw in the barn.

By the time the sun had risen above the horizon the house was engulfed in flames. The barn roof, burning fiercely, collapsed suddenly, sending sparks and embers flying. A section of house wall wavered, and fell outward. With the added oxygen the fire intensified.

Well upwind and hidden by some trees, Wilf and Reichard watched.

"Michael was right." Reichard mused. "We should have opened all the windows and doors to give it air."

"Aye, but no matter. The fire's done it for us now. Ho! What have we here?" Wilf pointed to several men coming down the lane at a trot. "That's Toby Beresford leading them."

"They've come to fight the fire. They're carrying buckets." Reichard passed over his binoculars.

The two watched as the newcomers stopped well away from the burning structures. Beresford set his men to searching around the yard.

"Looking for your family, I'd wager," Reichard muttered.

Just then, a large piece of the kitchen wall fell and the flames parted. Through the binoculars Wilf could make out the outline of his brother's burning body before the flames roared up again. From the stir amongst the men in the yard, they'd seen it, too.

"More men coming." Wilf handed the binoculars back to Reichard. "And from the direction, it's Hampford."

"Yes, Geoffrey is the one on the horse. He's only got eight men with him. Two of them were here before. The rest are new. They don't look happy."

They watched as Toby Beresford approached Geoffrey Hampford, every stride telegraphing anger. Beresford reached up and hauled Hampford off his horse. Between gestures and the occasional shouted word that they could hear, Beresford was accusing Geoffrey of murder and arson.

"Well, that's interesting." Wilf mused. "I think we'll not have to worry about pursuers now."

Reichard chuckled. "Your neighbor has given you a better revenge than you'd planned."

Wilf leaned against the stable wall, watching his brother and Lannie Clark in the round pen. A smile threatened to split Robin's face. The horse circling them had stopped and turned back to run the opposite way when Robin stepped toward him. Lannie was grinning, too. Robin stepped forward and the horse switched directions again. A minute later the horse stopped and faced Robin and Lannie. Joy radiated from Robin.

"He's a natural, Wilf." Rob Clark spoke quietly. "Lannie's already got him doing stuff it took me months to catch onto. I'm going to have to change his job description."

Wilf glanced at the up-timer, uncertain about what he meant.

"I'll bump him up to assistant trainer in a couple of weeks. By summer he'll be ready to take over training the young stock. His riding needs polishing but he's quick there, too, and we're working on it. When the riding school opens he'll be my senior instructor."

"His future's settled, then."

"As long as he wants. Heck, Wilf, in four or five years he could set up his own riding school."

"I don't think that he's likely to. Jane loves this place and so does Little Will."

"I hear that your new house and stables are well under way. What does Marta have to say about it?"

"A great deal." Wilf smiled gently. "She's fussing over the plans."

"Ah, and do I now get to tease you about your upcoming wedding?"

Wilf turned his attention back to his brother, ignoring the grinning young man beside him.

EDITOR'S NOTE, by Eric Flint:

I usually write just one story for these *Gazette* anthologies. But as I was getting ready to turn in the manuscript I became aware of an awkward problem. Walter Hunt and I had just finished the manuscript for the next 1632 series novel, *1636: The Cardinal Virtues*—which is coming out this July—and asked our usual circle of readers to check it for errors, continuity lapses, that sort of thing.

Alas, a rather major glitch was discovered. Walter and I had forgotten that Cardinal Richelieu was afflicted so badly by hemorrhoids that he was usually unable to ride a horse. And since one of the pivotal episodes in the novel *requires* him to ride a horse...

There were only two solutions.

1) Do a major revision of the first dozen or so chapters of the book.
2) Write another short story for *Gazette VII*—which, by good fortune, was coming out before the novel—that would explain the changed situation.

I would have chosen the second option no matter what. But I did so with positive glee because how often in a writer's career does he get to write a story about hemorrhoids?

When I posed that question to my publisher, Toni Weisskopf, her reply was terse and succinct:

"Let's hope it's only once."

She's probably right. So think of what follows as a unique opportunity.

A Cardinal Relief

Eric Flint

Mike Stearns squinted at the figure sitting across the table from him. "Are you serious? Richelieu actually made that a condition of signing the peace treaty?"

Then, remembering that the person he was addressing was not only a king and an emperor but something called a "high king" to boot, Mike added—somewhat lamely and two seconds too late to probably do much good—the phrase "Your Majesty."

Happily, Gustav II Adolf was in a jovial mood.

"Oh, yes. He did. It's not that surprising, Michael. You probably aren't familiar with the history, but the cardinal's problem with hemorrhoids is well known across Europe. He'd be a laughing stock because of it except laughing at Richelieu is dangerous if you're a Frenchman and unwise if you're anyone else."

Immediately belying his own words, the king of Sweden, emperor of the United States of Europe and high king of the Union of Kalmar, now issued several guffaws.

"Ha! Ha! Imagine! He had to be carried to the siege of LaRochelle on a litter while lying on his stomach. Ha!"

As big as he was, Gustav Adolf had an impressive guffaw. Several more followed.

"They say he once visited the reliquary of Saint Fiacre hoping for relief if they let him apply the bones to his malady. Ha! Ha!"

"I'm not familiar with Saint Fiacre."

"He's the patron saint of hemorrhoid sufferers. Ha! Ha!"

Hemorrhoid sufferers had their own patron saint? Well, why not? If Mike recalled correctly, there was a patron saint for just about everything including coffeehouses, gravediggers and prostitutes.

The monarch's ribaldry having subsided, Mike returned to the subject at hand.

"And he insists that Dr. Nichols has to perform the operation?"

"Oh, yes." Gustav Adolf nodded solemnly. "He was quite adamant, I'm told by my envoys."

Mike tugged at his earlobe. "But . . . why? James is a thoracic surgeon. I grant you, he's become something of a medical jack-of-all-trades since the Ring of Fire. But . . . *hemorrhoids?* So far as I know, he's never done a hemorrhoid operation in his life. It's a lot more likely that Dr. Adams has some experience with it."

Gustav Adolf shrugged. "It doesn't matter, Michael. No doctor in Europe—anywhere in the world—has the reputation of Dr. James Nichols. The fact that he's of Moorish ancestry just adds to the legend. The effective ruler of France is not about to settle for anyone else."

Knowing how much James was going to dislike the idea, Mike tried the last option he could think of. "Has Richelieu overlooked the small detail that he *lost* the war? He's in no position to be making demands in a peace negotiation."

"No, he's not—and if we resist him on the issue he will eventually back down. But I don't want the delay because I want the situation with France settled as soon as possible."

Gustav Adolf's blue eyes, under a lowered brow, bore a marked resemblance to those of an eagle who has spotted an exposed rodent. "I want to settle accounts with that bastard John George of Saxony and my worthless brother-in-law in Brandenburg. I can't march on them until I'm sure our western border is secure."

He didn't add what Mike knew he could have, which was: *And I want to settle accounts with Saxony and Brandenburg quickly so I still have time this year to settle accounts with that bastard cousin of mine who claims to be the king of Sweden as well as the king of Poland.*

The Hatfields and McCoys had nothing on the family feuds of European royalty.

"I'll talk to James. But I warn you, he may dig in his heels."

In point of fact, Nichols was sure to dig in his heels. But Mike thought he could probably get him to come around. Once the doctor's squeeze Melissa Mailey—no, he wasn't being sexist; Melissa herself relished the term—got wind of the proposal.

"Oh, yes!" exclaimed Melissa. She barely managed to keep from clapping her hands. "You have to do it! I love Paris!"

James Nichols didn't look nearly as pleased. "Yeah, great. You get to see the Eiffel Tower and I get to look at a cardinal's ass."

"Don't be silly. The Eiffel Tower won't be built for another two hundred and fifty years. And you'll get to see more of the Palais-Royal than I ever did. Most of it was off limits to the public when I visited Paris but in this day and age it's Richelieu's own palace. I'm sure he'll give you leave to go anywhere you want. See if you can get me invited."

"Why would he do that?"

Melissa gave James the look schoolteachers give a student who is a sweet kid but something of a dimbulb. "You're going to be carving up his tush, dear. Of course he won't deny you anything. What if your hand should slip during the operation?"

James shrugged. "Big deal if it does. Cardinals are supposed to be chaste and celibate anyway."

"True, true. So far as I know, it's even really true when it comes to Richelieu. So what? I don't know any man who doesn't have an unreasonable attachment to that equipment whether they ever use it or not."

She frowned. "The real problem is that ice cream hasn't been invented yet. Well, we have it here in the USE, but I doubt it's spread to Paris. And what's the Île Saint-Louis without ice cream parlors?"

Two days later, Melissa was considerably less pleased.

"That's preposterous!" Her face took on an expression that Mike Stearns remembered well from his days, thankfully long past, when he'd been one of her high school students. And not one of her favored ones, either.

Are you responsible for this?

He spread his hands in a gesture that conveyed—tried to, anyway—complete and total innocence.

"Don't look at me, Melissa. Gustav Adolf came up with the idea all on his own."

"I find that hard to believe. Why would he pick me to be his ambassador plenipotentiary?"

Mike couldn't stop himself from grinning. "He said it's because after the way you blew up the Tower of London he figures nobody will be tempted to hold you hostage."

"That's ridiculous! And *I* didn't blow it up. That was the work of that vandal of yours, Harry Lefferts."

"Just telling you what he said."

Melissa and James now both being disgruntled, they were determined to spread the grief.

"Gee, I don't know, Ms. Mailey." Ron Stone was a lot younger than Mike Stearns and his memories of the Schoolmarm from Hell were a lot more recent. There might eventually come a day when he'd be comfortable calling her "Melissa," but that day was still in the future. "I did look into it, once. But it turns out that stuff is a lot more complicated than it looks."

Missy Jenkins frowned. She'd been visiting Ron in his office at the Lothlorien Farbenwerke when Melissa and James showed up.

"*That* stuff?" she asked. "Preparation H? I figured it was just—" She waved her hand. "You know. Mostly petroleum jelly or something of that sort."

"I think that's probably what Dr. Phil mostly puts in that stuff he's been selling as a general-purpose ointment. I've heard people use it for hemorrhoids but I'm skeptical that it works that well. There's a whole line of Preparation H products, each with its own set of ingredients, some of which are pretty weird."

Ron shook his head bemusedly. "You wouldn't believe what a witches' brew it can be, Missy. Almost literally—some versions have witch hazel in them. That's an astringent from a shrub that doesn't grow in Europe so far as I know and while it did grow in Appalachia I'm not sure if any came through the Ring of Fire."

"Find out," Melissa commanded, in much the same tone Ron could remember her telling him the research on his term paper wasn't up to snuff.

"But there's lots of other stuff, too." He furrowed his brow, bringing up a somewhat faded memory. "Let's see... If I remember correctly, it usually includes a vasoconstrictor—phenylephrine, I think. Sometimes it has pramoxine—that's a topical anesthetic. And all sorts of protectants. Mineral oil and petrolatum, I know. Something else, too. Oh, yeah. Shark liver oil."

His expression became simultaneously aggrieved and dubious.

"Not too many sharks in Thuringia. Being as we are landlocked and two hundred miles from any coast." He looked at Nichols. "And why do you need it, anyway, since you're going to be operating on him?"

Nichols shrugged. "I've never done that operation. Thankfully, one of the nurses in town has some experience with it and she agreed to go along. But even if I was the world's foremost butt surgeon there's no guarantee the problem won't flare up again later. So we want some backup." He smiled. "So to speak."

Ron still looked dubious. "It seems like a lot of work for an end result that doesn't— I mean, how many people really need that stuff anyway?"

Missy looked at Melissa, smiling. "You got to make allowances. He's young, not overweight, and has no expectation of bearing children." When she looked back at Ron, the smile had gone away. "*Some* of us, on the other hand, are looking at worse odds and might someday find it handy to have the stuff around. So get cracking, buster."

Of course, even if he was successful in finding a reasonable facsimile or substitute for Preparation H, it would take Ron months before he had it in production. Still, Melissa was in a better mood when they flew off the next day in a Jupiter made available by King Fernando. The ruler of the Netherlands undoubtedly felt some regret at the prospect of a peace treaty being finally signed between France and the USE. It had been close to a year since a cease-fire put an end to the fighting between the two nations. In that interval, Fernando had taken advantage of the inevitable uncertainties and obscurities to nibble away at the odd bishopric here and the small principality there. Seventeenth-century rulers grazed on territory as naturally as cattle and sheep grazed on vegetation.

But all good things come to an end. Since a peace treaty was now inevitable, it was to the advantage of the Netherlands to play the role of an honest and helpful assistant, if not exactly a broker. So he'd made one of Royal Dutch Airlines' big transports available. Fortunately, there were two of them in operation at the moment so he could spare one.

The airfield just outside Paris was a bit on the rough side, since the French hadn't had any experience with building one. But Jupiters were sturdy aircraft even if their engines were prone to malfunction. (There were four of them, though, so no one worried too much.) The landing was bumpy but otherwise uneventful.

To Melissa's delight, she and James were provided with quarters—damn luxurious quarters, too, leaving aside the plumbing—in the Palais-Royal itself. Or Palais-Cardinal, rather, as it was called in this day and age. Richelieu had built it for his own private residence in the capital. Allowing for seventeenth-century cardinals-who-rule-whole-countries values of "residence."

While James went about his assigned task, Melissa tried to do the same. But as it turned out, Richelieu was being stubborn. Until his hemorrhoids were fixed, he wasn't agreeing to nothing, nohow, noway.

That suited her fine. She went off sightseeing.

Paris in the year 1635, of course, wasn't the Paris she'd visited up-time. Not even close. There was no Eiffel Tower. There was no Arc de Triomphe and Place de la Concorde—and no Champs-Élysées connecting them, for that matter. The area that would someday hold one of the world's most magnificent boulevards was nothing but fields and kitchen gardens.

On the other hand, not only did the Tuileries Gardens exist in the here and now but so did the Tuileries Palace. It had been built by Catherine de Medici, the widow of Henry II—the French one, not the *Lion in Winter* guy—in 1564. But Melissa had never seen it before because in her up-time world it had been burned down by the Paris Commune in 1871.

Notre Dame was there too, of course. So, to her surprise, was the Pont Neuf, the gorgeous bridge that led to the Île de la Cité where the medieval cathedral was located. She hadn't realized it dated back that far, probably because her French had been good enough that she'd known the name meant "New Bridge." Being an American, it just hadn't occurred to her that anyone would slap the label "new" on something built almost four centuries earlier.

To her delight, the Île Saint-Louis was there. She hadn't been sure it would be, at least in any way she'd recognize. She knew the island was partially man-made, but she hadn't been able to remember the history, if she'd ever known it at all. The few guide books in Grantville on Paris were sadly deficient in that sort of detail. As well as being completely out-of-date, of course. Using the term "out-of-date" in the upside-down way so many terms got used because of the Ring of Fire.

Overly-in-of-date? Ahead-of-date? Chronologically premature? Perhaps someday an enterprising analog of Dr. Roget would develop a special thesaurus for the purpose.

Unfortunately, while the island was there and was occupied—some of the buildings even seemed to be ones she remembered—it wasn't the delightful place she remembered, wandering from shop to shop with a pair of college friends while slurping on ice cream cones.

In the year 1635, as it turned out, the Île Saint-Louis was a brand new residential area which had been designed and built for the city's elite. Shops? Be serious. When the elite wanted something, they sent their servants across the bridge to get it from the commercial areas of Paris. Which were damn well somewhere else, with their nasty smells and nastier smelling inhabitants.

"We'll see about that!" Melissa vowed.

The next day she set out into those selfsame nasty-smelling parts of town. Without even thinking about it, she headed for the Left Bank.

In the here and now, the Left Bank wasn't what it had been in her day either. The Boulevard Saint-Germain didn't exist yet. Neither did the Boulevard Saint-Michel; not, at least, in the form she remembered. But its predecessor did exist, which they called the Rue de la Harpe. More importantly, the Sorbonne was there and so was the Latin Quarter—and in this day and age, the students lounging about *did* speak Latin.

Fortunately, some of them spoke English and German as well. Melissa's French could most charitably be described as rusty, and her Latin was downright laughable.

It took a while to make clear what she wanted. Perhaps an hour. Then another two hours while the students she'd intrigued with her proposal found local artisans who might be able to bring it to life. The rest of the day was spent closeted with the two artisans who'd been willing to give it a try and the four students whose interest hadn't flagged.

She'd had to show them the money first, of course. Left Bank or no, seventeenth-century artisans—students weren't much different—didn't gamble on a new venture unless the investor could come up with hard cash.

Hard cash, Melissa had. Being the squeeze of the world's most famous and sought-after doctor had its perks. James did a lot of work *pro bono,* to be sure. But the rest was generally well-paid and some of it barely escaped the label *shameless gouging.*

For the next three days she had to suspend her involvement in the project. James had finished the operation—quite successfully, he told her, sounding a bit surprised—and Richelieu was ready to start dickering over the peace treaty.

Dicker he did, too. Every bit as unscrupulous as his reputation said he was, the cardinal used the needs of his recovery as an excuse to stall, delay, postpone and equivocate wherever he found it convenient.

"God, that man's a pain in the ass," Melissa complained to James. Sourly: "And don't even *think* about telling me that's because he does have a pain in the ass. I hear that from him at least eight times a day."

But, try as he might, in the end Richelieu was overmatched. Partly, because the recovery did in fact distract him; mostly, because the objective reality was starkly in Melissa's favor: France had, in point of fact, lost the war—and lost it quite resoundingly. The defeat Torstennson had inflicted on the French army at Ahrensbök had been one of the worst defeats any army had suffered since the wars began in 1618. (Up-timers called it *the* Thirty Years' War, but down-timers saw the period as one of a multitude of overlapping and intersecting wars. Melissa thought they were probably right.)

But there was a third factor involved, too. Melissa wasn't consciously aware of it but Richelieu soon came to understand the phenomenon—and suspected that Gustav Adolf had realized it from the beginning. A man might become a king by good fortune, but he doesn't parlay that happenstance of birth into an empire—two empires, really—unless he's exceptionally shrewd.

Schoolmarms From Hell have a number of characteristics. One of them is a fiendlike ability to penetrate excuses and a pitiless attitude toward them. In the end, so far as Melissa was concerned, all of Richelieu's diplomatic wiles and stratagems amounted to *the dog ate my homework* and she was having none of it.

She wound up getting all that Gustav Adolf had instructed her to get and a fairly sizeable chunk out of the cardinal's hide as well.

"The woman is a horror," Richelieu complained to his *intendant* Servien. "But I least I can sit across the table from her and not be in constant agony of the behind as well as the mind."

☆ ☆ ☆

It was done. The treaty signed. Melissa spent two days giving James a tour of the city before spending her last day in Paris at what she had come to call The Mission.

They were making progress, she was pleased to see. The results so far were...

Encouraging, was the word she settled on. It was certainly better than James' assessment: *goopy slop.*

"Where do they get the ice?" he asked.

"So far they've been scraping it up here and there from small suppliers. But they'll start importing it from England if the business takes off. There's a pretty big ice harvesting industry in the Thames Estuary. People have had iceboxes for... oh, a long time. Centuries, I suppose. All I did was suggest building a really big one."

James looked around the facility. "They all look busy, I'll say that."

Melissa sniffed. "That's because what you called 'goopy slop' will soon be the talk of Paris. I'm just sorry I won't be here to see the first lines form outside the shop. Which they will."

She sounded extraordinarily sure of herself. That being, of course, one of the other characteristics of Schoolmarms From Hell.

James wasn't inclined to argue the point. Arguing with Melissa was an activity he saved for things he really cared about. Really, really, really, *really* cared about. It was too exhausting. He almost felt sorry for Richelieu.

They were greeted upon their return by a prestigious delegation at the Magdeburg airport. Gustav Adolf himself came out to welcome them back.

Well... not really. Mostly he came because his daughter Kristina was waging a relentless campaign to be allowed to take flying lessons and he hoped that he could forestall her by taking her on visits to the airport. He was coming to the conclusion, though, that as diplomatic tactics went, this one was probably backfiring.

"You were successful, I trust?" he said to Melissa, once she climbed down from the plane.

"I certainly was. Ice cream has come back to Paris. And"—she made a rude noise—"*ffftt* to those snobs on Île Saint-Louis."

"I was referring to the treaty."

"Oh. That."